First published by Skepdek Publishing in 2010

Copyright © Andrew Crawford, 2010

The right of Andrew Crawford to be identified as the author of this work has been asserted.

Catalogue details of this book are available from the National Library of Greece.

ISBN 978-960-99296-0-8

andrewmccallumcrawford@hotmail.com

Typeset, printed and bound by Epi Chartou

ANDREW McCALLUM CRAWFORD

Drive!

Σδ
Skepdek Publishing

Acknowledgements

Thanks to Chrysostomos Chrysostomidis for the typesetting, printing and binding.
Babbis Konstantinidis for the office space.
John McCaughie and Janet Paisley for helping out way back when.
Dave Jones for reading the manuscript when he had better things to do.
Finally, thanks to Lizzie and Elene for their love, faith and encouragement
– I couldn't have done it without you.

For Elizabeth Boyle McCallum

The silence of the fish – how boring!
　　　　　　　　　　　Plato

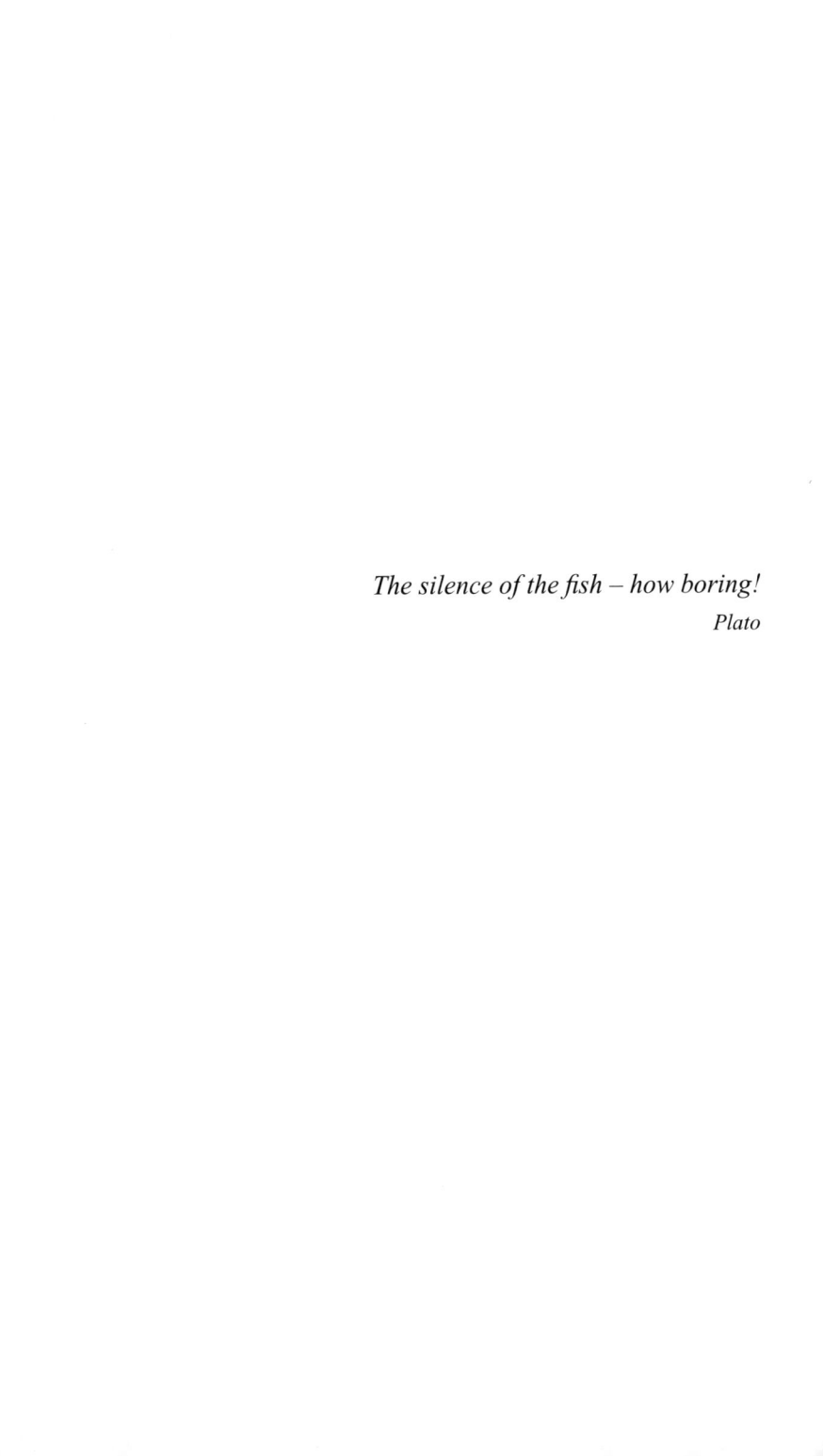

CHAPTER 1

Terry was in The Confessional. It was only lunchtime, but he was already on his fourth double.

His father was after him.

He drained the remainder and slapped the bar.

'More whisky here!' he said. He watched Sean pour another generous measure, then raised the glass to his lips. The warm fumes smelled like... like... something was missing...

'I know!' he said. 'It's time for a sing-song!'

The Confessional was full. Some of the patrons turned to look.

'I am the *spawn*!' he wailed, 'Let's be *fair*!'

He raised an arm, whisky lapping over the sides of his glass as he tried to incite the reluctant choir.

'Of a *shaman* pathologica-a-lly *vulgar*!'

The babble of conversation, he was pleased to note, had begun to trail off.

'And it's all over!' he laughed. 'Now!'

Silence at last. He closed his eyes and let the appreciation wash over him. Yes, he thought. They love me.

The silence continued. His audience seemed to be waiting for something. Perhaps the second verse... they didn't think he was a comedy act, surely? If it was a punchline they were expecting...

Oh, Christ, he thought, and turned carefully round.

Dennis McCleaver was standing right behind him.

'Well, well,' said Terry, the corner of his mouth suddenly trembling. 'I've been expecting you.'

Dennis just stood there, all camel hair coat and sinister grins. Even though nothing was funny, Terry knew that things were about to get very sinister indeed. A cordon sanitaire was already forming. He managed to check the trembling in his lip, but his legs began to shake.

'I suppose this is about my father?' he said.

Dennis just grinned.

'Look,' said Terry, 'you know, if he's...'

Dennis just grinned. Then grinned some more. The only sound in the pub was Sean's duster polishing a nervous hole in the counter. Terry knew he had to say something. To, what was it, take the initiative.

'Sean,' he said. 'Fill a glass for my friend here.' He would have asked Dennis if he had any particular preference, but when he looked at him all he could see was teeth.

A glass was pushed under the nearest optic.

'God, no, not the Grouse,' said Terry. 'Top shelf... a drop of my usual, I think.'

Dennis leaned in slowly.

'You've to get out of the flat,' he said. 'Give me your key.'

Terry did what he was told.

'Thank you,' said Dennis. He brushed aside the front of his coat and dropped the key into his trouser pocket. He was still grinning.

Terry risked a sigh of relief. He gestured at the glass Sean had just laid on the bar.

'Your whisky,' he said. 'It's from Jura, noted for its...'

He felt something skewer his thigh. He glanced down, his eyes wide, expecting to see the hilt of a knife buried in his leg. But it wasn't a knife. It was Dennis's knee. Terry's chin bounced off it as he crumpled to the floor.

Dennis tipped back his whisky.

'Let that be a lesson,' he said.

Terry, rolling around quietly on the carpet, watched Dennis's shoes disappear out the door. That it should have come to this. He had done his best to blend in among the Doctors, Lawyers and Professors who frequented the place. He was always immaculately dressed, and he had that essential Scottish Private School accent. They had kindly agreed to overlook the long hair and the fact that he was merely a third year student of Agriculture. What an embarrassment.

He groped his way up the front of the bar.

'Justice!' someone shouted.

A heckler? Terry thought, just as he got his elbows onto the counter.

'You okay?' asked Sean.

'Never better,' said Terry, and caught the eye of the Dean of the Faculty of Science, whose cutlery was poised over his bridie and beans. 'As you see, Professor, The Lord and my father work in mysterious ways!'

He limped out into the street. The screech of brakes, and he was sprawled over the bonnet of a car. He heard the driver's door slam.

'There's no need to do this,' Terry mumbled, his mouth smearing blood onto the cold windscreen. 'Tell my father I'm sorry...'

'You young bastid! I've joost put this through the car wash! Look at the bleemin mess!'

He was pulled round by the shoulder.

'You should bleemin well look where you're... Terry?'

It was Roy Sugden, his Director of Studies.

'It's my leg,' Terry groaned.

Sugden gasped.

'God, it's not broken, is it?!' He peeled Terry carefully off the bonnet. 'Not to worry,' he said. 'The Infirmary's just across the road. You hang on to me and we'll get you sorted out in a jiff.'

'No, you don't understand,' said Terry. 'My leg's okay... I think.'

He tried to put his weight on it and an explosion of pain nearly blinded him. He had to lean on the car.

'Any chance of a lift up to the Queen's Building's?' he said; his bottom lip felt like jelly. He needed to get Dug's key.

'Oh, yes,' said Sugden, and looked at his watch. 'Of course, it's your...our...'

'Eh?' Terry tried to back away from the arm that was being draped round his shoulder, but the man was all over him.

'It would be an honour and a privilege, young man. Slowly, now.'

They sat there, Terry massaging his thigh while Sugden harped on about the building work at the new Kinlochleven Suite of laboratories, nudge, nudge, wink, wink, the kind of sycophancy that was blatantly targeted toward career advancement. Sugden had been honing his approach for the last three years. But there was no point trying to curry favour with Terry. Not any more, there wasn't.

He was gently guided down the corridors of the Chemistry building, but had to stop every few paces. His leg was killing him.

'Do we really have to go through with this?' he said. They both knew it was a charade, the last in a furtive series of transactions that had been going on all summer.

'Now, now,' Sugden smirked. 'Got to make sure we've got all the paperwork in order. They're very thorough down at Admin, you know. Ah, here we are.'

He was nudged into the laboratory. The door clicked shut behind him. He looked at his labcoat hanging there on its peg. In a lighthearted moment, before the current mess, he had inscribed the following legend over the breast pocket:

TERENCE KINLOCHLEVEN
CHEMISTRY 1B
83-84 XX
84-85 XX
85-86 X?

The apparatus was already set up. Chromatography. He would make sure that his ink dots were placed correctly on the blotting paper, then set the paper in the solvent and wait. It was so easy they had started teaching it in Primary schools.

He was taking the class for the sixth time.

Mr Kwak approached, muttering. He was another failure, but only of the first year kind. He was mustering his language skills in order to indulge in his weekly perusal of Terry's counterfeit goods.

'Wha' you ge' fo'?' he asked.

Mr Kwak had failed the class due to his tenuous grasp of English.

Terry reached into his pigeon hole and removed the writeup of the previous week's practical. They had been distilling various mixtures of chemicals to find the boiling points of the fractions. Something like that, anyway. His results were presented in a graph – complete with error bars! He had to laugh. Dr Rimmer had failed him five times, but this year someone else was in charge of the resit class. And someone had started leaving faultless laboratory practical writeups in his pigeon hole.

He wasn't complaining.

Mr Kwak squinted at his own effort.

'Yes,' said Sugden, and plucked the sheet of paper out of his fingers. 'Indeed you do look confused.'

He winked at Terry.

'Once again Mr Kwak he do his *glaph long*!'

Mr Kwak frowned, and pointed at Terry's graph.

'Yes, that's right,' said Sugden. 'The *temperature* goes on the y-axis. Nice work, Terry!' He fashioned a copperplate *A+* in the corner of the page, and underlined it twice. He hesitated, then added an exclamation mark.

'But it no matter, surely?' said Mr Kwak, swivelling and twisting his graph, then folding it in half so that the line with the temperatures ran vertically up the page. His English was bad, it was true. His graphs also needed working on.

'Ah,' said Sugden, and turned to Terry. '*Surely*. The stock plea of the lazy undergraduate when confronted with his ignorance. Even though he has *tloubre plonouncing* it, he tends to use the word a lot.'

'But it...,' Mr Kwak began.

Sugden stopped him with a raised palm.

'Best to stick to convention,' he advised. 'Before you get stuck in first year.'

Terry was grateful for the writeups, but he felt there was no need for Sugden to be quite such a git. He started clicking his pen on and off.

'What's that noise?' said Sugden.

Terry laid the pen on the bench.

'Oh, that,' he said. 'Perhaps it's the sound of Nemesis slipping two bullets in her gun.'

Mr Kwak applauded immediately, crushing his graph.

Sugden smiled, but it was forced.

'And why would she be doing that?' he said. It was clear he didn't have a clue what Terry was talking about. His English was only slightly better than Mr Kwak's, and he was all too aware of this inadequacy; Terry had caught him on more than one occasion in his office copying out lists of synonyms from Roget's Thesaurus.

Sugden scratched his head.

'Er, Shakespeare?' he said.

Unfortunately, Roget's was pretty weak on contemporary Scottish poets.

'No,' said Terry. 'Norman MacCaig. And I must insist on using my own pen for the Chromatography.'

Sugden was blushing.

'Why?' he said.

'I'm trying to find the poetry in Chemistry 1B,' said Terry.

'Well, yes,' Sugden simpered. 'Aren't we all?'

He flattened Mr Kwak's homework on the bench and scribbled a C somewhere at the bottom.

'Ooh, by the way,' he said. 'I bumped into your, er, flatmate. I gave him your message.'

Yes, thought Terry. Of course you did.

The canteen at the Institute of Animal Science was so large that it was occasionally used as a theatre. It had been the scene of Terry's triumph in 'No Sex, Please, We're Scottish', in the Agrics' traditional second year performance. His rendition, in third year, of the Selected Works of Norman MacCaig – all three hours of it – had been hailed in the student rag as 'chilling'. He was a 'natural performer'. There was even a rumour that he had been offered a part in 'Accidental Death' at the Lyceum. But it was only a rumour, like so many others he knew circulated about him. The latest being that the only way he would end up in the poor house was if he poked his father's wife, thrice.

He laid Mr Kwak's tea on the table.

Oh, yes, he was the envy of one and all, one of those students who never seem to study but always end up with the highest marks in the class, exemption after exemption, leaving him with plenty of time to indulge in his hobbies and interests. What a CV he would have when the Milk Round came to town!

But that was next year. This was now, and he was in the shit.

He left Mr Kwak in the corner mulling over his cup of stewed leaves and stood at the window. As Sugden had faithfully reported, the building work was certainly coming along. The sun disappeared behind a cloud and he found himself staring at the reflection of someone who was in quite a state. He had a fat lip, and the beginnings of a black eye. The lapels of his suit were ripped. And what was that hanging out of his breast pock...

Someone tapped him on the elbow.

'All right, Terry?' said Dug, and pointed to the mess outside. 'And one day all this will be yours, eh?'

'Lay off,' said Terry, and turned round. 'I need your key.'

Dug's shock at the state of his best friend's face couldn't have been more apparent.

'What the fuck happened to you?' he said.

Terry straightened his jacket on his shoulders.

'I had a visit from Dennis,' he said.

'What?' said Dug. 'Did he give you a kicking? I told you he...'

'No,' said Terry, and removed a piece of rubber from his breast pocket. It was a sliver of windscreen wiper blade. 'I got hit by a car.'

'What?! He ran you over?!'

'No, that was Sugden.'

'What?!'

'Long story, Dug. I'll need to get over to the flat.'

A squad of workmen came bustling through the door.

'Ah,' said Dug. 'Your employees.'

'Shut it,' said Terry, perhaps a little too sharply; Dug's mouth had immediately gone into a pout. 'Listen.'

The foreman dumped a plastic bag on one of the tables and executed a playful soft shoe shuffle over to the serving hatch. One of the other workmen, a young guy wearing a Rangers scarf, pulled a pair of drumsticks out of his sleeve and started keeping the beat on the wood. The foreman cleared a space with his elbows and laid down five polystyrene cups.

'Frankie,' he said. 'D'ye fancy goin' ootside an' playin' them oan the grass?'

The drumming stopped.

'Eh?' said Frankie.

Terry smiled to himself. He'd been wanting to punch someone since The Confessional.

'Now, the lot ae yez,' said the foreman. 'Pay attention.'

The plastic bag was full of electronic locks, each one with a numeric keypad. He explained how to install them without getting locked in.

'Make share yez've got the plastic swipe card wi' yez at all times,' he stressed.

He looked round, then lowered his voice.

'Between me, youse lot an' wee Mavis through the hatch there, any piece ae plastic wi' a magnetic strip'll dae the business till they've got the security codes worked oot.'

'Whit, ye mean like a library ticket'll open it?' said Frankie.

'Check him oot!' shouted one of his workmates. 'Since when've you hud a library ticket, Frankie?'

'Frankie boy,' continued the foreman, 'ye can yaze yer platinum American Express card if ye want, as long as it's got a wee black strip doon the back. Jist make share ye've got somethin' wi' ye. Ah dinnae fancy landin' unpaid overtime tae come doon here tae let ye oot.'

Frankie scratched his scarf with a drumstick.

'Is that like a train ticket or whit?' he said.

'Oan ye go, Frankie!' they laughed.

He smiled, but it was obvious he was sick of it. He started twitching, his eyes darting around the canteen.

He clocked the foreigner sitting in the corner.

'Who let the Chink in?' he said.

Before Terry knew what he was doing, he felt his fingers tightening around Frankie's throat.

'That's enough,' he said with remarkable clarity, given that he was holding Frankie two feet off the floor with one hand.

'Hehh, hehh, that'll dae,' said the foreman.

'Cccc...ccannae...br...eathe...,' rasped Frankie.

It was strange, thought Terry. Even though it was Frankie getting strangled, it was the foreman that was shitting himself.

'Pit that laddie doon,' he said. He didn't sound very persuasive.

Despite the pain shooting through his thigh, Terry smiled.

'Make me,' he said.

They didn't dare.

When he was sure he'd got the reaction he was looking for, he let go, and Frankie fell to the floor in a heap, tugging at his scarf.

Sugden came beetling into the canteen.

'Ah, Terence,' he said, and started wringing his hands. Terry couldn't help but notice that the man's gaze was directed over his shoulder; for an opportunist like Sugden, the rugged pillars sprouting inexorably from the reinforced concrete deck held a certain ocular magnetism. 'Good news,' he said. 'You've passed your Chemistry practicals. Would you like to join me in a celebratory cup of the Institute's finest Tetley?'

'Sorry,' said Terry. 'Too much to do. Thanks for the key, Dug.'

Sugden looked like a wounded animal.

'Why don't you treat Dug, Dr Sugden?' said Terry, and watched with a certain amount of satisfaction as his DOS took in the scene:

A young man was writhing on the floor, being stared at by a group of workmen.

Mr Kwak was in the corner, smiling and murmuring like an imbecile.

Sugden's eyes came to rest on Dug, and he shook his head slowly.

'No,' he said. 'Oh, for goodness' sake, no.'

CHAPTER 2

The Kaptain's Kabin was going wild. Sammy flammed the cymbals, and a shower of sweat erupted off his head onto his drums.

This, he thought, *is better than sex with* any *woman*.

Mich threw him a towel.

'Cheers, doll!' he shouted.

She blew him a kiss.

There was shoving room only at the bar. Fat Edgar, sitting at the table directly in front of the stage, had four pints of Guinness in front of him.

'Dae *Layla*!' he shouted for the hundredth time.

Baz bowed to the crowd and started tuning up. Something went Ping!

Christ, thought Sammy. No again. He watched Baz loping towards him, that stupid grin all over his face.

'That's ma top E away again,' he said.

Sammy glared at him.

'Well fuckin' chainge it!' he said.

Fat Edgar started slapping his knees. A low drone of Layla! Layla! started to hum round the bar.

Baz pushed his guitar down and round and strutted to the front of the stage. He tugged the microphone out of Bear's hand.

'Laydeez and genewmen!' he announced. 'Now fur somethin' yez've never seen before!'

He reached inside his jacket and pulled out a harmonica. It flashed gold under the lights.

Whit the fuck is this? thought Sammy.

'This song's called *Layla*,' said Baz, and nudged Bear out of the way. He cupped his hands over the mike and went straight into the riff. Then the rhythm part. Then back to the riff. He turned, jumped and did the mid-air splits. When his feet hit the floor, Sammy and Mich came in, thumping and chugging.

Fuckin' hell, thought Sammy. This is brilliant. The crowd were loving it. Fat Edgar had his hands raised over his head, all praise to Baz, the Master!

Of course, there was a problem. Drive! were a one microphone band, and all too soon it was time for Bear to come in with the vocal. He tried to wrestle the mike out of Baz's hand, but he was too well into the song, and so were the punters, all two hundred of them. They were going mental. He was frantically jumping up and down, like a spoiled kid on a trampoline that won't bounce, trying to reach the mike, but there was no way Baz was going to hand it over.

Fat Edgar got to his feet. He chased Bear all over the stage, but the wee man was too fast. Someone kicked open the fire escape, and he pelted into the car park.

Drive! finished the set as a three-piece. Back in the van, Baz wanted to do a three-way split.

'No way,' said Sammy. 'Ah'll hang oan tae Bear's share. Ah'll gie it tae um next week when ae comes roond tae the flat.'

Bear didn't come round to the flat. Sammy bumped into him on the Tuesday morning.

'When ye comin' roond fur yer money?' he asked.

'Fuck the money!' said Bear. 'That's me, man, the show's over. Ah'm goin' back tae the waiterin' doon Rose Street. Nae cunt hunts me fae ma ain gig!'

There was something else, Sammy knew, that was bothering him even more.

'Fuckin' upstaged by a mooth organ, tae!' said Bear. 'Ye kiddin'?!'

'Ach, ye ken whit Baz's like,' said Sammy. 'Always got tae be the centre ae attention. Ye shouldae came back in.'

Bear looked at him as if he was a total clown.

21

'Whit aboot Friday?' said Sammy. The sun was out, but he felt something cold blowing down his neck.

'Get rid ae Baz an' ah'll think aboot it,' said Bear, and hobbled off down the street.

They missed the Friday gig. Barring holidays, it was the first time in three years. Sammy made up an excuse about Bear being sick. The fact was that Bear had disappeared. Sammy had gone round to his flat, and the front door had been lying wide open, not a scrap of the wee man's chattels in sight.

He knew they were in trouble.

Mich was trying to prop the couch against the door. She almost had it vertical when it swayed to the side, scraping three cardboard egg trays off the wall.

Sammy caught the glare out of the corner of his eye, but kept his head down. It was his birthday. He was not having a good time. Watching Mich destroy the flat wasn't helping matters. Bear still hadn't shown up, but that was the least of his problems.

The landlord's representative had paid him a wee visit that morning. He had known what the message would be, because it was always the same. Fair enough, the neighbours had every right to complain about the noise; living next to a flat where a rock band practised three times a week must have been a bit trying on the nerves. But Sammy had, he felt, done his part to remedy the situation. That's why there were cardboard egg trays stuck all over the walls. They looked exactly like the soundproofing they used in recording studios. It was a pity they refused to stick to the plaster, but at least he was trying. The landlord didn't think he was trying hard enough. He wanted Sammy out.

And what had Mich given him for his birthday? A fucking clicktrack! She would have been as well telling him his drumming stank. A slap across the face would have been less painful. He'd thrown it into a drawer in the bedroom when she wasn't looking. It would be staying there.

He adjusted his snare so it was in exactly the right spot. It wasn't difficult. He only had two drums, two cymbals and a hi-hat. The snare alone had cost him the best part of five hundred quid. His next purchase was going to be a good stool. He was making do with an unopened parcel of DHSS blankets until he got enough money together for the deposit.

The couch crashed to the floor.

Baz looked up. He had his guitar sitting across his knees. He had just broken his top E, again, and was busy carrying out a repair that would probably last well into tomorrow.

Mich propped the couch against the door. Another egg tray slid down the wall.

'Oh, for God's sake, Sammy,' she said. 'I told you this was a waste of time.'

'Ah dinnae hear the neighbours complainin',' he said. He started tapping out sixteenths on the hi-hat, TktkTktkTktkTktk, watching Baz's pathetic performance with the guitar string. He threw his sticks into the corner behind the drums.

'Fuck's sake, Baz!' he said. 'You take the biscuit, man! Look at ye!'

Baz threaded the string through the body of the guitar and started twisting the end with a wee pair of pliers.

'Whit ye oan aboot?' he said.

Sammy leaped off his blankets and thrust his hands into his pockets, rummaging around. It was only for effect. His pockets were empty. But he'd had enough of Baz acting skint. While he was investing thousands in top of the range drums, Baz was still using a Telecaster copy he'd picked up at a police sale for a fiver.

'How much is a new string?' he said. 'Ten bob? Go doon tae Jackie's an' get a new yin. Fuck's sake...ah, fuck it!'

Baz plugged his guitar into his amp. He started tuning up, laying his pinkie gently across the strings and teasing out the harmonics with his plectrum. He turned slowly to Sammy. His voice was calm.

'Sit doon, Sammy,' he said. 'Ah've fixed it.'

Sammy drew two new sticks out of the velvet pouch on the front of his bass drum. He battered the snare, segueing his anger into one of the band's standard covers, 'Stick It Where The Sun Don't Shine'. Mich was right on it, and Baz joined in, slightly late, but perfectly in tune. Sammy felt the weight lift from his shoulders as the music took over.

The song reached its usual, deafening finish, Sammy flamming the cymbals while the guitarists slid their hands down their fretboards.

Sammy closed his eyes. Aye, he thought. That'll do.

'That endin's shite,' said Baz. 'It sounds like the theme tune off Weekend World. We hud tae watch that every Sunday...'

Sammy's drums went DUH-DUH-DUH-ttsschohhhh. He wasn't in the mood for more tales of Baz's painful childhood. Maybe it was a good job Bear wasn't there. That would have been too much.

Mich leaned on her bass.

'Why don't you try the click-track, Sammy?' she smiled.

'Fuck that,' said Baz. 'Where's Bear?'

Sammy skelped out the intro to 'Love Will Tear Us Apart'. Mich was immediately into it. It would be a great song to play at weddings, just before the fighting started. He shook the thought out of his head. Drive! weren't a wedding band, and never would be. They were a rock band, the best in Edinburgh.

Baz lifted his packet of 10 Regal off the mantelpiece and took his time firing one up. He stuck it into the neck of his guitar and eventually joined in, playing in a different key to Mich and at a different tempo to Sammy.

They sounded like an ice cream van reversing fast down a tunnel.

Sammy threw his sticks into the corner. The plaster was pock marked with hundreds of small black streaks. It was the only place they hadn't bothered to stick egg trays. They would have had even less chance than the ones round the door.

Mich stopped, too, and stared at Baz, who was still playing. After a moment, he lifted his head.

'Whit?' he said. 'Ah telt ye tae play it in E so's we could yaze the harmonics.'

He withdrew the cigarette from its holder and took a series of short, sharp puffs.

Sammy had had enough. He swung the couch to the side. Another egg tray flapped to the carpet. The area round the door was now clear.

'Ah'll huv a cuppa if ye're makin' yin!' Baz shouted at his back.

Sammy tried to fill the kettle, but the spout was rattling too much against the tap.

'Calm down,' said Mich, and hugged him. 'You know what he's like.'

He laid the kettle on the draining board and turned to face her. The sound of Eddie Van Halen riffs came dive-bombing down the loby.

'Whit're we goannae dae, doll?' he asked her.

She kissed his nose.

'We've still got each other,' she said.

That was true, but it wasn't enough. It never would be.

She was smiling. It sounded like Yngwe Malmsteen was having a creatively epileptic fit in the living room.

Hang on, he thought. What if she meant... The three of them were still together. Fine, Bear had a voice like an angel, but it was Baz that was special. Everybody knew it. Guitarists in Baz's league came along once in a generation. Comments had been doing the rounds of the local music scene comparing him with the greats – Hendrix, Clapton, all of the black bluesmen. It would have been easy to dismiss it all as exaggeration, as so much hot air, but Sammy had been around long enough to know that *his* guitarist in *his* band was the business. The guy was a one-off, a fucking phenomenon.

So why were they still playing cover versions once a week in the Kaptain's Kabin, Dalkeith?

Sammy's dream was to land a regular gig at the Prezzie Hall, Edinburgh's premier venue. If they got in there, everything else would be inevitable. But one thing had been holding them back. Bear was not star quality. They had started calling him the Danny De Vito of Edinburgh pub rock. If they ever did get a spot at the Prezzie Hall, they'd be laughed off the stage, they'd be regarded as a novelty act, like the fucking Black Abbots or worse. And Sammy had to admit it, Bear had been boring him for a few years now with his reworkings of bog standard Joe Cocker and Dire Straits numbers. What they should do was use his absence to start writing their own material again, like in the old days, before age, familiarity and complacency – and Bear – had taken over.

He reached for the kettle.

'Where's the writin' pad?' he said.

He laid Baz's tea gently on top of his amp.

'There ye go,' he said.

He knew he would have to tread carefully. The last thing he wanted was Baz legging it down to Rose Street begging for forgiveness and dragging the singer back into the fold. The Bear days were over.

'Aboot yer question earlier oan there,' he said, and blew on his tea. 'Bear's jacked the band.'

Baz looked at him, his cup half way to his mouth.

'How d'ye mean?' he said.

Guid, thought Sammy. Ae looks betrayed. Play oan that.

'Chainge ae heart or somethin'. Said ae wis pissed off daein' covers.'

'The cunt!'

A wave of tea lapped over the side of Baz's cup. He held it away from him, letting the hot liquid splash onto his amp.

'If ae wanted tae write ae could've said! Ah'd've been intae it!'

Oh, you good thing, thought Sammy.

'Ma thoughts exactly, Baz,' he said. 'But there ye go.'

He scratched his nose.

'Ah bumped intae um doon the street. Ae's mind's made up. 'That's it,' ae says. '*Dinnae try tae get me tae come back.*'.'

Baz looked as if he'd just been told about a death in the family. He leaned his guitar against the fireplace and stood at the window, thinking. Sammy didn't want him thinking too much. He wanted to get him involved in the plan.

'So the next step, as ah say, is tae find another voice. Ah'm talkin' aboot goin' fur it this time, Baz, the fuckin' works, the full monty.'

Baz continued to stare out of the window.

'Startin' right now,' said Sammy, and flapped the piece of writing paper.

'Not going to use your click-track, Sammy?' said Mich. She did not look chuffed. Hell, thought Sammy, the writing pad must have been in the drawer in his bedroom.

'Aye, eh, maybe later, doll...'

'Whit's that?' said Baz. His eyes were red.

Sammy flapped the paper again. He felt like he was waving good-bye to Mich, who had walked out.

Back to business.

'We're goannae write an advert an' pit it in Jackie's windae,' he said.

Baz's eyebrows creased.

'Fur a new singer,' said Sammy. 'We cannae jist sit...'

Baz was having none of it.

'Ah say fur the three ae us tae go roond tae Bear's an' get this mess sorted oot. Ah mean the band...withoot Bear...it's...'

'Ae's done a bunk,' said Sammy.

'Eh?'

'Oh, not again,' said Mich. She was standing just outside the door. She's forgotten about the click-track already, thought Sammy. Great lassie.

'Like ah say, though,' said Sammy, 'ae's mind's made up, so in the meantime...'

'If Bear's oot,' said Baz, 'ah'm takin' a walk.'

'...that *of course* we've got tae dae everythin' tae get um back intae the band.'

Shite.

'But listen tae this,' Sammy went on, improvising as if his life depended on it. 'In the meantime we let um cool off. Then...get this... we find somebody an' work oot a set. Nae covers. Original stuff. Then when we've got ten or eleven songs ready we say choorio tae the dull cunt an' gie Bear a shout. Ae'll be back in a flash.'

Even Sammy could have believed it. But by the time they had a set worked out with the new singer, whoever it was, Bear would be a distant memory. Then the sky really would be the limit.

Baz was mulling it over.

'Ah'll think aboot it,' he said.

'Well, that's aw ah'm askin',' said Sammy, and coughed lightly into his fist. He felt sweat on his top lip.

'Let's dae it, then,' he said.

He wasn't sure, but he reckoned it was going to cost him a small fortune in Embassy Regal to keep the boy onside. Added to that, if they couldn't find a replacement soon, then the show, for the lot of them, definitely would be over. For good.

Jackie was at the back of the shop, ham-fistedly demonstrating 'Smoke On The Water' to a skeleton with strange ears. He clocked Drive! approaching through the valley of Marshall cabinets and thrust the Strat copy into the eager hands of the glaikit youth.

'But I only know three of the chords,' the boy whined.

'That's only yin less than me,' said Jackie.

He shuffled forwards, and Mich stepped behind Sammy.

'Sammy! Mich! Awright?!'

He reserved his handshake for Baz.

'An' you, ya fly divil, ye! Where the hell did ye learn tae blaw a harp like yon?'

'Awright, Jackie?' said Baz. 'Aye, it wis a bit special, eh?'

Sammy tried to keep his expression in check, although he was sure Mich was having trouble. She couldn't stand Jackie, for two reasons. Firstly, he had a 'detestable character'. Secondly, and more importantly, he always gave off a damp pong of household waste and semen. She blamed it on the overflowing rubbish skip that had taken root outside the shop, and the way he was always fidgeting with his nuts.

'Where's Bear?' he asked. 'Still walkin' up the road, eh?'

Sammy cleared his throat.

'Aye, ae's, eh, left the band, Jackie.'

Jackie looked shocked. He fidgeted with his nuts.

'Dinnae tell me ae's away in the huff cos the boy here...'

Sammy cut him off.

'Naw, Jackie, ye ken how it is. Musical differences an' aw that.'

'Aye. So!' said Jackie, and clapped his hands together. 'Ye'll be lookin' fur a new singer?'

Mich had told Sammy to be ready for this. Bearing in mind the size of his tab, it would be difficult to refuse. He still owed three hundred and fifty quid for the snare. Mich, bless her, had got his birthday present further down the road, at Music Mart. She'd already forgiven him.

'That's right, Jackie,' he said, and handed him the slip of paper.

Jackie laid it on top of a stack of amps and squinted at it. His fingers were once again tickling the ivories. Maybe ae's been learnin' boogie woogie piano oan the sly, thought Sammy. Ae's certainly got a busy left hand.

'If ye could pit it in the windae, Jackie. We're lookin' fur a new face. Somebody that isnae already oan the scene.'

Smelly shopkeepers whose only musical ability is making a till go 'Ching' once a fortnight need not apply.

Jackie was still trying to read the note.

'"No Time Wasters', eh?'

He looked at Sammy.

'This you slappin' the Bear's wrist?'

Baz had wandered off to give a few hints to the young boy, so Sammy drew Jackie into a corner. His heart missed a beat when he saw the dishevelled form of Gruff Plangent, Scotland's top rock music producer, checking out a display of sequencers.

'Is that who ah think it is?' he whispered.

'Gruff Plangent?' said Jackie. 'Aye, ae comes in here a lot.' He sniffed. 'A compulsive browser – unlike your good self, Mr Livingstone!'

'Aye, look, Jackie,' said Sammy, getting to the point. 'Ah telt Bear tae take a hike. It's time ma guitarist got the recognition ae deserves.'

They looked round to make sure Baz was out of earshot. He was tuning up the guitar for the young guy, another of those musical tasks that Jackie had never been able to master. Sammy inhaled deeply, put his arm round Jackie's shoulder and pulled him a few feet closer to Gruff Plangent.

'Drive! are about tae go stratospheric,' he proclaimed. 'Can ye dig it?'

He knew that within half an hour of leaving the shop, the news would be all over town that Drive! were still a viable entity, and were about to hit the big time.

Gruff Plangent winked at him.

'Right y'are,' said Jackie. He grinned, and his fingers did the Fandango all over the front of his jeans.

CHAPTER 3

Rimmer was sitting on the toilet, enjoying a post-ejaculatory Gauloise and ruminating on that new catchphrase that was being bandied about everywhere – Safe Sex. He was a practitioner, of that there was no doubt. No one would be transmitting viruses to him, oh, no. He was, and would remain, as clean as a whistle. He stroked his appliance, which was balanced on his knees. Meticulous aseptic technique, that was the key.

He nicked the end of his ciggie and slid it behind his ear. The solitude of toilets. Peace and quiet to get on with one's business, even if there was that rhythmic clackety-clack of the wheels...

Something creaked and the door imploded; a male torso crash landed at his feet. His appliance rolled off his knees and hit the intruder in the face.

The train charged into a tunnel.

'Er...,' Rimmer said. 'I haven't actually finished yet.'

The inverted face looked vaguely familiar. Then he noticed the hair, splayed out over the floor like a distressed shampoo advert.

'Terry? Well, well. I never had you down as a fan of toilet sports. One lives and learns.'

He offered a bony hand and helped his student to his feet. The toilet was suddenly very cramped. Of course it was; British Rail had designed it for the exclusive use of solitary stunted children, never mind two fully grown men. And young Terry was a strapping example of the fitter line of Scottish chromosomes. It was a pity half of them had come from Eck Kinlochleven, Rimmer reminded himself, but then Eck Kinlochleven seemed to be the poison at the root of every positive thought these days. He pulled a yard of paper off the wall and attempted to sponge away the mud, or worse, damage to Terry's tresses.

'I'm sure this will bring good luck,' he said, and stepped outside to give the boy more room. 'Like a pigeon pooing on you from a height.'

He gestured at Terry's suit. His performing a backwards roll into the toilet could in no way have accounted for the state he was in.

'Been gardening at all?' he asked.

'No,' said Terry, trying to wipe some of the muck off his sleeve.

'Ah,' said Rimmer. 'No accidents with large lawnmowers, then? Your falling into one, I mean?'

Perhaps he was being a tad too flippant. All this contrived humour and glib sexual innuendo had been wearing a bit thin lately. Oh, it was fine during lessons – nothing gave him more pleasure these days than watching a Fresher blush at one of his insinuations. But he was growing tired of it. He knew they spoke about him behind his back, the disgraced army MO who, like so many of his patients, had been subject to a dishonourable discharge. The sight of all those privates, as it were, standing to attention, had proved too much. He had groped the gunner's glans on one occasion too many and been shown the door.

It was all so long ago. So long ago, but the undercurrent to his everyday thoughts. One of the undercurrents, in any case. The boys being...

He stood back and took stock of the situation *in toto*.

'So,' he began. 'Terry gets onto the packed train, pushing and jostling his way to the other side of the carriage with his...what, is that Nike, is it?...with his Nike holdall. Nike, or 'Nikeh' as our classicists would have it, of course being the Greek goddess of Victory. This is a young man who will not be denied.'

An old woman in a crocheted cap, one of the many passengers crammed into the space between the carriages, began to tut. Rimmer stooped and retrieved his appliance from the floor. Don't worry, dear, he thought. I'll deal with you shortly.

'He props his bag against the door,' he continued, 'and sits down, but Alas! He is such a sturdy fellow that his weight proves too much for the flimsy latch and he lands with a thump at the feet of his venerable mentor.'

The tutting had stopped, but he could feel the old woman's eyes burning into the side of his head. Her stare was likely to reignite his Gauloise, the blackened end of which, he knew, stank. Rimmer was a man who did not like being silently stared at. God knows it was bad enough during tutorials, never mind on an overcrowded train. His motto over the years had become 'The silence of the fish is strictly for the fish', a line he'd borrowed from Plato, and improved upon. He returned the old woman's stare with tenacity. She tried to wriggle away, but it was too late. He'd hooked her.

'Excuse me, madam,' he demanded. 'But could you tell me what you are so insistently gawking at?'

Everyone was looking. The old dear's head lolled on her shoulders. How bloody predictable, he thought. She would probably contrive a fainting fit to avoid a scene.

'It's that thing you're holding,' she lisped, eventually. 'It looks like a rare wee hoover!'

She was referring to his appliance; cradled along the length of his forearm was a large leather cylinder, with rubber attachments at either end. To the uninitiated, he supposed, it probably did resemble a small vacuum cleaner, of the type used to clean the interiors of cars.

'Oh, my dear woman,' he laughed, loudly. 'This isn't a *hoover*. It's an artificial *vagina*, used for collecting *sperm* samples at the University of *Scotland*!'

Her eyes widened, trying to take in the full dimensions of the sperm sampler. They were at risk, Rimmer noted with awe, of popping out of their sockets, something that he had always considered an anatomical impossibility.

'I'd like to meet one of your students, then,' she faltered, and began to swoon.

Terry emerged from the toilet.

'Speak of the devil!' said Rimmer, and leaned into her. He lowered his voice to a seductive growl. 'He's a big boy, I'll grant you, and when he ejaculates, you lucky woman, he'll blow your woolly hat off.'

She fainted. It wasn't contrived.

Rimmer alighted one stop before the terminus, at Haymarket. He was feeling pleased with himself. He had lit, partially smoked, nicked and stored a Gauloise on the slow train from Glasgow to Edinburgh without it going all soggy on him, which was a first, he was sure, in anyone's book. He skipped up the steps to the exit, where he was met by another of his students. They would spend the rest of the afternoon at the Institute of Animal Science taking sperm samples from General Charles de Gaul, who was a really, really big boy, and when he ejaculated, he ejaculated in buckets. And in artificial vaginas, if they were handy. The kind of performance *de rigueur* for a prize Charolais, in fact.

* * *

The ambulance creamed black marks into the asphalt. It had taken longer than the projected two minutes to arrive because the driver had been supping Guinness in The Confessional, and had had his radio switched off. Central control had phoned through to the pub that there was a 999 down at Waverley station. The patient would be in no danger, he reassured himself as he dragged the gurney out the back door. Guinness was supposed to be good for you.

He got the old lady loaded into the wagon and hooked her up to the machinery. He immediately started tapping on the glass screen of the ECG. According to the display, she had a pulse of 220 and was well on the way out, but she had a smile on her face that was more indicative of recent orgasm than impending death. Just to be on the safe side, he gave her an injection of something mellow. It wouldn't do to ignore the readout.

He gunned it back to the Infirmary. He still had half a pint sitting under the counter across the road, and he didn't want it to get too warm.

* * *

Terry hoisted his bag onto his shoulder and headed for St Andrew Square. Dug was waiting for him beside a red double decker bus.

'I thought they only had these in London,' he said, and gave Terry a clap on the arm.

'All right?' said Terry. 'What's new? Apart from the haircut?'

'Like it?' said Dug. 'There's a great barber's down Drummond Street.'

Terry looked, and tilted his head. He didn't say anything.

'It's a flat top,' Dug explained.

'Yeah, right,' said Terry. 'Come on, here's the driver.'

He had spent the last fortnight with friends in Glasgow, well out of reach of his father's hardman. He was still recovering from a party he'd been to the previous night, in Linlithgow, people he knew from the University theatre.

They took the front seats on the top deck. Some wag had vandalised the passenger information sign over the window; they'd changed one of the letters. 'SHITTING PROHIBITED', it said.

'So, Terry,' said Dug. 'That's quite a lot of grass stains on your suit.'

He'd ended up roughing it on the grass slope next to the Palace. There had been a bit of argy-bargy. He'd get changed when they got to his mother's.

'Any more visits from Dennis?' he asked.

'Not since you moved out,' said Dug. 'I planked most of your stuff in my wardrobe.'

'Nice one.'

'By the way,' said Dug. 'Sugden mentioned something about the money for the French trip. Well, to remind you about it, anyway.'

'What?' said Terry. 'He actually spoke to you?'

'Yeah, right,' said Dug. 'I think I've kind of fucked up there.'

The bus trundled through Edinburgh, then out and over the Forth Bridge and into the Kingdom of Fife. Within half an hour they had reached the village of Numpty, built on its succession of steep hills. As they got to the far edge of the village, the bus began to slow down. Terry smiled to himself and gripped the rail that ran the length of the front window.

'Hang on, Dug,' he said. 'You'll love this.'

Terry wasn't one to use public transport, but he had recognised the driver from years back, from the time his mother used to take him shopping in Edinburgh. Maybe she'd been trying to show him how the other half lived. They slowed to a crawl at the crest of the penultimate hill. The final peak was no more than fifty yards away, but the valley in between was twice as deep. The driver floored it, and the engine screamed as the wheels lost contact with the road. They hit the trough of the valley in a storm of sparks and the bus roared, clawing itself up the other side of the hill.

Dug had banged his head off the ceiling. He was lying on the floor.

Terry stepped over him and made for the stairs.

'I do the same thing when I'm in the Quattro,' he said.

He thanked the driver and stepped onto the pavement. Old men were out cutting their hedges. Middle aged women pulling tartan shopping trolleys stopped to stare at the two strangers.

'Eh,' said Dug, rubbing a red mark on his temple. 'Is this where you live?'

Terry looked at him.

'Come on,' he said. 'It's this way. I hope you feel up to a walk.'

They hiked out of the village. Soon they were scaling a small mountain. The dust off the track and the smell coming off the pine trees made it difficult to breathe.

'Hang on,' said Dug. He stopped and lifted his bag carefully off his shoulder. 'This strap's rubbing me raw.'

Terry strode on, but waited for him at the summit.

'We're here,' he said.

Loch Leven stretched out to the horizon, the islands a blaze of green, their verdant grandeur shimmering in the reflection off the water.

Dug wasn't looking at the islands. In fact, he wasn't looking at the loch at all.

'That's a nice wee aeroplane parked next to your castle,' he said.

Terry saw the look on his face.

'It's just a house,' he said. 'Come on.'

He understood why Dug felt awkward. Terry had spent a weekend chez Lloyd at the end of second year. The Saturday evening's entertainment had consisted of watery beer at the Grangeburn Dockers' Club followed by a fish supper and an argument back at the house between Dug and his dad, who was slumped in front of the telly with a bottle propped between his legs. It was the first time Terry had seen someone drinking whisky out of a cup. Dug had described it as an average weekend. It was why he didn't go home very often.

The lawn at the back of the house had recently been manicured. Dug nearly broke his ankle on a croquet hoop.

An overalled backside was protruding from the front of the aeroplane, and a huddle of teenage boys was gathered round, sniggering and nudging as the well-proportioned rear jerked and wobbled. Terry threw his holdall down and strode across the grass.

'Right, you lot,' he shouted. 'Have you not got your work to go to?'

The boys sprang to attention. When they saw who it was they sloped off round the corner.

There was a shout from the engine compartment.

'Mum!' said Terry. 'It's me!'

'...anner!'

He started scouring the area of trampled earth around the plane.

'...anner! God's sake!'

A large silver spanner was jammed in behind the front wheel. Terry left it where it was and climbed onto the bottom rung of the ladder at the side of the engine.

'It's me, mum,' he said.

The writhing stopped, and his mother pushed herself out into the open.

'Terry!'

He helped her down the ladder. He would have given her a hug, but she pushed him away.

'You've been in the wars,' she said.

'Yes, it's a long...'

She looked over his shoulder.

'Who's your friend?' she said.

Dug was examining the family coat of arms carved into the stonework in the west wall.

'Dug, come here, will you?'

He approached them slowly across the grass, his eyes scanning the ground. Maybe he didn't want to trip over another croquet hoop. When he looked up, he stopped dead in his tracks.

'Hello,' he said, and stared.

'Hello,' said Terry's mother.

'.....'

She turned to her son.

'Is he ill?' she said.

Dug blushed.

'Eh, aye,' he stammered. 'I do a bit of writing.'

She turned to Terry again.

'Hannah Gordon!' said Dug.

She wiped an oily palm on her overalls.

'Marie Stuart,' she said, and offered her hand.

'No,' said Dug. 'God, sorry, it's just...Ann Bankroft!'

'Oh, I get it,' she smiled. 'Strange, but on a good day I always think I look like Jean Alexander.'

She had to leave. She had an important appointment in Scotlandwell.

'Are you still towing at the gliding club?' said Terry, cringing at the forced small talk. Fair enough, though. The request for cash could wait till later.

'Not that I want to, Terry,' she said. 'But it pays the bills.'

'That's it!' said Dug, and pointed to the ramparts forty feet over their heads. 'It's Linlithgow Palace, isn't it?'

They looked at him.

'You forgot the space-age spire, though,' he added.

'Not quite, er, Dug,' said Marie.

God, thought Terry. Not the family history. Bugger off to Scotlandwell and get back here with your cheque book. There was no stopping her, though.

'The spire that everyone mentions belongs to St Michael's Kirk, next to the Palace. Thankfully, it wasn't added until 1964. If it had existed any earlier, I'm sure my father would have scraped up the funds from somewhere to graft it onto the house. He was a bit of a Mary Queen of Scots buff, hence my…'

'The legend under the coat of arms...,' Dug interrupted.

Marie turned to Terry.

'Speaking of churches,' she said. 'I hear your father has been setting himself up as quite the Calvinist man of morals of late.'

'Yes,' said Terry. 'I want to talk to you...'

'Later, dear,' she said, and cast a baleful glance at the aeroplane. 'Must rush. If you see Mac, tell him to take a look at the distributor cap. He's so much more adept at these things than me.'

The Green Monster backed slowly into the yard. Mac applied the handbrake and lowered the discs onto the asphalt.

Terry jumped onto the footplate.

'All right, Mac?'

'Oh, hello, there, Terry. This you back on your vacation?'

Mac had been working on the farm since before Terry was born. If anything needed fixing, he was the man. He ran the place.

'Just back for a couple of days,' said Terry. 'I need a favour.'

'Fire away.'

'Any cutting jobs going?' said Terry. Dug was scratching dust into the asphalt with the sole of his training shoe. 'It's for my friend.'

'Aye,' I see him, said Mac, and cut off the power. He screwed his bunnet further down on his brow. 'He's a braw lookin' chookie.'

A change of clothes had been in order. Terry had found an old pair of overalls in the workshop. Dug had stripped down to a T-shirt and camouflage shorts. His legs were so skinny and white they were transparent.

'Just a few weeks,' said Terry.

'A few weeks!' laughed Mac. 'He might last half a shift!'

Terry shouted him over.

'The boys are up at the D-field,' said Mac. 'I'll take you up later.'

'Nice one, Mac.'

'In the meantime, take this contraption up to the Flatcard. I'll be along with the Rotovator shortly.'

Dug was sizing himself up next to one of the tyres. It was level with his shoulder.

'Oh, and Terry,' said Mac. 'If you get lost, just take a deek at your mate's legs.'

The three of them looked.

'Like a bloody road map,' he said.

They had to laugh. Large blue veins were visible criss-crossing just under the milky skin.

'Plenty motorways, anyway,' said Dug.

'Aye, right enough,' said Mac. He climbed down from the tractor and got into the Subaru. 'What's your name again, son? Dug? It's a good job you've got a fast tongue. You'll be needing it.'

He peeped his horn and disappeared in a cloud of dust.

Dug stepped back and looked at the tractor.

'Big, eh?' said Terry.

'Yeah,' said Dug. He looked nervous. 'I didn't know they made them with a chimney on the bonnet.'

'Come on,' said Terry. 'Get in.'

Terry pushed down the passenger seat for him. Dug was impressed.

'Fuck's sake,' he said. 'You could go your holidays in this thing.'

Terry took a minute to figure out the right combination of gearsticks from the six that were jutting at all angles between his legs. He was soon back into the swing of it. He took the back road up to the Flatcard. Dug was quieter than usual.

'Something up?' asked Terry.

'Eh, no,' said Dug. His arm was hanging out the window, his fingers drumming on the side of the wing mirror.

'Come on,' said Terry. 'Worried about your results?'

Dug sniffed.

'Aye, that'll be right,' he said. 'That's a done deal. I was wondering about the coat of arms on the side of the castle.'

'It's not a castle,' said Terry. It was time to get this out of the way before it started getting on his nerves. 'It's just a big house with a fancy outside.'

'Yeah, okay,' said Dug. 'But the motto – you know I did Ancient Greek 'O' Grade, right?'

Of course he knew. Everyone did. One of Dug's more amusingly annoying habits was interrupting Rimmer's lectures with uninteresting morsels on the etymology of almost everything.

'Well,' said Dug. 'I've worked out the 'eureka' part, but the other bit's got me wondering.'

'Most people round here don't need a translation,' said Terry. 'They know what my grandfather found.'

Dug shifted in his seat.

'It wasn't gold, was it?' he said.

'Spot on,' said Terry. He didn't want to talk about it. Past glories.

'But the mine's closed, right?' said Dug.

Yes, that's right, Dug. It closed many years ago when my daddy fucked off and left us, taking most of the family fortune with him.

'So, basically, your mum's running an estate...'

Terry stepped on the brakes.

'We're here,' he said.

The Flatcard was a huge field with a telegraph pole in the middle. Terry manoeuvred just inside the gate and switched off the engine. He jumped down and checked the discs. They were brand new. He could smell the paint off them.

'Right,' he said. 'This is called the headrig. You do both ends first before you start on the field. It gives you somewhere smooth to turn the tractor.'

'Got you,' said Dug.

'Want a shot?' said Terry.

'Eh...'

'Come on.'

'Look, Terry,' said Dug. 'I haven't even got a provisional driving licence...'

'It's a field, for Christ's sake,' said Terry. 'You're not going to crash into anyone.'

'Yeah,' said Dug. He was looking at the discs.

'Get in,' said Terry.

He stood on the footplate and gave directions through the window. Dug was scanning the dashboard, trying to look professional.

'What's a Blinklicht Zugwagen?' he asked.

'Never mind,' said Terry. 'You won't be needing it. Start her up.'

There was a black button with a dymo label stuck next to it. 'Depress clutch pedal to start,' it said.

'That's your left foot,' said Terry.

Dug depressed the clutch pedal. Nothing happened.

'Press the button,' said Terry.

The tractor roared into life, setting the cap on the chimney flapping.

'Sugden!' Dug shouted. 'If you could see me now!'

He lifted his foot off the clutch and they lurched forwards. It was a good job Terry was hanging on. He'd been expecting it.

'You should always make sure it's in neutral before you start,' he laughed. 'Come on, that's enough.'

Terry took over. He would have to get the field finished before Mac turned up with the Rotovator. He took off at a fair clip. It was strenuous work. The earth was baked hard, and they were bouncing around all over the cab, like balls in a pinball machine.

He managed to wallop the telegraph pole.

They got out to inspect the damage.

'That's quite a gouge,' said Dug, as the overhead cable hummed in the heat.

Terry couldn't have cared less about the pole. The discs were fucked. The last six feet were bent out of shape, pointing up at the sky.

Mac came charging across the field, shaking his fist.

'Hell's bells,' he shouted. 'There's only one stick in the park – and you hit it!'

He kicked the machine.

'Bloody part timers,' he growled.

Dug looked offended.

'Take it easy,' said Terry. 'It was me that was driving.'

'Aye,' said Mac. 'I ken fine it was you that was driving – I've been watching you for the last ten minutes. Did you think it was your mammy's Quattro or what?'

'I thought...'

Mac spat a thick wad of catarrh onto the ground.

'Don't think, Terry,' he said, and started raking through the toolbox. 'Take the Subaru and get up the D-field. I'll get this abortion up the road.'

'What's the problem?' said Terry. 'She can buy a new one.'

Mac stopped what he was doing and glared at him.

'I think you should talk to your mother,' he said.

Their steps across the field were punctuated by the clanging of a ball pane hammer against the discs.

The scene up at the D-field was like something out of Dickens, just as Terry had known it would be, with all the skinny little bodies darting in, on and around the machine.

'What a fucking shambles,' he said, and marched into the field.

The laddies were cutting cabbages, throwing them onto the conveyor belt that had been hooked up to the back of the tractor. Judd was boxing them. He was fifteen, and the spitting image of Popeye. He copped Terry approaching.

'Too many wee yins!' he shouted, and started chipping tennis ball sized cabbages back into the field.

Terry reached under the rear wheel and shut off the power. He looked at what was in the boxes.

'These are way too small, Judd,' he said.

He held up an example of an acceptable cabbage and showed it to the boys standing behind the machine.

'If they're any smaller than this,' he said, 'leave them.'

'Right y'are, Master Terry,' said Judd.

The laddies started pissing themselves.

'That's enough o' that!' Judd snapped. 'Dougal! Gie 'er some turns!'

The driver revved the engine and slipped the tractor into gear.

They progressed slowly through the field. After a while, the conveyor belt started filling up with golf balls.

'Too many wee yins!' shouted Terry.

'That wot oi be telling 'em, Master Terry,' said Judd.

Dug let out a snort.

Terry stared at him.

They trundled on.

'Here, Terry,' said Judd out of the corner of his mouth. 'If yer mate was any thinner, he'd only need yin eye.'

Someone sniggered 'Road Map' under their breath.

Dug was trailing along behind the boys. He wasn't doing any cutting – no one had given him a knife. He started whistling 'I'm Popeye The Sailor Man'.

The tractor stopped abruptly. All the wee faces turned toward him. Then the eyes were on Judd.

He stood up, slowly.

'Aaaahhhh – gagagagagag!' he laughed, and threw a cabbage in Dug's direction.

They finally cleared the field. The sun was beating down. Terry told them to take a break, and they pounced on a 2-litre plastic bottle of water that appeared out of the back window.

'Thank fuck,' said Judd. 'Ma tongue feels like the Mahatma's flip-flop.'

Mac parked the Green Monster at the fence. The discs had been removed. He walked into the field and climbed onto the machine, where he started counting the boxes.

'Right, that'll do yez,' he shouted.

He turned to Terry.

'Your mother's waiting for you in the house,' he said.

Judd had a transistor radio pressed to his ear.

'Get this, youse. This Mr Angry from Purley cunt. It makes me so angry! And he's daein' the David Bowie yin, tae...pawk sausa-geez!'

Mac looked up from the box he was holding.

'Judd,' he said. 'You'd gie an Anadin a sair heid.'

Judd turned off the radio.

'All aboard the Skylark!' he shouted, and the laddies, including Dug, climbed aboard for the ride back to the farm.

Terry was about to get into the Subaru, but Mac stopped him.

'No, Terry,' he said. 'You take the Merc up the road. And try not to hit anything. Right?'

She was waiting for him in the library, in the wing-backed chair under the portrait of his grandfather. On a small table at her elbow sat a whisky decanter and two glasses. There was going to be a serious talk. It probably wouldn't last very long, though. Terry noticed that she was wearing an olive green lambswool sweater over a tartan skirt. Her 'bridge' clothes.

'Sorry about the machine,' he said. He sat in the chair opposite, and leaned forwards. 'I was trying to get the field finished quickly because Mac...'

She raised a hand.

'It's alright, Terry,' she said. 'He's already fixed it. Luckily it was only minor damage.'

'Oh, good,' he said.

'Although I'll have to get onto the electricity board about their pylon.'

'I thought it was a telegraph pole,' said Terry. 'That was lucky. Not getting electrocuted, I me...'

'Yes,' Marie continued, 'Mr Bank of Scotland has his noose tightening around our necks. I don't think asking him for more money to replace damaged machinery would be quite as painless as you intimated to Mac.'

'.....'

'And thank you for forgetting to tell him about the distributor cap. No, no, quite all right. He's seen to that, too. Now. Let's get this sorry mess sorted out.'

She knew?

'It's not often you turn up in August unannounced, Terry. And your suit looked like you've been sleeping in it.'

'Well,' he said. He cleared his throat. 'There's two or three things.'

'Let's take them in order, shall we?'

He felt about ten years old.

'Dad threw me out of the flat,' he said.

Marie smoothed out an imaginary crease in her lap.

'You'll be looking for a new one, then,' she said.

'That was two weeks ago,' said Terry.

'So you *have* been sleeping in your suit. How perspicacious of me.'

He made a movement with his neck; a twitch.

'I got a visit from Dennis McCleaver,' he said.

Marie raised a hand to her throat.

'Really?' she gasped. 'I hope you had a box of Elastoplast handy.'

'He assaulted me in public!'

'Of course he did, Terry! Thousands of people could tell the same story. That's what your father pays him to do.'

What the hell was wrong with her? Was she deaf?

'I'm signing on,' he lied.

She laughed.

'It's 1986, Terry! There's a lot of it about.'

'I get fifteen quid a week,' he said. He'd got that information from Dug.

'Well,' she said. 'I suggest you do what your friend is doing.'

'What?'

'Get a job, Terry. The new MAFF wage rates are out. Ninety pounds a week. Don't tell the boys. Goodness knows we could do with someone to keep an eye on them. At the first chance they're off standing under the sprayer drinking Iron Brew.'

This was not an option. There was no way he was going to come and work on the farm. It was like being stuck in an adolescent sitcom, typecast as the butt of every joke. The worst part was that he was supposed to be the boss.

'You could at least give Dug some help until he finds his feet,' she said. 'He doesn't look as if he's done much manual labour.'

There was something else.

'But, mum, the Festival…'

'Yes, I know, Terry, you've missed the first week. Oh, did I tell you? I managed to get a Saturday seat at the Tattoo. Those Saturday tickets are like, ahem, gold dust. You have to book them months in advance.'

'.....'

'Forward planning, Terry. That's the key.'

'But, mum...'

'Oh, don't whine,' she said. 'Fortunately, I think I can help you out.'

Her hand moved to the table. Perhaps her cheque book was tucked in behind the decanter. It wasn't. She poured herself a whisky.

'Hasn't it occurred to you just to move back into the flat?'

'What?' he said. 'Haven't you been paying attention?'

She sighed.

'Terry,' she said. 'How old are you?'

'What?'

'How old are you?' she repeated.

'What's this got to do with...?'

'You are twenty years old, Terry. Look at you. You must be six foot four in your stocking soles, and you have the build of a champion athlete. You are more of a man than you will ever be. And you're telling me that an oik like Dennis McCleaver has got you running scared?'

45

She obviously didn't know that Dennis had form.

'I remember when your father used to bring him up here, just after we got engaged. Your grandfather couldn't stand the man – but then he couldn't stand your father, either, so that was to be expected. It's the way men are round here. They're miners, don't forget. Stand up for yourself. You graduate next year, Terry. How are you going to keep your employees in check if you're afraid that some middle-aged nyaff is going to punch you?'

It was time to put her in the picture. Maybe then she would understand.

'He's been in prison, mum,' he said.

She coughed.

'Attempted murder,' he added. That's what he had heard, anyway.

She started ironing out another crease.

'Yes,' she said. 'He was released after three years, if memory serves.'

'What?' he said. 'You know?'

'Yes, I know,' she said. 'Your father had a very good lawyer.'

For a second she looked uneasy. She took a large mouthful of whisky.

'Do you know who he tried to kill?' she said.

'What does it matter?!' Terry shouted. 'Maybe I'm next!'

'I doubt it,' she laughed mirthlessly. 'He only goes for the weaker sex.'

'Eh?'

'He's a wife-beater, Terry. He tried to kill his wife.'

Terry had had visions of Dennis being involved in some kind of Edinburgh gangland tit-for-tat kneecapping scenario. Fair enough, it wasn't that, but it was still serious – maybe more so. If he was prepared to get rid of the mother of his children, if he had any, then what would he be capable of doing to a complete stranger like Terry? Especially if, like Marie had said, he was getting paid to do it.

'I was there when it happened,' she said.

Terry was gasping for a drink, but he couldn't move.

'In fact,' she went on, 'it was me who pulled him off.'

'.....'

'Then I smashed him in the mouth with a torque wrench – he's had false teeth since he was thirty two, did you know that?'

The famous grin, thought Terry. Sterilised in a glass every night. But this was all extraneous detail. It didn't solve the problem.

'Dad's cut off my allowance,' he said. 'My cash card's useless – the account's been closed. What am I supposed to do for money?'

'I've already told you,' she said, and drained the last of her whisky. Bitch.

'Now,' she said. 'All of this is just so much beating about the bush, isn't it?'

Ah. Yes. He'd been wondering when she was going to ask.

'That's right, Terry,' she said. 'Why did he throw you out?'

'It's a long story,' he managed, finally, his eyes on the carpet. He raised his head and looked at the portrait of his grandfather. Those steely eyes, and that huge beard half way down his chest, like an Old Testament prophet. It scared the shit out of Terry just to look at it. It always had.

'What do you think he would make of this?' he said. 'He saw you alright, didn't he?'

Marie slammed her tumbler down so hard that the other glassware was set chiming.

'God, you're just like your father! All you can think about is getting your hands on other people's money! If you want to know, Terry, what my father would have to say about this, then I'll tell you. He'd be right behind me, telling me to keep my hands in my pockets until you make something of yourself.'

'But, mum...'

'Oh, get to the point, for goodness' sake!'

She moved her wrist in front of her face and looked at her watch.

'It's a long story,' he said. 'I wouldn't want you to miss your bridge club.'

'No hurry,' she said. 'I'm all ears. And don't be cute, there's a dear.'

The story wasn't long at all, in fact it was extremely short. He chose his words with practiced care, which wasn't difficult, as he'd gone over what had happened countless times in his head.

His father had started going around with – being seen with – a young lady. She was from China. Miss Chang. God knows where

47

he had found her. The only possible connection Terry could think of was that his father had served in Korea during his national service. Maybe he was trying to make amends for some kind of atrocity he had been involved in, like a good Christian. Anyhow. He had brought her round to the Institute, ostensibly, Terry had assumed, to show her the building work, but really just to show off. He had looked like a lecherous old pervert. Terry had been careful to merge into the background as the students and dignitaries came to shake hands and ogle. It was the first time Terry had seen him in years.

The next day, someone had made the 'poor house' crack within hearing distance in the canteen. Terry had made sure that the culprit wouldn't be making it again. It was only then that he realised his father had got married. The Reverend Kinlochleven, in his role as Church of Scotland Minister, had performed the betrothal himself.

'I don't know how it stands legally,' said Terry.

Marie didn't look as shocked as he'd hoped. In fact it struck him that perhaps she knew all the details already, and was enjoying making him go through this. It didn't make the telling any easier.

He took a deep breath.

'She came round to the flat a couple... three weeks ago. I don't know how she found it...'

Marie blew her nose into a tissue.

'Sorry,' she said. 'Go on.'

'I don't know what she wanted,' said Terry. 'Her English isn't very good.'

Marie nodded.

There was nothing more to tell. Apart from the end of the story. The punchline. He was looking everywhere but at his mother. Out of the corner of his eye, he saw something move. Maybe it was his grandfather shaking his head.

The sound of teenage laughter suddenly filled the room. The laddies must have been down in the yard.

'I poked...,' he blurted.

He looked up, and saw the door close quietly.

His mother was gone.

Dug was holding court. He was showing the laddies something that looked like a butter paddle. No one seemed to notice that Terry had joined the edge of the group.

'Ah still dinnae believe it,' said Judd.

'No, it's true,' said Dug. 'The barber shoves it into your hair and shaves off whatever sticks through.'

The spirit level, he explained, was the secret of the perfect flat top.

Judd flapped away the eager hands of the other laddies and grabbed the comb. He turned it this way and that, checking the bubble.

'Did ae huv a limp?' he said.

'Eh?'

'The barber. Maybe yin ae ae's legs wis shorter than the other.'

Dug looked uneasy.

'How do you mean?' he said.

Judd delivered the bad news.

'Yer flat top's squint,' he said, and the laddies, right on cue, cackled like baby hyenas.

'Aye,' said Dug, and slipped the comb into his back pocket. 'It goes with my ears.'

'Doctor Spock!' one of the boys squeaked.

'No,' said Terry. 'Just plain Mister. They don't do PhDs on the planet Vulcan.'

'Oops,' said Judd, as if he'd just noticed that Terry was there. 'Stand by yer beds!'

Terry pulled Dug to the side.

'I need your key,' he said. 'I'm going back to Edinburgh.'

49

CHAPTER 4

People were staring, openly. Some of them, the younger ones especially, were even pointing. The Reverend Kinlochleven tucked a fold of his robes under an armpit and ostentatiously consulted his wristwatch.

Dennis was late.

At long last the Rover rolled into view, traversing the diagonal from the Waterloo Place junction to the polished slabs outside the North British Hotel like a huge, graceful, ocean-going liner. Then the front wheel smacked the kerb and the car mounted the pavement, ruining the image completely.

'Sorry, Eck,' said Dennis, jumping out of the driver's seat and pulling the door open. 'Bit of a queue at the Texaco. What's new, eh?'

The Reverend knew nothing whatsoever about the vagaries of Edinburgh city centre petrol stations, nor did he want to. He burped quietly, and a subtle memory of Isle of Jura filled his nostrils. He liked to indulge in a spot of tea followed by a single malt before business. He pulled his robes around his knees, his suit trousers showing, and arranged himself on the back seat. Today he was mixing church business with business business.

The car pulled out into Princes Street.

'Dennis?'

'What's that?'

'When we're in public, didn't we say that you were to address me as 'Reverend'?'

'Oh, aye, sorry, Eck…Reverend.'

The Reverend sighed.

'Yes, Dennis, when we're in public. We're in the car now.'

'Right, y'are.'

Within minutes they were on The Mound, then down Victoria Street, where they took a slow left at the bottom of the hill. They parked across the road from an abandoned tenement block, eight storeys high.

The Reverend smoothed his robes along his knee. Church business. His accountants had told him about this place, along with the fiscal benefits of setting up a hostel for the Christian homeless of the capital. It made sound financial sense; you could still turn one flat into three and raise the rent as high as you wanted – Lothian District Housing Department were very understanding of these matters. But, according to his accountants, Mr Tax Man was beginning to insist on rather more than his fair share. As much as he would have liked, even The Reverend Alexander Kinlochleven was unable to hold any sway with the Inland Revenue. The answer was to set up a charity. Seemingly, charities were in some way exempt. The first step, then, was to find premises, hence the visit to this particularly murky corner of the city. The next would be to sack his accountants for not unearthing this gem of a money spinner earlier.

There was a fly in the ointment, however.

He looked at the building, and began drumming his fingers on his knee.

'Forgive me if I'm wrong, Dennis,' he said. 'But it looks shut.'

Dennis looked around. The street was empty.

'Don't worry, Eck, I told him to be here at half past three. He'll be inside, don't worry.'

Dennis pounded on the front door. It was one of those establishments that are permanently shuttered against the light, and open for business at around eleven in the evening. Catering for the vampires of the night, thought The Reverend. That reminded him – he'd have to get PestKillers round to the church. They had bats in the bell tower.

Dennis continued hammering, drawing stares from a group of young women going into the shop next door. He mouthed something at them and made a rude gesture with his fist.

The door opened, like a yawn in a toothless mouth.
The Reverend waited to be escorted from the car.

* * *

There was only one other customer in Proctor's, leaning against the bar and toying with the remains of a pint. His hair was a feather cut left long at the back. He was wearing a black T-shirt, and had black combat trousers tucked into little furry boots. He had said to Sammy on the phone, 'You can't miss me. I look like Bono.'
Sammy tapped him on the elbow.
'You Percival?' he said.
'Yeah…Sammy, right? Fancy a drink?'
The boy was making an early impression on the judges.
'Aye, ta. Pint ae Special.' He looked over at Baz and Mich, who had just sat down at the table in the bay window. 'An' two pints ae Fosters.' He noted that the round was ordered without so much as a huff or puff. The boy was obviously flush. That would be a new departure for the band, having someone in the immediate circle that they could bum off.
'So is this where you usually meet before practices?' Percival asked.
Aye, thought Sammy. Every lunchtime.
'Ye could say that, aye - ah, this must be mine.'
The barman laid a pint of special and a pint of Fosters on the towel. Sammy carried them over to the table.
'That's Percival gettin' a round in,' he said.
Baz made a grab for the lager, which had been meant for Mich.
'Ask um if ae's Spitfire's ootside,' he said.
Right enough, thought Sammy. The boy's boots were a riot.
All eyes were on Percival as he approached the table with the remaining beers. Before anyone had the chance to make introductions, he was offering to put money in the juke box.
'Sounds?' He nodded to himself. 'Yeah.'
He loped over to the box on the wall and studied the racks before inserting a pound coin. And then another.
'Well?' said Sammy.

Mich smiled into her pint; Baz was patting his jacket pockets.

'Rock 'n' Roll!' shouted Percival, strumming furious air guitar to the opening of Queen's 'One Vision'. This was unfortunate, for two reasons; firstly, there is no guitar during the opening of 'One Vision', and, secondly, Drive! were not a band who liked Queen.

He pogoed over to the table.

'Is that a bottle ae black nail varnish in yer pocket,' said Baz, 'or are ye jist glad tae see me?'

Percival looked down at his combat trousers. He was still gripping his invisible axe.

'No, man, just the keys to the flat, y'know?'

'Aye, so,' said Sammy. 'Everybody meet Percival…'

'Perce,' Percival corrected him.

'Right. Perse.' The way he had pronounced it in his Edinburgh private school accent had made it sound like an Englishman saying 'purse'. Things were definitely looking up.

'Perse, this is Baz, and Mich.'

'Hi there!'

'Awright?'

'Hi.'

'So, Perse,' said Sammy. 'How much experience ye got in bands?'

He was still laying riffs. He was impressing no one, Sammy knew, especially Baz, who had been known to stop mid-song if he spotted folk doing air-guitar near him. He hammered-on up the imaginary fretboard and shook his head to get the imaginary hair out of his eyes.

'Yeah, mostly round the universities, y'know?'

'How old are you?' asked Mich.

'N-n-n-n-nineteen,' he laughed. 'I look older though, eh?'

They sipped their beer.

Percival was not what they were looking for. He would not go down well with the punters at the Kaptain's Kabin. Too young and cocky by half. Then again, you could never tell. Even Bear had been accepted after a while.

'So, we going to go to your practice room for a jam or what?' he said. He was keen. 'Hang on,' he said, and held his guitar ready. 'This is the best bit.'

Drive! sat in silence as Percival did his Brian May impersonation to the middle eight of the song. It certainly was a twiddly bit of fingerwork.

Mich looked at Sammy and shook her head slowly.

Baz had his eyes closed, as if he was concentrating.

'Ye've no got a fag on ye, huv ye, Perce?' he said, when the boy finished the lick.

Sammy had been waiting for it.

'Nah, don't smoke, man,' said Percival. 'But, er…' He shoved his hand into his side pocket, and threw a five pound note across the table. 'I think they do fags up at the bar.'

Baz studied the wrinkled piece of paper, then, rising from his seat, picked it up.

'Yes, Percival,' he said, crossing the empty floor to the counter. 'They certainly do.'

Back at the flat, they ran through a couple of new numbers they had been working on, Percival sitting on a pouffe in the corner listening to what was what. Sammy noticed that he was paying particular attention to the drumming, as well as Mich's bass lines, tapping them out with his wee boots. A good sign, he obviously had a bit of co-ordination about him.

'Jist join in whenever ye feel like it,' Sammy told him. 'The mike's sittin' oan top ae Baz's amp.'

Percival picked up the mike and immediately started looking awkward, like he'd never seen one before.

'When ye're ready, Perce.'

'Yeah. Er, where will I plug this in?'

It was a good question. There was no PA for the singer; they used Baz's amp for the vocals during practices. Even the most basic Public Address system would have been too powerful. They couldn't have afforded one, anyway. The vocalist would get plugged into the real McCoy at the Kaptain's Kabin. Even so, it was a pretty standard setup for band practices – for any band.

Baz had just lit a cigarette.

'Ye can use ma amp,' he said, after a pause.

'Yeah…er…sure,' said Percival. 'Where does the jack go?' He was studying the front panel of the amplifier. There were two holes in this panel. In one of the holes was the jack for Baz's guitar. The other hole was empty.

'Eh, Perce,' said Sammy. 'How long did ye say ye've been singin' in bands?'

'Me? Singing?' he laughed. 'Nah, I'm a drummer, me.'

Sammy burped slightly, and a stale taste of Bell's whisky filled the back of his throat. Baz had invested the change from the fiver in a round of shorts.

'FFFWWHHHH FFFWWHHHH... ONE... TWO... TESTING ONE... TWO... BBBREAD, BBBUTTER, TTTEA, TTTOAST. YEAH SEEMS TO BE WORKING.'

Percival wasn't a singer, but he'd been to plenty of sound checks.

'If ye jist want tae turn it doon a peep,' said Sammy.

'Er, yeah…'

The room was filled with a shrill, ear piercing whistle.

'Stand behind the amp!' shouted Mich, her hands over her ears.

'Er, yeah, feedback. Right.'

Sammy turned to Baz.

'You dae it when we start,' he said.

Baz jammed the fag into the end of his guitar and started the riff to another of the new songs, provisionally entitled 'Chick-a-lick-a'. Just as Sammy and Mich were about to come in, Percival waved a hand. The guitar ground to a halt.

'Look,' he said 'Can we try something I can actually join in on?'

The three looked at each other.

'Do you know any Queen? Bohemian Rhapsody - I know that one.'

'We're no a four part harmony band,' said Baz. 'An' besides, the piano's away gettin' tuned.'

'Aw, right. Well what about Lloyd Cole and the Commotions? Do you know 'Perfect Skin'?

He sang the hook line. It reminded Sammy of the Pub Singer on the Steve Wright Show. A fucking good impression of Lloyd Cole, in other words.

'Nah, don't know that one, either,' said Baz.

Mich was shaking, trying to suppress the laughter.

'Joy Div?' said Percival.

They cranked up the drums and guitar.

'Mind an' play it in E!' shouted Baz.

Mich finally got it together.

They were off.

Percival struck a moody pose, The Thinker, and came in, albeit slightly late, with the vocal.

It was the Pub Singer meets Sid James. On helium.

Sammy had to lean forwards. He was battering the kick drum so hard that it was creeping away from him across the carpet. Baz had started missing chords, taking huge windmill swipes at the strings and jumping in the air to perform the splits. But he kept going – maybe he didn't want to miss the bit with the harmonics. Mich caved in. She collapsed against the wall, sending egg trays flying, and ran for the door. She threw the couch to the side, and managed a direct hit on one of Percival's boots.

'What's up with her?' he asked, rubbing his toes through the imitation leather. 'Looks a bit upset.'

'Aye, said Sammy, and laid his sticks unsteadily on his snare. 'Somethin' like that.'

'Shame,' he said. 'I was really getting into it. Y'know?'

Baz crash-dived into the lick from the middle of 'One Vision', slicing the strings to imitate the percussion. He made it go

CHUGGA-CHUGGA-CHUUUNG!
Waaaah!
CHUNG-CHUNG-CHUNG-CHUNG!
Fee-weedly-deeeee!
Feedle-eedl-eedl-eedl-eedl-eedl-eedl-eedl-eedl-eedl-eedl-WWAAAAOOOOOWWWWWW!!!

like a ten-player Galaxian machine on turbo.

Percival's jaw dropped.

Baz stooped and pulled the microphone out of his amp.

'Aye, Perce,' he smiled. 'We'll let ye know.'

* * *

As had been faithfully reported, it was a dive. The furniture consisted of what appeared to be leftover classroom chairs, and the tables could have been out of the Numpty miners' welfare hall. The Reverend shook himself; it wasn't a pleasant memory. Even the tinny music was the same. And there was a funny smell hanging in the air, like burnt Caramel Wafers.

'So, eh, Reverend,' said Dennis, guiding him over to the bar, which resembled the serving hatch in a canteen. 'This is the man I was telling you about. Mr Plato.'

'We meet at last,' beamed The Reverend.

Plato took a sip of wine, then offered a reluctant hand.

'The Reverend Kinlochleven?' he said, and tested the cloth on The Reverend's sleeve between thumb and index finger. 'Very.'

'I must admit,' said The Reverend, 'I was expecting someone slightly more… Greek?'

'Really?' Plato sniffed. 'One hundred per cent on my mother's side, I assure you.'

'…..'
'…..'

Dennis coughed into the silence.

Scratching.

An old man in a donkey jacket was sweeping the floor in the corner. He definitely wasn't getting paid by the square yard. The most animated thing about him was the ribbon of smoke spiralling from the roll up stuck to his bottom lip.

'Don't mind him,' said Plato. 'He is conveniently hard of hearing.'

'Do you think you could turn off that noise,' said The Reverend, and pointed at the loudspeaker that was nailed to the wall next to his head.

Plato looked at him with disdain.

'It's Cliff Richard,' he said.

'I know perfectly well who it is,' said The Reverend. 'But it is, let's face it, the devil's music.'

'What an old poser!' Plato laughed. 'You, obviously, not Cliff.'

'He told you to turn it off,' said Dennis.

Plato drew him a long look.

57

'Sid not with you today?' he said. 'No need to answer that, Dennis, it was a rhetorical question. I enjoy expressing the obvious interrogatively in order to induce discomfort. Other people called it sarcasm.'

Dennis looked away. He sniffed.

'He had to go for a skin graft,' he said.

Plato laughed.

'Now there's a line that would go down well in any primary school sick note. It would make a change from 'sickness and di-a-ho-ree-ho-ha'. Well done, Dennis.'

The Reverend placed one hand on Plato's shoulder and the other firmly on the back of Dennis's head.

'The Lord works in mysterious ways,' he said, and nodded gravely at the filthy bartop.

'Ah,' said Plato. 'The non sequitur as harbinger of our imminent approach to the crux.'

'I told you he was a talker,' said Dennis out of the side of his mouth.

'Yes,' rejoined Plato. 'What is it they say? The Lord will provide. Did He provide you with your toga, or did you get it mail order?'

'He got it next door,' said Dennis.

The Reverend glared at him. It was an InVestments-4-U 'High Altar' ¾ length, and it had cost nine hundred pounds.

Plato was shaking his head slowly.

'Next door?' he said. 'I seriously doubt it. And isn't that a pair of Bovver Boots peeking out shyly from your turn ups, Father? Very New Testament chic.'

'Functional,' said The Reverend, and cleared his throat. What on earth was Dennis playing at? They were supposed to be telling Plato to get out of the building, not playing word games with him.

The music was still blaring.

'And please don't address me as Father,' he said. 'I find it blasphemous. As it says in the good book, we have only one Father. God.'

'Ah, that old chestnut,' said Plato. 'I was quite forgetting that you Presbyterians take offence. Of course, it does pose the problem of what one is supposed to call one's old man. 'Hoy, you' isn't exactly respectful. 'Dad', presumably.'

The Reverend leaned on the bar.

'I believe Dennis has acquainted you with my offer,' he said.

'Indeed he has,' said Plato.

The cassette clunked itself off. The only sound was the brush scratching the floor.

'Well, come on now, Plato,' said The Reverend. 'Even the ass moved out of the way when it saw the angel of the Lord.'

Plato laughed.

'And a damn lot of good it did him!' he said.

'Yes,' said The Reverend. He attempted a sneer. 'He was given a bit of a slap, wasn't he?'

Dennis rolled his shoulders inside his coat.

'Yes, he was given a slap because he *moved*,' said Plato. 'God, I loathe debating Scripture with men of the cloth. This pose of having all the answers when in fact the only knowledge you have is a veneer of chapter and verse numbers gleaned from a skim read of the bits on your theology course. I understand fully why you are revered by the illiterate hordes.'

The Reverend glared at Dennis, who was obviously having trouble deciding if this was an insult or not.

'But come, come,' Plato continued. 'We're really not here to dissect the root meanings of Numbers Chapter 22, are we?'

'So you've read...?'

'All of it,' said Plato. 'More than once.'

A match flared as the cleaner got his roll up burning.

Plato nodded.

'Anyway, I'm sure, Father...oops, sorry, Reverend, Mister or however the blazes you fashion yourself, that you had quite enough of that Old Testament blood and guts when you were swatting for your L.Th. last year.'

'Well perhaps you'd prefer something a little more current?' said The Reverend. He could feel his face reddening. 'Let us ponder on the conversion of Paul on the road to Damascus. "*And he fell to the earth, and heard a voice…*".'

'Yes, let's,' Plato interrupted. 'Something about it being hard to kick against the pricks, isn't it?'

Dennis unbuttoned his coat.

'And don't quote me the New Testament,' Plato said. 'You seem to forget it was my lot that wrote it.'

There was no arguing with that.

'I'm not saying that the original can't be improved upon,' he continued. He sipped wine. 'Take John, for example.'

Dennis shot a glance at the old cleaner, causing both Plato and The Reverend to roll their eyes at the ceiling.

'"In the beginning was the Word. And the Word was with God. *And God was the Word*.".' Plato sucked air through his front teeth. 'A bit jarring on the ear, that last bit. One might venture that it actually gains something in the translation – I'm talking King James, of course. But then it's more to do with the word order in Greek than any difficulty with the translation *per se*.'

The Reverend conceded a smile.

'You seem quite the biblical scholar,' he said.

Plato humphed.

'Hardly. Do I look two thousand years old?'

It was rather embarrassing. The Reverend had been caught out by the same piece of vocabulary when he was studying for his Licentiate in Theology at New College – not last year, but six years ago.

'I think you should show The Reverend some respect,' said Dennis.

'You haud yer wheesht!' said Plato.

Even the cleaner turned round.

'Good, eh?' Plato smiled. 'Some people collect stamps. I collect dialects. Although dialectics is really the bag I'm into.'

'That's not funny,' said Dennis. 'My mother had that. It's no joke having to inject insul...'

'Let's get down to business, shall we?' said The Reverend. God, Dennis was a spare part.

'Yes, let's get into the roast, as it were,' said Plato. 'Don't worry, Dennis, that's not a dig at Sid. It's a Greek idiom. Do forgive me. I realise it must be over your head.'

'Well, I'll make you an offer free of idioms,' said The Reverend. 'Greek or English. Fifty thousand and I'll even say a wee prayer for you.'

'You'll say a prayer for me?' Plato laughed. 'You jumped up gold digger. I'll tell you what. Have you heard that joke about the woman on the bus with her ugly child? The punchline goes, 'And would you like a banana for your monkey?' So. Go away, feed your baboon, and I just might light a candle to your eternal estrangement from my establishment.'

'Don't talk to The Reverend like that,' said Dennis.

Plato raised his glass to his lips.

'I've just worked out what it is, Dennis,' he said. 'You scare me.'

'I hope so.'

'Oh, you're so *boring*. We have a word for people like you. Tsaba Mangas. Which is two words, but you're not to know that. It means someone who thinks he's tough when in fact he's as hard as the baby Jesus's first bout of di-a-ho-ree-ho-ha.'

The Reverend winced.

'And stop banging that ashtray off the edge of my bar, Dennis. You might chip the formica.'

'My offer remains on the table for the next fortnight,' said The Reverend. 'After that you'll be negotiating directly with Dennis and…eh…'

'Sid,' Plato prompted.

'…and Sid. There are easier ways to do this, you know.'

'Well of course there are,' said Plato. 'You could graciously accept my refusal and bugger off forever.'

'All right, then. Fifty five thousand. That's my final offer. Period.'

Plato had just taken a mouthful of wine. The guffaw which erupted from his mouth sent it spraying over the front of The Reverend's robes.

'Fifty five thousand? Your final offer? Period?' He dabbed The Reverend's chest with a big white hanky. 'You seem to forget I'm not selling. Do you dry clean this or does Miss Chang do it for you in the sink?'

Dennis flicked back the front of his coat.

'Oh, look,' said Plato. 'Dennis is going for his knee.' He looked at The Reverend. 'And you should be ashamed of yourself, sending an arsehole like this to attack your son in a public hostelry.'

The Reverend was making for the door.

'My associates will be in touch,' he said.

'Ooh, here we go again,' said Plato. 'Look, I'm shaking. You'll be making me spill my drink.'

Dennis sprinted across the road and got the back door open, pronto.

'Did you get a load of the witness?' he said, trying to catch The Reverend's reflection in the mirror.

'What witness?' said The Reverend. He was seriously considering letting Dennis go. What a performance.

'The old guy, the cleaner. And what about that roll up, eh? Old Holborn. Reminded me of Nick.'

The Reverend sighed.

'And which particular Nick would that be?'

'All of them,' said Dennis. 'Saughton, Bar-L, Inverness for a while…'

Plato had been right about one thing. Dennis was a bore. But his torpor inducing conversation was beside the point. The real problem was that this pose of ex-con hardman had worn very thin. It had had no effect on Plato whatsoever. It was time for Dennis's strong arm to get some real exercise. The Reverend would wait until he was at a very discreet distance before issuing any orders, though. He wasn't stupid.

* * *

Sammy was on his way to Jackie's with an instalment on his snare. He'd had to hit the bank and withdraw fifty quid from his savings account first, but Mich had insisted he cross Jackie's palm with silver. He'd been on the phone twice asking if they'd found a singer yet. Mich reckoned money would make him back off. At least it would reduce the hold he had over Sammy. Temporarily.

That wasn't the main problem, though. They'd had to cancel another gig at the Kaptain's Kabin, and informed sources had told him that the replacement band, a group of forty-year-old builders called 'Treads 'n' Risers', had gone down a storm. After seeing Jackie, he would jump on a bus and get down there to see what was what.

Jackie was sitting on a Marshall amp, tuning up a guitar. Even with the wee plastic tuner plugged in, he could only do it badly. He handed it over to a skinny teenager, who got stuck into Smoke On The Water, with mistakes.

'Does that no get on your wick?' said Sammy. He already had his hand in his back pocket, wanting to get the business over with. If the truth be told, however, he also wanted to keep Jackie sweet. If push came to shove and they couldn't find a singer, then Jackie was it whether they liked it or not.

'Whit, The Dirge?' said Jackie. 'Nah, ah'm used tae it. It'd help if ah wis deef, eh?!'

Ah thought ye were, Sammy couldn't stop himself thinking. Ah've heard ye singin'.

'Aye, right enough.'

He produced the tube of folded notes.

'A wee bit ae luck oan the gee-gees,' he said. 'That's fifty.'

Jackie's face fell. He counted the notes and slipped them into his breast pocket.

'Nice one, ma man,' he said. 'So, eh, nae chance ae sittin' in wi' the band?'

Sammy knew he would have to play this carefully. Jackie might have been tone deaf, but when it came to gossip he had ears like a minesweeper.

'Ach, Jackie, ah'd love tae, but we've narrowed it doon tae a couple ae new faces. No fae Edinburgh, like.'

'That right?' said Jackie. 'A wee burd tells me they've no exactly been batterin' yer door doon.'

Cunt, thought Sammy. Time to leave.

'Anyway,' he said. 'Ah'm just oan ma way doon tae Dalkeith tae see Alec Dick...'

Something went Beep Beep Beep. It was probably the guitar tuner, but it could easily have been Jackie's ears.

'...so ah'll catch ye later, right?'

'Hang oan, man,' said Jackie, and fiddled with his nuts. 'Ah'll chum ye.'

Sammy checked his wrist, but he wasn't wearing a watch. He never did.

63

'Aye, there's a bus due...'
'Nae problem,' said Jackie. 'Ah'm closin' fur dinner anyway.'
He shouted over to the teenager in the corner.
'Right you, thingwy. We're shut.'
'Five minutes?'
'Oot!'

* * *

The Reverend had removed his robes. This was business business.
'So. Dennis. Where is everyone?'
If negotiations with striking workers are to be entered into, it helps if the so-called aggrieved party is sitting across the table from you. In the large room on the second floor of the Kinlochleven Suite, there wasn't even a table.

They looked in the other rooms. They were all empty. They were also extremely draughty, on account of the windows not having been put in yet.

The Reverend started pacing up and down the corridor with his hands in his pockets.

'Well?' he said.

Dennis opened his arms wide.

'Nobody's here,' he said.

'Oh, for God's sake, I can see nobody's here!'

'Eck, I phoned the shop steward and told him to be here at 4.30 sharp. It's not my fault if the boy's late.'

'Well, it certainly isn't mine,' said The Reverend.

'Will I go over the road and phone him?' said Dennis.

'Oh, don't bother,' said The Reverend. He was going to pay Rimmer a visit, anyway. He'd give the shop steward, whatever his name was, a phone from Rimmer's office.

No. He wouldn't.

'Right, Dennis,' he said. 'I've had enough of this crowd. Get onto Group 5 and tell them to get a crew down here as of now.'

'But Security Success have got a two year contract, Eck. They're on strike. You'll be causing problems...'

The Reverend held up a hand, in the manner he used in bible study groups whenever his take on the Gospels was being questioned.

'Dennis?' he said.

'What?'

'Just do it.'

* * *

The poster had been stuck on the wall with black insulating tape. It was squint.

'SISTER CLARA'S HOME IMPROVEMENTS,' it said. 'ITS AMAZING WHAT A NUN CAN DO WITH A HAMMER DRILL!'

Moose was on the door.

'Awright, Sammy?' he said.

'Awright, Moose? You no supposed tae be at school?'

Moose was fourteen, but built like the side of a house. Apart from doing the door at the Kaptain's Kabin, he worked Sunday mornings in a slaughterhouse, killing pigs with a hammer.

'Nah,' he said. 'Suspended.'

'How many 'O' grades is it ye're daein' again?' said Jackie.

Sammy glared at him.

Moose scratched his head and looked at his shoes.

'Eh,' he said. 'Nane.'

Sammy had one foot over the threshold but turned back when he heard a hand hitting somebody in the chest.

'That's two pound,' said Moose.

'Eh?' said Jackie.

'Fur the stripper.'

'Ah'm wi' Sammy,' said Jackie, and tried to take another step.

'Two pound,' said Moose. 'Cough up or fuck off.'

Jackie started raking through the side pockets of his denim jacket.

'Who's yer favourite band again?' he said.

Moose scratched his head.

'Eh,' he said. 'The Smiths.'

Jackie handed him something.

'See that?' he said. 'That's yin ae Mark Knopfler's picks. Ae threw it intae the audience, Caley Palais, '85. Dinnae say ah'm no guid tae ye.'

The Kaptain's Kabin was stowed. Alec must have been making a mint.

'Mind yer backs!'

Sammy had to duck as a Crawford's bakery employee came swaying through the door with a tray of pies on his shoulder. Sister Clara was already well into her routine. She made a paintbrush disappear. She writhed. She produced a grouting spatula on a chain. Although the place was packed, Sammy had a good view. Someone had screwed a mirror to the ceiling.

'Paul Daniels eat yer heart out,' rasped Jackie.

Sammy looked at him. Jackie's hands were in his pockets, keeping time with the disco beat that was pumping out of the PA system.

'Whit the fuck ye daein'?!' said Sammy. This was unbelievable.

'Interior decoratin',' said Jackie. 'Jist like every other cunt in here.'

Sammy looked around.

'You're the only yin wankin',' he said, and pushed his way into the wall of bodies.

Mich would not be happy about the stripper. He'd say what he had to say to Alec, and leave. He dodged to the side to let the Crawford's employee out. The tray of pies had been left on the bar, and it looked like it would be staying there. The customers were giving their undivided attention to Sister Clara, who, she announced, was about to start her 'Living Room' routine. It was like a boxing match, with chairs gathered round a raised platform in the middle of the pub, while the punters brayed like donkeys. A lava lamp, complete with three-pin plug, was at that moment being passed over their heads, and those at the back were climbing onto their seats to get a better view, because the lads in the front row were on their feet, and the mirror had steamed up.

Alec was in his office, round the side of the bar. He was in conversation with a greasy looking character dressed in a jacket with a dozen pockets, and trousers to match.

'Ye're holdin' a knife at ma throat,' said Alec.

'Ah'm just lookin' after ma client's interests,' said the man in the jacket. 'Takin' yer clothes off in pubs is a career wi' a short life span. Think butterflies, ma man. Think flowers in full bloom. 'Ephemeral' is the word ah'm lookin' fur.'

Alec clocked Sammy standing at the door, and winked.

'Ah'll tell ye what, Malcolm,' he said. 'We'll reduce the programme slightly. The lads werenae too keen oan the number wi' the food mixer. Able Mabel in The Busker's Howf's done that yin tae death.'

Malcolm exhaled, slowly.

'Yer askin' me tae fuck wi' ma artist's art, Alec...'

Alec loosened his tie. Whatever Malcolm had asked for, thought Sammy, he could forget about.

'Let me put it this way,' said Alec. 'Ah'm fucked if ah'm goannae hand over mair than forty notes fur a lassie that shoehorns household objects up 'er fanny. It's a pub ah'm runnin' here, no a fuckin freak show. Get me?'

Sammy rapped the door jamb.

'Sammy!' smiled Alec. 'Where've ye been?'

He turned to Malcolm.

'Discussion's over. Ah've got an appointment wi' the boy here.'

Malcolm hummed something then limped out of the office, leaning on a walking stick.

'He wi' the stripper?' said Sammy, and parked himself in the armchair Malcolm had just vacated. It was warm.

'Never give in tae a cripple in a safari suit,' said Alec.

That was Alec Dick all over. You didn't get to rule the roost at the Kaptain's Kabin, Dalkeith, by being a soft touch. Alec was a manager who kept a shillelagh over the bar, in full view of the customers. It wasn't an ornament. It was a warning.

Sammy was glad they were on the same side.

'Now,' said Alec. 'What can ah do ye for?'

Sammy coughed.

'It's aboot the residency, Alec,' he said.

'Whit?' said Alec. 'Ye mean the gig your wee band does here maist Fridays?'

'Aye,' said Sammy. He moved slightly on the cushion. 'It's jist ye know the trouble wi' Bear an' that.'

'An' how is the wee fella?' said Alec, and started looking through a pile of bills.

'Fine, aye,' said Sammy. He felt like he'd lost it already. 'No, it's just that ah wis wonderin' if ye could maybe cut us some slack, ye know, till we find a new singer.'

'Treads 'n' Risers' drummer sings,' said Alec, still rifling through his bills. He made it sound like a personal challenge, as if it was a... a battle of the bands or something.

It was.

Sammy gripped the arms of the chair.

'And, eh...,' Alec looked directly at him. 'Ah hear they're lookin' fur a guitarist.'

'Alright, Alec, ma man?'

Jackie came through the door and parked himself next to Sammy. Alec ignored him completely.

'So ah'll see ye aboot that later, Sammy,' he said.

Sammy took the hint. He would have got up and left, but he couldn't feel his legs.

Alec produced a bottle and three glasses from the bottom drawer of his desk. As he poured the whisky, he launched into a story about a divorce hearing up at the court.

'So McIver's brief says tae 'er, 'Did you or did you not fellate Mr Davidson in the car park?' 'Fellate him?' she goes. 'Ah didnae even ken ae hud a puncture!'.'

Sammy wasn't laughing.

Jackie drained his glass, and started on his theory of whisky.

'Ye'll huv noticed there are three kinds,' he said. 'Family names, objects fae nature, an' place names. In ascendin' order ae quality. Think oan it, yer Bells, yer Mackinleys, yer Queen Mary's – the bottom end ae the market, right? Then the objects – yer Four Roses, yer Wild Turkey...'

He raised his glass and grimaced.

'...yer Famous Grouse. Then ye've got yer up-market brands, ye know, the kind that come in a biscuit tin, yer Laphroaig, yer Balvenie, yer Glenfiddich…'

Alec let him finish what he was saying.

'Ah'll bet ye didnae pay fur yer ticket, either,' he said, staring at the glass in Jackie's hand.

'Eh?' said Jackie.

Bastards, thought Sammy.

'Did ye blag yer way in tae see the stripper?' said Alec.

'Aye, well Sammy hud a bit ae business wi' you...'

'Fuck off, Jackie,' said Alec. 'Yer patter's garbage.'

Sammy struggled to get out of the chair.

'See ye oan Friday!' Alec shouted at his back.

The bar was strangely silent. Some comedian barked 'Ah need a new three-piece suite!' Nobody laughed. It must have been Fat Edgar.

He let the door bang shut behind him and leaned against the wall, his forehead touching the cold bricks.

Someone poked him on the arm.

'Here,' said Moose, and shoved the plectrum under his nose. 'Since when did Mark Knopfler play wi' The Smiths?'

* * *

'So. Roger. That's the package I'm offering you.'

Rimmer reclined and hoisted his feet, slowly, onto his desk.

The Reverend regarded the soles of Rimmer's shoes. Fair enough. He was allowed to put his feet on his desk. It was, after all, his desk. The Reverend didn't own it. Not yet, anyway.

Rimmer looked at him between his shoes.

'And a very generous offer it is, Eck.'

Dennis cleared his throat.

'Tell me,' Rimmer continued. 'How many prime chunks of Edinburgh real estate will I be able to get my hands on out of forty grand a year?'

'Oh, come on, Roger, I...'

'No, let's explore this. Perhaps I could just about manage to get on the premium property ladder if you gave me let me think ah yes thirty five years back pay. On second thoughts, it would still be a tad off the pace, don't you think?'

The Reverend sighed.

'Take it or leave it,' he said.

Rimmer removed his feet from the desk with a grunt and stood up.

'You've got a fucking nerve,' he hissed.

69

'No, Roger,' said The Reverend, 'but I used to, I'll grant you that much. It's never too late to make amends, though, is it? Think it over.'

Rimmer had already turned his back, and was unbuckling something that looked like a leather flask.

'If you'll excuse me,' he said. 'My appliance needs washing.'

The Reverend watched him disappear into his cubby hole, and cocked an indifferent eyebrow at the floor. He'd made the offer. If Rimmer didn't want to take up the position of Director of the Kinlochleven Suite, which would be the crowning glory of his career, then it was a decision that would have to be respected. But what was wrong with the man? Surely after all these years he had managed to put two and two together and work out that it was Eck Kinlochleven, putting a word in the right ear here, letting a name drop there, who had engineered his rise from disgraced doctor to University Lecturer. Ingratitude was something that The Reverend could not abide. It wasn't very Christian. Neither was stealing a man's wife from under his nose, but that had all turned out for the best – and then failed, admittedly, but it was all water under the bridge.

He glanced at his watch.

'Dennis,' he said. 'Bring the car round.'

'Right, Eck.'

It was almost visiting time at the Infirmary. What a liability Miss Chang was turning into. Still, she was his other half, so he'd have to go. At least in hospital he could be sure that she was behaving herself.

And, of course, there was that other niggling problem. Rumour had it that his son had moved back into the flat, no doubt on the instigation of his mother, who had been sticking her nose into church affairs of late. To hell with both of them. He would let Terry get his feet comfortably back under the table then send Dennis round to sort him out. Permanently, this time. He'd have to make sure he ended up in a different hospital to Miss Chang, though. The Devil only knew what they would get up to if they found themselves together again, broken bones or not.

CHAPTER 5

'It's aw a Masonic plot, man. Ah'm tellin' ye.'

The computer screens were orange. Geeky, sitting at the next terminal to Terry, was sure that the dark forces of Protestantism were trying to convert the temping staff by stealth.

'Maybe it's just cheaper to make orange screens,' said Terry.

'Aye,' said Geeky. 'Tell that tae the Marines.'

They tapped in their data until lunchtime.

Terry found a quiet spot in the corner of the canteen, and unwrapped his chicken roll. He was glad to be on his own. Fine, his neighbour could come out with some fantastic lines, but he could also be a bit wearing on the nerves.

Geeky stopped in the doorway and scanned the room. He had a carton of juice sitting squarely in the middle of his tray. Terry tried to hide behind his roll, but there was no getting away from this boy. Geeky parked himself on the other side of the table, and looked around to make sure there was no one within hearing distance.

'It's aw set up,' he said.

Terry chewed a mouthful of chicken.

'What is?' he asked.

Geeky looked around again. He lowered his voice.

'You ken...the...'

His voice softened to a whisper.

'The A.R.M.'

Besides being scared to death at the thought of enforced Sunday school, Geeky was also concerned about what was being done to animals in the name of Science. He was sure that the next step was bodysnatching – maybe that had already started. He had been a member of the Animal Rights Movement for almost two months, and wanted Terry to join.

'Are you still trying to convert me to your cause?' Terry asked.

Geeky sipped his juice seriously.

'We could dae ye a favour, Terry,' he said. 'After whit ye telt me aboot you an' yer dad.'

Terry had thought about getting back at his father for all of five minutes. What was the point? He'd been a bad boy, he'd got his wrist slapped, now it was time to move on. He didn't think he would be needing the services of the A.R.M.

Geeky pulled a pepperoni stick out of his back pocket and bit off a mouthful.

'Come roond the flat the night,' he said. 'We're huvvin' a meetin'.'

Terry watched him chew. There was, of course, no way he would be going round to Geeky's flat. He'd been there once already for a 'meeting', and he hadn't been at all impressed. The place stank of boiled cabbages and soya pepperoni – the members of the A.R.M., all three of them, were strict vegans, and wore their smell like a badge of honour. They had informed him that they were a clandestine organisation, but Terry was sure that one day, sooner or later, the stench would give the game away.

In any case, Terry had other plans.

Tracey from Accounts.

The latest.

There wasn't much of the summer left, but he was making the most of it. The young ladies working the terminals at Scottish Death had been unable to resist the charms of that hunk on the third floor, the guy with the hair, the shoulders and the nice wee bum. Those who had been unable to get into his jeans – both male and female – had labelled him the office slut. He was loving it. If anything, he was actually encouraging it. He wasn't intending to hang around to take advantage of the generous pension plan.

Yes, it had been a fantastic summer, and it was a shame it was coming to an end. But he had his Honours Year to think about, and after that the world was his oyster.

Geeky burped.

'So, we oan, then?' he asked through the garlic haze.

'Some other time,' said Terry. 'I've got a prior engagement.'

He could hear splashing. Dug was in the bath. He'd better leave enough water.

Mr Kwak was sitting at the kitchen table, paring his nails with a Swiss Army knife. He smiled when Terry walked in.

'Hi, there,' said Terry. This was a surprise.

The sound of The Smiths' 'How Soon Is Now?' came throbbing out of Dug's room.

'Morrissey!' said Mr Kwak.

Dug appeared in the kitchen. Despite the sunburn, he was pale.

'Ah, Terry,' he said. 'Am I glad you're here!'

Terry looked their guest up and down.

'He's not causing problems, is he?' he said.

'God, no,' said Dug. 'Mr Kwak has saved the day.'

A loud gurgle as the bath plug was removed.

'You've got visitors,' said Dug.

The bathroom door opened, liberating a cloud of steam into the hallway.

'Dug!' shouted a woman's voice. 'You haven't got another towel have you?'

Terry glared.

'What the fuck's my mother doing here...in the bath...?'

'It's not your mum having the bath,' said Dug. She's helping...'

'Oh, hello, Terry,' said Marie. 'Quick, Dug, get another towel for Miss Chang.'

* * *

He put in a solid eighteen hours a day for the next four days learning how to play and sing at the same time. The neighbours were loving it. Neither the cardboard egg trays on the walls nor the couch propped against the door could stop the sound of Sammy permeating the whole building. Band practices were cancelled until he thought he was good enough to perform in front of the others.

He told them to come round on Friday.

He brought the tea through and sat behind his drums.

'Did they get a replacement band last week?' asked Mich.

Sammy was ready.

'Aye. Get this. Treads 'n' Risers.'

'Eh?'

He repeated the name slowly.

'Treads. 'N'. Risers.'

'What, are they German?'

'No, they're builders.'

He coughed.

'Their drummer does the vocals.'

'Arseholes,' muttered Baz. He was repairing his top E.

Sammy hesitated.

'So, eh, that's why ah've been locked away aw week.'

Baz was unravelling the coil of wire that was wrapped around the machine head. He stopped.

'Are you serious?' he said.

Mich jumped in.

'I don't think we've got time to have a disagreement,' she said.

'Aye,' said Sammy. 'Alec said we could huv the gig the night if we've got a singer.'

'But we huvnae got a fuckin' singer!' said Baz.

Fair point.

'We'll keep the vocals doon and crank up the guitar,' said Sammy. He knew that Baz would be into anything where he was pushed to the front of the performance. 'Nae ballads, jist fast, rockin' numbers.'

Baz twisted the string with his pliers.

'A band should huv a front man,' he said. 'Okay, the Bear's a dwarf, but ae kens how tae jump aroond a stage an' get a crowd goin'.'

This was true. He couldn't jump very high, right enough, but he was quick over the ground.

Sammy adjusted the hi-hat.

'It's a temporary measure,' he said.

'Till we find a singer,' echoed Mich.

'So we make arses ae oorsells till then?' said Baz. 'No way.'

Mich slung her bass round her neck.

'I think we should at least hear what Sammy's like before we go making snap judgements,' she said.

Thanks, doll, he wanted to say, but his eyes were on his knees. He was shiting it.

Baz took his time with the string.

'Sultans ae Swing,' said Sammy. The lyrics were more spoken than sung, and the guitar was well to the front. Just as Sammy was about to come in with the vocals, Baz held up a hand.

'Wo, wo, wo,' he said. 'Yer mike's too high up oan the stand. Ye look like Phil Collins.'

It was difficult to play the drums and sing and not look like Phil Collins.

Sammy adjusted the microphone.

They started again.

'Wo, wo, wo. The way ye're hittin' the hi-hat. Ye look like Stewart Copeland.'

He could feel the anger rising. Baz must have known he was chancing it. *Nobody* told Sammy how to play the drums.

They started for the third time. Baz held up his hand again, but before he could say anything, Sammy threw his sticks into the corner. The eighteen hour shifts had caught up with him.

'Fuckin' pack it in, awright?!' he shouted.

Baz leaned over his guitar. He wasn't taking the piss.

'Ah'm preparin' ye fur Fat Edgar,' he said.

Mich slapped her bass.

'Come, on, let's do it,' she said.

Sammy clicked his sticks: 1 – 2, 1-2-3-flam.

He was good.

Sammy was very good.

Mich broke into a smile.

Baz gave a workmanlike performance. It was all that was being asked of him. He soon got into it.

* * *

Mr Kwak was singing along to Morrissey.

Terry waited until the end of the song.

'Dug,' he said. 'Turn that racket off, will you?'

'Got you,' said Dug.

Miss Chang was standing over by the sink. Even though her arm was in a sling, she still looked like the front cover of Vogue. The 'Injured Supermodels' edition, perhaps.

'And that,' said Marie, 'brings us right up to date.'

Marie had received a phone call. She had come to town looking for Miss Chang. She could have come sooner, of course, but she had a farm to run. It hadn't been too difficult to find her; there weren't too many six-foot Korean women with fractured limbs and minimal English in Edinburgh's hospitals. She'd been in the Infirmary. Dug had got in touch with Mr Kwak to act as translator. Mr Kwak was Korean, too, it turned out. The plan was to take Miss Chang back to the farm, where she could recuperate. After that, it was up to her what she wanted to do. If she wanted to be repatriated, Marie would organise it.

She looked at her watch.

'You'll have to excuse me,' she said. 'I'm not really *au fait* with the legalities, so I'm seeing my lawyer. It shouldn't take longer than an hour.'

She stood up, and Miss Chang reached nervously for her. She started speaking to Mr Kwak.

'She want to know where...'

'Tell her I have to go and see someone,' said Marie. 'Don't worry, you poor girl. Everything will be all right.' She would have hugged her, but Miss Chang drew back. 'Oh, yes, your arm, pet. Sorry.'

* * *

He had only managed to prepare eight numbers, but he was sure the punters would understand. They might even be impressed. Anyway, they could repeat the set after the break, changing the order. If they wanted an encore then Baz could do 'Layla' on the harmonica till closing time.

'Ye're late,' said Alec, as Sammy carted his bass drum into the lounge. 'Ah wis jist away tae give that other crowd a tinkle.'

'Everythin's cool,' Sammy assured him. 'My, my, my, have we got somethin' special fur you the night.'

'An' whit wid that be?'

'Wait an' see.'

He could feel someone watching him as he taped his drum to the floor.

'Ah've got a wee surprise fur the punters an' all,' said Alec.

'Aye?' said Sammy.

'Aye,' said Alec. 'Sister Clara's goannae be givin' a DIY demonstration in the interval.'

Sammy froze with the tape stretched across his mouth. His eyes scanned the bar. The mirror was still screwed to the ceiling. Mich was coming through the door with the snare.

'Jist kiddin',' said Alec, and clapped him on the shoulder. 'Friday night is rock night in the Kaptain's Kabin!'

* * *

The sound of a key in the lock.

Marie didn't have a key.

Before Terry could get to the mortise, the door jamb splintered, and Dennis was standing, gasping, in the hallway.

'Well, well,' he said. 'We meet again.' He stood to the side. There was someone behind him. 'Sid said I should try the key first, but it looks like the locks have been changed.'

He grinned.

'That's naughty.'

His overcoat was draped over his shoulders.

'That's not a shotgun, is it?' said Dug.

Dennis pumped it.

'Oh, shite,' said Dug.

Terry suppressed a smile; he'd seen what was written on the side of the gun.

'Right,' said Dennis. 'Get in the kitchen.' He worked his dentures on his gums. 'And no funny business.'

Miss Chang screamed when she saw him. She backed into the corner, whimpering, when Sid came in. He was swinging a golf club gently between thumb and forefinger. It was Sid they'd have to watch out for, Terry knew. Christ, but he was ugly. He looked like he'd been in a fire. Maybe they'd tried to give him a skin graft. If so, the operation had only been a partial success. His left ear hung like an empty scrotum.

Dennis barked something in a foreign language, and Mr Kwak's hands nearly went through the ceiling. Miss Chang struggled to raise her good hand – the one that wasn't in a stookie.

Dennis grinned.

'Aye,' he said. 'The Numpty Fusiliers, Pakchon, '50. The best days of my life.'

Mr Kwak started stammering something, nodding at Sid.

Terry hoped he wasn't making a crack about his ear.

'Nice top!' Mr Kwak managed, eventually.

Sid was wearing a red and black T-shirt. There was a picture on the front, Dennis the Menace giving it to Beryl the Peril, doggy style. 'Menace me, Dennis,' ran the legend.

Dennis pumped the gun again.

Terry laughed.

'A few more times, I think,' he said.

'No!' said Dug.

'Don't worry,' said Terry. 'Webley don't make shotguns.'

It was an air rifle.

'Careful, Dennis,' he said. 'You could take someone's eye out with that.'

Dennis ignored him.

'Sid,' he said. 'Bring Miss...Mrs Kinlochleven over here.'

Mr Kwak began the translation, but it was drowned out by Miss Chang's screaming. He stood up, blabbing away, trying to calm her down, and he got Sid's elbow in his face. Terry took a swing at Sid's head, but the boy had been practising his golf strokes. He stepped back and caught Terry a beauty across the knee caps.

Terry went straight down, squealing like a pig.

Sid grabbed Miss Chang and marched her to the door. She started shouting again. Terry blinked the tears out of his eyes and saw Dennis lean into her. He pressed the butt of his gun into her sling.

'Any more noise,' he hissed, 'and Sid will break it. Again. Got it?'

Sid pushed her into the hallway.

'And you, young yin,' Dennis added. He was talking to Terry. 'You should learn to take a telling. Get out of the flat. And fucking stay out.'

* * *

'It's Ke-vin God-ley!'

Sammy was unfazed. Kevin Godley was a terrific drummer, with a voice like an angel. And Kevin Godley had a beard, whereas Sammy didn't. Well done, Fat Edgar. Spot-on, as usual.

'Shut it, you,' came a voice from the back.

'D'ye make videos as well, Sammy?'

Aye.

'That's enough!' shouted somebody else. 'Gie the boy a chance.'

He could have done without the moral support. Gie the boy a chance? Sammy was thirty five years old and had been playing in bands since he was fifteen.

'Is it a video nasty, Sammy?'

He ignored it.

They played the opening number in hushed silence, the regulars taking slow mouthfuls of beer. Then they started nodding at each other. Then they started tapping their feet.

The applause was adequate.

Fat Edgar clapped, too.

'And ten makes a hundred,' said Alec, handing over the night's pay.

Sammy folded the money and slipped it into his pocket. He usually counted it, but didn't want to give offence.

'So, eh, we'll see ye next week, then?' he said.

Alec reached into his desk for the bottle of Grouse. He loosened his tie.

'Look, Sammy,' he said. 'Ah'm no sayin' ye're no good. Ah think ye've got a lovely singin' voice. But, eh...'

If he was going to give them the brush off he could at least get it over with quickly.

'...ah'm runnin' a business here. Ye with me?'

'Oan ye go.'

'Drinkers sittin' oan their arses don't drink. They sip. Ye get me?'

'Oan ye go.'

'Christ's sake, Sammy, ye're no makin' it very easy!'

'How long is it we've been playin' here, Alec?' said Sammy. 'Three year? Say forty gigs a year. That's a hunner an' twenty. Ah think that adds up tae a fair wad ae beer money.'

Alec shifted in his seat.

'Point taken, Sammy. But ye need a front man. If there's a clown prancin' aroond oan the stage, it makes other clowns prance aroond between the tables...aw the way up tae the bar.'

Sammy couldn't let him get away with that. Not after all the sweat he'd put in.

'Ah thought ye said the drummer oot ae Treads 'n' Risers sings?' he said. 'Whit ah mean is they huvnae got a front man, but you're sayin'...'

'But he's better than you, Sammy,' said Alec.

'.....'

It was hard to draw breath.

'So, is this it, then?' said Sammy.

Alec looked at him steadily, then straightened his tie. He downed his whisky in one.

'Okay,' he said. 'Ah'll tell ye whit.'

He produced a battered desk diary from his drawer, and flicked through the remaining pages.

'Ah'll let yez play till the end ae the month. If ye cannae get it the gether by then...'

'Treads 'n' Risers.'

Alec clapped the diary shut.

'Sammy,' he said. 'Ah couldnae gie a fiddler's fuck who's yodellin' through the lounge there. As long as the punters are neckin' their pints, ah'm happy. So. The end ae the month. If ye cannae come up wi' the goods...'

'Ye've got a business tae run.'

'Precisely. Now, finish yer whisky ya mouthy wee bastard.'

They were waiting for him in the van.

'What was that all about?' said Mich.

There was no avoiding it.

'We've got four weeks tae get oor shit the gether,' said Sammy.

Mich sighed, and turned the key in the ignition.

Baz sparked a match behind them. He leaned through the gap between the front seats.

'We goannae divvy up or whit?' he said.

* * *

'Eh, I think we've met,' he said, and offered a hand. 'The name's Vic.'

It was the medic who'd helped the old woman at Waverley. He was still drunk.

He burped.

'You drink in The Confessional, don't you?' he said.

'Right,' said Terry, and showed him into the kitchen.

Mr Kwak was slumped under the table. Vic tried to start CPR. He was having trouble keeping his balance, even though he was kneeling on the floor.

'He's breathing,' he said, and looked up. 'That's always a good sign.'

He put a drip into Mr Kwak's arm and hooked up a finger to an ECG monitor. Terry recognised the machine from his Physiology 2h class.

'But surely you should attach the leads to his chest,' said Dug. He'd done Physiology 2h, too.

'Shut it, Dug,' said Terry.

Vic pushed himself up, one hand on the table and the other on the wall.

'I'll drink to that,' he said, and pulled a bottle of Guinness out of his anorak pocket.

The line on the screen went flat, and the machine started to whine.

Dug gasped.

Vic's eyes were darting around the kitchen. He grabbed the Swiss Army knife off the table.

'Great things, these,' he said. He tucked the bottle under his arm and opened the knife. 'A blade for every occasion. Pure Genius, if you ask me.'

He prised off the stopper and took a swig.

Dug was staring at him.

Vic wiped the neck on his sleeve.

'Sorry, mate,' he said. 'Want some?'

Dug pointed a trembling finger at Mr Kwak.

'Oh, him?' said Vic. He gave the machine a kick. It bleeped. 'He'll live.'

He raised the bottle once more.

'Cheers,' he said, and emptied the contents down his throat.

They carried Mr Kwak down to the ambulance, Vic holding his legs, Terry his torso, and Dug bringing up the rear making sure that the drip and the ECG didn't bang into anything.

Vic was sweating.

'He's a heavy little fucker, eh?' he panted.

He stopped behind a white Ford Escort van with a wee blue light on the roof, and looked at Terry.

'Thatcher's Britain, mate,' he said.

He had to bang the tailgate a few times to get it to stay shut. Terry rubbed a hole in the back window. Mr Kwak was still unconscious.

'What on earth...?'

Terry made to brush past her, but she caught hold of his arm.

'Don't fucking touch me,' he said.

'But, Terry, what...?'

The ambulance farted smoke and pulled out into the street. The wee blue light came on okay, but the siren sounded like it needed winding up.

'We had another visit from Dennis, mum. He took Miss Chang with him. He's slightly more dangerous than you made out.'

His knees were still throbbing.

'Dennis didn't actually hit anyone, though,' Dug piped up. 'It was his mate, Sid, that did all the damage.'

'Oh, I can't be doing with all this!' said Marie, and made her way out onto the road. 'I've got...'

'Yeah, mum, you've got a farm to run. Well, you're fucking welcome to it!'

Dug breathed a sigh of relief.

'It's a good job I'm moving into Duddingston Halls,' he said.
Terry rubbed his kneecaps.
'Bully for you, Dug,' he said.

CHAPTER 6

The close stank. Geeky was obviously in, and cooking.

He was sticking posters to the walls of his room. A pot of broccoli was bubbling next to the bed.

'This is the guid thing aboot the joab,' he said, and tore off another strip of sellotape. 'Apart fae the free hoalidays, like.'

He'd just been taken on as a trainee at Travel Ecosse.

He stood back and admired his work.

'It covers up the damp patches an' aw,' he added.

The saucepan boiled, leaving a film of condensation over everything. Terry wiped his brow. The happy holidaymakers were glaring down at him. They looked like they were sweating.

'Ah've got plenty mair if ye want some,' said Geeky.

Terry had moved in next door.

'No, you're okay,' he said.

They shared a bowl of greens.

Terry steered the conversation in the direction of animal rights, which wasn't difficult. He told a story about sheep being screwed to the walls at the Institute, and was rewarded with exactly the result he was looking for.

Geeky's face changed colour. Flecks of saliva formed in the corners of his mouth, and they were soon showering across the table. He was ranting. He began to smash his fist into the table, oblivious to the fact that he was mashing his pepperoni stick into the woodwork.

'It's a fuckin' abomination!' he screamed.

Do I really want to get involved in this? Terry asked himself. He pulled a bottle of Jack Daniel's out of his pocket. Geeky calmed down immediately. He looked impressed. Terry had jacked his job, and had started shoplifting life's little luxuries.

There was only one cup in the flat; it was mottled purple, and matched the bowl. Geeky pushed a mound of wet underpants to the side of the wash hand basin and rinsed it under the tap. Terry drank from the bottle.

'So ye've thought aboot ma proposition?' said Geeky.

'I'm still thinking about it,' said Terry.

'Here's the deal,' said Geeky. 'Ah've got an address fur a possible client. It's yours if ye want.'

'What do you mean?' said Terry. If there was going to be any terrorist activity, he was quite sure that he'd be spectating from a safe distance. And what did he mean by 'client'? He'd read about animal rights fanatics in the paper – he'd always thought of them as free agents.

'It's the 1980s, mate! The grapevine's buzzin'. Ye've got tae cater tae the market.'

'What, you mean people actually pay you to...whatever it is you do?'

Geeky shook his head and held out his cup.

'Folk huv got problems, right? So they come tae us an' we take care ae thum.'

'How much do they pay you?'

Geeky looked offended.

'Nothin',' he said. 'We dae it cos it's right.'

They drank more whiskey.

'We'll get roond tae yer daddy later, Terry. In the meantime, ye'll huv tae prove yersell.'

He held out his cup again.

'Look oan it as a kind ae initiation ritual,' he said.

He told Terry where to go, and who to ask for.

It was called The Left Bank, but it had more in common with a greasy spoon than coffee time at the Sorbonne. He had no problem finding it. It was next door to the second hand clothes shop that was famous throughout the University. The bar was full of what had to be History and Politics students wearing black polo necks under the overcoats they had recently purchased from the shop. My goodness but they thought they were cool. Geeky had told him that the owner of the shop also owned the bar. This would have explained the dress code. Presumably, you didn't get in unless you were wearing one of the guvnor's minging Crombies.

Terry was wearing his suit, but he was blending in nicely – the jacket had contracted mildew from the wardrobe in the flat. He had probably smoked half a pack of regurgitated Gauloises by the time he pulled up a stool at the bar. The barman greeted him in French. Terry stared at him, then pointed at a bottle of Newcastle Brown in the cooler. Everyone else seemed to be drinking it.

He had been told to ask for Plato. Code names already.

He leaned over the counter.

'I want to see Plato,' he said, slowly.

'Quoi?'

The taped accordions were loud.

'Tell Plato I want to see him,' he said. He opened his palm and showed the barman the letters A.R.M.

'Ah, got it,' said the barman. 'Did Geeky send you?'

'Eh?'

'Look,' he said, and moved his head closer. 'I joined last week – do you know how much the cunt charged me for subscription?'

Terry sipped his beer.

'Plato?' he said.

The barman winked.

'Go and sit at that table in the corner,' he said. 'I'll, eh, see if he's in.'

Terry made sure he was facing the wall. All those arseholes in their overcoats were making him sick. He flicked through a pamphlet on the table, two sheets of A4 stapled together. Upcoming arts events. The Mummers. Shut Up and Mime. The only thing worth looking at was a thing called Rock Angers, a music festival in France. Hang on. That was where the Agrics were going for their final year trip. Some time in Feb...

A wheelchair bumped into his table. A joker in a corduroy suit was in it. He was wearing a monkey mask.

'You can fuck off for a start,' said Terry, and tipped the last of his beer into his glass.

The monkey was saying something. Terry couldn't make it out. The mask was muffling it. And those accordions!

A bottle of wine and two glasses were placed on the table.

The man removed his mask.

'Rosé d'Anjou, '84,' he gasped. 'Bloody sweaty thing – the mask, of course, not the wine.'

Terry had a vague idea he had seen him somewhere...

'I'm Plato,' said the man. 'The last time I saw you, you were rolling around on the floor of The Confessional.'

'Sorry?'

'Someone had just kneed you in the balls.'

Ah.

'It was my leg, actually,' said Terry.

'Balls, legs,' said Plato, and filled their glasses. 'It's all the same, isn't it?'

'Well...'

'Sore when people stick their knees in them, I mean.'

Terry looked at the wheelchair, and Plato performed a rapid tap dance on the footrests.

'Believe it or not,' he said, 'I'm going for the sympathy vote. Have some wine. Or ur ye stickin' wi' the Newky Broon?'

Terry blinked. He sounded exactly like Dug's dad.

'Yes,' Plato said. 'Falkirk. Give or take a few miles. Although it's a shame how Glaswegian has pervaded East Central Scotland argot. I blame Billy Connolly, but then that's the fashionable thing to do these days. From hanging his arse over a railing on the Clyde to nibbling cucumber sandwiches round the back of Buckingham Palace. Guaranteed to upset people...especially those who hate to see you getting on.'

Terry tried the wine. He felt grit between his teeth.

'The soil from the vineyard leaves a pleasant aftertaste, don't you think?' said Plato.

87

Terry swirled the wine round in the glass. Maybe there had been some kind of mistake.

'Do you mind if I ask you something?' he said.

Plato smiled.

'Fire, ahem, away,' he said.

Terry leaned in closer.

'I was given your name...'

'Of course you were,' said Plato. 'Don't worry, Terry, the, er, grapevine can be trusted.'

'You know my name?' said Terry.

Plato tilted his head slightly to the side.

'Oh, yes,' he said.

Fair enough, thought Terry, if he was a regular in The Confessional. But his cover was already blown. This was verging on the downright reckless.

A frumpy girl whose belly filled the hem of her jumper loomed up behind the wheelchair. She was wearing a monkey mask, and didn't seem sure whether to lay her fingers on the handgrips or run them through Plato's hair. She made do with putting a hand on his shoulder, but withdrew it immediately when he shrugged.

Plato turned to look.

'My dear,' he said. 'You can dispense with the ape face. You may have noticed that I have deemed our disguises *perittés*. Terry is one of us.'

She dutifully removed the mask. She looked at Terry.

'You used to work at Scottish Dea...,' she began.

'Yes, well I'll see you later, Morag,' said Plato.

'But I wanted to ask you...'

'Yes, I'm sure you did, Morag. It's time for you to go now.'

She sloped off and leaned against the wall, kneading the mask in her fists. Then she put it back on.

Plato poured the last of the wine into his glass.

'All the young ladies for me,' he chuckled.

Terry wasn't impressed. He'd been through dozens of women at Scottish Death – but he'd made sure to steer clear of the ugly ones.

'You'll have to excuse Morag,' Plato said. 'She's been on my case for what seems like...well, for a lifetime, really. I'm treading very carefully. She isn't well. Pierre was telling me, and Pierre is a barman who studies Psychology in real life, that she suffers from a condition known as Mild Turettes by Proxy.'

'Really?'

'Yes,' said Plato. 'She is apt to make people curse under their breath.'

It doesn't change the fact that you're a dirty old man, thought Terry.

Plato took a large draught of wine.

'My enemy's enemy is my friend,' he said, and fixed Terry with a stare. 'The most dangerous expression in the language. Would you agree?'

'I thought that was 'There's no smoke without fire',' said Terry.

'Touché!' said Plato. 'And so apt!'

He reached down into his wheelchair and placed a battered paperback book on the table.

'As you can see,' he said, 'it's The Assistant, by Mr Bernard Malamud.'

Terry picked it up.

Plato was nodding.

'I've marked the pages I think are germane to our conversation,' he said.

Terry flicked through the book. The text on page 187 was underlined in red biro.

'Fire insurance?' he said.

'Perhaps it would be better to read it later,' said Plato. 'I think we should talk a little. Firstly, I'd like to know what on earth is going on between you and your f...'

There was a sudden lull in the noise level. Even the accordions seemed to get quieter.

Dennis and Sid had just walked in. They were slowly surveying the scene. Sid was swinging his golf club lazily at his side, like a pendulum. He wasn't in a hurry.

Terry turned his attention to the grime inlaid etchings on the surface of the table. He hadn't realised they were following him.

'Don't worry,' said Plato, and put his wheelchair into reverse.

'I've got some business to attend to. Do your homework. You know where to find me.'

Terry could feel Dennis's eyes boring into the back of his neck. He turned.

They had disappeared. They must have gone to look in the toilet. He grabbed the book and made a sharp exit.

CHAPTER 7

He was in Dug's room, drying himself with a towel. He looked out of the window. The girl in the room directly opposite smiled at him. She removed her jumper. She kept smiling.

The joys of the Duddingston Halls of Residence. The water in the flat was on the blink. He'd come over to use the shower facilities. He'd brought his washing with him, too. Dug was in the drying room, hanging it up.

* * *

The Prezzie Hall was stowed, but Sammy was alone, nursing a pint up at the bar. He'd had a bastard of a day.

He was looking for Bear.

* * *

Sugden wanted to see his students about their Honours theses, but Dug insisted on ducking into the music shop on Mayfield Road to have a look at the guitars first. The money he'd saved over the summer was burning a hole in his pocket.

'There's a Strat copy I've been looking at,' he said. 'I hope it's still there.'

Dug wanted to be a singer/songwriter. He'd explained that there was a problem – he only knew three chords. Getting the guitar would help him hone his craft.

'The owner's called Jackie,' he said. 'You should hear him playing Smoke On The Water!'

The shop was empty. Dug marched straight over to the second hand section. Just as he put his hand on the guitar, a wee head popped up from behind the amps.

'Alright, Jackie?' said Dug.

'Oh, it's you,' said Jackie. 'Nice haircut.'

He looked at Terry.

'Who's this?' he said. 'David Coverdale?'

Terry had used Dug's hair dryer.

Dug took the guitar down off the hook.

'Can you plug this in for me?' he said.

Jackie grimaced.

'Geeza break, man,' he said. 'That Deep Purple Appreciation crowd fae the Uni were in aw mornin'.'

Dug looked disappointed.

'Dinnae worry, mate,' said Jackie. 'Ye'll hear the sustain better if ye play it acoustic.'

'Aye,' said Dug. 'But I'm thinking about buying it.'

Jackie had the connections done in a flash, and gave them a free demonstration.

This is really, really bad, thought Terry.

Dug bought the guitar.

Terry noticed that Jackie was well pleased, if the way he was rubbing his crotch was anything to go by. He even threw in a wee 3 watt practice amp for free.

Dug strummed the guitar all the way up Mayfield Road, the little amplifier slung over his shoulder like a telephone receiver. It crackled away, as if someone was crumpling paper long distance.

'You might need to practise,' said Terry.

'Rock 'n' Roll!' wailed Dug. He tried a bit of Pete Townshend, and nearly sliced his fingers off.

* * *

A summons had come through from Tollcross DHSS. He was to appear before a Mr Goodbrand at 11 am on Wednesday. Sammy had actually turned up early, so keen was he to make a good impression. If it was anything to do with undeclared paid employment, he'd deny it. Where was the photographic proof? The last stranger to take a picture in the Kaptain's Kabin had left on a stretcher with his camera rammed up his arse. The DHSS knew to give the place a wide berth.

Fair enough, they were auditioning someone that afternoon, but Mr Goodbrand wasn't to know that.

He thought that they would at least have shown him into an interview room. He had to stand at the counter. Mr Goodbrand was on the other side, a big book open in front of him.

The meeting had nothing to do with working on the side.

'Do you know a Michelle Wendy Birkett?' he asked.

Sammy was right on it.

'Eh, aye, ah do, but if ye're...'

Mr Goodbrand looked in his book.

'We had a report that Ms Birkett is resident at...'

'Look, mate, we can cut the shit right now...'

Sammy had been on the dole since he was sixteen. He knew how to talk to these fuckers.

Mr Goodbrand started scribbling.

'It's no a cohabitation deal, awright?' said Sammy. 'She stays at her sister's!'

The book was closing.

'But it's no a cohabitation deal!'

The book was closing.

'It's no, ah'm tellin' ye!'

Mr Goodbrand clicked his pen and put it in his inside pocket.

'The book's closed, Mr Livingstone,' he smiled. 'We'll be in touch in due course.'

There was no point arguing. They'd probably cut his money. Or Mich's. Probably both. Bastards.

He walked the length of Lothian Road down to the Caledonian, then all the way back up to the other end; twice he had to duck into shop doorways to sort himself out – he had a lump in his throat the size of a golf ball. He sat on his arse in the Meadows and watched a squad of foreigners putting up a stripy tent. The novelty of that lasted about ten minutes.

He went back to the flat.

There was a smell of aftershave in the living room. He looked around. Baz had combed his hair, and was wearing a clean jumper.

Right enough. The audition. Mich had organised it – a woman, no less.

'Ah hope she's good lookin',' said Baz.

'No idea,' said Mich, and tutted. She'd put up an ad at her women's rights group.

'She's no a dyke, though?' said Baz.

Sammy could tell he was taking the piss.

'Mind you,' Baz went on. 'It'll be awright if she looks like Suzanne Vega, eh?'

'Suzanne Vega isn't a lesbian,' said Mich.

Baz laughed like a drain.

The practice was for one o'clock, but they gave up waiting at half past. Sammy went to the kitchen to put the kettle on, and heard something scratching at the front door. He opened it. She'd probably been standing there for half an hour, pawing the wood.

'Hello,' she whispered. 'I'm Morag.'

She didn't look like Suzanne Vega. She looked like that lassie off Scooby Doo, not the ride, the other yin, the wee fat yin with the glasses, the yin that Scooby Doo himself wouldn't have gone near.

She had an acoustic guitar in a polythene bag.

'Aye?' said Sammy. He'd tell her she had the wrong address.

'I'm here for the...'

He was already closing the door. Mich kicked his ankle.

'Hi!' she said. 'Are you Morag? We've been waiting for you!'

She showed her into the living room.

Baz started playing the music off Cartoon Cavalcade. Loud.

Morag stood against one of the walls. An egg tray slid down the back of her leg.

'Oh...sorry,' she whispered.

'Doesn't matter,' said Mich.

'So, eh, whit kind ae music are ye intae?' asked Sammy. He was dying to hear the answer.

Morag looked at the carpet.

'I like that 'Wordy Rappinghood',' she said. 'That's a good one.'

Twang-ang-ang, went Baz's guitar.

'Gary Davies plays it on his Bit In The Middle,' she explained, then gave them a stammering rendition of the first verse, complete with a jerky little dance, the buckles on her sandals making a clinking sound.

'Sister,' said Mich, and touched her on the arm. 'You don't need to do this.'

Sammy sighed. This was a complete waste...

'I've written a song!' she said.

She put her guitar round her neck. It was a rigmarole; she couldn't get the strap over the hood of her duffel coat. She started tapping out the rhythm on the wood, and Sammy got in behind his drums. You never knew – maybe she'd been winding them up. He kept it soft, hi-hat and rim shots. It sounded okay. It would never do for the band, but well done, Morag, you've had a go at writing a song, it's quite good, now it's time for you to fuck off.

Baz came in with some chords; a wee bit of chorus. He started improvising.

Mich picked up her bass.

Very soon, it became clear that Baz was picking out the theme tune to Scooby Doo.

He looked at Morag, and winked.

'We're really jammin' now,' he mouthed.

Morag stopped. She looked at Sammy.

'It's supposed to be a waltz,' she said.

Sammy bit his lip, and nodded.

'A waltz is jist 6:8 slowed doon,' he informed her.

She blushed.

'Can we try it without the drums?' she said, and looked at the other two. 'Just till you hear what it goes li...'

Sammy walked out. He didn't throw his sticks into the corner. He didn't have the energy.

* * *

'Oh, my God,' said Sugden. 'It's Elvis Presley.' He locked his car. The Morris 1800 was shiny, although somewhat dented around the bonnet.

Dug unwound the chord from his shoulders and shoved the amplifier into the pocket of his camouflage jacket. He seemed at a loss concerning what to do with the guitar.

Sugden tutted.

'Glad to see you could make it, Terry.'

'Dr Sugden.'

Dug was trying to keep his guitar from scraping on the gravel.

'Now, both of you,' said Sugden. 'You might like to come and help me with something.'

'Can I go and leave this in my locker?' said Dug.

Sugden looked at Terry, and smiled.

'No,' he said. 'Now, let's go and give a few pointers to the Freshers.'

Terry looked at his watch.

'Didn't you say you wanted to see us at two o'clock?' he said.

Sugden put his hand on him.

'All in good time, Terry,' he said. 'All in good time.'

He led them round the back of the Institute, to the animal research station.

'Christ,' said Dug. 'Not this.'

A crowd of first year Agrics were milling around the door, cracking jokes about rabbits smoking forty a day, and wee dogs running around with human heads. There was also a sizeable group of what Dug called The Quinties – the Quintessential Agrics – as there was every year. Dug reckoned they bred them at a secret location just outside Edinburgh. What they were wearing wasn't quite smocks, but most of them had hair like straw, and each one had a bumper crop of boils on the back of his neck.

Sugden moved to the front of the mob.

'Now, then, my fine friends,' he intoned. 'Not a word of this to anyone. We don't want those animal rights conshies wrecking our experiments, do we?'

Don't we? thought Terry.

Sugden slid a card into the lock in the reinforced door; the Quinties were already jostling for position. When everyone was inside, he approached Dug.

'Come on, Mr Lloyd,' he said. 'You know you like this.'

Dug was looking decidedly queasy.

'I'll just wait outside if it's all the same,' he stammered.

Sugden turned to Terry.

'Bring your friend inside,' he said. 'Even though it's a bit late, he might learn something.'

The shed, in semi-darkness, stank as farms do. Sheep were tethered along the walls with chains round their necks. Sugden gestured for the students to gather round one of the pens. The Quinties made sure they were at the front.

A ewe was munching contentedly on the lawn clippings in her trough. She turned, unconcerned, as Sugden approached. Terry remembered him giving exactly this performance at the beginning of his own first year. It was what he'd told Geeky about.

'Observe the system / environment interface!'

There was a piece of white plastic jutting out of the side of the sheep. It was like a fitting you'd find under a wash hand basin. Sugden unscrewed the cap. The pipe was stitched into the animal's skin, providing a direct route to the stomach. He pulled on a thread lying on the lip of the plastic. On the end of the thread was a small perforated bag.

From out of nowhere, he flourished a teacup.

'Anyone for Lapsang Sooshong?' he said, and popped the little bag into his cup.

The sheep bleated, then took another mouthful.

'So, this is how we test the digestibility of grass,' he said, 'for those of you who haven't yet grasped the gist of our visit.'

Dug was leaning unsteadily on his guitar.

'Mr Lloyd!'

Everyone turned to stare.

'If you can stave off your obvious nausea, be a man and join us next door.'

He beamed at his students.

'We have cows, too,' he said.

The Agrics liked Sugden. The Quinties loved him. He was off the wall. Unlike the sheep, which were, of course, screwed to it. So were the cows. Their anatomical bathroom fitting had more in common with a dirty toilet seat than the plumbing under the sink.

Sugden rolled up a sleeve and lowered his arm into the side of his preferred bovine, puffs of steam moistening his beard as he rummaged around. Slopping sounds were audible, which added to the entertainment.

There was a clatter as Dug's guitar hit the floor. He had just lurched for the railings.

Sugden produced a handful of dark brown sludge. He raised his hand to his nose, droplets of stinking mulch dripping down the front of his shirt, and filled his nostrils.

'Eeee, that's the stuff, eh lads?'

Terry had his arm round Dug, keeping him upright.

'Get it together,' he said. 'Don't give him the satisfaction.'

Sugden had mounted a hay bale. He had one of the toilet seats round his neck.

'Where I come from, they call this 'Gurning',' he said, and made his face turn inside out.

How the Quinties cheered!

Dug dry retched into Terry's shoulder.

The Agrics were dismissed, although a few of the keener Quinties lagged behind hoping to pick Sugden's brains about dietary supplements. He shrugged them off, and approached Terry, who was still trying to keep Dug off the floor.

'Both of you,' he said. 'My office. If you please.'

Terry knew exactly what was going on. This was Dug's rap on the knuckles for doing badly in his exams. Humiliation to make him mend his ways in his Honours year. Doubtless the performance in the shed had been entirely for Terry's benefit – why else would Sugden have insisted that he watch? He wanted to show Terry that he could be ruthless when the situation called for it. A Quintessential Manager.

What an arsehole.

Terry manoeuvred Dug into a chair in Sugden's office and made for the door.

'No, Terry, please stay,' said Sugden.

'I'll wait outside,' said Terry.

Sugden closed the door.

'Please be seated,' he said. 'Then we'll begin.'

He stood at his desk and slowly regarded his two charges.

'Aye,' he sighed, and reached into the inside pocket of his jacket. He produced his pipe, a huge, creamy briar, stained yellow round the edge of the bowl, the kind of pipe that only exists in fairy tales. He tamped down a wad of thick black twist and popped the stem into his mouth.

'No rush,' he smiled, and struck a match.

It was all faintly disgusting, with his lips moulded around the plastic and that incessant putt-putt-putting, like a moist anus. He disappeared into a cloud of smoke. When the fug had cleared, he was sitting at his desk, his back to a bookcase whose shelves sagged under the weight of countless books, folders, periodicals, government reports, departmental research missives and tractor advertising pamphlets. A spiral bound document was hanging tentatively from the middle shelf, held in place by the weight of Roget's Thesaurus.

Terry glanced at Dug. He was still ill. The reek from Sugden's pipe wasn't helping.

'Now,' said Sugden. 'We'll start with Mr Lloyd, methinks.'

Terry got out of his chair.

'No, no, park yourself, Terry. We'll call it a learning experience, shall we?'

'But if you want to talk to Dug...'

Sugden took a few sucks.

'Oh, him?' he said. 'We'll be finished with Mr Lloyd shortly.'

'Yeah, sit down, Terry,' said Dug. He looked like he could do with the support.

'So,' said Sugden. 'Mr Lloyd.'

Dug moved around in the chair.

'No need to be so formal,' he said.

Sugden puttered on his pipe.

'You should learn to enjoy it,' he said. 'Hearing those letters on the front of your name, I mean. The way things are going, you'll be testing the bounds of probability to leave this place with any ont back of it.'

'Well, I...'

Sugden swivelled in his chair and pulled a folder from the pile on the shelf. As he did so, the spiral bound document flopped like a cowpat to the floor.

'Now, let's see.'

He opened the folder. The title page was embossed thus:

Douglas Lloyd, BSc (Hons), 1987

He obliterated the (Hons) with an index finger.

'That's more like it,' he said. 'N'est pas?'

There being nothing to say, Dug kept his mouth shut.

'So, first year. Biology, IPM, Chemistry 1B.'

Sugden winked at Terry.

'Mr Lloyd – exemptions in all three? My, we did get off to a flier, didn't we?'

'Thank you,' said Dug.

Sugden turned the page.

'Second year. Biology, Ecology, mmm-hmmm. Physiology – 51% borderline pass...ooh, the first sneeze of the disease. Agriculture – fail, but 49.5% on the resit, and, seeing as you passed your Introductory Physics with Maths, you know what happens to 49.5%, don't you? It gets rounded up to 50 and you pass the class.'

He puffed.

'The patient is weak, but clings to dear life by his fingernails. Christ knows why.'

Dug was squirming again. Terry looked at him.

The page flapped.

'Third year,' said Sugden. 'Make your mind up time, as someone once said. Animal Reproduction...'

He sniffed.

'That's Rimmer's class, int it? 75%. Advanced Physiology – 64%. Ooh, looks like a sliding scale to me.'

His pipe had gone out. He laid it carefully in its little rack, which had been glued onto the side of a trophy of a boy swimming past a lighthouse. There were a few more of the same dotted about the room.

'And now, ladies and gentlemen. The moment we've all been waiting for.'

He produced two pink exam scripts from a drawer.

Putt-putt-putt, went Dug's anus.

Sugden opened the first script. The page wasn't even halfway covered in writing. The booklet had eight pages.

'Farm Business Management,' he said. 'Although a more appropriate title would be Suicide Note.'

He could barely conceal his glee, so he decided not to, and a yellow smile twitched within the depths of his beard.

'Question – you were asked to elaborate on the quarterly maintenance costs of a medium-sized dairy herd. Answer – and you will forgive me while I paraphrase your, er, paragraph. One day, you heard a Quinty...'

He looked up.

'A 'Quinty', Mr Lloyd?'

Dug smiled weakly.

'...you heard a *Quinty* mention the words 'margin over concentrates'. You then explain that you haven't got a clue what this means. Your answer ends with the words, 'My Tippex requirement is low, low, low'.'

He looked up again.

'Nil pwah,' he said, pronounced as if the Eurovision Song Contest had gone to the north of England and got bored. 'I won't bother with the other paper.'

'Thank you,' Dug whispered.

'Your answers were supposed to be terse, cogent and salient,' said Sugden. 'But do you know what they are?'

Dug shook his head.

Sugden took a deep breath.

'Pyoh. Fooking. Shah-eet,' he said.

You cunt, thought Terry.

'Any chance of a resit?' said Dug.

'In third year?' Sugden laughed. 'Thou jestest!' He began groping for a large tome on the shelf.

Dug got unsteadily to his feet.

'Going somewhere, Mr Lloyd?' said Sugden. 'Hang on a tick, I'll give you a map.'

He tossed the bulky volume across the desk. It landed with a thud, falling open at the section entitled First Year Courses.

'It's the University Calendar,' he said. 'Pick a card, any card. Keep it to yourself, mind, although they tell me Moral Philosophy is a bit of a doss.'

101

'But what...'

'Yes, Mr Lloyd, you'll be spending the rest of the year down at Charles Square with all the other hippies. They might even let you strum your guitar during lectures.'

'But my degree...'

'You need seven credits to graduate with an Ordinary,' Sugden sneered. 'You're on six. Fair thee well.'

Dug was counting on his fingers.

'But I've passed nine classes,' he said. 'What's all this about only having six credits?'

'Second and third year are all half-courses, you prannet.'

'But my Honours thesis...'

'No Honours for Mr Lloyd, I'm afraid. You'll be plain old BSc General Science. Nothing to shout about by any manner of means, but this is a good university, so I'm sure you'll find something when you leave. Goodbye. Now, Terry...'

Dug wasn't finished. Terry nodded at him. Perhaps there was still a chance.

'Look,' he said. 'I know I haven't been applying myself. Perhaps I'm a bit...disaffected, what with the ethical aspects of animal husbandry and...'

Sugden exploded.

'Oh, get a fucking grip man! You fooked oop! Disaffected? Let's see what Roger's got to say about it!'

What was this? thought Terry. Surely Sugden wasn't on first name terms with Dr Rimmer. They couldn't stand each other.

The thesaurus came crashing down. Immediately, Sugden was rifling through the pages, whole chunks of the book flapping back and forth.

'Let's not get bogged down int semantics,' he said. 'Now, let's see...disaffected...disaffected...ah, here it is...*disaffected...disloyal, unfaithful...aloof.*'

He hoisted the book across the desk.

'Face it,' he said. 'You've been a waste of fooking spess in 'ere since you walked in back in '83, so spare me your self-joostifahin', self-pityin' claptrap.'

Terry could see clearly that the complete entry for *Enmity*, in a hand so heavy it had scored the page, had been underlined in green ink. Both columns of it.

'Now get out of my sight.'

The phone rang, tolling the knell of Dug's demise as he sloped out of the office.

He had to come back in for his guitar.

* * *

He didn't know where Bear was working, but he had a fair idea. A new place had just opened down Rose Street – Mandela Bites. It sounded right on, the kind of place that would go out of its way to give someone like Bear a chance. He was right. When it came to waiting on tables, Mandela Bites was an Equal Opportunities Employer. It said so on a huge poster in the window.

He went round the back, to the kitchen.

A bucket of swill missed his feet by inches. Someone shouted.

'Fuckin' watch where ye're goin'!'

This looked like someone who was in charge of personnel.

'Excuse me,' said Sammy. 'Ah'm lookin' fur Be...' He didn't know Bear's real name.

'Whit?' snapped the man with the bucket. 'Ah've got a kitchen tae run here.'

'Ah'm lookin' fur, eh...' Sammy made a gesture with his hand, at thigh height.

'Whit, the midget?' The man was half way back into the kitchen. 'Ae got ae's books, the cheeky wee fucker.'

'Any idea where...?' said Sammy.

'Ah hear there's a circus settin' up doon the Meadows – ye might want tae try there.'

Ha. Ha. Ha.

Sammy turned away.

The man shouted after him.

'Here, ye're no lookin' fur a waiterin' job, ur ye?'

* * *

103

'Speak! Yes, this is he.'

Sugden's demeanour changed in an instant.

It crossed Terry's mind that it might have been polite to step outside so that he could take his call in private, but he stayed exactly where he was. Sugden was a total misanthrope. He wondered if he'd underlined that in the thesaurus, too.

'Ooh,' he simpered. 'That would be an honour... most acceptable.'

His eyes were all over Terry, and he was nodding.

'...how much?!...aah, most acceptable.'

There was a tapping sound. Sugden was clicking his heels together under the desk.

'Yes, anything you like, of course, Reverend.'

Terry felt as if a jug of ice had just been poured down his neck.

Sugden smiled at him like an imbecile.

'...yes, Reverend, indeed I have, in fact he's with me at the moment, large as life and twice as...'

The smile froze on his face, and he turned slightly in his seat. He pressed the phone closer to his ear.

'...sorry, what was that?'

Little beads of sweat sprung out on his brow.

'Yes, but why...I don't see how I can...yes, they're in my files, but the other marks are in the computers down at Admin in Charles... well, yes of course I do...sorry?...Dennis who?...no, no need for that…no, no, I assure you, Reverend...yes, yes...I'll see to it. Leave it to me…not at all, Reverend…thank *you*.'

He put the phone down. There was a stunned expression on his face.

'Well, you never know the minute, do you?' he said.

He started collecting his papers, paying special attention to the student folders and exam scripts – the rest he brushed into his briefcase with his forearm. He seemed to be in a hurry.

'Terry,' he said. 'You might want to have a look in there when Lloyd's finished.'

Terry looked at the thesaurus.

'No, not that one,' said Sugden. 'The other one.'

The University Calendar was still open at First Year Courses.

'What?' said Terry.

Sugden glanced at the phone.

'You 've failed your exams, too,' he said, and made for the door.

Terry got there before him.

'Not so fast,' he said, and twisted the lock.

'Oh, come on, now, Terry, I've got to be...somewhere else.'

Terry gripped the lapels of Sugden's jacket.

'What was my father saying to you on the phone?'

'Now, now, Terry.' His briefcase was bunched up in front of him, covering his chest like a shield.

Terry squeezed harder. He could feel his knuckles on Sugden's collar bones.

Sugden winced.

'That...was a... personal call,' he said.

'Which had something to do with me,' said Terry.

'I'm...not at liberty...'

Terry shoved him. He stumbled back into the desk, and his pipe rack fell to the floor.

'Oh, look what you've done!' he cried. He stooped to pick up his pipe and his briefcase fell out of his hands, his papers scattering everywhere.

'Aye, that's you all over,' said Terry. 'Get down on your knees, you fucking parasite.'

Sugden, his jacket askew on his shoulders, was trying to stick the pipe rack back together, but the dowelling was broken.

Terry took a run, and kicked it out of his hands.

* * *

And here was Sammy, languishing at the bar in the Prezzie Hall. He looked around. As far as playing live went, this was the gig to get. Some of the biggest names in Edinburgh rock had played here, most of them twice – once on the way up, and once on the way down again. The place oozed atmosphere. Of course it did, it was a converted 16th century church. The pulpit was still there, although the walls were covered in black and white photographs of all the famous acts who'd graced the stage. As usual, the island bar was being leaned on by everyone who thought he was anyone in the Edinburgh pub rock scene.

Including Sammy.

The Blues Domination Society were a four-piece. They had been playing the Wednesday night residency for nigh on five years, and would probably be there for the next five. It had to be admitted – they were a tight outfit, but then again most bands that had the neck to put on a show were able to keep in time with each other.

The noise they made never failed to set Sammy's teeth on edge. Who gave a fuck about the music, though? You only had to look at them.

The lead guitarist was an old timer who went by the name of Fast Chuck. He had long, grey, straggly hair, and a beard to match. At least once a month some young prick in the crowd shouted 'ZZ Top!', but it was well wide of the mark. He looked more like Catweazel after a night on the piss. All his gear was home made, the guitar, the effects pedals and the amp, but he was too experimental for Sammy's tastes. The received wisdom was that Eddie Van Halen had ripped him off; Fast Chuck was way ahead of his time. It was probably true – he was squatting in a caravan in Balerno.

The drummer was good, too, but he was sitting behind the biggest drum kit in Great Britain. It should have had a wee flag sticking out the top, like Ben Nevis. There were twenty six drums, and he made sure he hit all of them. Complete overkill.

It was the bass-player-cum-singer who was the weak link in the chain, and the strange thing was that he was the acknowledged leader of the gang. He was always dressed in blue and white Nike trainers, stone-washed jeans and a yellow and green Hawaiian shirt. Like Fast Chuck, he was a man who knew his fingering. The bass should have added an extra punch to the rhythm, but it didn't. He was far too busy. The noise he made was nothing more than a blur.

Sammy nearly forgot – there was a rhythm guitarist, too. Mr Invisible. If you looked hard enough you could usually find him, standing behind something. He chugged along, doing his thing, getting ignored by the other three. He was the only one that Sammy rated.

It would have given Sammy no end of pleasure to bump them.

Mick Robertson, the bar manager, was perched in his usual position, over the till. He caught Sammy's eye.

'Sammy! It's yerself! How goes it?'

'Fine, Mick, fine.'

He locked the cash drawer and came over.

'Ah see this lot's still daein' Wednesdays,' said Sammy.

'An' the customers are lovin' it, as per,' said Mick. 'Ah hear Danny DeVito took a walk.'

It had always been a bone of contention, and it had always annoyed Sammy. Mick had told them that they could have the occasional gig as long as Bear was kept in the dark. At first, Sammy had been upset about the blatant racism involved, if that was the word. But the fact had to be faced. Bear wasn't just a hindrance to the band. He was a hindrance to Sammy.

So much ae a hindrance, ya hypocritical wee cunt, that ye're goannae beg um...

'No exactly, Mick,' he said. 'Ah gave um the shove.'

'An' aboot bloody time! Who ever heard ae a band wi' a midget fur a singer – apart fae the Oompah Loompahs.'

He stabbed the counter with a finger.

'No in this bar,' he said.

He stepped back and inhaled deeply.

'*No chance.*'

Sammy swirled his beer.

'Aye, well, times they are a-changin',' he said. 'We're audi...'

One of the bar staff was trying to get into the till.

'Back in a minute, Sammy,' said Mick. 'Heh, sir, whit the fuck...?'

Sammy looked in his glass. He only had dregs left.

The band went into another of their standard covers, 'Walking On The Moon'. The bass player liked to use it as a showcase for his lightning fingers. He had substituted Sting's sparse bass line with a succession of arpeggio runs. Never mind 'Walking On The Moon'. It sounded more like 'Knees Up Mother Brown'.

Sammy wanted to climb onto the bar and scream 'This band are fucking shite!', and watch the audience come round to his way of thinking.

But as he tipped the last of the froth down his throat, he suddenly realised something.

107

The Blues Domination Society had the gig.

Sammy didn't even have a band.

Being in a three-piece didn't count, unless you were The Police.

Without a band, a real band, Sammy was... Sammy was nothing.

He was on his way out when he saw Bear standing in the alcove next to the fag machine. He was smiling and yapping away quite the thing to a crowd of women. Sammy thought he saw a few faces from the Kaptain's Kabin, but he didn't stop to check.

He couldn't do it.

He couldn't ask Bear to come back.

Bear had obviously moved on.

Sammy knew that he would have to do the same.

* * *

'No!' shouted Sugden, and shoved his fingers under his armpits.

'What?' said Terry. 'Was that sore?'

Sugden's face was purple.

'I'll report you for this!' he hissed. 'Just you see if I don't!'

Terry yanked the door, but it was locked. He twisted the knob and got out of the place, leaving Sugden scrabbling around on his knees. He marched to the other end of the building. Before he had turned the final corner, the corridor began to fill with the sickening smell of formaldehyde. The door was lying open. A huge saucepan was bubbling away on a camping gas burner.

The laboratory seemed to be empty. Just as he was about to give up, he heard an extended groan from the cubby hole behind the blackboard. Rimmer appeared a few moments later, wiping his hands on a paper towel. He seemed surprised to see Terry standing there.

'Oops!' he smiled, uneasily. 'You almost caught me with my trousers down. Just indulging in a quick Jodrell before the afternoon dissection.'

'No, you're okay, Dr Rimmer, I...'

Rimmer wasn't listening. He began poking the contents of the saucepan with a glass rod. He turned off the gas.

'No need to be coy, Terry. We all do it. I've been wanking in University toilets since I was an undergraduate. Just like you.'

Terry was in no mood to listen to Rimmer's confessions, nor offer a denial of what Rimmer seemed to be suggesting.

'Dr Rimmer, I wanted to see you about...'

'Yes, indeed,' he continued, pouring the contents of the saucepan into a metal strainer. 'There isn't a toilet on campus I haven't christened. Toilets, shower cubicles, Wellington boot defumigation footbaths...'

He held up the glass rod, as if conducting his train of thoughts.

'Have running water, will self-abuse, that's what I say. Although I hasten to add I draw the line at kitchens.'

'And trains,' said Terry. What the hell.

Rimmer scratched his nose with the rod and smiled wistfully.

'Well, I don't know...'

'You could do the Inauguration at the Kinlochleven Suite,' said Terry. He wasn't being funny.

'Now, there's an idea,' said Rimmer. He set down a polystyrene tray bearing a dissected worm. 'What do they say? Here's one I prepared earlier? Yes, Terry,' he said, and became serious. 'That's Roger Rimmer for you. An Old Wanker.'

'Our resident onanist.'

'Onan wasn't wanking,' Rimmer corrected him. 'It was a clear case of *coitus interruptus*.'

They regarded the glistening *Lumbricus terrestris* pinned open for inspection on the tray.

'Joke's over,' said Rimmer. 'What's up?'

Voices far off down the corridor. Sugden was throwing a tantrum.

'It's my exam results,' said Terry. 'Something's going on.'

Rimmer sniffed.

'That's Roy Sugden's area, if I'm not mistaken.'

'Yes, but he says I ploughed my exams. No chance. I've just been in his office, and everything was fine until he got a phone call from my father.'

'Ah,' said Rimmer. 'Your father.' He started distributing the boiled worms out of the strainer, one worm for every pair of students.

'Do you know anything about it?' said Terry.

Rimmer stopped what he was doing and placed both hands on the bench. He turned slowly, and straightened up.

'Young man,' he said. 'I think it's time you and I had a chat.'

He took Terry's arm, and guided him to the cubby hole.

CHAPTER 8

The plot thickens, thought Rimmer. Something had been going on with young Kinlochleven's results since way back, but he'd thought it better to keep his mouth shut. So had everyone else at the Institute; Eck was a man who had lots of money to spend. Terry was a bright boy, but his performance, Rimmer thought, had always been average – below average. The ongoing saga with his Chemistry practicals bore testament to that. He just couldn't get the hang of filling a burette to the bottom edge of the meniscus. So it was strange that he was always top of the class. And now he had failed his exams? He certainly hadn't failed Rimmer's.

It was Sugden who phoned the results down to Charles Square.

'Let me be absolutely frank with you, Terry. Are you sure you want that?'

Terry nodded.

'Fine. If your father is behind this then you can forget all about it. No one will lift a finger.'

Terry frowned.

'Not even you, Doctor Rimmer?'

'Well, I...'

'Dr Rimmer, there is no way I failed my exams. I know I didn't.'

Rimmer fastened the clips on his artificial vagina and moved it further along the bench. Terry couldn't take his eyes off it.

'Ah, my appliance,' said Rimmer. 'It's not what you think, you know…'

'My exams?' said Terry.

111

'Look,' Rimmer said. 'Your father and I...we go back a long way...'

'What?'

'...right back to the beginning, in fact. We've, er...let's just say our relationship has had its ups and downs over the years, shall we?'

'God, he hasn't got you in his pocket as well, has he?'

Wouldn't Eck just love to think that, thought Rimmer, but he could honestly say that he had never fudged any of Terry's exam results, even though the hint had been dropped by Kinlochleven pater at the beginning of first year.

His students were coming into the lab. He'd have to get to them before they started poking around with the worms.

'Terry, look. This is all a bit... I can't imagine why your father is behaving like this.'

Apart from the fact that he's a bastard, and always has been, he didn't add.

'Have you thought about talking to him? That would seem the obvious thing to do.'

* * *

He could have caught a bus down to the New Town, but decided that a walk would give him time to cool off. How wrong he was. He felt the rage rising with every step.

It took him an hour to get there. The sweat was running down his back; he was knackered. The fact that all he had had to eat over the past two weeks was the scraps Dug could smuggle out of the Refectory wasn't helping.

He needed a drink. It didn't matter where.

He could hardly see through the smoke. All the tables were occupied, a bulging Filofax on every one. He shouldered his way into a space at the end of the bar, next to a girl who was perched on a stool. She was scribbling in a notebook, but looked up when he ordered a double Isle of Jura.

He knew she was smiling at him.

'I've got the feeling we've met,' she said, the pencil tracing invisible lines on her bottom lip.

'Fuck off,' said Terry.

He gulped the whisky. His intention had been to drink until there was nothing but coppers left in his pockets. When he'd paid for the second glass, there was nothing left in his pockets at all.

He'd have to do it sober.

Even from half a mile away, the church filled the horizon. The architecture was something that Stalin would have been proud of. A massive cube of blackened concrete dominated the end of the road, with a crenellated bell tower rising from dead centre.

It looked like a clenched fist giving the world the finger. Forget Praise The Lord. This was Fear The Minister.

The entrance, a cold maw of forty steps, yawped its silent displeasure at his approach. He shivered as he climbed to the huge doors. He'd been here before, when he'd first come to Edinburgh. Curiosity. Back then, he hadn't dared go inside.

He placed his hand on the wood, and pushed.

His heels echoed round the empty vestibule; a cold stench of disinfectant and old bibles. His throat rasped. The inner doors were locked, but there was a flight of stone stairs on the left.

Another door. He could hear voices. He pressed softly and looked inside. The voices grew louder, but he couldn't see anyone.

It was a balcony.

He crept inside, making sure his head was below the level of the seats, and peered over the edge.

It looked as if Caligula and his court had come to Edinburgh and found God. A cross of gilded timber was suspended from overhead cables. The centre of the wood was inscribed with the letters 'Au'. His father was sitting on the throne underneath, swathed in multi-coloured robes.

A door crashed open. Terry turned, but no one was there. The commotion was downstairs, in the chamber. He pushed himself up. There must have been a hundred people there, all of them standing against the walls, all of them dressed in white nightshirts. They were watching Miss Chang, who was prostrate at his father's feet. The only sound was the sound of whimpering.

'My wife!'

'Hallelujah,' someone said.

'Praise Him,' said someone else.

'My wife has decided to repent! She has decided to turn! Come in, wife! Come and join the body of the kirk!'

Miss Chang raised herself on an elbow. She stretched out a hand to the silent, approaching horde, pleading, beseeching them...

'Look! She wants to be saved! She wants to turn! Let us rejoice! Let us sing!'

The congregation moved slowly across the floor and formed a tight circle, three deep. Terry's father stepped down from his throne, his robes flowing, and pulled Miss Chang to her feet.

Everyone joined hands.

'Ms Tonner – when you're ready!'

A harmonium began to wheeze. Terry saw that it was very old, but not as old as Ms Tonner, who was so ancient that her hair was the colour of methylated spirits. There was a bellows at the side. Dennis was pumping it. He was wearing a nightshirt, too.

Terry recognised the tune. He rested his head on his hands. He didn't know what he had been expecting, but he hadn't been expecting this. It was an action song, and everyone had to join in. His father made sure Miss Chang performed with gusto.

He made the world	(make a big circle with your arms!)
He gave us hands	(show your hands)
He made the big, big world	(bigger circle!)
He gave us hands	(show those hands again!)
He made the world	(Great Big Circle)
He gave us hands	(Look at our HANDS!)
He made the world	(STRETCH!!)
And He gave us hands	(HELLO THERE!!!)

Dennis looked like he was glad he only had to pump the organ.

The song suddenly stopped. A few people expressed concern that Mrs Kinlochleven seemed to be in some pain. She was alright, Terry's father assured them; she'd had her stookie removed two days ago.

They began another verse about a tiny little baby, but Terry missed most of it. Something touched him gently on the shoulder.

He turned his head.

Arnold Palmer 9 was written on curved metal.

'Come oan, you,' said Sid.

Terry was prodded all the way down the stairs. When he reached the door to the chamber, the one that was locked, Sid poked for a final time, and let the golf club rest in the small of his back.

'Wait a minute,' he said.

There was murmuring in the chamber.

Then a sudden voice.

'Turn or burn, wife!'

Other voices began to join in.

'Turn or BURN!'

'TURN or BURN!'

'TURN OR BURN!!'

A woman screamed.

Then silence.

He had to strain to hear what was being said.

...forgive us our debts
as we forgive our debtors...

They were praying like good Scotsmen.

...and the fellowship of the Holy Spirit...

'Hang oan,' said Sid. 'This is the best bit.'

On the count of three, we break for tea. One...Two...Three!

A warm round of applause, and laughter. Terry imagined them all hugging each other, leaving Miss Chang to get on with her nervous breakdown in the middle of the floor. The doors slid open, and the congregation poured out into the vestibule. Cups rattled in the distance. They headed in that direction.

'Right, move,' said Sid, and poked. Terry wanted to grab the stick out of his hand and ram it down his pubic earhole, *Arnold Palmer 9* end first, but that would have to wait.

His father was standing under a huge painting, his hand on Miss Chang's shoulder. He was trying to explain the picture. She was crying her eyes out.

Terry felt metal on the back of his neck. Sid yanked back on his collar. His father was saying something about doors, but it was difficult to make it out over the soft music that had started up on the harmonium. Dennis, in mid-pump, clocked Terry. He looked embarrassed.

'I see you've found your metier,' Terry joked, suddenly feeling brave. What a fucking circus.

His father turned.

'Yes?' he said. He was looking over Terry's shoulder, at Sid.

'Ah caught this yin hidin' up in the balcony, Reverend.'

Terry was given the once over.

'What, another homeless person looking for accommodation? Can't Dennis handle it?'

'It's...yer...son,' Dennis gasped. Ms Tonner had started practising her scales, and was using up the air really fast.

Miss Chang was pointed in the direction of the door, and given a gentle shove.

'Tea, wife. Now.'

Terry had his eyes on her, but she didn't dare look at him.

His father inhaled deeply, puffing up his chest to its full girth. Terry was a big fellow, it was true. It was unsettling to see that his father was even bigger.

'And what can I do for you, young man?'

There was no handshake, no fatherly hug. It was the first time they had been face to face for fifteen years. Maybe they shared the same last memory. It was the day his father had stormed out of the house for the last time. He had kicked Terry out of the way because he was playing with his modelling clay in the doorway.

Not that Terry had been expecting a handshake, let alone a fatherly hug.

'I've come to apologise,' he said.

His father laughed. It didn't last long.

'Apologise?' he said. 'Apologise for what?'

'You know,' said Terry. 'Miss Ch...your wife.'

'Why?' he asked, and looked from side to side, as if he'd lost something. 'What did you do to her?'

Terry wasn't going to get involved in this. He'd say what he had to say, and leave.

'I want you to stop what you're doing at the University,' he said.

'But I'm in the middle of a building project...'

'You know what I mean.'

'…it's not something that can be turned off like water…'

'Just please stop…'

'Silence!'

Ms Tonner kept going.

Terry felt tears welling in his eyes.

'For your information,' his father said, 'the Kinlochleven Suite was conceived as a gift for my only child. The fruit of my loins. Perhaps one fine day you would have found yourself in the Director's chair. No chance of that now, of course.'

He clapped his hands lightly together, and left them there, in a gesture of prayer. He turned.

'Can you see this painting?' he said.

Of course Terry could see it. It covered the wall, right up to the roof. A bearded gentleman in robes was holding a lantern. He was standing at the door of a cottage. Warm light could be seen behind the small panes of glass in the window.

'Do you know who this is?' his father asked.

Terry looked at the painting, then at his father.

'You with a beard?' he said.

'No. Close, though. It's Jesus Christ. The Son of Man. Our Saviour.'

The harmonium wheezed, then died. Dennis was shagged.

'Notice the door,' his father went on. 'There's no handle. What does that tell us?'

'....'

'You have to ask him to come in. You have to *invite* him.'

'So?' said Terry. What was this? Did he think he had come here to join his church?

'Inviting someone to step into your private world is very important, don't you think?'

'.....'

'Look around you. What do you see?'

117

'.....'

'This is *my* private world.'

His voice hardened.

'Did I invite you to come in? No, I didn't. You came creeping in like a thief, didn't you?'

Terry felt his shoulders being gripped. His father looked at him straight between the eyes. He looked like a maniac. *You're not my dad, you cunt. You never were! Reverend? What a fucking...*

Something flapped up in the rafters.

The Reverend looked up.

'I may have bats in my belfry,' he said, 'but I'm far from insane.'

Terry could have broken his nose with one swift movement of his head.

The Reverend's voice quaked.

'You and I, Terry.'

'Let go of me, you bastard.'

'You and I, my boy!'

His shoulders were being squeezed out of joint.

'You just don't understand, son!'

The pain was blinding him.

'We're!'

Squeeze.

'Fucking!'

Squeeze.

'Finished!'

Terry tried to butt him, but he was too fast.

'Si-id!'

There was no need for Dennis to shout. Terry saw out of the corner of his eye that Sid was already in mid-swing. The upper part of his right arm exploded.

He collapsed to his knees.

'Yes!' hissed The Reverend, his fist slapping into his palm. 'Do unto others as they would do unto you!'

Terry keeled over.

'Exodus, Chapter 20, verse 12: *Honour thy father and thy mother that thy days may be long upon the land*! Not *Humiliate thy father and fuck thy stepmother that the old goat will keep you in clover*!'

Terry had banged his head off the floor. Blood was flowing away from him across the parquet.

'Now,' said The Reverend. His voice sounded far, far away. 'Will someone *please* get this mess out of my sight?'

CHAPTER 9

They registered for classes on the Monday morning. Terry couldn't have cared less; in fact, he slept in. He was woken by Dug pounding on his door, shouting that if he didn't get his name down for something soon, he'd be as well kissing goodbye to his degree.

Dug nipped his head all the way to the University, explaining what a 'buoyant' mood he was in. He felt like he'd escaped from a sinking ship, and was about to start studying something that he thought was worthwhile. He'd just been elected JCR President of his House, too.

They eventually reached the Administration building. Dug nudged him on the side of the arm.

'Careful!' said Terry. Although it wasn't broken, his arm was still aching.

'Sorry, mate,' said Dug. 'Check this.'

A squat army officer, looking angry in a kilt, was swishing towards them.

'Atten-shun!' said Dug, like a pillock, and saluted.

The officer stopped dead in his tracks and glared at them.

'Pray to God they give you a job at the Milk Round,' he said, and spat on the pavement.

The old woman at the computer scowled at him. Terry raised his hand to the side of his head, but there was no way he could get the dressing to stick in place. He'd checked it that morning. The sellotape was full of hair.

'And if you'll give me the name of your awarding body,' she said.

'Sorry?'

'Your a-war-ding bo-dy,' she enunciated, and stabbed the application form. The course cost £195.

He didn't have a clue. His father's accountants had always taken care of this stuff.

'Just tell her you'll be paying it yourself,' Dug whispered.

The woman sighed.

'Look, Dug,' said Terry, 'it's a lot...'

'Don't worry about it,' said Dug. He leaned on the counter and wrote out a cheque. 'You can pay me back when you're rich and famous.'

'Thanks, mate,' said Terry.

Then it was Dug's turn.

'And your awarding body?'

'That's the Scottish Education Department,' he said.

She clicked the information into the computer. From where he was standing, Terry could see that the screen was orange.

'There seems to be a problem,' she said.

Dug shook his head.

'Not again,' he said. 'I told my dad to get his books in on time this year.'

She scanned the screen.

'Don't blame your dad,' she said. 'Your grant application's been rejected.'

'Eh?'

'An Ordinary degree is only funded for three years,' she said, and licked her lips. 'But I'll take a cheque.'

'Skint again,' said Dug as they made their way out. 'Maybe I should start busking.'

Yeah, thought Terry. They'll throw coins at you to make you stop.

There were plenty of second hand copies of The Republic in James Thin's in Nicolson Street, Dug informed him, but the commentary that went with it was sold out. Sugden had been right – Moral Philosophy was the doss course of choice for Freshers.

The concourse outside the lecture theatre was teeming. Even though they were in the open air, the noise of all those shouted, enthusiastic first-year conversations was echoing so much that he could feel a headache coming on. It didn't help that he didn't want to be here.

A servitor pulled open the doors, and there was a surge for the best seats. Dug joined it. He waved to Terry from up the back. The lecture hall filled quickly. Strange coats were in abundance. Well, they would be. They were now in the Faculty of Arts. Dug looked like a complete dork in his flat top and camouflage gear, but he was keen. His A4 pad was open, the date was scribbled in the corner of the page, and his pen was poised.

Terry hunched down in his suit and waited for the boredom to commence.

A stern looking man in a jacket, tie and jumper walked in. He placed a hand on the lectern and slowly surveyed all, waiting for silence.

What the fuck is this? thought Terry, and sank down further into his seat.

Pockets of isolated noise persisted in various parts of the theatre, mostly young English guys with floppy hair.

'Eeeeek!' screeched a posh girl down the front. 'Pippa's got a starfish!'

Uneasy laughter rippled round the room. Terry's side of the hall was getting stared at, at the spot where the commotion was being caused. Someone – Pippa? - had half a pail of water sitting on the bench.

'I would ask Pippa,' boomed Plato, deadpan, 'to leave her starfish at home in future. Despite the recent disbanding of the GLC, I do feel that the phylum *Echinodermata* has little to contribute to the ethical debate.'

The student body hummed their appreciation at his little joke.

'Would that it were otherwise, Pippa, but that's the world we live in.'

He turned his back on the students and stared, motionless, at nothing. A faint titter ran round the theatre. Plastic grated on wood as Pippa pushed her pail along to the far end of the bench. Various small blisters of conversation were beginning to break out.

A chain was pulled and a huge blackboard sprang up, hitting the ceiling with an almighty clatter.

Dug nearly jumped out of his seat.

'I am Plato!' boomed Plato.

What? thought Terry. It wasn't a codename?

'No, not him,' said Plato, and flicked his head at the word 'REPUBLIC' scrawled in large letters on the board. 'Plato Buchanan, and as far as The Republic is concerned, I'm it. Book 1. Is it so much to ask?' He sounded like he'd been teaching it for years.

Terry noticed that a good few of the keener students were copying down what was written on the board. Dug was doing the same.

'Now,' Plato continued. 'I'll be honest with you. I've got most of a glass of Rosé d'Anjou parked under the bar across the road as we speak, so let's get on with it. I think we'll start with you,' he pointed at Pippa, 'removing that stinking bucket from my *locus operandi*.' His jacket had swung open, revealing that his other arm was in a sling.

Pippa started to say something, but she was abruptly cut off.

'All right, all right,' said Plato. 'Animal rights. How would *you* feel if some hair-brained floozy was carting *you* all over Charles Square in a polyurethane dustbin? Hmmm?'

Dug was bent over his notepad, trying his hardest to keep up.

'And where can you find sea water in the middle of Edinburgh? Puurlease!'

All eyes were on the young lady. Terry's certainly were. She was a looker. Some of the slower students were looking at the pail. Dug was still scribbling.

'Rhetorical!' Plato laughed, but no one knew whether to join in. 'I do that a lot. For those of you not *eksikiomeni* with Greek, or indeed English, let's just say that a rhetorical question is not a question at all, but a rather nasty habit I have of talking to myself when I think someone is being an arse.'

Pause.

'They tell me Socrates did it a lot, too.'

Dug underlined that bit.

Pippa stood up. The pail was dragged back to her end of the bench. She lifted it and hobbled to the exit, water sloshing over the side.

'There she goes,' said Plato, almost to himself. 'Pippa and her starfish. I ask you.'

Terry switched off for the rest of the lecture. It was no big deal. He'd get Dug to photocopy his notes in the library. What the hell was Plato doing lecturing in the department of Moral Philosophy? That was easy enough – it was his job. And it would also explain the rendezvous in The Left Bank. It was easy for him as a lecturer to get involved in underground student politics. But why did he need the services of the ARM? What was that book he had given him? Something about an old loser burning down his house for the insurance money.

He felt a smile smearing its way across his lips.

Perhaps it wouldn't be necessary to get a copy of Dug's notes after all. There were other ways of passing the class.

The lecture finished with a round of applause. Plato busied himself with his papers, ignoring a huddle of keen freshers who were trying to gain his attention.

Dug strode right up to him and laid his pad on the bench.

'Hello, Doctor Buchanan,' he said, and offered a hand. 'I'm Dug Lloyd. I'm in your tutorial group.'

Terry waited by the exit. The hall was almost empty.

'Please,' said Plato. 'That's Professor. I think I've earned the right. Oh, don't blush, for goodness' sake!'

'Sorry, Professor,' said Dug. 'I just wanted to say...'

'Yes, yes, yes,' said Plato. 'Dug, is it? The Confessional.' He strode for the door, right past Terry. 'You can come, too,' he said.

The conversation died when Terry walked in. Perhaps it had something to do with the fact that he was guzzling whiskey out of a bottle.

Plato came barrelling out of the gents and took up a place at the bar.

'Sean! Is my wine still under the counter? Oh, Christ, not again! That was the last bottle!'

Terry pushed Dug forwards.

'Ah, you made it,' said Plato. 'Drink?'

Dug was looking nervously around. He probably thought the stares were aimed at him, and not at Terry, who was swaying in the middle of the floor. He'd managed to neck most of the whiskey on the way across Charles Square.

'Eh, pint of Dog's Leg?' said Dug.

'Ah, a man who appreciates his Scottish porter. Sean! Make that two Dog's Legs, will you?'

Terry caught Sean's eye, and winked.

Two pints of frothy purple liquid were laid on the bar.

'Do you come here often?' asked Dug.

Plato shot him a sidelong glance, then burst out laughing.

'I beg your pardon?'

'No, I mean, I've never been in here before, it's not really for the likes of...'

'Dug,' said Plato. 'I'm in here every effing lunchtime.'

Terry burped raucously.

Dug handled the introductions.

'Ah, Professor Buchanan, this is Terry...'

'Hello,' smiled Terry, and snorted a laugh. 'Professor.'

'And hello to you, too, Terry. I must say that you look worse than I feel – and I feel like shit.'

'But your legs are all cured?' said Terry.

Plato rubbed his sling.

'I seem to remember intimating that there was in fact nothing wrong with them,' he said.

'Yeah, right.'

Dug was following this like a tennis match.

'Have you two already met?' he said.

'You could say that,' said Terry, and took another swig.

'I would have offered to buy you a drink, Terry,' said Plato, 'but I see you're ahead of me.'

Terry cackled.

'You've got that right,' he said.

Plato turned his back and started doodling in the head of his pint with a cocktail stick.

'I liked the way you got a bit of Biology into your lecture,' said Dug.
'What?' said Plato. 'Oh, the aquatic quip.'
'Yes,' said Dug. 'How did you know that starfish belong to the phylum *Echin...*'

Plato sighed.

'Why does a Greek draw an Irish flower in his porter?' he said.

'I'll bet this is a rhetorical question,' sneered Terry.

'Think football clubs,' said Plato. 'Think green and white, and I'm not talking about Celtic. Anyway, it's a fleur-de-lis, not a four-leafed-clover.'

He looked at Terry.

'No, it's not rhetorical,' he said.

'Maybe you wish it was Guinness,' said Dug.

'Good guess,' said Plato. 'But it's not Irish, and I mentioned football. Am I confusing you?'

Dug took a mouthful of beer.

'Your arm,' he said. 'Is it broken?'

For Christ's sake, thought Terry. Dug's fawning small talk was starting to annoy him.

'Indeed it is,' said Plato. 'In two places. A bizarre golfing mishap, would you believe.' He looked at the dressing on Terry's head. 'It looks as if you've caught the wrong end of something, too,' he said.

Terry laughed like a maniac, then stopped abruptly. Like a maniac.

'You could say that,' he said, and peeled back the sellotape. 'The result of a nine iron to the humerus. Would you believe.'

Plato took a second to respond.

'Really?' he said. 'An accident on Bruntsfield Links? Or something more premeditated?'

'There's a madman on the loose,' said Terry.

'Ah, yes,' said Plato, and raised his glass slowly to his lips. 'I think I might have met him.'

A pall of steam hung over the clothes piled on the floor. It was like a jumble sale for the dispossessed. Terry tried on an overcoat and looked like he'd just walked off the set of a Gothic movie. Dug tried one on, too. He looked like he'd just been to a jumble sale.

* * *

Plato was sitting in a wheelchair in the middle of his office. He wasn't kidding this time. His left foot was in a plaster cast. His students were arranged in a row in front of him. He directed their attention to the small table at his elbow. A chess clock was sitting on it. One side had been removed; there was a hole where the clock face should have been.

Enough was enough. They'd been at it for three weeks. If they went any slower, they'd be going backwards.

'This is my Boring Clock,' he said. 'If someone starts to bore me, I will press this button. The little flag will fall after a total of five minutes Boring Time. I will then go off like a bomb. However, if you can come up with something, anything, that drags me back from the brink of unconsciousness, I will press this other button, and the clock will stop. A good tutorial is a tutorial where the flag fails to fall. A great tutorial is one where there is no sound of ticking in this room.'

Dug took a sip of tea and replaced the cup on its saucer, being careful not to dislodge the dainty biscuit teetering over the edge.

'What happened to your foot?' he said.

Plato was unfazed. He looked at Terry snoring in the corner. He seemed to spend most of the tutorials looking at Terry, trying to fathom out what was going on. According to Rimmer, the boy was kosher.

Things could have been worse, he supposed. They could have broken both his ankles.

'Another golfing mishap,' he said. 'I'm beginning to think I'm going to be in for a lot of those over the coming months.'

'Your handicap's getting worse,' said Dug.

'Although I have a fair way to go before I retire,' said Plato.

'Indeed.'

'And you,' said Plato, gesturing at the sail-like proportions of Dug's overcoat, 'are looking very Bohemian today.'

'Thank you.'

'Yes, I noticed when you walked in. You do of course realise that it hangs on you like a Durex on a pencil?'

127

'.....'

'Just kidding. Terry is also looking very James Dean, although you could perhaps lend him your hairstyle. So. If we have sucked the tea from our ginger snaps, who's, er, going to tee off?'

Daniel jumped straight in. He was thirty five years old, and had had enough of the girlies examining the floor. He was all for sexual equality, sure, and would never have called himself sexist, but the two bints in the group didn't have much to say for themselves, and seemed to be determined to destroy the tutorial proving it. At least, this was Plato's take on Daniel's psychology. Plato was a teacher who prided himself on knowing his students' inner thoughts before they knew them themselves.

Terry remained the exception, unfortunately.

'I think we should begin by raising a couple of points raised in this week's lectures,' said Daniel.

'Do you, now?' said Plato, and smiled.

Daniel was in no mood for confrontations, Plato could see. He'd had enough of those in his job, before he jacked it for this. He'd thought that University was a place where he'd be encouraged to express his thoughts freely. Plato, however, always seemed to be on the brink of a quarrel, ready to jump down your throat given the slightest chance.

'Firstly,' said Daniel. 'Justice is the interest of the stronger.'

Plato adjusted his sling and broke a ginger snap in two. Perhaps he snapped it in two, which amounts to the same thing, but would have sounded repetitive. He held both halves over his teacup and deliberated over which half to dunk first. This one? Or this one?

He became conscious of a post-snap silence in the room.

'We are listening with bated breath, Daniel,' he said.

'Well, it's obviously wrong...'

'You don't say!' Plato laughed.

Something shuffled in the corner.

'I think I know what this means,' whispered Morag.

At last, thought Plato. Perhaps Morag realised that the Boring Clock was down, in part, to her. Fair enough, she had taken his advice and visited Tony Randall at the student health centre, but all he'd done was encourage her to take up guitar lessons. A charlatan if ever there was one. Plato had found the splintered remains of the guitar he'd bought her in the wheelie bin that very morning.

'Has it got something to do with self-interest?' she asked.

If he hadn't been holding the ends of his ginger snap, and if his arm wasn't still broken, he would have applauded.

'Yes, it has!' he said.

'S'right,' slurred Terry, who had momentarily snored himself awake. 'S'good to be bad.'

Terry was looking haggard. He had dark circles under his eyes, and his overcoat, despite Plato's earlier comment, looked like it had been slept in. There was, of course, a bottle hanging out of the pocket. He hadn't done a stroke of work since the first day. Dug, however, had been handing in typed essays in the name of Terence Kinlochleven. Plato had decided to see where it would lead. He'd made sure to have Terry in one of his tutorial groups, and sources had informed him that Terry and Dug were a package. Why spoil a winning formula?

Plato popped a semicircle of biscuit into his mouth.

Daniel shifted in his seat. He had been beavering away in the library, and had prepared a little speech, a little Socratic question and answer script, and the adolescents were taking over the conversation. He moved around in his chair and stole a furtive glance at Pippa's legs. She was a girl whose pins went all the way up to her midriff. Today she was dressed from top to toe in green. When she'd walked into the room, she'd looked like a six-foot strip of chewy spearmint. It wasn't a criticism, it was...

Plato chuckled to himself. God, he thought, what an overactive imagination I have.

'It depends if we're talking about expediency or moral good, you know, Right and Wrong with capital letters.' Thus spake Dug, Philosopher.

Plato hmm-hmm-ed his agreement, and was disconcerted to find that he was snorting crumbs through his nose, always a danger if you forget to dunk your ginger snap before masticating.

Morag hesitated.

'Yes,' she whispered. 'I agree.'

Plato's hand hovered over the clock. For him, 'I agree' was Boring. With a capital letter.

'Now, now, Morag,' he said. 'One more twee outburst like that and the clock starts ticking.'

Morag blushed. Her eyes began to shine.

'Oh, don't be such a bully!' said Pippa, and brushed crumbs off her lap.

'Ah,' said Plato. 'I think Pippa wants to say something. It would make a change.'

'Don't patronise me.'

'I'm not patronising you. It's called sarcasm. Haven't you noticed that I'm rather good at it?'

'So what Thrasymachus is saying...,' Daniel began.

'Oh, fuck Thrasymachus!' said Plato. He laid his cup and saucer on the table because he was becoming tempted to throw them. 'We've got the makings of an A-1 discussion here, and you want to drone on about Thrasymachus? Bo-RING!'

He thumped the clock with his good hand.

Morag sobbed.

'You're okay, Morag,' he said. 'I'm not shouting at you.'

Tears in the tutorial, now that would be something new.

'I don't think swearing in a Philosophy tutorial...,' Daniel began.

'Fuck Philosophy,' said Pippa, and folded her arms across her chest.

Dug smiled.

'This is so much better than Farm Business Management,' he said.

'Pippa,' said Plato. 'If you want to leave, no one is stopping you.'

'I'll stay,' she said. She tried not to let her eyes wander over to Terry, who was slumped in his chair, eyes closed, mouth open, at the other end of the row. God, he was worth one.

Steady on, thought Plato.

'I've seen this before,' said Daniel, the man who stood up for women whenever he wasn't imagining the warm, damp furrow nestling in the gusset of their tights. Pippa was, and who could blame him, his current obsession, although doubtless he was trying to conjour up a senario for Morag, who'd been occupying his thoughts...

130

Plato shook his head suddenly. Cut it out, he berated himself.

'I think you should treat your students with more respect,' said Daniel.

'But Terry just said it was good to be bad!' said Plato.

There was no reaction from Terry – he was well out of it.

'You know what I mean,' said Daniel.

'Be specific,' said Plato.

Pippa couldn't have cared less, but Morag had started twitching.

'Okay, I will,' said Daniel. He pulled his chair forward. 'Morag, tell him to apologise.'

'I apologise to neither man nor woman,' said Plato. 'Period.'

Terry emerged from his slumbers. He opened one lazy eye.

'S'sucks when y'get found out,' he croaked.

Everyone looked at him, apart from Morag, who was trying to climb into her satchel.

'It's what Thrasymachus is saying,' said Dug. 'Do what you can to better yourself, but don't get caught. And if you do get caught, so what? Because there's no such thing as Right or Wrong with capital letters. There's just Me.'

Plato nodded. His hand was already over the table. He pressed the button, and the thick ticking of the chess clock stopped.

He looked at Daniel.

'I hope that clears up any lingering confusion,' he said.

'*Thrasis* means 'cheeky' in Greek, doesn't it?' said Dug.

Plato frowned.

'Ye-es,' he said.

Pippa looked at her watch, and yawned.

'Bored, Pippa? Dug doesn't mean 'cheek' in the facial or indeed gluteal sense. He means it in the sense of 'I've had enough of your cheek, young lady'. Perhaps he is striving to understand, although I must say his attempt is rather contrived, how Plato – you know, the other one, the famous one, the one that isn't me – is perhaps using a dramatic device, and is thus trying to explore our reaction to what *Thrasy*machus is being made to say.'

'Whatever,' she said.

'I know!' said Dug. 'Let's talk about Durkheim's definition of suicide. It'll go well with the milky tea.'

Plato smiled. You had to hand it to the boy – he brightened up the tutorials. More of a *malakas* than *thrasis,* but there you go.

Terry grunted in his sleep.

Daniel sniffed, then cleared his throat. Doubtless, Durkeim was the second point he'd wanted to raise, and he'd prepared a wee speech for this, too.

'Well,' he said. 'What Durkheim is saying is that it can only really be counted as suicide if there's the element of intent.'

Plato scanned the faces of the other students.

'Daniel,' he said. 'We know what Durkheim is saying. What we need to do is explore the theme. It's called Moral Philosophy. I really do expect more from a mature student.'

'Oh, for God's sake!' Daniel hissed.

Morag still had her head buried in her satchel. She probably thought the clock was still ticking.

'Perhaps... Morag would like to say something,' Plato ventured. He kept his hand fastened to his knee. Perhaps the Boring Clock hadn't been such a good idea after all.

'Doctor Debrett said something about The Deerhunter,' she stammered, although it came out rather muffled.

There was a long pause.

'And...?' said Plato. Christ, it was like pulling teeth.

Pause.

The satchel moved. Muttering.

Plato looked at Dug.

'What did she say?'

'She hasn't seen it,' Dug reported.

'Ah,' said Plato. 'She hasn't seen it.'

'Oh, don't sigh,' said Pippa. 'She's trying, you know.'

'Forget The Deerhunter,' said Dug. 'In Bernard Malamud's The Assistant, there's the part where the old man turns the gas on and goes to bed.'

Plato shot a glance at Terry, but there was no reaction.

So Dug had been into the past papers? From the 70s? Malamud had been dropped from the curriculum, as it was felt that references to him were becoming too 'pat'. Plato had been all for reinstating him this year – he had passed away only last April. His argument had been that the man's credentials were impeccable. Anyone who was anyone on the Moral Philosophy reading list was, it had to be faced, dead.

'That's right,' said Plato, his voice low. 'But it was an accident, wasn't it?'

'But this is the point,' said Dug. He placed his cup and saucer on the floor and leaned forwards in his seat, clasping his hands between his knees.

What a pompous little git, thought Plato.

Dug was on a roll.

'The old man, Morris, is in a real dilemma. Later on in the book, he tries to burn his shop down for the insurance money...'

Oops, thought Plato, and glanced at Terry again. This is getting a bit too close for comfort. Perhaps it's time to wind things up before the boy surfaces and starts making drunken allusions.

'Even if he had died from gas poisoning,' Dug continued, 'it wouldn't have been suicide, surely?'

Pippa yawned and started putting her things away.

'Going somewhere?' said Plato.

'I'm meeting some chums in the Cheviot Carvery at twelve...,' she said.

'...ah, yes, and there's always a queue, isn't there?'

'Bernard who?' said Daniel.

Morag removed her head from her satchel, presumably having confirmed that the thing that didn't exist that she'd been pretending to look for wasn't there after all.

'If he'd wanted to kill himself he could have done it in other ways!' she chirped.

'You seem to speak with some authority!' joked Plato.

Morag turned pale quicker than you could say 'Durkheim'.

'Oh, sorry,' he said. 'I didn't...'

He was all too aware of Morag's innate fragility. He worried about her, as any father would, and was concerned about what she had said she wanted to get involved in. He'd fix the Boring Clock and send it back to the chess club, unless he could think of some other use for it. He certainly wouldn't be playing chess with it. Chess was Boring.

133

Terry slowly pushed himself up by the armrests and glared round the room, as if he despised everyone in it, including himself.

'So here's your assignment,' Plato said hastily. 'Make a bus journey through the centre of Edinburgh without paying for your ticket, then describe, in one thousand words, the reactions of your fellow passengers, with reference to Book 1 of The Republic.'

Concrete Philosophy, he called it. It was another of his little hobbies.

CHAPTER 10

He pulled the curtain to the side and craned his neck. The rain was pounding off the roof of the Tollcross DHSS bunker, just across the street. The flat was a tip. It had been a tip when Terry moved in, but now it was even worse. Empty Jack Daniel's bottles were strewn all over the floor, along with clothes and stained tinfoil cartons, the contents of which were in varying states of decomposition.

The whole building hung heavy with the stench of boiled cabbages.

Terry was lying drunk on the bed. The door had been lying open.

The carry out food had been paid for by Dug. Terry had stopped eating. The only thing he put into his mouth these days was sour mash whiskey. A bottle plus twenty fags and his dole money was gone. He stole from supermarkets. In a way, it was a good thing; if he didn't have to walk around to find shops where they didn't know his face, he wouldn't have had any reason to get out of bed.

Dug tried to pull the curtain back into place, but the nail that was holding it into the wall fell out and ticked across the lino, under the sink. Sure, it was a hike from Duddingston Halls to Tollcross, but someone had to do it. It wasn't a chore. It was, however, hard work to get Terry out of the flat and up to Charles Square for lectures; he had recently given up. He'd been writing essays for him since the beginning of term. His handwriting might have been an issue, so he'd located a typewriter on the 6th floor of the library. He made sure not to copy word for word, and the essays were more of a summarisation of what he himself had written. Sugden would have been proud of him. His essays had suddenly become cogent and salient. The stuff he was handing in for Terry was certainly terse.

He looked at Terry lying there in a heap. He'd been sleeping in his overcoat since he'd bought it. He looked like a huge chrysalis, his chest rising and falling, pumping the metamorphosis along. What was going to emerge when he eventually got through this crisis was anyone's guess.

* * *

The pounding on the door started again.

Sammy stood in the loby, straining to make out how many people were on the landing. He was due a visit from Dennis.

'Who is it?' he said.

'I phoned about the advert,' came the reply.

Nae need tae shout, thought Sammy, and rubbed his ear. They could have done with a new front door. It was made of balsa wood or something. Maybe he should have a word with Sister Clara…

He made sure the chain was in place and opened it a crack.

It wasn't Dennis.

Sammy told him to come in, and went to the bedroom to give the other two the all clear. When he stepped into the living room, the boy was standing in the middle of the floor looking like a right dork, with a shiny new vinyl guitar case over his shoulder. That wasn't what Sammy was staring at, though.

'Who's yer mate?' he said.

There was a big fucker slumped on the pouffe next to the telly. He looked like David Lee Roth working on a death wish. He started snoring.

'That's Terry,' said the boy. 'Don't mind him. He's harmless.'

'Anyway. Ah'm Sammy. Baz. Mich.'

'Dug. Alright?'

'Hi,' said Mich.

'Awright,' said Baz, and raised an index finger. 'Jackie's, right?'

'Yeah, that's right,' Dug blushed. 'You've tuned up my guitar a couple of times.'

Fuck the small talk, thought Sammy, and sat down behind his drums. There were only five days left till the deadline, and he'd had it up to here with no-users. If this guy was another one, they might as well get it over with.

Mich plugged in the microphone.

'Eh,' said Dug. 'God, this is a bit embarrassing. You're not looking for a guitarist, are you?'

Fuck it, thought Sammy. Another time waster.

'The advert said we're lookin' fur a singer,' he said, and put his sticks back in their pouch.

'Aye,' laughed Dug. 'But I can't sing. Believe me.'

'Well, that's jist too bad,' said Sammy.

'Gie the boy a chance,' said Baz.

Sammy stared at him.

Dug got his guitar out. He had to wipe his hands on his coat. When Sammy saw the practice amp, all three watts of it, he almost felt sorry for him.

Baz must have felt the same.

'Ye can plug intae mines if ye want,' he offered.

'Are you sure?' said Dug. He looked as if Princess Diana had just given him permission to touch her fanny.

'Aye,' said Baz. 'Oan ye go.'

Dug approached the amp, but stopped short. His skinny guitar lead was dangling in his fingers. It looked like a Walkman would have fried it.

'Where does the, eh...?'

Christ, thought Sammy.

Baz did the connection, and cranked up the volume to ten. They watched Dug tuning up. It was nearly as bad as Jackie.

He took a deep breath.

NUH – NUH – NUUUGH

It was The Dirge.

NUH – NUH --------------- NUUUGH

Sammy coughed.

NUH – NUH – NUUUGH

NUUGH – NUUUGH

It was shite.

Baz was sympathetic.

137

'It's a mistake a lot ae folk make,' he explained. 'They think that if they get plugged intae a ballsy amp, they'll sound better. Doesnae work like that. It's still shite. Jist louder.'

'We'll let ye know,' said Sammy.

'Gie the boy a chance!' said Baz.

'Whhh?' said Sammy. 'It's a singer we're lookin' fur, no a rhythm guitarist!'

'Ae says ae cannae sing!' said Baz.

'Ae cannae play the guitar, either!' said Sammy.

Terry started awake and vomited gently down the front of his coat.

'Whit aboot yer mate?' said Sammy. 'Can he sing?'

Dug put the guitar back in its case.

'Ye might want tae work oan that other chord,' said Baz.

Sammy went to the kitchen. He heard Baz and Mich do the intro to Milk and Alcohol, Baz chopping the strings and punching the wood to fill in the rhythm. It was amazing, as usual, and it was all for fucking nothing. They'd never find a singer before Fri...

Someone came in with the vocals, and a shiver went right down Sammy's spine.

He dropped the kettle.

It sounded like Beelzebub himself had appeared in the living room and was at that moment barking down the microphone.

He ran through and got in behind his drums.

Terry took another slug of whiskey. He had the bottle clenched in his fist, and there were slavers running down his chin. They didn't stop running till the end of the song, when he wiped his mouth on his sleeve.

Mich was applauding before the last note had died out.

'You've done this before!' she smiled.

'Whit wis yer last band?' said Sammy. The boy obviously had form, but he didn't like the way Mich was beaming like an idiot.

'I'm not a singer,' Terry slurred. A gob of saliva detached itself from his bottom lip and dripped onto the rope that was holding his coat shut. 'I just came with...'

Dug had left, and nobody had noticed.

Baz started the intro to Punch and Judy. They would see if he could really sing on this one. It started off in 7:8, which was enough to throw anyone off. Sammy glanced at Mich. She had always wanted to do the song. She felt that domestic violence was an issue that wasn't taken seriously enough. They'd done the song live, but only once. Fat Edgar had latched onto the puppet theme. He'd wanted to know whose hand was up Bear's back.

Terry knew it. He came in bang on time. Most of the idiots who'd been round to audition thought that singing in a band meant jumping in whenever you felt like it. Total hairbrush pop stars. Not a clue.

Terry was good.

By Christ, he was good.

'You're better than Fish,' said Mich.

All three of them knew he was better than Bear.

As far as Sammy was concerned, he was in.

'D'ye write?' said Baz.

'Eh?'

'The advert said we're lookin' fur somebody that can write songs.'

Terry thought about it.

'You'd need to see Dug about that,' he said.

'Oh, dear,' said Baz, and pulled the mike out of his amp. 'We're lookin' fur a writer.'

Shut it, you, thought Sammy.

Terry was engrossed in the label on his bottle. He turned his head slightly and stared down at Baz with bloodshot eyes.

'I said you'd have to see Dug about that.'

Personality, too, thought Sammy.

'Right,' he said. 'We've got a gig this Friday. Practices are every day at one. And, eh, fifty pee electricity money.'

Terry burped. He worked his jaws.

'Fine by me,' he said, and drained the bottle.

Mich dropped Sammy off at the Kaptain's Kabin and drove round to a friend's house for a loan of a string. They could have got one at Jackie's, but Sammy didn't want to be anywhere near the guy. He'd only have wanted to tag along and give his expert opinion on the new singer. Terry had said he'd get the bus out later because he had to go and see someone in Drummond Street, whatever that meant. Baz, as usual, would show after all the gear had been set up.

Sammy sat at the bar and had a good look at the set list. At their fourth and final practice, Terry, who had sobered up a bit, had insisted on opening with a Sex Pistols number.

'Is ae serious?' Baz asked the carpet.

'Yes, he is,' said Terry, and put on a cassette.

It had been a while since any of them had heard the track. All three of them were amazed at how weedy it sounded, even when Sammy turned up the bass on his stereo. They had it down note perfect in ten minutes. Sammy rearranged the intro. He speeded the song up, a lot, and battered the snare where he was supposed to hit the toms. Baz grudgingly reworked the guitar parts, but it was brilliant. Mich thrummed her bass with a hard plectrum half way up the neck, making it growl.

It sounded fucking mental.

Everything had gelled immediately, and Terry's vocals were spot-on. Baz was still shaking his head, though. It wasn't that it was punk; Alec Dick had a plaque behind the bar that testified to the fact that he'd been the subscriptions secretary of the Dalkeith Sex Pistols Fan Club, '77-'78. But he was sure that Fat Edgar would have something to say about a tall guy with hair like a wind machine doing a Johnny Rotten number. He didn't know how Terry would handle the slagging in front of a crowd of paying punters. If he bottled it, it wouldn't just be the singer that looked like a cunt.

Fat Edgar was, of course, installed in his seat, and had three empty Guinness tumblers lying on the table.

Sammy ordered a pint, but was having trouble catching Alec's eye. There seemed to be something urgent needing polished at the other end of the counter. After another glance at the set list, he folded up the paper and shoved it in his pocket.

The door slammed, and a big stranger in a donkey jacket, with a commando bunnet rolled down over his ears, crossed the floor, heading straight for the jacks.

Alec unhooked his shillelagh.

'Got tae keep the scruff oot, eh, Alec?' said Sammy.

'Back in a minute,' Alec sniffed, and disappeared into the bogs.

Sammy ordered a packet of scampi fries to go with his Special, and suddenly noticed a small pair of hands gripping the stool next to him. Amidst much puffing and panting, a neatly coiffured head strained up and over the cushion.

Unbelievable, thought Sammy. It had been a matter of time before he came back, begging.

'Awright, there?' said Sammy. 'Long time no see.'

Bear manoeuvred himself into a comfortable sitting position; he placed both hands between his legs and pushed himself up, his feet jutting out at right angles. He looked like a Junior Olympian mounting the pommel horse.

'Still waiterin' doon Rose Street?' Sammy smirked. He could afford to be smug. He'd discovered Terry.

Bear took a minute to get his breath back, then looked at the edge of the counter. He was too far away to lean on it.

'Nah, Sammy,' he said. 'Ah jacked it.'

'That right?' said Sammy. 'Whit happened?'

'A misunderstanding.'

Sammy knew about those.

Alec Dick was back behind the bar. He was as white as a sheet.

'You look like ye've jist seen a ghost,' said Sammy.

Alec jerked a tumbler under an optic until it was full.

'So, Bear,' Sammy continued, all concern. 'Whit happened?'

Bear cleared his throat, as if he'd rehearsed the next bit.

'This guy comes intae the restaurant wi' ae's wife, right? So ah serve their table aw night, right up tae well past closin' time. Ae pays the bill an' ah bring um ae's chainge. Then ae shouts me over again, the cheeky cunt.'

Sammy had already guessed where this was going. He let Bear finish, though.

'"Ye've made a mistake,' ae goes. 'Ye're short.'.'

Poor wee bastard. But that was Bear all over; too sensitive by half.

'So ah gave um a slap an' walked oot.'

Sammy took a sip of his pint and handed Bear the packet of scampi fries, seeing as he couldn't reach it.

'So is this you idle again?' he said. It was a cruel world right enough.

'No,' said Bear. 'Ah'm singin' in a band. We're playin' here the night.'

141

'.....Eh?'

'Treads 'n' Risers. Ah hear yous're strugglin' as a three-piece.'

The fire door swung open and a drum kit that wasn't Sammy's was being carted in. Sammy shot a glance at Alec, who was trying to fill a glass with vodka and make a phone call at the same time.

He must have felt Sammy staring at him.

'Ah've got a business tae run,' he said, and emptied the tumbler down his throat.

Sammy was straight over to the stage.

'Who's the drummer?' he demanded.

A middle-aged guy in overalls laid down the hi-hat.

'Frankie! Boy here wants tae see ye.'

A young guy was struggling towards the stage under the bulk of a bass drum. It looked brand new, top of the range with solid mahogany trim. He laid it gently on the floor.

'Aye?'

'No football colours in the bar!' shouted Alec. He sounded drunk.

Sammy was raging.

'Whit the fuck's goin' oan?' he said.

Frankie looked around and loosened his scarf.

'How d'ye mean?' he said.

Sammy pointed at the array of drums and cymbals that were rapidly multiplying round his feet. Frankie pulled a stick out of his sleeve and scratched his head. Jackie came through the fire door with a snare drum. He set it down on the floor and immediately his fingers were hovering like Clint Eastwood.

'Eh...ah'm a drummer,' said Frankie.

'Ah can fuckin' see ye're a drummer!' said Sammy.

Pause.

'Ma band's playin' here the night,' said Frankie.

'No it's fuckin' no!' said Sammy, and stabbed himself in the chest with his index finger. 'MA band's playin' here the night!'

There was a lot of shouting. Very soon it was Sammy against the five members of Treads 'n' Risers. Bear was keeping out of it.

The Kaptain's Kabin regulars, some of them with their wives, had started drifting in. One group had taken a table right in front of the stage, and were already into their second round of drinks.

The toilet door slammed.

'It's Dun-can Good-hew!' shouted Fat Edgar.

Everyone turned to look.

Someone was loping towards them. His head was shaved, and his eyebrows were gone, but that was the least of what everyone was staring at. He had thick mascara round his eyes, and there were trails of red ink weeping from the corners. His nipples, belly button and appendix scar were circled in green, transforming his torso into a twisted face.

He looked like something that had escaped from a locked ward.

The shillelagh he was wielding only added to the effect.

Something rattled at the bar. Alec was back at the optic.

'What's up, Sammy?' said Terry, and leaned his stick against Fat Edgar's table.

When he had recovered from the shock, Sammy told him. Treads 'n' Risers, as a unit, began to look very sheepish indeed. It was all Sammy could do not to smile. The old guy was shaking, but trying to look hard in front of the youngsters. As for Frankie, he was sniffling something about not wanting any bother.

Terry stretched his arms over his head, as if he were preparing for a high dive. The ladies at the table began to coo, and it was no wonder. Terry had quite a body, the massive shoulders tapering down to the muscular stomach...

'Ah telt yez it wis Duncan Goodhew,' said Fat Edgar.

In one fluid arc, Terry's right arm swooped down and grabbed the shillelagh, which flew up and over and down, down down...

The only person who moved was Jackie. He ripped off his shirt and lunged towards Frankie, who was jerking around on the floor, screaming, his hands clutching his head, trying to hold it together. Blood was spewing out between his fingers, covering Frankie, the floor and Fat Edgar's shoes. His scarf had quickly become a sodden rag of red, red and brown.

The other members of Treads 'n' Risers, it was noted, did not jump in to help their mate.

'Well, that settles that!' shouted Alec. He slapped his hands together. 'Anybody fur a wee yin?'

Bear tried to take a swing at him and fell off his stool. He picked himself up and stomped towards the fire exit.

'Move! Move!' shouted Jackie.

'The boy's right,' said Fat Edgar, checking the blood damage on his shoes. 'Ye'd better phone an ambulance, Alec.'

Alec laughed.

'Ah'm well ahead ae the game the night!' he shouted.

'Move! Move!' shouted Jackie. His shirt was bunched up in his fist, and he was frantically scrubbing the solid mahogany trim. 'Move, ya deef cunt! That's a twelve hunner pound drum kit yer bleedin' oan!'

Baz appeared at the fire exit.

'Wis that Bear ah saw ootside?' he said.

The sound of an ice cream van in the car park.

Vic swayed to a halt beside Baz.

'Evenin' all,' he said. 'Like ma chimes?'

Fuckin' hell, thought Sammy. That wis quick. Whenever there was a fight in the Kaptain's Kabin, the ambulance took at least half an hour to get there. Longer if Vic was driving.

A drip was shoved into Frankie's arm, and wires were taped to his chest. His skin, the bits that you could see through the blood, was pale.

'Will ye be needin' blood donors?' asked Fat Edgar.

'No,' said Vic, taking stock of the situation. 'I'll just wring out this scarf.'

'Ah don't want tae die,' murmured Frankie.

Vic patted his wee box.

'According to this machine, you're already dead, son. Mind you, it's been on the blink for months.'

He lifted a fresh pint of Guinness off Fat Edgar's table and downed it in one.

Frankie passed out.

. . .

By the time the gig started, the place was heaving. There had been a queue at the payphone all night, people phoning friends and family, telling them to get down to the Kaptain's Kabin to see this crazy new kid on the block. So many people were crowding and shouting round the phone that the message was sometimes garbled. A minibus of teenage girls from Penicuik screeched to a halt outside at ten to ten because they'd heard that an American boy band were playing.

Their disappointment didn't last long. At ten o'clock sharp, Drive! crashed into their opening number and the singer came storming, bare-chested onto the stage.

'This song is called – Anarchy...'

They were already on their feet, roaring.

'D'ye think that's real blood oan ae's airms?' shouted one of the girls into her mate's earhole.

Her mate was too busy screaming to hear.

The rumours were starting already.

'They ca' um The Surgeon,' shouted someone up at the bar.

'That's right, ae wis a student doctor,' shouted someone else.

'Ae killed yin ae ae's patients!' shouted his mate.

'Gross negligence?'

'Naw, ae didnae like ae's face!'

Alec knew the song well. He was waiting for the fourth verse. He put down his glass and reached for his shillelagh – but The Surgeon was swinging it round his head.

The microphone was turned to the crowd.

They all thought it was the K.K.!!

Everyone joined in. Even the regulars. Especially the regulars.

People were going wild, and it was only the first song.

Alec smiled. He wouldn't be needing his stick after all.

They played a blinder.

A star was born.

CHAPTER 11

There was no stopping them. It was like being on an express train to the top of the world. At least, that was how Sammy had described it one night, when they were sharing out the money in the van. It was all Terry could do not to laugh. Fair enough, it might have been an express train, but Terry was sure as hell who was driving. He could feel himself improving with every performance. Goodness, but he knew how to work an audience. He had them baying for more at the end of every gig. It was obvious that the Kaptain's Kabin had never seen anything like it.

Alec Dick asked them to do Saturdays, too.

Drive! duly obliged, but they also had other fish to fry. Terry's ties with people at the university theatre got them hooked into a series of college tours in and around the city. They were a hit and run kind of affair, no stopovers, just out and back again the same night, but the money was good and, more importantly, they were becoming a name in Edinburgh. What was it Sammy had said? They were 'a force to be reckoned with'.

Terry wondered what planet Sammy was living on.

By Christmas, Alec was turning away people at the door.

Terry was going to have to watch himself, though. It was common knowledge that he was shagging half of the regulars' wives. So far he had been lucky. He was trading on his reputation as a bit of a nutter, and had avoided numerous kickings because of his skill with the shillelagh, which he now carried around with him like a walking aid. Mich had actually given him gyp about it after one of the practices at the flat. 'Exploitation of women', she called it. What a couple she and Sammy were, a quote for every occasion. Terry knew where she was coming from, though. It was obvious that her relationship with Sammy was on the skids. It was a matter of time before Terry stepped effortlessly in to show her what she'd been missing.

Mich might have been forty, but she was fit.

And the only thing Sammy cared about – really cared about – was his drums.

* * *

They turned the corner into Victoria Street.

The blackboard outside the pub read, in fluorescent chalk:

Tonite – The Blues Domination Society.

'This is the crowd ah wis tellin' ye aboot,' said Sammy.

Terry was studying the name.

'Do they give you a kicking if you don't clap hard enough?' he said.

Sammy smiled. This was going to be good.

The band were on their break, huddled round a wee table in the pulpit. Fucking prima donnas. They sank their pints and mounted the stage. There was no banter with the audience. They got straight into the second half of their set. That was one of the good things about Terry, he always got the punters to shut up and pay attention before they started. This crowd were acting like it was a fucking chicken-in-a-basket cabaret setup.

Mick Robertson was perched over the till, checking his receipts.

Sammy had been doing a lot of thinking lately.

Things were about to change. Big time.

There are three things that determine whether a band is going to make it. The name, the look, and, above all, the music. As far as the first factor was concerned, this lot were off to a good start – even Terry had noticed. He would let Terry use his eyes and ears to make up his mind about the other two. Sammy was going to wet the boy's whistle and listen to what he had to say. Then he was going to tell him why the Blues Domination Society were shite. Then he was going to tell him how Drive! were going to bump them.

The first song rattled along.

'Whit d'ye think?' said Sammy.

Terry sipped his whiskey. He'd started drinking out of a glass in public.

'I think the old guy on the guitar could blow Baz off the stage any day of the week,' he said.

Sammy ground his teeth together. He was trying to come up with a line about the difference between Baz and Fast Chuck, about, what was it, how less is more, but Terry had turned away. He wasn't even looking at the stage. He seemed to be giving his undivided attention to the bloke sitting over in the corner, behind the mixing desk.

'Aye,' shouted Sammy over the noise of Fast Chuck's distortion pedal, 'this is a professional setup. It's the best gig in toon.'

Terry looked at him.

'I thought that was The Jailhouse,' he said.

Sammy's jaws were grinding again.

'Strictly fur wee laddies wi' guitars oot their mammy's catalogue,' he said.

Then he had to smile.

They had started playing Walking On The Moon.

It was time to explain how Drive! were going to knock the Blues Domination Society off their perch.

He was looking at the back of Terry's head again.

There was a crowd of wasters hunched round a table behind the sound boy. Sammy had them down as scoundrels straight away, fucking parasites of the worst order, all manky anoraks and glazed expressions. They were passing round a wee brown medicine bottle and taking snorts.

Terry couldn't take his eyes off them.

'Amyl Nitrate,' said Sammy.

'Is it a good hit?' asked Terry.

'Aye, it's a good buzz,' said Sammy. 'If ye want tae feel like ye've jist been runnin' fur a bus.'

Terry was an alcohol man. The fact that he had never seen poppers before showed an innocence that was alarming. His experience of hard drugs was probably three Alka Seltzer after too much of that

Jack Daniel's. He'd have to be careful. Sharks were circling, and they liked the taste of virgin flesh.

One of the ne'er-do-wells, a right dodgy character in a blue cagoule, had caught Terry's eye.

'It'd be better if ye didnae stare at folk,' said Sammy out of the corner of his mouth.

'He's staring at me!' laughed Terry, just as the man rose from his seat and started heading for the bar. He veered off suddenly to the jacks, scratching his nose with his pinkie.

Terry tipped back a mouthful of whiskey.

'Back in a minute,' he said.

Of course folk stared at Terry. He looked like a fucking space alien. The shaved head and eyebrows were bad enough, but now he'd taken to sporting a pair of pointy Midge Ure sideburns. They looked more like dirty marks than facial hair. But he was the singer in a band, so it was allowed.

So were recreational drugs.

He was back. His eyes were birling.

'Good hit?' said Sammy.

Terry had his hand inside his coat, rubbing his chest.

'Does this last long?' he said.

Sammy said nothing.

Terry reached for his glass, and a tiny tinfoil package flipped onto the bar.

Sammy nodded.

'Whit's this?' he said. 'Huv ye hit the big time already?'

Terry placed his hands slowly on the counter.

'Don't worry,' he said. 'I'll not be injecting it.'

'That's right,' said Sammy, and reached for the package. He ripped it open and shook the powder onto the floor, then rubbed it into the carpet with his boot.

Terry swung him round and pushed him up against the bar. Sammy felt the end of the shillelagh getting pressed into the flesh under his chin.

'Who the fuck do you think you are?!' Terry hissed. 'My father?'

Mick Robertson.

'Evenin', gents.'

'Oh, hello, there, Mick,' said Sammy. It was difficult to look casual with his back bent over the counter. And the nobbly bit of the shillelagh was pressing into his windpipe.

Mick took a good look at Terry.

'This cunt bothering you, Sammy?' he said.

It wasn't supposed to be like this. They had missed Walking On The Moon. Terry was supposed to be listening to Sammy's plan. Terry was supposed to be shaking hands with Mick Robertson, saying, 'Hello there, I'm the singer in Drive!. We can do Wednesdays no problem.'

Terry stormed out.

'An' fuckin' stay oot,' said Mick.

Sammy rubbed his throat. Christ, it was sore.

'Na, ye're awright, Mick,' he coughed. 'A friend ae mine, that's aw.'

* * *

The rain was pishing down. He ducked into a shop doorway and shook the water out of his coat. A polythene bag was trapped in an eddy of wind in the corner. He folded it this way and that and planked it on his head.

He marched down the street, the rain bouncing off his shoulders, running off the bag onto his shoulders. Is this what he'd become? Fair enough, he had money in his pocket, but there was no future, no long-term future in this. The way Sammy was acting, the band was the be all and end all, the *raison d'être.* And where the hell did he get off telling Terry what to do? The last thing he needed was a Sammy-shaped chaperone keeping him on the straight and narrow.

Hang on.

The band had landed in his lap, he reminded himself. It was a gift. Perhaps it was a sign.

Sammy might have had plans, but Terry had an agenda.

The rain had eased off. He tossed the bag into a bin outside the Commonwealth Pool. He hunched down into his coat and walked through the main entrance to the Halls. A servitor was standing on guard duty outside the office block. Terry bid him a good evening and continued on into the compound. Dug's House was right at the back. There was a black and white photograph of Dug in the foyer, along with all the other pictures of JCR Presidents of yesteryear.

Terry rapped on the door. He thought he heard a voice inside, so turned the handle.

It looked like a tip. Empty lemonade bottles were all over the floor, and there were even more on the workbench, in front of the window, sticking out of carrier bags. Perhaps Dug had invested in Barr's Ltd.; there was an Irn Bru duvet on the bed.

Something moved under it.

'Dug?'

It stopped moving.

Oh, Douglas, thought Terry. You naughty boy.

The door opened. Dug walked in. He looked like he'd been caught fiddling with himself.

'Oh! Terry,' he said, and his eyes darted to the bed.

'Evening,' said Terry. 'I was just passing...'

Dug was holding the door open.

'Aye, right, well, if you want to come down to the common room, it'll be a bit more comfortable...'

'No,' said Terry, and cleared an arse-sized space on the workbench. 'I'm fine.'

Dug's face was a picture.

'What's going on here?' said Terry.

'Eh?' said Dug.

'Has the university bottle bank been set up in your room?'

Dug grinned nervously.

'Oh, right, I see what you mean,' he said, and added a pile of coins to the stacks that were arranged along the top of the fireplace. They looked like rows of little silver pillars, although they were supporting nothing.

'Waste not want not. There's 5p back on the empties. We're on slot electricity.'

As if to prove he wasn't lying, he slid a coin into the box next to the fire and twisted the lug. The bar hissed then creaked, the scent of burning dust filling the room.

151

'It smells like you haven't used it for a while, Dug,' said Terry. 'Perhaps you've found some other way of keeping warm in winter?'

A hand appeared from under the duvet and padded about until it came to rest on a pair of Joe 90 glasses.

Terry smiled.

The hand disappeared back under the duvet. With the glasses.

'She hasn't got a torch under there, has she?' Terry laughed. 'That would be kinky.'

Dug pulled the door open.

'If there's nothing I can help you with...' he said.

His guitar was leaning against the wardrobe. A battered acoustic, held together with sellotape, was lying next to it.

'I was wondering why you haven't been out to Dalkeith to see my band,' said Terry.

'Fucking good line, Terry!' said Dug.

Now, now. Temper. Although his jealousy is understandable. I stole his gig.

'We're really good,' said Terry. 'So the ladies keep telling me.'

Dug was looking flushed.

'Aye, well,' he said, 'I've been working part time in the ref bar on Fridays, clearing tables.'

'We do Saturdays, too.'

'Fuck off, Terry! I'm fucking skint, man!'

Oh, yes. Terry was forgetting.

'I had to beg Sugden to give me back the money I paid for the French trip,' said Dug. 'That was gone in a flash – do you know how much the rent is...'

'When is that?' said Terry.

'Eh? In about a month,' said Dug. 'What, you're not thinking about go...'

'Now there's an idea,' said Terry. 'Sorry, I interrupted you.'

'Anyway. The rent. The part time job. Studying.'

Terry stood up. Something glinted under the top of the duvet.

'What's your point, Dug?' he said.

Dug's hand disappeared into his pocket. He produced another clutch of coins.

152

'Do you know how fucking embarrassing it is going round the Halls asking folk for their empty lemonade bottles? This is the University of Scotland, Terry. Nobody here takes back their empties – nobody.'

He jerked his thumb at the door.

'Most of these arseholes have never seen a fucking ice cream van!'

'Yeah, yeah, yeah, Dug, you're a working class hero, a real martyr. What's your point?'

'Are you kidding?' said Dug.

'Let me think,' said Terry. 'Er, no.'

'The hundred and ninety five quid, Terry! I'm fucking suffering here.'

Terry pulled his coat tighter.

'You'll get your money, Dug,' he said. 'Don't worry.'

There were tears in Dug's eyes.

'But I need it now, Terry,' he said.

Terry felt sorry for him. He didn't know why, but he did.

'I'll tell you what,' he said. 'Give me some of your songs and I'll see if we can do anything with them. I'll give you full credit for the lyrics.'

Dug beamed like a child.

Goodness, thought Terry. The boy is like putty in my hands. Like a nubbin of Play-Doh.

'Would you?' said Dug. 'God, that would be... I've been practising with...'

Black spectacle frames emerged from the duvet; the eyes were huge through the lenses.

'Hello again,' she stammered.

Terry thought for a moment.

'Oh, Dug,' he said. 'Really.'

CHAPTER 12

Everything was set for the Scotch On de Rocks gig, a showcase for new Scottish and Irish bands that was to take place in the park behind Salisbury Crags. Terry had been shaking from the moment he found out it was going to be televised. There was a lot riding on this.

'What's with the 'de'?' he asked.

'Good question,' said Sammy.

'There's a lot of Irish bands taking part,' explained Mich. 'The theme is Eamon de Valera. All the artwork is supposed to be based around that.'

Baz took a sip of his tea.

'Ah thought the guy that painted the Mona Lisa wis Dutch?' he said, hesitantly.

Terry smiled. What a fucking arsehole.

'Whit artwork?' said Sammy.

Mich tore open the six-pack of DHSS blankets that Sammy had been using as a stool. It was no longer required. He had recently been urged by Jackie to try out the new Tamaha 'Bevvy Powell' Assprop, with lockable piston. Top of the range, naturally. There was no rush about the money. Jackie knew they were on the rise.

'We put one big letter on each blanket,' she explained.

'There's five letters in 'Drive',' said Baz.

'Plus the exclamation mark,' said Terry. 'I like it,' he added, though he didn't.

'The whit?' said Baz.

Mich sighed.

'It's like an upside down 'i',' she explained.

'Got ye.'

'So, Sammy,' she said. 'Where's the paint?'

'Eh?'

'Oh, don't say you forgot! I told you at least three times!'

Sammy looked round the room. There were more egg trays on the carpet than on the walls. The plaster was stained with streaks of sellotape and blu-tac.

'I thought ye were droppin' hints aboot the state ae the flat,' he said.

Terry helped him to salvage four half empty tins of paint from a skip at the end of the street.

'It's luminous green fur fuck's sake!' Baz protested, and took another slug of tea.

Mich hesitated.

'That can be the Irish theme,' she said.

This is fucking stupid, thought Terry. It's my face I want on the telly, not badly painted blankets.

Terry, Sammy and Mich did the letters. Terry suggested that Baz do the exclamation mark. A line and a dot were just about his level. Baz took his time about it, his head bent over the blanket with his tongue poking out, almost touching the material, as he smeared on the paint with the side of an empty fag packet. There hadn't been any brushes in the skip.

Someone pounded on the front door.

'Shit,' said Sammy. 'This is aw we need.'

* * *

It was just the two of them, slouching comfortably in their wickerwork armchairs. Plato had suggested this ad hoc tutorial, and Dug had been only too willing to accept.

Of course he had.

Plato had checked his countenance that morning in the bathroom mirror. He had decided that a shave would have been too painful. His face looked like a NASA photograph of the moon: grey, full of craters, and with little criss-cross marks all over it.

'If you're in the business of handing out sore faces, that's one to be proud of,' said Dug.

Plato thoughtfully scratched the ladder of stitches on the side of his head.

'Jimmy Boyle?' he said. 'You *do* do a lot of reading in the library.'

'Not really,' said Dug. 'I got his autobiography as a birthday present.'

'Why? Was someone trying to mend your evil ways? As hints go, it's not very subtle.'

Dug laughed, but caught himself short.

Very polite, thought Plato. The boy knows there's a lot at stake, and doesn't want to fawn too much. This was money in the bank.

'Did you get mugged or what?' Dug asked. 'Don't tell me it was another golfing accident.'

'No, that's changed,' said Plato. '"Here's something for your stamp collection," was how my assailant put it.'

Dug, man of the world, sighed.

'"Ta panda reh-ee",' he said. 'As Heraclitus put it.'

Things were indeed in a state of flux. But Dug was getting all cocky again. Plato couldn't help himself.

'You do of course mean 'Ta panda *ree*'?' he said.

Dug had done 'O' Grade Ancient Greek, or so he claimed. He was, he felt, qualified to argue the toss.

'"Ta panda reh-ee". Surely?'

'Oh, really,' said Plato, acting the part of injured party very well, he thought. 'Try taking a trip to Athens and talking like that.'

Dug wanted to say something, but Plato just talked right over him.

'It's the difference between 'hoy anthropoy' and 'ee anthropee',' he said. 'Or, if you'd prefer, 'the peh-o-pleh' and 'the people'. I don't think you'd get very far.'

'But it's Ancient Greek pronunciation we're talking about,' said Dug.

The boy was tenacious, something which Plato found encouraging.

'And how would you feel, Dug, if a Greek were to correct your pronunciation of, for example, a Robert Burns poem? *Wee, sleekit, cow'rin, tim'rous beastie...*'

Plato sat back in his chair and inhaled deeply. Any linguist who knew his poetry, and his cartography, could have pinpointed the accent as belonging somewhere along the B7204. The road that goes through Alloway, in other words.

'Any comments, Dug?'

The boy decided not to labour the point, and nodded his acquiescence. His eyes, Plato noticed, were on his essay, which was lying on the desk.

'You are right, of course,' said Plato. 'They teach it all wrong in Greece. You really should stick to your guns, old son.'

Dug smiled like a loon.

'Although you must realise,' Plato continued, 'that an undergraduate telling me in a comical Grangeburn rat-a-tat squeak how to pronounce my ancient tongue is a little hard to stomach.'

That got rid of the smirk.

'Tell me,' said Plato. 'What do you intend to do after graduation?'

'Well...'

It was time to get this conversation back on track.

'Merchant banking,' said Dug.

Plato laughed.

'Yes, Dug,' he said. 'But seriously.'

'.....'

'You're serious?'

To his credit, Dug turned crimson.

* * *

Mich and Baz quickly folded up the blankets and tiptoed into the bedroom, while Sammy hid the paint tins and fag packets behind the sofa, which he shoved right up against the wall. Terry was trying to gather up the newspapers that were scattered all over the floor without making too much noise.

'What's up?' he whispered.

'Ah'll tell ye later,' said Sammy, and pointed to the kitchen.

Since the wee argument in the Prezzie Hall, they had had an unspoken agreement. As long as Terry showed up for practices and gigs, no questions would be asked. In any case, Sammy wouldn't

157

have dared make his mouth go. He knew only too well that Terry was the backbone of the band. If anything, Terry *was* the band. Everyone knew it.

More hammering on the door.

'Who is it?' Sammy shouted.

Terry was watching him through a gap in the kitchen door. He was having a final look round the living room to make sure everything was cleared away. Whoever the unexpected caller was, Sammy obviously didn't want him tipping paint over his drums.

'Rent!'

Sammy pulled the door open slightly, keeping it on the chain.

'Dennis wants tae see ye,' yapped a voice.

Eh? thought Terry, and drew back quickly as the wedge of space in the doorway was filled by Dennis's teeth.

'Is Sammy in?' Dennis asked Sammy. 'If he's not, I'll come back later.'

Terry watched the two visitors loping into the living room. What was he supposed to do? He'd stand where he was and let Sammy do all the talking. After all, it was the rent Dennis had come round for, not Terry.

'Ah hud an interestin' conversation doon Tollcross a while back,' said Sammy, his voice shaking. He sounded like a complete whelk.

Fuck this.

Terry strode into the living room doorway. Dennis was just lowering himself onto the sofa, gathering his coat around his legs as if he didn't want it getting soiled on the cushion covers.

Sammy looked at Terry, and made a high pitched noise in the back of his throat.

'Ah,' said Dennis. 'I see Yul Brynner's here. Awright, big yin?'

Terry was keeping his eyes on Sid.

Dennis started poking around the sofa. He picked up a cushion and looked underneath.

'What's that smell?' he said.

Sammy was a bad actor.

'Whit smell?' he said. 'Ah cannae smell anythin'.'

'Fucking Dulux emulsion,' said Dennis. 'Don't tell me you're decorating this dump?'

'There's paint tins and that behind the couch,' said Sid, and parked himself on Sammy's new stool. The rubber handle of a golf club was protruding from the cuff of his leather jacket. He pulled it out and propped it against the wall. The shaft had been shortened, and sharpened to a point. It was obvious that pitch 'n' putt was not on today's agenda.

Terry had left his shillelagh at home. Sammy had started cowering at the sight of it. In the same way he was cowering at the sight of Sid's spike.

'Ah hud an interestin' conversation doon Tollcross a while back,' Sammy repeated. There was even more of a tremor in his voice.

'I heard you the first time, Sammy,' said Dennis.

'Aye. Somebody's been tellin' wee stories aboot me bein' shacked up wi' some lassie. Cohabitin', like. Ma money…'

Dennis puffed out his cheeks and exhaled.

'I think that's terrible,' he said, 'folk grassing up other folk to the social. I mean the next thing you know your money's getting cut and then where are you? But that's no a problem for you, is it, Sammy? According to my, eh, clients in Dalkeith, you're fucking raking it in.'

Sammy stared at him.

'And, anyway,' Dennis continued. 'It's a bit of a liberty folk describing your bint as a lassie. She's at least fifty, isn't she? What do you think, Sid?'

Sid's hand was under the stool. He was fiddling with something. Probably the lockable piston. Sammy was keeping his mouth shut. Telling him to leave it alone would only have encouraged him.

Dennis sat back on the sofa and crossed one elegantly trousered leg over the other.

'Piece of advice, Sammy,' he said, and jerked his thumb in Terry's direction. 'You want to watch this yin. He likes shagging married women.'

'So they tell me,' said Sammy, and attempted a fly smile.

Dennis laughed slowly.

'Aye, Sammy,' he said. 'They told me you were slow. Anyway, about your tenancy.'

Sammy swallowed.

'Aye?'

'I've been getting complaints.'

'Oh, aye?'

'Oh, aye. They tell me you're a noisy neighbour.'

'Ah'll make sure an' turn ma stereo doon, Dennis.'

Sid gripped the snare by the rim and started rattling it, as if he wanted to see what was holding it together.

Dennis laughed.

'Have a look in that wee pouch,' he said.

Sid removed a long, red drumstick and held it up to his nose, sniffing it. Sammy whined again. It was a Tamaha 'Captain Scarlet' classic heavy, twenty notes the pair. He'd spent a boring couple of minutes informing Terry that a titanium rod ran through the centre of the wood, which went a long way to explaining why it was the favoured stick of heavy metal drummers.

Sid tried to break it across his knee.

'What was I saying?' said Dennis. 'Oh, aye, about your tenancy. When is it you're leaving again?'

'Ye cannae throw us oot,' said Sammy. 'Ah took a walk doon Waterloo Street. They telt me ye've got tae gie six months notice. Come oan, Dennis, we've talked...'

Dennis silenced him with a wave of his hand.

'Yes, you're right again, Sammy. I can't throw you out.'

Sid was still trying to break the stick.

'But he can.'

The snare drum was battered, once, and there was a sharp crack as the drumstick snapped in half, the thin end somersaulting across the room and clattering off the front of the telly.

'Rimshot!' squeaked Sid.

Terry's eyes were on the golf club. He took a step towards it.

'Now, now,' said Dennis, getting to his feet. He shook his coat. 'There's a time and a place for that sort of thing.'

He patted Sammy on the elbow.

'Right place, some other time, though, eh? Come on, you.'

Sid pushed his spike back into his sleeve and followed him down the loby. They stopped outside the bedroom door.

'It's all right, Mich,' Dennis shouted. 'You can come out now, I'm leaving. Have a word with that man of yours, though. He's starting to give my arse the toothache.'

He pulled open the front door then pushed it shut with a thud.

Mich came out of the bedroom.

'Boo!' said Dennis, and laughed in her face. 'Just kidding. I wasn't really leaving. And hello, hello, isn't that Baz hiding in the shadows?'

He turned to Sammy.

'Your bint was in there with a sex-starved guitarist. Did you know?'

He gave Mich the once-over.

'Nah, you're okay,' he said. 'I don't think he'd stoop to her level.'

Mich was looking at Sammy.

'Cheerio, hen,' said Dennis. 'And, hey...' He stroked her upper arm, making her recoil. 'Don't worry. I really am leaving this time.'

He winked at Terry on the way out.

'Give her one for me, eh?' he said.

Terry slammed the door behind them.

Sammy was standing at the window, raging. Mich had an arm round his shoulder.

'It's okay,' she said. 'He can't put us out – you know that. Come on, let's get the gear packed up.'

Baz was crouched down at the telly, examining the broken drumstick.

'Here,' he said. 'Ah thought ye said these were indestructible?'

Sammy locked himself in the toilet. It was time for them to get up to the Crags – they were playing sixth from the top of the bill, and they'd need to get the blankets and the rest of the gear loaded into the van. Although Sammy had taken things badly, Terry couldn't help feeling that Dennis's visit had been just the spur he was looking for. Terry was about to give the performance of his life. He poked his head into his bag to make sure he had all his make up with him. Exposure of a televisual nature beckoned. And not just for Terry.

He smiled.

The Reverend Alexander Kinlochleven was about to become a household name.

161

* * *

'Let's turn to your assignment, shall we?' said Plato.

The essay rejoiced in the title 'Does An Agricultural Philosopher Believe That A Pig Has A Soul?'. The theme, admittedly contrived, had been Plato's idea, but it was a good, solid piece of writing, drawing parallels and contrasts between JS Mill, Hume, Bentham and Kant. Dug had even managed to embroider the expressions 'means-end reasoning', 'better Socrates dissatisfied', and 'pork futures' into the same paragraph. And Kant wasn't even on the Moral Philosophy 1 reading list, so that put it down as a pass straight away. Depending on how Dug handled himself over the next few minutes, it was going to get an A+.

Dug looked pleased with himself. The essay, which Plato was smoothing out on his knee, was immaculately presented, written on five sheets of A4 held firmly within the transparent covers of a plastic folder.

The expression of self-satisfaction was noted. What a git, thought Plato. You'll do splendidly.

He tossed the folder back onto the desk.

Dug stared, his mouth hanging open.

'My dear boy,' Plato began. 'Do you really think I asked you here to talk about your homework?'

* * *

Fat Edgar was already installed in the front row of swaying bodies, with two six packs of Guinness round his neck on a length of washing line.

The Scotch On de Rocks festival was being sponsored by McNab's Beers, so there was plenty of lager sloshing around backstage for the performers. Terry was in no mood for any of it. He wanted to keep a clear head. He spent his time in a corner, checking out the inflated egos of the fledgling pop stars. Drive! were on after a folk rock outfit called Jock Ma Ceilidh, who had been described in RockPress as Falkirk's Next Big Thing. He had got talking to the drummer, a teenager called Grant. The conversation soon got round to band personnel, and Grant started slagging off their latest bass player, a big, lanky guy in full highland dress who played the bass like Nick Heyward played the guitar, high and fast.

'Ae's intae fusion,' he grimaced. 'Andy Stewart meets Haircut 100.'

'So why don't you give him the shove?' said Terry.

Grant's expression was serious.

'Ae's dad says ae can get us oan Wogan,' he said.

They were approached by a John Cooper Clark clone wearing a frock coat. He had a single dreadlock sticking out of the front of his head, between the freckles. He cadged a fag off Grant, then returned to a group of wee lassies dressed in mini skirts and Doc Marten boots. One of them had shiny Elastoplast all over her knees; probably a recent fall off her tricycle.

'I've got him down as a wanker straight away,' said Terry. 'Who is he?'

'Ma brother,' said Grant. 'He's the singer.'

Jock Ma Ceilidh were booed on. Half way through their first number a hailstorm of disposable lighters descended on the stage, some of the cheaper ones exploding with a crack off the front of the singer's guitar.

Then he took a direct hit to the face.

'Fuckin' blood claaahhhht, ya bastards!' he wailed into the mike, in an accent that was pure Rastafarian Falkirk.

Grant had already left the stage. The bass player had to be dragged off.

Drive! had five minutes to organise themselves and get the backdrop hung. The stage was a flurry of activity, two of the McNab's employees sweeping up the lighters while Mich and Terry hung the blankets behind the drum riser.

'Make share they're in the right order!' shouted Sammy over the noise coming from the audience. They were a tough crowd.

'Get oan wi' it!'

Sammy was rushing, trying to get his drums taped to the floor.

Baz got a loan of a harmonica and dazzled them with Layla in blues style, reggae, and finally in waltz time for fifteen minutes. When everything on the stage was ready, he still showed no signs of stopping. Terry grabbed the mike off him and shoved his guitar into his hands.

'Anarchy! In! The! KKKKKK!!!! KKKKKKKKKKK!!!!!'

They got off to a blistering start, but in the roar of applause at the end of the song, Terry could tell that something was wrong. The crowd were chanting something, and he was straining to make it out. He knew from previous gigs that it was likely to be 'Sur-geon! Sur-geon!', or even 'Baz! Baz!', but it was neither. It sounded like 'Dribble! Dribble!'

Mich had a foot on her monitor, leaning over at Fat Edgar. He was pointing at Sammy. She turned round with a look of horror on her face, pointing to somewhere above Sammy's head.

Terry got a fright – he thought the lighting rig was falling. He didn't get as big a fright as Sammy, though, who jumped clear of his drums.

It wasn't the lighting rig. Mich was still pointing. She crossed the stage and gave Baz a sharp poke in the ribs.

It was the backdrop.

Sammy had been playing the drums under a huge sign which read, in bold, luminous green,

Drivel

'I told you it was an upside down 'i'!' Mich screamed.

'It *is* upside doon!' said Baz. 'It looks the same the other way roond an' aw!'

It was a capital 'I'.

Terry was on it. He grabbed Sammy's insulating tape and quickly tore off a few strips, sticking them three quarters of the way down the blanket. The 'I' became an exclamation mark.

'We're Drive!,' he shouted into the mike. 'And this next song's for people who have a problem with punctuation marks. Right, Baz?'

The crowd cheered.

Baz tuned his guitar, loudly.

'But before that...,' said Terry. He could feel the words forming in his throat, and a huge weight seemed to lift from his shoulders. 'There's something I'd like to say.'

'Oan ye go, Terry!' shouted Sammy. 'The gift ae the gab!'

Terry looked straight into the camera that was in the pit at the front of the stage.

'My father is the Reverend Alexander Kinlochleven,' he said, slowly.

No reaction.

'He owns a huge church in St Vincent Street.'

A small spatter of applause, like water pishing out a pipe.

'He's shacked up with a woman from Korea.'

Ooooooooohhhhh!

'He's keeping her prisoner.'

Awwwwwwwww!

'He beats her up.'

Uuuuuuuuuugggggggghhhhh!

It was like a kiddies pantomime, even Terry could see that. All that was missing was the crowd shouting 'He's behind you!', and a troupe of dancing midgets. They wanted to hear music, not some crap about the singer's daddy.

'He's been trying to destroy my life ever since I fucked her!'

That got some Oohh-errs, and a few laughs.

What was happening? He'd practised this. They were supposed to be baying for his father's blood.

'He's got two jokers that go around...'

'Get oan wi' it!' someone shouted.

'...one of them carries a golf club...'

A disposable lighter bounced off his head.

Sammy started Milk and Alcohol. Baz and Mich were straight in.

So was Terry. He ran all over the stage, twisting, turning, rolling around on the floor, the vocals incomprehensible, trying to get something out of his system, but it was going nowhere. He felt the blood, sweat and tears streaming down his face.

Something, however, sprang into his mind with clarity.

Fuck, he thought. I've flipped.

* * *

He was on his feet, pacing the floor, and came to an abrupt halt in front of the fireplace. He'd been doing a lot of pacing up and down lately, trying to figure out his escape route.

'You could have been good. Oh, yes, you could have been bloody great. Philosophy. Keeping up the rhetoric when everyone else is falling asleep in their chairs. God knows you're good at it. But then you know that, don't you?'

'Well...'

'You think it's nothing but an undergraduate talking shop, don't you? How many times do I have to say that people should be out there, *doing* it? Haven't you learned anything from my Concrete Philosophy workshops?'

Of course he had, the poor boy. He'd learned not to try and blag his way onto LRT buses through the front door. He had explained what he was up to, and the driver had told him to either purchase a ticket or get off. Dug had got off. Perhaps he should have effected entry through the middle doors. Still, he'd milked 1037 words out of the experience, and got an A+. But Plato knew what he was up to. As far as Dug was concerned, Ethics paled into the shadows at the thought of the forthcoming Milk Round.

'I suppose I'm doing it as a hobby,' said Dug. 'You know, to pass the time till I finish.'

Plato gasped and put his foot through the front of the fire, sending shards of porcelain heating element pinging across the carpet tiles.

'Fuck!' he shouted. 'That was a new pair of Hush Puppies!'

'Well, I'm sorry if...'

'Oh, don't say sorry, for Christ's sake!'

He began to pace the floor, but had to lean on his desk because his ankle had begun to throb. So had his head, and his stitches felt dangerously close to bursting point.

'Sorry is what you write in a four page epistle to your spouse's lawyer, copied in triplicate and stamped by a notary public because you dared to violate her labia in these days of intolerant, pre-menstrual, post-feminist sexism.'

'Look, I know that...'

Plato grasped the essay in both hands.

'Do you know what this is?' he said. 'Eh?'

Dug suddenly looked ready to cave in.

'It's a safe wee piece of writing,' said Plato, 'nothing more. Oh, it's good, I'll grant you that, but that's all it is, it's little black marks on a piece of paper. Sometimes...'

Oh, get on with it you old waffler, he said to himself.

'Dug,' he said, and sat down heavily in his chair. 'There's something I want you to do.'

Dug still had his eyes clamped on the essay. One more A+ and he would be exempt from the end of year exam.

Plato lifted his pen.

'It might be a tad...*antinomian*,' he said.

'Well, I...'

The pen was describing small triangles in the centimetre of space above the paper.

'At least tell me you'll think about it,' said Plato.

'Look,' said Dug. 'I think you should tell me what...'

'A+' was scribbled in the corner of the page. This elicited a sound from somewhere in Dug's vicinity, as if a minor orgasm were being suppressed.

'That's that settled, then,' said Plato. 'Now. Do you remember mentioning Bernard Malamud a while back? Yes. Of course you do.'

He handed Dug a brand new copy of The Assistant.

'I've marked the pages which I think are germane to our conversation,' he said.

* * *

Terry was huddled in a corner. Mich had her arm round him, and Sammy was swaying about behind her, looking awkward. Baz had fucked off.

If she keeps her arm there any longer, thought Terry, Sammy's going to start getting jealous.

'Don't worry, Terry,' she said. 'At least the crowd seemed to like it.'

It had been weird, like it wasn't him who had been writhing around all over the stage like an idiot. What an embarrassment. Half way through the number he'd come to his senses. He'd realised he was making a total arse of himself, but kept up the act and rolled off the side of the stage. Baz had immediately started playing Layla on his mouth organ, but someone had knocked it out of his mouth with a lighter.

Mich squeezed his shoulder, and pressed up against him. There was the sudden overpowering stench of beer and soiled underwear.

'Ah'd like tae pit you oan ma books,' a voice grunted into his ear.

Terry drew back.

Some old jakey was leaning into Mich, slicking his hair back with a fat hand. He was wearing a safari suit. Sammy punched him, and he collapsed like a punctured bin bag.

Mich mopped up the blood with her guitar cloth. She was looking daggers at Sammy, who was hyperventilating.

The man struggled to get his hand inside his jacket, and handed Terry a small card. Although the words were smudged red, he could just make them out.

Malcolm. A & R. Smashing Records.

Terry handed the card to Sammy, who started frantically wiping the front of Malcolm's jacket, but only succeeded in spreading the bloodstains around. He helped him up, making sure he had a good grip of his walking stick. The safari suit was soaked in lager, but Terry guessed it had been like that before he hit the floor.

The apology was accepted.

Malcolm looked at Mich. He licked his hand and slicked back his hair.

'Ah ken a class act when ah see yin,' he said.

CHAPTER 13

Malcolm was holding the latest copy of RockPress open for them all to see. Page 8. The title was 'Drive! Got Their Motor Running!'

Sammy looked chuffed as fuck. He was probably wondering where his scissors were. The article would soon be taking pride of place stuck to an egg tray over the fireplace. He could look at it while he was drumming.

''...to wow the audience...',' read Malcolm. ''...a bravura performance to rank with all the greats. The band's original material went down a storm...'.'

Original material? thought Terry. Maybe it was referring to his rant about his father. There certainly hadn't been anything else. He had rolled off the stage before they'd had a chance to do Dug's song. The article was total exaggeration. No, it was more than that. It was complete fiction.

Malcolm folded the paper in half and ran his fingers over the words.

'Which famous rock journalist wrote the article?' asked Terry.

'Get tae fuck!' said Malcolm, and handed the paper to Sammy. 'Ah wrote it masell – but it'll dae the trick, you mark ma words.'

The review was printed on the letters page.

'Now,' he said. 'The next step.'

He wanted them to come along to the Hoochie Coochie Club to see an Australian band called The Middlemen.

'The support band are local,' he said. 'Well, Grangemouth. Go by the name of Blowfly.'

169

'I don't know anything about The Middlemen,' said Mich, 'but I've heard of Blowfly. Their bass player used to be in the Cocteau Twins.'

'No way!' said Baz. 'If ah want tae listen tae taped music, ah'll stick oan a cassette. An' it willnae be the fuckin' Cocteau Twins.'

'That's what I'm saying,' said Mich. 'Blowfly are a 4-piece...'

'Anyway,' said Malcolm. 'That's no important. It's this other crowd ah want yez tae watch, the Aussies.'

. . .

Baz stood in a corner of a dive in Bread Street and watched a fat woman doing squat thrusts until he was sure the support band were finished. When he got to the club, the song The Middlemen had just started ground to a halt. Someone had swiped their oboe off the edge of the stage. They got it back after a five-minute shouting match. Oboes, he thought. A fucking backing track would have been better.

Sammy was right down the front, getting into it. The drummer looked about twelve, but he was handy. Malcolm had said their drummer was a lassie – maybe she was ill or something. Maybe Malcolm was wrong – there was a lassie all right, but she'd been playing the violin earlier on. She was a cracker. And here she was again. She'd just got her oboe back. There was no doubt that this lot were good, but their sound was too...what was the word? Big? No, that was Simple Minds. Over the top? No, that was the Blues Domination Society. Arty? Arthouse! That was it, they were too Arthouse, there were too many orchestral instruments on the stage. Violins and Oboes. And the guitarists took turns singing!

Mich loved the lyrics.

Lullaby folly illegal palls
Silly dolly falling balloons

She couldn't imagine Terry singing those particular lines, which was unfortunate. You never knew, though.

Terry couldn't take his eyes off the girl. She had the oboe between her lips. Christ she was good looking. And that smile she had, like she was doing exactly what she wanted with her life, and was loving it, loving just being there.

. . .

Malcolm got them into a huddle after the gig, when the sweeping up was going on. His suit was fastened right up to his neck, but the top button wouldn't stay in – it was too greasy. He wasn't carrying his walking stick, but for some reason he had a big shoebox tucked under his arm. From the way he was leaning to one side, it must have weighed a ton. Maybe it was a counterbalance to correct the limp.

'Ladies and gents,' he puffed. 'Yez huv jist heard the next generation ae Edinburgh rock.'

'I thought that was Goodbye Mr Mackenzie,' said Terry. He wanted to get this over with and get backstage.

'They're a blown entity,' gasped Malcolm. He was having trouble keeping the shoebox off the floor. It seemed to be getting heavier.

'Whit's an Australian band playin' classical music got tae dae wi' us?' asked Baz.

The shoebox bleeped, massively. Malcolm stepped back and pulled out an aerial. He hoisted the box onto his shoulder.

'Lex, ma man...LEX, MA MAN...aye...awsome, aye...eh?...SAY AGAIN...nah...EH?...aye, right next tae me...aye, they're intae it... Lex, ye're bray...YE'RE BREAKIN' UP...ah'll catch ye later...aye... the landl...THE LANDLINE...RIGHT...'

'Over and out,' said Baz.

Malcolm pushed the aerial back in. He got Sammy to give him a hand to lay the telephone on the floor. He was sweating.

'Whit ah'm sayin' is this,' he said. 'If youse can be like The Middlemen, yez've got it made.'

Sammy looked wired.

'Got ye,' he said. 'Change ae direction. That mate ae yours, Terry, the skinny guy wi' the ears? Chase um up. We'll need mair songs.'

Terry knew it was a non-starter. The singer, the tall one, looked like the boy out of the B52s, complete with the candyfloss hairdo. Maybe Malcolm wanted him to wear a wig.

'Why don't we just poach the violinist?' he said.

'Come roond the office oan Monday,' said Malcolm. 'We'll get the contract sorted oot.'

Sammy looked like he'd just won the pools.

171

'Ye no hangin' aroond fur a drink?' he said.
'Whit?' said Malcolm. 'Fuck that fur a laugh.' He looked down at his phone, and shook his head. 'It's a two mile hike back tae ma mother's,' he said.

* * *

He'd been locked in the office since the back of five. The bolt was fastened securely. There would be no interruptions.

The outer doors banged shut. He waited another ten minutes, his ears straining, until he was sure he was completely alone.

The roll of cellophane was in the top desk drawer. He pulled off a generous length and deposited the roll in his rucksack, which he immediately put over his shoulder. He didn't want to leave any clues, and that would have been a rather large one. He slipped the book of Left Bank matches into his pocket and switched off the light.

* * *

Terry was late. He sauntered into the office just as the deal was being done. There was a party atmosphere. Malcolm, with his arm round Mich's waist, was slobbering all over Baz's head. Sammy was leaning forwards, signing his name on a piece of paper that was being gripped by a grim looking man in a business suit. There was a plastic name holder on the desk.

Lex Lodestar
President
Smashing Records

'Youse lot ur goannae be fuckin' huuuuuuge,' he growled.
'Say cheese!' said Malcolm, and pressed a Kodak Instamatic to his good eye.
Sammy looked up from the contract, and the moment was captured for the archives. Terry imagined him asking for a copy to go over the fireplace, next to the cutting from RockPress.
A cork popped. Asti Spumante, Terry noticed. Very classy.
'Here's tae us wha's like us,' said Malcolm, and filled a line of paper cups.

Sammy closed his eyes, and a tear plopped into the bubbles.

'This tastes like cider,' said Baz, and held his cup out for a refill.

Lex and Malcolm had some other business to attend to. They left Drive! alone in the office to contemplate the future.

'How much?' asked Terry.

Mich's face was red. Maybe it was the wine.

'Five thousand pounds,' she said, and started giggling.

Sammy fingered the outline of a fat envelope in his pocket.

'Lex gave us two grand tae be goin' oan wi',' he said.

Fair play to you, Sammy, thought Terry. Don't spend it all at once.

* * *

It was hard to breathe. The air was thick with smoke, that aromatic French stuff that everyone had been choking themselves with.

The fusebox was through the back, in a cupboard under a staircase that led nowhere. He slowly prised open the door, but he fumbled it and it fell with a clunk at his feet. The fuses were vintage, from the dawn of electricity. They were the size of egg cups, and made of porcelain. Maybe they were *egg cups, and the 19th century electrician that had installed them had been improvising. He located the shaft at the back of the cupboard, and stuffed the cellophane into the space. He held his match poised, and thought of Morris Bober.*

The window! It was a good job he'd read the whole book, and not just the bit that had been marked in red ink. He knew that no one would be jumping out of the shadows to save him if anything went wrong.

Something had changed. He sniffed the air. Biscuits. Caramel Wafers.

Shuffling and scratching in the bar.

He stuck his head round the door.

An old man was sweeping the floor, a ribbon of smoke rising from the rollup stuck to his bottom lip.

Dug utilised the window. He'd tell Plato that he'd filled his end of the bargain, which was true. Concrete Philosophy. It had never been his intention to go up in flames with the building. He wanted nothing to do with killing himself, nor with roasting a pensioner who was sweeping up.

After this, he decided, he wanted nothing to do with Plato, either.

* * *

'Heard the latest?' smiled Alec Dick.

'Whit's that?' said Sammy.

'Whit d'ye call an openin' act that's also the main turn?'

'Ah give in.'

'A stripper!' laughed Alec, and pushed himself back in his chair to give him room to slap his thigh.

'Aye, that's a good yin,' said Sammy.

Alec had a hanky pressed to his eyes to stem the tears. He blew his nose and buried the material in his pocket.

'So, Sammy,' he said, still chuckling. 'Whit can ah do ye for?'

Alec had had to take on extra barstaff. Fridays and Saturdays were Drive! nights, and that meant lots of clowns prancing around getting thirsty, making everybody else thirsty.

He'd recently increased the ticket price to two pounds.

'Eh, ah'd like tae talk aboot a raise,' said Sammy. 'Let's say two hundred a gig.'

Alec laughed. He loosened his tie.

'Ye can say anythin' ye fuckin' like, Sammy!'

'Come oan, Alec. It's only an extra twenty five quid each.'

'So it's no goannae make much difference? We willnae bother, then.'

This was what Sammy had been expecting. But it was the hike in the ticket price that was bothering him more than anything.

'Fine,' he said. 'Whit aboot a percentage ae the box office?'

Alec smiled like a lizard.

'Oh, Sammy,' he said. 'We're coming out with the big words now.'

Of course, there was no 'box office'. McNab's Beers' policy was to have free music in its pubs. Alec was putting the ticket money straight into his pocket. And Sammy knew that Alec was fucked if he was going to start spreading it around.

Sammy shifted on his cushion. He had no choice but to put the screws on. Malcolm had assured him that it was only a matter of time before they'd be playing Victoria Street.

'Well, Alec,' he said, 'ah huv tae tell ye that we've landed the Wednesday night gig at the Prezzie Hall.'

Alec cocked an eyebrow.

'Ye wouldnae be tellin' porky pies, now, would ye?' he said.

'No, Alec,' said Sammy. 'Straight up.'

'Ye tryin' tae tell me ye've bumped the Blues Domination Society?'

Sammy sniffed.

'Aye,' he said.

'Well, if that's true,' said Alec, 'ye deserve a pat oan the heid. An' a pat oan the heid's what ye'll huv tae settle fur, because ye won't be gettin' anythin' else off Alec Dick.'

Sammy took a deep breath, trying not to make it look too obvious.

'Robertson's payin' us three hunner a night,' he said.

Alec laughed.

'Aye, Sammy,' he said. 'In yer dreams ae is.'

Sammy knew he shouldn't have tried this line – it was Mich's idea. As far as paying bands was concerned, Mick Robertson was as tight as a nun's cunt on a Sunday. Strangely enough, the word was that Sister Clara had landed a lunchtime spot at the pub.

'Ah'm jist lettin' ye know things are changin',' said Sammy.

'Well done,' said Alec. 'Yer diary will soon be bulgin'.' He started looking through a pile of bills. 'So ye're movin' oan tae pastures new, Sammy?'

Sammy swallowed. The aim had been to squeeze some extra cash out of him, not get shown the door.

'It's no that, Alec. The Kaptain's Kabin's been guid tae us. As a band, like.'

'Aye.'

'We'd like tae go oan playin' here...'

Alec looked at him, and a sneer flashed across his face.

'A wee bit ae advice,' he said. 'Don't try tae play five card stud wi' yer uncle Alec.'

'Eh?'

'Yer bluff's jist been called, Sammy.'

'.....'

'Anyway,' he said. 'There's somethin' ah wis wantin' tae ask you. There's a story daein' the rounds that you've suddenly come intae a fair wad ae money. As a band, like.'

Their picture had been in RockPress. Page 8. Sammy had shown it to all the regulars, before he cut it out and taped it over the fireplace.

'Ah'm no askin' ye tae comment oan it,' said Alec. 'But, eh...hypothetically. Ye're no goannae try an' leave auld Alec Dick high an' dry, are ye? After aw, as ye said yerself, the Kaptain's Kabin's been guid tae ye. Ah've been guid tae ye, in other words.'

They couldn't afford to lose the Kaptain's Kabin. The five grand was for a single and an album, and they'd be paying all the recording costs out of it. They'd have to husband the cash. Plus the costs of this French gig Terry had mentioned. And Baz's head was somewhere else completely. Sammy had clocked him sitting hunched over a beer in Proctor's – with Bear. They had to get their material perfect before going into the studio. Recording time came in at a hefty three hundred an hour, and there would be no room for messing around doing retakes.

'Look, Alec. Ah'm jist tellin' ye that Robertson's...'

Alec looked at him.

There was a rap on the door jamb.

'Malcolm!' said Alec. 'It's yerself!'

Malcolm hobbled into the office, bent double over his stick.

'Awright, Sammy?' he wheezed.

'Malcolm.'

Alec was all smiles.

'No got yer walkie talkie the day?' he said.

'Fuck that, Alec. Strictly fur emergencies fae noo oan. If it's a choice between walkiein' an' talkiein', ah'll be walkiein'.'

Sammy decided it would be wise to leave. Malcolm had made it clear from the start that he would take care of the business end. And he had enough trouble getting around without Sammy treading on his toes.

He caught the beginning of the conversation.

'Chance ae a lifetime, Alec. Scantily clad matriarchs – wi' mops an' buckets.'

Sammy pulled the door shut quietly behind him. He had to get down the post office and get a passport sorted out.

CHAPTER 14

Terry looked across the aisle at Sugden. Even in his sleep, his lips were going putt-putt-putt.

The motorhome that Malcolm had hired had broken down in Portsmouth. He'd got a lift back to Edinburgh in the cab of an RAC lorry. He said he'd be in touch with them later.

Rimmer had offered them a lift to Angers. The Agrics were going there, too.

The coach was quiet. It made a welcome change after the drunken night on the ferry. An old couple had been vomited over, and the culprit was lying full stretch along the back seat, wrapped in a large P & O towel nicked out of first class.

Sugden grunted, and was immediately patting his pockets. He looked over at Terry and smiled.

It didn't last long.

'You shouldn't bleemin well be here...you and your...friends taking up all the bleemin space.'

Sammy and Mich were further down the coach. Terry looked over the back of his seat and caught Sammy in mid-fidget. He hadn't slept a wink all night, and had kept Terry awake with his constant yapping about the gear, which was in the hold, where he couldn't keep an eye on it. Mich was enjoying the scenery, her fingers pressed to the window.

It was Baz who was crashed out on the back seat.

By mid-morning, the Agrics had stirred. The Quinties were immediately up for laughs. A kilt landed on Rimmer's head. Half of it fell over Terry's left shoulder. He helped Rimmer to remove it.

'Really, boys,' said Rimmer. 'If you insist on throwing items of clothing at me, do try to find something a little more feminine. De spite the absence of crotch, kilts do tend to harbour the guff of sweaty male arses.'

He handed the article back to its owner.

'Said guff does not light my fire.'

The comment was repeated until it reached the back of the bus, by which time it had been transformed into the triggering mechanism for a communal rugby song.

The maid of the mountain,
She pissed like a fucking fountain,
And the hairs on her dickie-die-doh
Went down to her knees!
One black one, one white one,
And one with a little shite on,
And one with a fairy light on
To see in the dark!

'Shut the fuck up!' shouted Baz, who had managed to prop himself up on an elbow. 'Fucking wankers.'

He was soon buried under a shower of kilts.

Rimmer was sitting on the plastic fascia next to the driver, swapping old army stories.

'Yes, Vic, those Wee Willie Winkies could smell Uncle Sam coming. No need for high powered binoculars. Blame it on all those bloody stogies they used to go around with stuck in their mouths. And you can forget the old yarn about never lighting up three ciggies – or cigars for that matter – with the same match. The Chinks could get a bead on them from the stench alone. You know how many faces I had to stitch back together because of sniper fire? Bloody dozens. And do you know what they used to say to me? 'Doc, it wasn't even lit'. Assholes. Then they would offer me a cigar. Yanks? A bloody liability, the lot of them. Now, I remember a time when I was over in Berlin...'

Vic wasn't saying much. Then again, Rimmer wasn't giving him a chance. He just sat there bent over the steering wheel, intermittently rubbing the wings and dagger tattoo on his left forearm, and licking his lips.

The sound of a match sparking on sandpaper.

'I say, Vic,' said Rimmer. 'Can't you enforce the no-smoking policy?'

Terry looked over at Vic, who was shaking his head. It didn't mean 'no'. It meant he knew that Sugden was a wanker.

Sugden huffed an imploding cloud of smoke into the aisle. It crept onwards until Rimmer's back was pressed against the windscreen. He inhaled a lungful of clean air before he was completely submerged in the fug.

'Dr Sugden,' he began. 'I really must protest at your lighting up in such a confined space when there is no air extractor and it is not feasible to open a window due to the fact that...'

Sugden puffed sedatedly. He was waiting for Rimmer to run out of oxygen.

'...and it isn't just me spare a thoughtfor allthenonsmokerspresent!'

He was waving his hands in front of his face, trying to fight his way out of the stinking cloud, but only managing to make it bigger.

Sugden clicked his pipe thoughtfully against his teeth, then gestured at Rimmer with the stem.

'You can't boss me about,' he said.

'Oh, put the damn thing out, man!' Rimmer shouted.

Terry glanced at Vic. The coach seemed to be accelerating. He could see clearly that the speedometer was at 70.

'If you'd use your eyes,' said Sugden, after another poot-poot-puff, 'you'd see that the ashtrays are screwed shoot.'

'And why are they screwed *shoot*?' said Rimmer.

'Ooh, you'd have to ask the driver that. I'm not a mechanic.'

'Put it out, please,' said Vic. They were up to 80.

'There's no ashtray,' said Sugden.

'Put it out,' Vic repeated. He sounded bored. 85.

'What, do you want me to empty the bowl ont floor? I'd start a bleemin fire!'

Vic pressed a big red button. Unfortunately, it wasn't an ejection seat. The door hissed outward, then slid along the side of the coach.

179

There was an onrush of air, and Rimmer lurched for the handle on the dashboard.

'Put it out!' Vic shouted over the noise of the hurricane coming through the door. 'Now!'

Terry reached across the aisle and tugged the pipe out of Sugden's mouth. He chipped it out the door, and it sailed end over end over the hedge that was speeding past, leaving a spiralling trail of smoke in its wake.

'Oh, well done, Terry,' said Rimmer as the door slid shut. 'I thought Vic meant 'extinguish it', not 'throw it away'. Those pesky phrasal verbs. I really should brush up. Does Roget's have a section on phrasal verbs, Dr Sugden?'

Sugden glared at them. His mouth was still puckered, but it slowly turned into a smirk. He probably had a spare in his suitcase, the git.

'Remind you of home, Terry?' said Rimmer. He was referring to the ornate chateau, the driveway of which they were now negotiating. Vic had to drop into first gear, the gravel was so deep.

The place didn't remind Terry of home at all. For a start, it was in good nick, and looked lived in. It had nothing whatsoever in common with the folly his grandfather had built. This was five-star accommodation to be sure.

The Quinties had noticed, too, and were grunting their pleasure. The coach slowed to a halt in front of the main doors, mighty slabs of carved timber set in weathered stonework. A small hatch inlaid in the wood opened, and an old man in dirty trousers emerged to greet them.

Rimmer stepped down from the coach and sank to his ankles in the stones. The old man was waving wildly. No translation was required.

'Round the back,' said Rimmer, climbing back aboard. He started poking the PA system. The old man was right behind him, scratching his vest and smiling like a lunatic.

'Round the back' was a shed. A large shed, admittedly, with a rusty fire escape connecting the floors. There was a collective groan from the passengers.

The old man started yapping.

'Okay, listen, please,' said Rimmer. He was holding his little microphone between thumb and index finger. 'Ooh, I suddenly feel very Sacha Distel. Can you hear me at the back? Well, shut up, then. There are plenty of beds on the ground and first floors. I trust you can work it out amongst yourselves.'

The old man poked him on the arm.

'What's that? Oh, and, yes, er, on no account are you to use the fire escape.'

Sammy's drums were the first thing to be unloaded from the hold.

'Dinnae touch them, Vic!' he said. 'Ah'll dae it masell.'

Terry got the guitar cases out, and the holdalls. Mich gave him a hand. They joined Sammy round the back of the coach. He seemed to be waiting for something.

'What's up?' asked Terry.

'Whit's up?' said Sammy. 'Ye fuckin' kiddin'?'

Baz was wandering about, his eyes on the ground, as if he'd never seen gravel before. He still had the towel wrapped round his body, which was a good job, because he wasn't wearing anything else.

Mich brought him over and opened his holdall.

Terry picked up his bag and made for the shed.

'Where ye goin'?' said Sammy.

'We'll need to get a room organised,' said Terry.

'Fuck that,' said Sammy. 'We've got a gig tae dae, an' somethin' tells me it's no takin' place anywhere near this castle.' He turned to Vic. 'Any chance ae a lift intae toon?' he said.

Vic licked his lips.

'Good thinking, Sammy,' he said. 'I've got a drooth. Maybe the frogs've started importing the black velvet since the last...'

Baz staggered into him.

'Ye've no got an Anadin oan ye, huv ye?' he said.

Vic thought for a moment.

'I'm on my holidays, Baz,' he said. 'It's a bus I'm driving, no an ambulance.'

Baz, tripping over the stones, trailed his sorry form out of sight.

'Serves him fucking right,' said Vic. 'That was some performance on the boat last night, eh, Sammy?'

Sammy spat on the ground.

'Somethin' tells me there's mair tae come,' he said.

The gig was to take place in the town square. Their contact was a M. Bertillon.

'Just in time!' he said. 'Telephone!'

The line was terrible.

'Sammy?...it...Malcolm...yez...the gig?'

'Malcolm? This is Terry. Did you get back to Edinburgh?'

'There's...b...fie...kk...lat......hear me...Sammy?... Yer...ats...urnt doon!'

The line hummed, then suddenly it was as clear as a bell.

Terry looked at the phone, then handed it to Sammy.

'Where did I put my pork sausages? They're in the sideboard, where I left them yesterday!'

Malcolm's phone was broadcasting Steve Wright In The Afternoon.

The gig was shambolic. Terry felt like he was the main attraction at a freak show. The kids stood motionless at the front of the stage, smoking and gawking. Baz was pissed again. He started doing his Pete Townshend, the acrobatic arms, the whole bit, and fell across Sammy's drums.

'Grrrock agrrround the clock!' shouted some little wanker.

They did four numbers then were replaced by a duo doing Soft Cell covers on an organ and a trumpet.

Terry gave Sammy a hand with his drums while the Bontempi squeaked.

A tomato hit Sammy on the knee.

'Cunts,' he murmured, and shuffled backwards off the stage.

They were there for three days. Baz was permanently out of his face on the cheap local wine. Terry couldn't blame him – there was nothing else to do apart from sit on the coach and listen to the Quinties singing about their sweet chariot. Sammy tried to phone Malcolm; maybe he thought he would come to the rescue in the Motorhome. Terry read the instructions in the phone box while Sammy squinted at a slip of paper with a 15-digit number on it. Malcolm had given it to him 'in case yez need me'. They eventually got through.

Whooh Gary Davies on your radio!
They didn't try again.
They had to get back for Friday.
'No problem,' said Rimmer. 'We'll be back on Friday morning. You will of course be joining us in Paris?'
Terry looked at the loving couple. Mich's eyes had lit up.
Sammy shrugged.
'Huv we got a choice?' he said.

He sat at a pavement café on the Rue de Bruin and sipped lukewarm coffee. It didn't take him long to work out why all the cars in Paris had mangled bumpers. He watched as an aged gent manoeuvred his Citroen Insect into a tight space. The space wasn't big enough, so he nudged the cars parked to the front and rear until it was.

No one used handbrakes, either, it seemed.

This, he thought to himself, is the life. He'd been to Paris before, when he was at school, but it seemed so different this time. He'd been a mere boy then, of course. His only real memory of the trip was the complaining about the lack of hamburger joints.

He was enjoying being on his own. Sammy and Mich had gone off somewhere arm in arm. Baz had disappeared drunk into the crowd along the Champs Elysees. As for everyone else, he couldn't have cared less. He was sure the feeling, or lack of it, was mutual.

A rusty Renault van coughed into life, sending a cloud of exhaust fumes across his table. The café owner ran out to remonstrate with the driver. No sooner had the car pulled out into the traffic than the space was taken by another car, complete with the bumper to bumper ballet.

This definitely wasn't Scotland.

He had money in his pocket. It would have been so easy not to go back to the hostel. He could just disappear. Although the idea was appealing, he know that he wouldn't – couldn't – do it. A leap in the dark? It wasn't his style. He had the beginnings of a plan sketched out, and his future glory, which he predicted would indeed be noteworthy, required his presence in Edinburgh in exactly one month.

Terry was preparing to come back into the fold. Big Time.

Time to get walking.

He stopped on a bridge. A young black guy was selling toy aeroplanes, the kind with a rubber band that spin the propeller. Terry bought one – it reminded him of his mother. He wound up the elastic and threw it into the air. It soared briefly then took a dive into the Seine. Terry laughed.

The ticket booth of the Eiffel Tower was built around one of the legs. The queue wound all the way round the other three. He pushed through a gap in the line and crunched over the gravel until he was directly beneath the centre. He looked up. It was just a mass of grey metal.

'It's amazing how many tourists do this.'

It was Vic.

'I've been watching them,' he said. 'It's about all I can afford to do. Have you seen the amount your man's charging for the lift?'

His SAS training had left its mark. Terry hadn't heard him coming. A dangerous man to be sure. And here was Rimmer stumbling over the pebbles.

'Are you two a couple?' asked Terry.

Rimmer looked at Vic and laughed.

'Yes,' he said. 'I suppose we are. Though it's a symbiotic relationship. Rather like you and your old mate, Dug.'

Good line, thought Terry. He jerked his head at the tower.

'You been up it?' he asked.

Rimmer was still smiling.

'Indeed I have,' he said, and rubbed his nose with a finger. 'Many times.'

They walked down to the road.

'So, Terry,' said Rimmer. 'How would you describe Paris?'

Terry thought for a moment and looked back over his shoulder.

'Flat, with a big prick in the middle,' he said.

'And when you're not in town?' said Rimmer.

'Flat!'

They laughed, and Rimmer hailed a taxi.

The sign said 'Isle de Feu'.

Rimmer coughed lightly into his fist.

'I'm just going in for a bit, as it were,' he said. 'Care to join me, Vic? Terry? They'd, er, be queuing up to meet you.'

Terry didn't doubt it. The doorman was a dead giveaway. He was wearing a leather mask and had a bullwhip trailing along the pavement.

'There's only one dick going up my arse,' Terry said. 'Mine.'

Rimmer touched him on the sleeve.

'Oh, you poor boy,' he said. 'Consensual homosexual sex is so much more than buggery between strangers – although that arena does have its patrons, so I'm told.'

Terry nodded.

'It was a beer I was going in for, Terry, nothing else. What was it someone once said? 'I'll try anything once, except incest and Morris Dancing'.' He looked at the doorman. 'I think they should have added Coprophagy to the list, don't you agree?'

Terry smiled. This was an old line of Rimmer's. He'd used it in a lecture way back, but it had stuck in his mind. None of the students had had a clue what he was talking about. Dug, of course, had been quick to fill everyone in.

Vic licked his lips.

'Do they do Guinness an' all?' he said.

Terry laughed out loud.

'Oh, I doubt it,' said Rimmer. He took Vic by the arm and led him to the tiny doorway.

'Mind out for the Coprophagy!' laughed Terry.

The doorman twitched his whip.

Vic stopped on the threshold.

'So what's this Copro...whatsit?' he said.

Rimmer was looking through his wallet.

'Well, you know Morris Dancing?' he said. 'It's a bit of an acquired taste.'

. . .

The sign said 'Isle de Feu'. Baz clocked the guy leaning against the door. Fuck it, he thought, and started raking through his coins. He was bored stiff.

. . .

185

It was hard to get a train of thought going. Someone was staggering about in the yard, pissed, and Sugden was snoring like a pig further down the corridor.

Rimmer came crashing through the door, waving a bottle in his hand.

'Terry! Terry! Wake up!'

He flopped down onto the bunk, and his head lolled between his knees, his dentures making a clacking sound.

'We...,' he said.

Terry tried to sit up, but his legs were trapped.

'We...,' Rimmer faltered, '...I...rather...need to talk.'

He sounded like he'd just committed a crime.

The bed began to pulse gently. Terry wondered what was going on, until he realised that Rimmer was crying.

Rimmer raised the bottle and looked at the wine. It was nearly finished.

'How's Plato?' he said. 'Still ranting on about suicide?'

This was a surprise.

'What,' said Terry. 'You know Plato?'

'Know him?' said Rimmer. 'I'm his fucking wine man.'

So that was why he had loaded up so many cases in Angers.

'At a very reasonable markup, too,' he added. 'But then that's me all over. Mr Bargain Fucking Basement.'

'I haven't seen him for ages,' said Terry. He managed to twist himself round on an elbow. 'He's a crook. He wanted me to burn something down for the insurance money, I don't know what, but...'

'Ah, yes,' said Rimmer. 'His pub.'

'Eh?'

'The Left Bank,' said Rimmer. 'A complete dive, by all accounts. And there we have it! The conversation is but seconds old and we've already mentioned your daddy!'

'What?'

Rimmer filled him in. Besides being Plato's wine man, it seemed that he was also his main confidante. He knew all the details. Fair enough, Terry knew that his father was involved in the dodgy property market – Dennis's visit to Sammy had been testament to that. But he'd had no idea what a slumlord he was.

It was starting again. Terry didn't need this shit. Not now.

'So the point is this,' said Rimmer. 'Plato either torches the place or he sells up to your father. I think it's called 'covering your bases'. Either way, he wins. I don't know. Maybe he's just a greedy fucker.'

'Hang on,' said Terry. 'Why are you telling me all this? Do you want me to go running to my father with the news?'

Rimmer laughed mirthlessly.

'Oh, Terry,' he said. 'I think you're the last person in the world who'd do that.'

He took a long pull on the bottle and slowly got to his feet, his knees cracking in protest. He pushed open the window.

'My life...,' he began, and rubbed his chest with the flat of his hand. 'My life...mind you, I had put Numpty behind me years before you came along.'

Terry pulled his legs round so they were hanging over the edge of the bed. They were numb.

'You've been to Numpty?' he said.

Another swig, the wine jangling against the glass.

'I was born there,' said Rimmer, and leaned his head against the wall. 'Did your mother ever mention me? No? No, no, I don't suppose she ever did. Why would she? I...'

He broke off. Someone had stumbled against a dustbin down in the yard. Rimmer looked carefully out of the window then began to talk more quickly, his eyes darting around the room.

'I was a father, Terry, did you know? A terrible father. A Bad Dad. I had two...but then that never worked out. They were…taken away from me after that Army business, you know, their mother, she couldn't...'

This was too much to take in.

'I was ready to make amends, then your fucking father...'

The main door banged shut.

'I rue the day I saved his life. Carrying him out of that swamp on my back. The Numpty Fusiliers, an outfit as risible as it sounds, believe me. Then he stole my Mary, my Queen of Scots...then the boys...then the mine...but he's been making up for it ever since. He thinks he's being a good Christian, but he's...it's all a fucking delusion, Terry! Sticking his oar in where it isn't wanted. Every job I've had, every promotion...and now he's doing the same to you, Terry! I saw your exam results. Not brilliant, but not a fail.'

'Yes, I know that,' said Terry. 'Sugden...'

'Yes, Sugden!' Rimmer shouted. 'And what did he get out of it, eh, Terry? Why would he do exactly what your father told him?'

Terry was trying to fit the pieces together...

'What?' said Rimmer. 'You don't know?'

'No, I mean I haven't been near the Institute since...'

'Sugden is the Director Elect of the Kinlochleven Suite, Terry. Your daddy told him the job was his as long as he fucked you up. Good, eh?'

Footsteps staggering in the corridor. Rimmer's eyes were darting round the room again, as if he were looking for somewhere to hide. There wasn't even a wardrobe. He tipped the last of the wine down his throat, and Terry stared in disbelief as he hit himself repeatedly over the head with the bottle. After the third strike, he crumpled to the floor. There was a thump, and his top plate shot across the linoleum and cracked off the skirting board.

Baz appeared in the doorway, and looked at the old man lying on the floor.

'Is his name Rimmer?' he slurred.

Putt-putt-putt.

'Aye, it's Rimmer all right,' said Sugden over his shoulder. 'Can't hold his liquor, by the look of it.'

Vic parked the coach in the loading area. He'd timed it perfectly. He turned to Terry, burped, and smiled.

'That Coprophagy's a bit special, eh?' he said.

'What?' said Terry. His mind had been consumed by criminal thoughts all night. He knew what Rimmer had been getting at, and realised what he would have to do. He'd have to force himself to go through with it.

Vic leaned on the steering wheel. He looked pleased with himself.

'I just had the four,' he said. 'Cos of the driving, like. Dr Rimmer was right about it being an acquired taste, by the way. He suggested a bag of crisps on the side, to take the edge off.'

Terry didn't want to hear this, but there was no stopping him.

'And the taste! A bit bitter, I'd say, and kind of chocolatey, like plain chocolate, you know, that Bourneville. Creamy as hell an' all. I've never tasted anything like it in my puff. I'd recommend it, though. Dr Rimmer left after a couple, but I stayed for the four. I'd've stayed for another, but you know, the driving, like.'

Rimmer emerged cautiously from his blanket. He looked like a corpse risking a second chance.

'Yes,' he said. 'Unfortunately, Coprophagy isn't a beer they sell in Scottish pubs.'

Poor old Vic, thought Terry. So credulous, like a child.

Rimmer pulled himself up and looked over the backrest. Terry turned round, too.

Baz was sitting right behind them, staring.

Rimmer sank back into his blanket.

'Ignore everything I may have been blethering about last night, Terry,' he whispered. 'A bit too much *veritas* with the *in vinum*, if you get me.'

Terry watched as he pulled the material over his head. It's a bit too late for that, he thought.

The airline style seat digging into his kidneys made it easier for him to stay awake.

The pain and patience paid off. Sugden started clawing himself for his pipe. It was in his jacket pocket. After a quick look round at the dozing students, he pushed himself up quietly and made for the exit.

Terry was right behind him.

The fog, which was billowing across the deck in gusts, stank of rancid oil. Rimmer was leaning over the stern, howling into the wake, his voice lost in the churn of the propellers.

Sugden strode right up to him, his pipe in his hand, and leaned on the railing.

Terry waited in the shadows. The last thing he needed was a witness. Certainly not Rimmer.

The two men faced each other, Rimmer gesticulating wildly with his arms as Sugden stood there, jerking, trying to get his pipe burning. He couldn't manage it, there was too much wind, and, besides, every time he bent his head and tried to strike a match, Rimmer poked him in the shoulder.

The guts of the boat grated rhythmically. It was impossible to make out what they were saying, although Terry could guess. Eventually, Rimmer, having said all there was to say, stormed off to the lower deck, leaving Sugden all alone with his pipe.

Terry waited a moment. Rimmer wasn't coming back.

He placed his hands on the railing.

'It's certainly a bracing night,' he said.

Sugden started, then squinted at him.

'You stay away from me,' he said. 'You hear?'

Terry smiled.

'You sound frightened, Doctor,' he said. 'There's no need.'

Sugden stabbed his pipe at him.

'You and your friend, Rimmer,' he said. 'And his ideas. And your hippy friends. I could still report you for assaulting me in my office.'

'Come, now, Dr Sugden,' said Terry. 'That's all in the past. And, anyway, what is it they say? Blood is thicker than water? My father might hate me, that's true, but I don't think he would be happy about you putting the police onto me.'

Sugden inhaled a lungful of spray.

'Well, yes,' he said. 'I'm glad to hear you'll let bygones be bygones. Perhaps you should have a word with Rimmer. His mind seems to be...anyway, Terry, you're right. You've got to look to the future.'

'My sentiments exactly!' Terry enthused.

Sugden had another go at his pipe.

'Can I have a look at that?' said Terry, and pulled the pipe out of Sugden's grip before he had time to react.

'Careful!'

Terry put the stem into his mouth. It tasted of ear wax.

'That's disgusting,' he said. 'Have you never thought about giving up, Doctor?'

Sugden snatched at the pipe, but Terry was too fast.

'Now, now, Doctor,' he said. 'Don't get upset.'

'Come on, Terry, give it back.'

'All in good time,' said Terry.

He had rehearsed the next part while sitting in the lounge. A true professional!

'This weather,' he said. 'It makes me feel all Thespian.'

Sugden wasn't taking his eyes off the pipe.

'Nemesis,' said Terry. 'Remember that one, Doctor?'

'What?'

'No,' said Terry. 'Thought not. Or should I say *null point*? Scottish poetry was never your forte, was it?'

'Come on,' said Sugden, and put his hand out. 'Give it back, there's a good lad. It was a present from me sister.'

'How does it go again?' said Terry. He clicked the pipe twice off the handrail. 'Oh, yes – something about Nemesis putting two bullets in her gun, isn't it?'

He let the pipe fall to the deck.

'Allow me,' he said, and stooped to pick it up.

He gripped Sugden by the ankles and hoisted him onto the handrail.

'What the hell...?!!'

'Feel the dampness seeping through your trousers, Doctor?'

Fog was billowing out of their mouths; the wake was churning

Terry had him exactly where he wanted.

'No need for two bullets, Roy!' he laughed, and pushed his problem over the back of the boat.

Sugden disappeared into the foam.

He didn't surface.

Terry looked around the deck. It was empty, not a soul. Dawn was breaking. Maybe he would manage a few hours sleep before Portsmouth. He'd try to ignore the seat digging into his lower back.

CHAPTER 15

He stacked his gear on the pavement and paid up. The driver made a quick getaway before he could ask him for a hand up the stair.

All he wanted to do was get to his bed. There had been a delay when they got to Portsmouth. Seemingly, one of Terry's old teachers had taken a dive over the side of the boat during the night. The ferry had been swarming with busies as soon as they got into the harbour. They had wasted two hours standing in a queue, then five minutes answering stupid questions. Vic, bless him, had floored it all the way up the motorway.

He would get his head down for an hour, then Mich was coming round to take him to the Kaptain's Kabin.

A skip had been parked on the pavement right outside the close door. It was stinking, full to the brim with old mattresses and fuck knows what else, a broken TV set and a couch, from what he could make out. Some wanker had put a match to the lot, and it was only blackened material and wood that was left.

Maybe it was time to move. This neighbourhood was getting dangerous.

Dennis came out of the close.

'Well, well, well,' he said. 'The wanderer returns.'

Sammy couldn't be doing with this.

'Pack it in, Dennis,' he said. 'Ah'm knackered.'

Dennis grabbed his arm.

'Come here, you,' he said, and pulled. 'You've got to see this.'

Sammy didn't want to leave his drums lying on the pavement. Sid was probably somewhere in the vicinity, waiting for the chance to jump on them.

Dennis pulled him across the road.

'You'll love this,' he said.

Sammy still had his eyes on his stuff.

'Check it out,' said Dennis, and pointed to the roof of Sammy's building.

The top flat was gutted. The windows were out. The charred remains of Sammy's living room curtains were flapping in the wind. The wall under the window was streaked black, all the way down to the rubbish skip.

'Shame about the old couple down the stair,' said Dennis. 'Your floor fell on them. The other tenants took the hint.'

Sammy slumped against Dennis's coat.

'There, there,' said Dennis, and gave him a shake. 'It could have been worse.'

Sammy managed to look up at him.

'Eh?' he said.

'Your drums could have been in there. Come on, I'll give you a lift round to your ladyfriend's in the Rover.'

He refused the Housing Department's offer of a hovel in Bread Street. He told them there was no way he was taking a flat next door to five strip joints. The area wasn't called The Pubic Triangle for nothing. He knew what they were up to. Try and get rid of the dumps that nobody wants, then move on to the accommodation that was almost humane.

He finally accepted a three-bedroom top floor flat in Marchmont. He was well pleased. The acoustics in the main room were ace, which probably had something to do with the seven layers of wallpaper he discovered when he was trying to stick up some egg trays; there was a butcher's just round the corner. In any case, soundproofing was not required. The neighbours were students, and spent all their time listening to The Smiths at full volume.

Mich seemed to like the place as well, although she was worried about the heating costs. She'd never seen such high ceilings. She spent most of the week standing in the smallest bedroom, watching one of the neighbours, the only one in Marchmont who wasn't a student, hanging out nappies.

Sammy knew what was on her mind.

Something had happened in Paris.

Maybe she was right. Maybe it was time to tie the knot. They soon had the place fixed up. The DHSS paid for the furniture.

He took a walk down H Samuel and had a look at the engagement rings. There was one that took his fancy straight away, a thin silver band with a cluster of diamonds. He nearly fainted when the assistant told him the price. He handed over the cash. It wouldn't have been right to pay for it on the never never.

He knew it would be worth it in the end.

* * *

There was a couple up ahead. The man was pushing a shopping trolley. People were turning and staring; you don't see many shopping trolleys getting pushed along Lothian Road. Not at this end, anyway, thought Terry.

The way Sammy was carrying on when they came to corners, lowering the trolley gently down onto the road, it could have been their first born child they were transporting. It wasn't a baby, though. Something was anchored under a tarpaulin.

'Lift it,' said Sammy. 'Fur Christ's sake, Mich! It'll bang oan the kerb again.'

Terry caught hold and pulled the trolley up onto the pavement. The doorman of The Caledonian, looking ridiculous in top hat and tails, coughed.

'Don't worry,' Terry smiled. 'We're not coming in.'

The doorman tipped his hat.

'You've got that right, sir,' he said.

They dragged the trolley over to the railings. One of the wheels had come off in the gutter.

'Cheers, Terry,' said Sammy, and did a double take. 'Nice duds, by the way.'

Terry hadn't seen them for a couple of weeks. Practices and gigs had been cancelled while Sammy got settled in to his new flat.

'Thank you very much, Sammy,' said Terry. 'I'm going for a change of sartorial direction.'

Sammy was trying to shove the wheel back into the leg of the trolley.

'Eh?'

'A change of style,' explained Mich. She was blushing.

And there we have it, thought Terry. What is it they say about leaving the best till last?

Sammy threw the wheel in beside the tarpaulin.

'Whit, ye mean like Michael Bolton?' he said, and rubbed Terry's lapel. 'Well dressed and dangerous. Ah like it.'

Terry laughed.

'I don't know about that, Sammy,' he said. 'I was thinking more along the lines of a hundred and eighty degrees.'

'Anyway,' said Sammy. 'Let's get this doon tae the studio. Time is money, eh?!'

There had been a note under Terry's door. Tuesday. 11 am. Studio in Drumsheugh Gardens. Terry had once aspired to a wee flat at the quiet end of the street. The idea was beginning to regain some of its appeal. For the moment, though, he was trying his hardest not to blend in too nicely with Sammy, who looked like a homeless person.

Upper Cuts.

'This wis Malcolm's idea,' said Sammy, and chained the trolley to the gate. 'An' ah must admit, it seems like yin ae ae's better yins.'

They descended the narrow stairs to the studio, Sammy taking care not to bang his snare off the walls. The place certainly smelled expensive, all fresh paint and new carpets.

Jackie was sitting in the control booth, twiddling the knobs on a stack of electronics.

'Awright, Sammy?' he said. He took a long look at Mich, who had just removed her coat. She was wearing a mini skirt and not much else. He twiddled another knob.

Terry stopped himself from doing the same.

'Awright, Mich?' said Jackie. 'Lookin' good.'

Sammy was still standing in the doorway cradling his snare.

'Common knowledge, ma man,' said Jackie. 'It's a small toon.'

195

Sammy did not look chuffed. Mich sat down in a chair opposite Jackie. She shut her legs like a nutcracker.

Jackie stretched out a hand.

'And, eh, hello, there, Scalpel,' he said.

Terry ignored him. It was Jackie's pet name for him. He'd told him he considered The Surgeon too 'obvious', the little prick.

Sammy laid his drum on the floor.

'Eh, Jackie, where's, eh...'

'Cludge,' said Jackie, and winked at Mich. 'Ae'll be back in two shakes.'

Sammy carried his snare carefully into the recording area, making sure not to dislodge any of the millions of little purple pyramids jutting from the walls.

Jackie pressed a button on the desk and leaned into a microphone.

'This is the real deal now, Sammy, eh?' he said.

Gruff Plangent came into the control booth, and slapped Jackie's hand away from the desk. Terry recognised him from his advert in the back pages of RockPress. The beard and the dungarees were just the same in real life. Unkempt, and needing a good wash.

Sammy bounced through the door, smiling.

'Jackie,' said Gruff. 'Go and make sure everything's miked up.'

Sammy stared.

'Assistant Producer,' Jackie smirked.

Gruff glared at him.

'Ah couldnae let ma mates doon, could ah?' said Jackie. 'No in their moment ae glory. An' it'll save yez a packet. Ah'm daein' it buckshee.'

Gruff looked out of the wee window into the recording area.

'Who's been fucking around with my drums?' he said.

Sammy sniffed.

'That wis me, eh, Gruff. Ma snare's got a special...'

'And you are?'

Sammy wiped his hand on his anorak.

'Sammy,' he said. 'Ah'm the dru...'

'Who's producing this record?' said Gruff. 'You or me?'

'Well...'

'Jackie, get the drums miked up. Let's get this over with.'

196

Sammy got in behind the drums and started tapping. Terry could see that it was a dry run for 'Bayonet Practice', one of the songs Dug had given them. Malcolm had deemed it 'definite single material', as if he knew what he was talking about. Terry had seen him hanging around Bread Street a lot lately, going in and out of a new strip joint that had just opened. 'Scrubbers', it was called.

Gruff was trying to calibrate something on the mixing desk, in between brushing away Jackie's hand every five seconds. He pressed the button and leaned into the microphone.

'Right, Sammy,' he said. 'When you're ready.'

Sammy winked.

The sound booth was filled with the sound of a clicking metronome, and Sammy started.

Straight away, Gruff pressed his wee button.

'Sammy,' he said. 'Try and keep up with the click track.'

Sammy adjusted his snare.

'Ah cannae use click tracks, Gruff,' he said. 'They pit me oaf.'

Gruff sighed.

'Sammy,' he said, 'we're going to be using sequencers on this track...'

'Straight oot ae Jackie's Music Emporium,' Jackie announced to no one.

'...they're not very forgiving about bad timekeeping.'

Sammy shifted on his stool.

'Ah ken how tae hold doon a beat,' he said through clenched teeth.

Gruff slapped away Jackie's hand, and pressed the button.

'Sammy,' he said. 'It's a machine. It can't hear your beautiful drumming. It's like a quartz watch. Accurate to a millisecond. You're not.'

He switched the click track back on, ready for the second take.

Sammy refused to use it.

Mich leaned into Terry. Her breath was hot in his ear.

'Just popping to the loo,' she whispered. Her hand slid down his thigh. When she got to the door, she glanced over her shoulder.

Sammy was still in conference with Gruff about his drumming, Jackie nodding away like a tosser.

No one noticed Terry leave. Not even Sammy, the poor wee bastard.

The toilet was tiny. A seat, and nothing else. There was barely room for Mich to squat.

'This is intimate,' said Terry, and pressed himself up against her.

Mich looked up at him.

'I love Sammy,' she said. 'Remember that.'

Terry stroked her cheek.

'Who said anything about love?' he said, and guided her hand to his zip.

Gruff was leaning back in his chair, his hands behind his head, looking at the clock over the window. Instead of numbers, it had wee pound signs.

Big time, thought Terry, and adjusted himself.

They started again. Gruff turned off the clicking in Sammy's ear, but they could still hear it in the control booth.

'Wo, wo, Sammy,' he said into the microphone. 'You're already half a beat slow.'

They started again.

Jackie leaned over and pressed the button.

'Yer draggin, wee man!' he said.

Sammy came charging across the carpet. Terry was immediately onto his feet, but he needn't have worried. Sammy's hands went straight round Jackie's throat.

'Who invited you, ya smelly bastard?!!' he screamed into Jackie's face.

Close, thought Terry. Gruff was staring through the window. A pair of sticks were embedded in the tiles behind the drums.

Terry broke up the fight.

'After aw the help ah've given yez!' shouted Jackie, tears and snotters mixing. 'Ya ungrateful...ah, fuck yez!'

He staggered to the door, rubbing his throat, and bumped into Mich, who was dabbing her mouth with a wad of toilet roll.

'An' ye can fuckin' forget aboot tick fae noo oan ya fuckin' dreamer!' Jackie shouted. 'Fuckin'...Clem Burke!'

The only sound was the click click click of the click track, and Sammy crying.

Baz stuck his head round the door. He looked like shit.

'Jackie's ootside attackin' a shoppin' trolley,' he said.

Gruff took a sip of coffee from a dirty mug.

'Who's this?' he said.

'The guitarist,' said Sammy, his arm around Mich's shoulder. 'Sorry, doll,' he said. He sobbed, and Mich dabbed his eyes with the bog roll.

What a performance, thought Terry.

'Right,' said Gruff. 'Get your guitars plugged in and let's get this done. I'm cutting a Radio Forth jingle after this. Their boy usually shows up on time.'

'Okay, Baz, that was better,' said Gruff. 'You need to tune up, though.'

Baz stared at him through the glass.

Sammy had got the drums down, playing along with Mich. Gruff had decided not to bother with the sequencers.

Something went 'Ping!'.

Gruff pressed his button.

'What was that?' he said.

Sammy shook his head.

'Eh...ma top E's away,' said Baz.

Terry had to laugh. Baz was standing there as if he was waiting for a bus.

'Are you going to fix it?' said Gruff.

'Kindae difficult,' said Baz. 'There's only a panel pin stickin' oot the machine head.'

'Christ!' said Gruff. He hadn't pressed the button.

'Ye've no got a spare guitar, huv ye?' said Baz.

Gruff leaned back and looked at the clock.

'That'll have to be that,' he said. He turned to Terry. 'I hope you can do the vocals in one take, big man.'

They adjourned to Screevers to celebrate. It was Sammy's idea. He knew a reporter from RockPress that drank there. They were old friends.

199

Terry remembered the place as soon as he walked through the door.

Drinks all round, and Sammy was buying. He sidled up to the girl perched on the stool at the end of the bar. She was holding a pencil over a thick notepad, probably trying to come up with her next article, Terry thought. Sammy suggested that everyone sit at the table that just happened to be adjacent to her stool. She seemed pleased to see him, especially after he bought her a drink. Mich was smiling. Too right she was, thought Terry. She knew she could trust Sammy. She could depend on him right down the line.

They sat round the table in silence. Everyone was smiling. Apart from Baz, of course.

Malcolm wheezed his way into the bar. He made a point of hobbling round the table to shake Sammy's hand.

'Sorry ah huvnae seen any yez since the ferry,' he said. 'Serious business entanglements doon Bread Street.'

He looked at Mich.

'Soapy water and sponges feature heavily,' he said.

He leaned on the back of a chair, then dragged it over.

'Oof!' he said. 'That's better.'

He propped his stick against the table.

'Sorry tae hear aboot yer fire, Sammy,' he said.

Sammy laughed.

'Nae bother, Malcolm. It's aw turned oot fur the best.'

'Ah tried tae phone ye wi' the bad news,' said Malcolm, and wiped the sweat off his brow with his sleeve, 'but it wis a really bad line.'

'Eh?'

'Ye hud yer radio turned up really loud,' he said.

Sammy laughed.

'By the way,' said Malcolm. 'Ah didnae ken ye could pick up Radio 1 in France.'

'Never mind,' said Sammy. 'We're aw back safe and sound, an' ready fur superstardom.' His voice was loud. The news was travelling unedited to the reporter. She was already scribbling. 'So that's the single done,' he said. 'Ah think ye did a brilliant job, by the way, Baz. You an' aw, Terry.'

'Aye,' said Baz.

'...yeah,' said Terry.

'Gruff'll probably fill oot the sound wi' synths,' Sammy informed them.

'As long as there's nae oboes oan it,' Baz mumbled.

Sammy laughed again, and turned slightly in his seat.

'Aye,' he said. '*Gruff Plangent* is sure it's goannae be a hit.'

The girl stopped writing and looked over. Then she started again, faster.

'So what happens next?' said Mich.

Terry coughed.

Sammy took a large mouthful of beer.

'Malcolm?'

'Well, as yez know, ah'll be takin' care ae the pressin' an' distribution. The single should be in the shoaps by the beginnin' ae May. After that...'

'What about air play?' said Mich.

Terry sipped his whiskey. She was trying not to look at him. As if the airplay of their wee record was what was on her mind!

Sammy studied the faces of his compadres and laid his hands on the table.

'Gruff's a producer who's oan the up,' he said.

What? thought Terry. He buys gear on credit from Jackie.

'Ae's got inside ties at Radio Forth.'

He records jingles.

'And Radio Clyde.'

They found him in the back pages of RockPress.

'Then it's Radio Scotland. Ae knows Tom Ferrie personally.'

They chatted over canapes at a function.

'So that's the BBC stitched up.'

He's put in a tender for the mid-day news.

'So we're lookin' at Radio 1. Peel...'

He never misses it.

'Even...'

Top Of The Pops? Oh, Sammy. Jackie was right. You are a fucking dreamer. Time to wake up.

Sammy reached into his pocket and placed a wee box on the table.

'Now,' he said. 'Ah've got a wee announcement tae make. Though it's mair ae a question than an announcement.'

He smiled at everyone, but his eyes skidded to a halt on Terry.

'Whit's up wi' you?' he laughed. 'We're supposed tae be celebratin'!'

Terry looked straight at him, then at Mich, who was hiding behind a pint of Fosters.

'I'm...,' said Terry

'Aye?' said Sammy. The smile was still there, but in the brief silence the corners started to tremble.

'I'm leaving...'

Sammy buried his face in his hands.

'No...No. Naw.' His fingers dragged skin along the sides of his head. 'Naw...NAW, NAW.'

'I'm leaving the...'

Sammy's fingers were in his ears, and his eyes were screwed shut. 'DINNAE...DAE...THIS...TAE...MEEEEEE!!!!!'

'I'm leaving the band, Sammy.'

The reporter's pencil snapped.

Mich went 'Oh!'.

Baz jumped out of his chair.

'Ah'll gie Bear a shout,' he said.

Sammy stared into his pint. He reached for the wee box.

Nobody said anything.

'Whit?' said Baz. He looked at Terry, and grinned. 'That wis the plan aw along, wint it?'

Malcolm wheezed loudly.

'Any chance ae a beer, Sammy?' he said. 'That wis a bit ae a hike fae Bread Street.'

CHAPTER 16

'You can put your stick away, Sid,' said Plato. 'I think we may be on the verge of a breakthrough.'

The sight of the baseball bat, complete with metal studs, had clinched the deal.

Sid looked at Dennis.

'He means he's going to accept The Reverend's offer,' Dennis explained.

Plato's fortitude had paid off. The figure was now seventy five thousand. He had just renewed his fire insurance, too. When this was over, which would be very soon, he was going to be very rich indeed.

Sid stroked his bat. He looked confused.

'But The Reverend said tae make share ae accepted it this time.'

'No need,' said Dennis, and offered Plato his hand.

Plato shook it.

'Strangely enough,' Plato said, 'it has been a pleasure.'

'Likewise,' said Dennis.

'Although there is one more thing.'

'What's that?'

'I'd like the payment to be effected in cash. Bank of England 20s.'

'Well...'

'Oh, come on, now, Dennis. After all the pain I've been through. I really think I'm within my rights to insist.'

Dennis thought for a second.

'I'll see what I can do,' he said. 'Come on, you. And stop banging that bat off the furniture.'

* * *

'Good morning to you,' he said.

The old woman glanced up at him. Seeing nothing worthy of her attention, she resumed typing.

'I'd like to see my file,' he said.

The woman sighed.

'Matriculation card,' she said.

He handed it over.

She looked at the photograph.

'Are you sure this is you?' she said.

'Oh, yes,' he said. 'A slightly more innocent version, though.'

She typed the details into her computer, and handed him a printout.

Biology, IPM, Chemistry 1B – so Sugden had sent his practical results down to Admin? How helpful of him. Biology 2h, Ecology 2h, Physiology 2h, Agriculture 2h. Animal Reproduction 3h – Rimmer's class, and Advanced Physiology 3h.

According to the piece of paper, he had failed Farm Business Management and Ruminant Nutrition. Both of Sugden's classes. Just like Dug.

It didn't matter.

He was on six credits.

There was only one more problem to solve.

* * *

The door opened quietly; there hadn't been a knock.

Plato had to look twice. The hair was extremely short, and he was sporting a very regal wee beard. The expensive suit was what clinched it, though. It was as if the Terry of The Confessional days had risen from the dead. The rest seemed to have done him the power of good.

'This is a surprise,' Plato said. 'Like the snow, as we say in Greece. It's been a while.'

Terry hitched up his suit trousers and lowered himself into a chair. He arranged the cuffs of his shirt sleeves so that they were just so.

'Nice cufflinks,' Plato observed.

'Yes,' said Terry. 'Damned expensive, too.'

There was an uneasy silence. Terry seemed to be in an unassailably chipper mood, if the determined grin was anything to judge by.

'So what brings you here?' said Plato.

'I'm glad you asked,' said Terry. 'I'm rather concerned about my degree.'

'So you should be,' said Plato. Even though Dug, the failed firebomber, had been faithfully handing in essays on Terry's behalf, there was the small matter of his absence from the examination room. It wasn't something that a nonentity like Dug could fix.

'Yes, Terry, you're in a bit of a pickle. The situation is of your own making, let's remember.'

'You are absolutely right,' said Terry.

'So there's really nothing I can do. Perhaps you should re-register and come back next year.'

Terry laughed softly. He removed a white handkerchief from his breast pocket and dabbed his lips.

'Roger Rimmer sends his regards,' he said.

'Really?'

'Yes, really. I hear you're having some trouble with my father.'

Not anymore, I'm not, thought Plato.

'Oh, that's all water under the bridge,' he said with a dismissive wave.

'Are you still thinking of burning down your pub for the insurance money?' said Terry.

'.....'

'Yes, I thought so. It would be rather awkward if word got out, don't you think?'

Holy Christ, thought Plato. He was going to ruin everything. He'd found someone to do the job. It was all arranged.

'I've told you, Terry, we've settled our differences. There's really nothing...'

Terry smiled, and toyed with a cufflink.

'Let me put it another way,' he said. 'I need my degree. I'm not asking you to do anything grand. Just pass marks for the Christmas exam and the forthcoming Easter paper. I'm sure that the essays

Dug has been writing for me suffice to secure an exemption from the June diet.'

'Terry,' said Plato. 'You can't come in here demanding that I falsify...'

Terry laughed.

'Please, Professor,' he said. 'Spare me your bullshit.'

'What?!' said Plato. A large, invisible hand was pressing him into his chair.

'Are we agreed, Professor?'

'Look, Terry, I admit...'

'That's excellent,' said Terry. He stood up and arranged his jacket on his shoulders. 'If you'll excuse me, Professor. I've got a rather important engagement with my haberdasher.'

* * *

All eyes on Terry when he breezed in. He scanned the faces, and imagined the mental calculations that were going on concerning how much he'd paid per yard for the cloth that had gone into his suit. The only sound was the creak of his patent leather shoes as he crossed the carpet. The fedora, at a cocky angle, was a flourish he had decided could only add to the flair.

A few ageing gentlemen nodded their approval.

'Hello, there, Sean. An Isle of Jura, please. Make it a double, eh?'

Sean filled the metal cup. And again. His hand was shaking. He put in an extra measure free of charge.

'There you go, Terry,' he said. 'It's been a while.'

Terry held the glass to his nose and savoured the aroma. He swirled the whisky around, admiring the way it adhered to the sides of the glass.

'Yes, it has,' he said.

Sean was fishing around under the bar. He produced a notepad and pen.

'I caught you at that gig in Jesters a while back,' he blushed. 'You were brilliant.'

Terry smiled, and made his mark on the paper.

'When's your next gig? I'd come down to the Kaptain's Kabin, but, you know, with working here and that...'

Terry took a small sip of his whisky.

'What would you say if I told you I was looking for a job?' he said.

'What, they didn't throw you out of the band, did they?!'

Terry had to laugh.

'No, Sean, nothing like that. I think it's time I joined the mainstream.'

'What?' said Sean. 'Like George Michael? Are you going solo?'

Terry finished his drink.

'See you later, Sean,' he said.

He crossed Charles Square, heading straight for the Appleby Hall. Excellent, he thought. Not too busy yet. The early bird...

A grey dustcoated servitor pulled the door open for him, and he was in.

The exam results noticeboard was just inside the main door. He smiled. It was where they used to congregate after their first year exams, before hitting the pub. But he wasn't here to look at results. He was here to get one.

The interior had been transformed into a labyrinth of felt covered display boards. This was the cutting edge of multinational graduate recruitment. The Milk Round had arrived.

He had narrowed his main options down to three, and had spent the previous evening going over the literature they had sent him. If they wanted his 'take' on their 'operations', whether 'at home' or 'abroad', all they had to do was ask. He had it all down pat. What a joke. It was easier than learning the words to a song.

The young man from British Allied Trading looked like James Bond: the white tuxedo, the black bow tie and the suntan. His name tag broadcast the fact that he was the Agricultural Investments Advisor (South Bangladesh), which caused Terry to wonder which manager's wife he'd been caught shagging; it didn't sound like a plumb position. Still, he thought, it would be an interesting first rung on the ladder.

Terry proffered a hand.

'Terence Kinlochleven,' he said, with what he knew was a winning smile.

'Jamie Arbuckle,' said the BAT man, and motioned for Terry to sit down.

It was all a game, a performance, Terry knew. His bespoke suit spoke volumes. The private school accent would lubricate the conversation. And, praise be, he was the best dressed man in the room.

It was obvious that Jamie liked the package that was on offer.

'So,' said Terry, and let it hang.

'Ah, yes, sorry...Terence, right?'

'Terry.'

'Right, Terry. So what can I do for you?'

'Well, I was rather hoping you'd offer me a job!'

Laughs all round.

'I realise,' Terry continued, 'that you must be a bit busy, what with British Allied Trading being such a popular career choice, so why don't you take a quick look at my CV?'

The document was immaculately presented. Dug had spent the better part of a week getting it ready. As Dug had predicted, Jamie turned directly to the back pages, those marked 'Hobbies and Interests'.

There was lots of coloured ink.

'Mm-hmm, mm-hmm,' Jamie hummed. 'A-hah. Yes, very impressive. You've certainly been keeping yourself busy.'

There had been no need to lie. His theatre experience, which was extensive, along with the details of his involvement with the band covered most of three pages. He'd left out any mention of his doings with his fans, however. Perhaps Jamie would find the omission worthy of extra brownie points, a sure sign of Terry's ability to show restraint where necessary. No one, after all, likes a loudmouth. Anyway, they would be able to discuss that at the second interview, in London.

It was all so much preamble.

Jamie squared a printed sheet of questions on the table.

'Would you describe yourself as a team player, Terry?' he asked.

'Well, I really should let my CV speak for itself...'

'Sure.'

'Sometimes I feel that 'team playing' is all I've been doing for the last four years...'

'Sure.'

'Although being the lead singer in a successful rock band does place some demands...'

'Got you.'

Jamie asked all the questions and ticked all the boxes. He added up the scores. Gentlemen, he wanted to shout, we have a winner! Heads would turn at HQ when this boy turned up!! It might even get him out of Bangladesh!!!

He picked up the CV and turned to the front page.

'What is it you're studying again?' he asked.

Terry coughed lightly into his hanky.

'Philosophy,' he said.

'Uh-huh.' Jamie turned to the 'Academic Qualifications' section, and frowned. 'It says here 'BSc General Science'.'

'Yes, that's right,' said Terry. 'In my final...'

'That's an Ordinary degree, isn't it?' said Jamie. He inserted a finger under his collar and craned his neck.

'Yes, you see in my final...'

'What I'm saying is there isn't an Honours degree in General Science, isn't that right?' He looked over Terry's shoulder.

Terry could feel a queue forming.

'Yes, that's right, but in my final...'

'Oh, I'm afraid that won't do,' said Jamie, and pushed the CV away. 'I'm afraid that won't do at all.'

'But the CV...'

'We're looking for Honours graduates, Barry.'

Barry?

'Yes, but in my final year...'

'It's not called an Honours Year for nothing,' Jamie sniffed. 'We're looking for a 2:1 and above. Sorry.'

Jamie, Mr Arbuckle, Our Man In Fucking Dhaka, the huge obstacle between Terry and some kind of future, was already welcoming the next candidate.

Terry was still in the chair.

'It's been lovely talking to you,' said Jamie. 'Do take an information pack.'

Terry tipped his hat further back on his head and stared at him.

209

'An information pack?' he said. 'I think you can do better than that.' He stood up, and his seat was promptly taken by a young lady dressed in a business suit.

Jamie was already into his introductory spiel.

Terry grabbed him by the bow tie, but it seemed that Jamie had been expecting it. Terry's wrist was wrenched round, and his shoulder felt like it was going to come out of its socket.

'Listen, you,' Jamie hissed. Maybe he actually did do a bit of James Bonding on the side. 'It's over. Now take an information pack like a good lad and bog off. An Ordinary degree after four years? You fucking time waster.'

A squad of servitors was approaching. Terry knew it was time to leave.

Dug came bounding up the main steps.

'All right, Terry?' he said. 'How did they like the CV?'

'They fucking hated it, Dug.' He moved his shoulder inside his jacket and felt it click back into place. 'They only want Honours graduates.'

Dennis was across the road, leaning against the Rover. He was smiling, as if things had gone exactly to plan.

'Aw, what's wrong?' he pouted. 'Does nobody want you?'

Sid was lifting the tailgate. Terry marched straight across the road and punched him on the side of the head.

He looked in the boot.

'Oh, dear,' he said. 'The game has changed.'

Terry might not have been what British Allied Trading were looking for, but he knew how to swing a length of wood round his head. He made sure Sid wouldn't be getting up for a while. When the whimpering had stopped, he turned to Dennis, who was trying to keep plenty of car between the two of them.

'What are you doing?' said Dennis, his voice shaking.

Terry said nothing. The time for words was over. He walked slowly to the front of the car and staved in the windscreen.

Sid was crawling along the gutter, in the opposite direction.

'Get up, you!' yelled Dennis.

Then the headlamps were gone.

A few dents in the bonnet.

Terry stopped for a breath.

'Careful, Dennis,' he said. 'I'm coming your way.'

Dennis jumped into the car and locked the doors. He tried to get the engine started.

The baseball bat went through the side window.

The engine screamed.

'I'll fucking get you for this you baaaa...!'

Dennis had put the car into reverse; it had just mounted Sid.

Terry leaned on his bat and watched. Dennis couldn't fold Sid up tidily enough for the back seat, so he made do with the boot. Having made sure Terry was at a safe distance, he pulled out what remained of the windscreen and threw it into the gutter.

'Give my father a message!' shouted Terry. 'This is just the start!'

The car made off in an Infirmary direction, the exhaust pipe grating along the tarmac. Terry was laughing. He couldn't stop himself.

The doors of the Appleby Hall banged open, and a body came tumbling down the steps. Three servitors stood wiping their hands on their dustcoats. They obviously wanted to make sure that Dug stayed out.

'You fucking elitist bastards!' he shouted, rubbing the grime off the knees of his trousers.

Terry helped him to his feet.

'Told you,' he said.

Dug brandished his CV.

'Three fucking days it took me to put this together,' he sobbed. 'Plus a subscription to The Scotsman. Cunts.' He shoved the CV into his pocket. 'Nice baseball bat,' he said.

Terry tapped the kerb.

'Fancy a drink?' he said. 'I need to do some thinking.'

'Yeah,' said Dug. 'I'll fill you in on Plan B.'

'You what?'

'Oh, yes,' said Dug, and tried to force a smile. 'There should always be a Plan B.'

* * *

The door crashed open. Terry was standing there. He was holding a baseball bat.

211

Plato cocked his head to the side.

'That's not Sid's, is it?' he said. 'Well done, Terry. It seems we have the same taste in nasty acquaintances after all.'

Terry lurched across the room and sat down heavily in the chair. He tried to prop the bat against the table, but it slid onto the floor. The whisky fumes wafting across the desk were almost visible.

'There's something else I need you to do,' he said.

'You what?'

'I need someone to carry something for me. That's all. Someone who can keep their eyes open and their mouth shut. I'm sure you can come up with someone.'

Plato was gripping the armrests of his chair.

Terry pushed himself up and placed his hands on the edge of the desk.

'Your pub is a side issue,' he said. 'In fact, I couldn't care less about it. There's something much more grand that The Reverend would miss.'

'But, Terry, I...'

'You will do it, Professor.'

'But...'

Terry buttoned his jacket.

'Have you heard of Doctor Sugden?' he said.

Of course he had. The silly bugger had been all over the front page of the student rag. The man was a laughing stock. What the hell did this have to do with anything?

'The question is this,' said Terry. 'Did he fall, or was he pushed?'

Plato was lost. Rimmer had told him about his contretemps with Sugden when he brought the wine round to the pub. He had looked oddly preoccupied – depressed, even. He hadn't mentioned anything about...

Oh, Christ.

'Don't tell me you were on the boat when...'

'I'll be in touch with you at a later date,' said Terry, and dragged his stick to the door. 'Goodbye.'

CHAPTER 17

The Joint Services Recruitment Office had a queue of desperate looking twenty year olds three deep along the railings. It seemed that 'Queen and Country' was a route well trodden by the University's failures.

Terry didn't have to wait long. Maybe the boys in front of him were only going in for information. When they came out, they all seemed to be clutching a pink piece of paper.

'Next, God damn it!'

He followed the rotund little man into the office. Too late, he realised he was whistling the tune to 'Donald, Where's Yer Troosers?'.

The wee bullfrog stopped abruptly and turned round. He rubbed the leather band on his wrist.

'Don't whistle in my office, son,' he said.

Affixed to the wall was a photograph of Her Majesty Queen Elizabeth II sitting on a horse. The frame gleamed. The name plate on the desk looked like it had been salvaged from a Scrabble board. It was even tackier than Lex Lodestar's.

WO1 RAYMOND BARR

'I didn't know they wore kilts in the RAF,' offered Terry by way of opening gambit. 'Tartan for the flyboys. Perhaps it's a new forces paradigm?'

Terry had had a few.

Barr sat down at his desk and regarded him with disdain he didn't bother to conceal.

'What's your story?' he said.

'Well, Colonel...'

'That's Sergeant Major,' said Barr. 'Christ!'

Terry smiled.

'Well, Sergeant Major,' he said. 'What I'd like from you today is some information about helicopters.'

Someone laughed. Terry glanced up at the picture of the Queen, but he knew it was only a voice in his head.

Barr leaned back in his chair. It began to rotate slowly. His feet had lost contact with the floor.

'Helicopters?' he said, and manoeuvred his fists until he was able to place them on the desk. 'You're the ninth one today.'

'Yes, I've decided,' said Terry, with massive gravity. His acting skills were being tested to the full. 'It's what I want to do.'

'And what makes you think the Army would give you a helicopter to go flying around in?'

'The RAF,' Terry corrected him.

Barr leaned back and started to rotate. He decided to stand, and swaggered, with a stocky swish-swish country dancing motion to the window. They were in the basement – the view was of a brick wall. Tragic, thought Terry. Barr had wanted the sharp end, and they'd given him this dead end.

'Where do the RAF train their pilots?' Barr said.

Terry didn't have a clue.

'At the same place as the Army,' said Barr. 'And the Navy, for that matter. Biggin Hill. I see you're well prepared for your interview.'

Terry reminded himself that this had been Dug's idea. Nonetheless, he'd thought that selling his soul would be easier than...

'What's your rank in the OTC?' said Barr.

'Well, I...'

'What, you mean you haven't been through the Officers Training Corps?'

Of course he hadn't.

'I did explain that it's the RAF I want to join.'

'Fine,' said Barr. 'Tell me about the University Air Squadron.'

'.....'

'The Royal Naval Reserve?'

214

'.....'

'The Boy Scouts?'

Terry hesitated.

'My mother flies a Piper Pawnee,' he said. 'Mainly for glider towing round Loch Leven. I've been up in it a few times.'

Barr smiled.

'I'll give you this,' he said. 'At least your line's original. Folk like you usually try to impress me with stories about being JCR Presidents. If another one comes into this office, I'll be able to open my own Halls of Residence.'

He hula-hooped back to his desk and took up position with his arms crossed on his chest. He fixed Terry with a hard stare.

'When you come in here,' he said, 'you're supposed to have something to show for your interest in the armed forces. But you're telling me you've done nothing over the last four years in connection with soldiering, sailing boats or,' he snorted, 'piloting aircraft?'

'Well, I did mention my...'

'Aye, well let's give your mum a big round of applause. But it's you we're talking about.'

'Look,' said Terry. The joking was over. He'd had a glass or three before he came down here, fine, but he'd thought they'd be falling over themselves to take him. He was offering himself up as cannon fodder for the old UK, for Christ's sake. If he couldn't get his foot in the door here...

All Barr could do was criticise him for not joining the right club.

'If you're telling me it's a game,' said Terry, 'you could at least do me the favour of telling me the rules.'

'Hark at it!' said Barr. 'You stroppy...'

'I mean, if you'd tell me the name of the game at least...'

Barr cut him off.

'Have you seen that programme The Paras on the telly?' he said.

'Sorry?'

'I think your aggression would go down better in the infantry than in a cockpit.'

'I didn't realise I was being aggressive,' said Terry, and felt the walls closing in on him.

215

'Aye,' said Barr, and started filling in a pink form. 'A short, sharp shock's what you need. Any idiot can fire a machine gun.'

Terry realised it was time to go over this little nyaff's head.

'If you'll just give me an appointment for a medical,' he said. 'I'll sort it out myself.'

Barr tossed the piece of paper at him.

'Already sorted, old bean. Now shut up and listen. A big lanky laddie like you would never fit into a helicopter. There's as much chance of them taking you as there is of them taking me. So take that railway pass and get yourself through to the Army Recruitment Office in Queen Street. That's Glasgow. Three pm tomorrow.'

'But I told you...'

Barr pulled the door open.

'Next, God damn it!' he shouted.

The RAF Medical Centre was on the first floor over a Pizza Hut. A bored man in a blue uniform was hunched over the Guardian crossword. Terry had to cough to get his attention.

'Oh, hello there,' he said, startled. 'Can I help you?'

There was a first aid kit on the shelf at his shoulder. You could have stored blankets in it. Under the red cross was the legend **FOR USE IN BOMB ATTACK**.

Terry swallowed.

'You couldn't tell me where the toilet is, could you?' he said.

The officer laughed.

'What, nervous before your medical? Don't be, it's all routine.'

'Yes,' said Terry. 'The toilet?'

'Down the corridor, second on the left.'

When he returned, the officer was still engrossed in his crossword.

'Postman's bag,' he said aloud, and tapped the page.

Terry gave it some thought.

'How many letters?' he asked.

'Bloody hundreds!'

'Sorry?'

The officer looked peeved.

'Bloody hundreds,' he repeated. 'How many letters in the postman's bag? It's a joke.'

Terry looked round the office. His eyes came to rest on the first aid kit.

'I'd like to join the RAF,' he said.

The officer took a slow sip from a Kit Kat coffee mug and studied the prospective new recruit.

'Are you a student?' he said.

'Why?' said Terry.

'Are you?'

'Yes.'

'Well, you should really go down to the office in Buccleuch Street. Raymond Barr will give you an appointment for this office for, let me see in my little book, some time next week.'

This was the game. Barr vets the students. If your face fits, he sends you here.

'I see,' said Terry. 'I didn't know that.'

He turned to leave. That was the impression he wanted to give, anyway.

'Look,' he said. 'I've walked all the way from Duddingston Halls. Could you fit me in some time this afternoon?'

'Ah, the University of Scotland!' said the officer. 'I'm an old alumnus myself.' He looked at Terry's suit. 'The University isn't really my jurisdiction...'

Terry knew they were on the same side.

'The thing is,' he said, 'I'm a bit behind in studying for my finals.'

'Ooh, the rigours of Honours Year!' said the officer. 'I remember it well.' He flicked back through the appointments book. 'We're a bit full this afternoon,' he said, 'but I'll tell you what. We usually have a few no shows. Why don't you go for a walk round Princes Street gardens and come back at three-thirty four-ish?'

'Splendid,' said Terry.

. . .

The waiting room was empty. Dug was trying to find something readable in an ancient copy of Railway Modeller that was hanging off the end of the coffee table.

217

His membership of the University Air Squadron had lasted all of a fortnight, way back in October. Raymond Barr had praised him on his initiative, though for some reason he hadn't seemed very impressed with Dug's JCR credentials. It was all about getting your foot in the door, Dug supposed, but he felt very alone indeed. He was still wondering about Terry. The last he'd seen of him was when he'd stormed out of the pub, drunk, after the débâcle at the Milk Round.

A hardnut in a denim jacket swaggered in and parked himself against the wall. He rejoiced in the kind of flat top that Dug had once aspired to – no matter how much he slouched, you *knew* it wasn't squint. Dug had given up on that long ago. He now sported the kind of platform quiff that Morrissey would have been proud of.

The hardnut didn't like getting stared at.

'Whit the fuck you lookin' it?' he said.

Dug's eyes darted back to the magazine, something about 00 gauge signal boxes.

The room began to fill up with bodies and smoke. The atmosphere was tense, as if all the fine young men had been coerced into it. Dug had had a pint of Dutch courage before coming, and was bursting for the toilet, but before he could make up his mind, the silence was broken by a fat man in a labcoat. There were three stripes on his arm.

'Right, three o'clock batch, move yourselves!'

They were herded into a laboratory. The benches along the windows were covered in test tubes and centrifuges.

'Name?' mumbled the Sergeant.

Dug took his time responding. He was admiring the man's toupee, which was glued to his head like a liquorice mat.

He was handed a beaker.

'Right! You've all got your little glass jugs. Fill them!'

There was a rush for the cubicle in the corner. Dug, by a miracle, got there first. Despite the pain in his bladder, however, he couldn't make himself urinate.

The curtain was pulled back sharply.

'What's going on?' barked the Sergeant. 'You wanking?'

Dug didn't know what to say.

'Next man!'

Dug was being stared at with an expression of disgust.

'Get in and see the doctor,' said the Sergeant. 'You useless article.'

. . .

He was swaying in the middle of the room, a cigar jammed in the corner of his mouth. Despite the smoke that was stinging his eyes, he couldn't stop laughing. It was impossible to keep the piss from running over the edge of the glass.

'I perform extraordinarily well in front of an audience, don't you think?' said Terry, and offered the overflowing beaker to the man with the stripes on his arm.

'Oh, you fucking animal! Get in and see the doctor!'

Dug stopped him in the corridor.

'All right, Dug! Plan B comes to fruition, eh?!'

Through the smoke, he could see that Dug looked worried.

'Look, Terry,' he said. 'Before you go in there...'

'What, is it true they squeeze your balls and tell you to cough?'

'Well, yeah, but that's not...he's talking about killing himself.'

'Wh...?'

The officer appeared.

'Come on, now,' he said. 'Chop chop. Lucky about that cancellation, eh? Just down the corridor on the right and strip down to your underpants. There's a dressing gown hanging on the wall.'

Terry swayed to the side and looked round, but Dug was gone.

'And, er,' said the officer. 'I'll take your cigar before you go in.'

The dressing gown was threadbare Paisley pattern. It barely covered his arse.

'Very fetching,' said the officer. He was still holding the cigar between thumb and middle finger, his elbow cradled in his other hand, giving Terry the once over. 'The doctor's ready for you. End of the corridor.'

He knocked and stepped inside. A two bar electric fire glowed orange at the other end of the room. A folding screen hid the doctor from view.

'Well, come in if you're coming in!'

He minced across the floor. The dressing gown had probably belonged to Twiggy. It had an amazingly sobering quality.

219

'Bugger me!' said Rimmer. 'If it isn't the other half of the glimmer twins!'

Terry stared.

'From the wasp-waisted Douglas Lloyd to the transvestite rugby player Kinlochleven. It's times like this when I think I've seen everything.'

He was sitting behind a metal desk that had been painted green. His labcoat was filthy, and he had a stethoscope round his neck. He lit a Gauloise with a Zippo and blew a cloud of smoke at the ceiling.

'I like to keep my hand in, Terry,' he explained. 'Sit down.'

The omens were good. All Terry had to do was call in the favour that Rimmer owed him. But he was sure it wouldn't come to that. He shifted on the seat and clawed a sudden itch in his bollocks.

'You're not moonlighting from the Institute, are you?' he said.

Rimmer chuckled a chain of smoke rings across the desk.

'Not at all,' he said. 'One can hardly moonlight from a job one has recently jacked.'

'What?'

'That's right. Straight out the door, and no compensation. Not that I'll be needing any where I'm going.'

'.....'

'And to add further embellishment to my response, I'm standing in for an old friend who's off sick. Now.'

'Yes,' said Terry. 'Let's get on with the medical. I've already handed in my...'

Rimmer cut him off.

'All in good time, old son,' he said, and took a long pull on his cigarette.

Terry felt as if the examination had already started. It would all be over soon, he reassured himself. He would let Rimmer have his jollies, then hit the nearest pub. Still, sitting there in that stupid dressing gown...

'The, er, incident,' said Rimmer.

Terry relaxed. He sat back in the chair and crossed his legs.

'What incident?' he said, and brushed the hair on his thigh with the flat of his hand. He was sure he looked like a butch homosexual, but so what? It would probably result in a higher mark.

'On the ferry, Terry. Sugden's telling everyone he slipped. Although how anyone slips over a barrier that's at chest height is a bit of a puzzler.'

Terry noticed that he didn't look very grateful.

'I thought I was doing you a favour,' he said.

Rimmer smiled, although it was clear he thought nothing was funny.

'A good job he had all those trophies for long-distance swimming, eh, Terry?' Puff. Puff. 'He was scooped out by a dredger off Selsey Bill.'

'So I read in the paper,' said Terry.

'So he'll be ship shape, as it were, Bristol fashion, hale, hearty and turning cartwheels in an anally Reverend direction when the Kinlochleven Suite opens in a fortnight.'

'Perhaps I should have hit him over the head with a bottle before I pushed him,' said Terry. 'How remiss of me.'

'See, that's you Kinlochlevens all over, isn't it?' said Rimmer. 'Always interfering in my life. There's really no need.'

'I've already handed in my urine sample,' Terry repeated.

Rimmer sucked long and hard.

'You are a very dangerous man,' he said. 'Remind you of anyone?'

Terry stood up. The back of the dressing gown was sticking to his cheeks like clingfilm.

'Perhaps I should find another doctor,' he said.

'No, no,' said Rimmer, and ground out his cigarette in a battered ashtray. 'Unfortunately, I'm it.'

He pulled open a drawer. His leather vagina hit the desk with a thud.

'Don't worry,' he said. 'I'm not going to ask you to fill it.'

His arm disappeared into the drawer again, and he produced something metal and medical with a flourish. He huffed on the dull surface and rubbed it on his sleeve.

'If you'll, er, follow me over to the bed, as it were.'

Terry lifted a knee onto the frame, which elicited a quiet laugh from Rimmer.

'No, Terry. Not yet. Just sit down.'

Terry perched himself on the edge of the mattress. It was made of rubber. The backs of his legs were already stuck to it.

'If you'll lean over,' Rimmer whispered, 'I'll have a quick look at your membrane.'

Cold pressure as Rimmer pushed and struggled to get the probe into his ear.

'Oooh, it won't go in. First time, is it, Terry? Shall we try some Vaseline?'

Terry batted the instrument away and stood up, dragging half of the mattress off the bed.

'Okay, that's enough,' he said.

'But you have to do your medical, Terry. Having your eardrums explode at forty thousand feet might cause problems. You could easily swerve into the path of an airliner full of drunk tourists. Think how you'd spoil their holiday.'

Terry raised a finger.

'And I have it from informed sources,' Rimmer continued, 'that Windolene and a duster are not standard issue for fighter pilots.'

Terry lifted the pack of Gauloise off the desk and helped himself. He took one drag and nearly choked.

'Careful, Terry,' said Rimmer. 'They're the dirtiest fags on the market.'

Terry persevered. He could feel his lungs turning yellow.

Rimmer sat down in his chair. He tossed the probe into the drawer.

'A little bird tells me you've pulled off an exemption from your final exams,' he said.

'Really?' said Terry. 'Has your boyfriend been filling you in?'

'Oh, very juvenile, Terry, although I believe you're referring to Plato Buchanan. Indeed he has. As always. We go back a long way. A shared interest in Robert Bruce, would you believe?'

'Scottish History by way of Athens?' said Terry, and rolled the stubby cigarette around in his fingers; it felt soggy. He could only guess what it was doing to his lungs, but his fingers were turning yellow before his eyes.

'No,' said Rimmer. 'Stock car racing in Cowdenbeath. And, of course, fine wines. It's not important.'

Terry laid the cigarette in the indentation in the side of the ashtray. Lighting it had been a bad idea.

Rimmer stubbed it out.

'I really have to ask you something, Terry,' he said. 'Forgive me for being quite so blunt, but what the fuck are you doing here?'

'.....'

'Oh, come on now, Terry. I've given you a graphic account of why I'm here. Let's hear what's on your mind.'

Terry sat down.

'I want to join the RAF,' he said.

Rimmer made a small pyramid with his fingers. It reminded Terry uncomfortably of his father.

'Yes, uh-huh, I can see that,' said Rimmer. 'A medical being the first step in the joining the RAF process. Just answer my fucking question, Terry.'

The merchant banks didn't want him. If they didn't want him, there was nothing else. Applying to join the RAF, it had to be faced, was scraping the bottom of the barrel marked 'Desperate'. Plan B.

There was something else, though.

He was looking for something that might save him from himself. Something that might save him from Plan C.

He wasn't about to divulge that nugget to Rimmer, though.

'Can we get on with the rest of the medical?' he said.

Rimmer smiled broadly.

'In days of yore...'

'Yes, lovely,' said Terry. 'Can we just get on with it?'

'Do you really want me titillating your helmet, Terry? I doubt it.'

Terry jumped to his feet.

'Okay, if I have to get my pants off, let's go!'

Rimmer sighed and reached for a notepad. He began to scribble with a silver pen.

'No need to go through all the rigmarole, Terry,' he said, and tore off a sheet of paper. 'You've failed.'

Terry gaped at him.

'But you didn't even put that thing in my ear!'

'Oh, Terry, Terry. That thing in your ear? I've seen everything I need to know. Everything *salient*, as a former colleague of mine might… You've failed the medical, Terry. It's over. Think 'Driving Test'. Or rather, don't think about driving tests, because they let you bask in the delusion of possible success even though you've already ploughed it.'

Terry gripped the edge of the desk. He clearly saw himself hoisting it, and Rimmer, out of the window.

'I demand a second opinion!' he said.

Rimmer nodded slowly.

'You're a chip off the old block,' he said. 'Will that do you?'

Something strange was happening. Terry felt a mask moulding itself over his face. A smile was creeping across his mouth.

'You do of course realise that I can't be held responsible for whatever happens next,' he said.

Rimmer flipped another ciggie out of his packet.

'Do me a favour,' he said. 'Go and talk tough to your daddy, not to me. I'm neither impressed nor intimidated nor anything else you might think. I've watched you change, Terry, and I abhor what you have become. In short, you make me sick to my stomach. But then, what could anyone expect from a Kinlochleven?'

Terry leaned all the way over the desk. The dressing gown wasn't funny any more. He watched his hand reaching for the old man's lapel.

'Just send in the next candidate,' said Rimmer, and flicked his Zippo. 'There's a good chap.'

CHAPTER 18

Rumour had it that Mick Robertson was out of town. Sammy took a quick walk down to the Prezzie Hall to confirm it. He ordered a half pint of special and got the SP from the young guy who'd been left in charge.

It was Wednesday.

Mick Robertson wouldn't be back till tomorrow.

* * *

Plato opened the door a crack and watched Terry sipping his whisky. The young man was early for their meeting. Plato had received a call at his office at the University. Terry wanted to see him about something 'incendiary', related to the chess clock that had appeared in one of his tutorials. At first, Plato had been surprised; if memory served, Terry had been unconscious during all of his lessons, before he'd stopped coming altogether. He must have got the information from his sidekick. Either that, or he hadn't been as comatose as he'd been making out.

Plato, of course, was ahead of the game. Concrete Philosophy? No, he was sure it was something slightly more dastardly. Terry, the poor, misguided boy, wanted to make an inflammatory statement. Things would soon be hotting up at the Queen's Buildings.

At long last he had worked out what was going on in Terry's head.

There was a huge whoop from the corner. The Overseas Students Soc, the whole lot of them, were laughing, singing and dancing round their usual table, which was awash, Plato was pleased to see, with empty bottles. Strange how they could find humour in a shared second language which none of them had mastered. Mr Kwak was at that moment being raised onto the shoulders of a brace of Nigerians, with a third giving a helpful push from behind.

He closed the door and went to admire his device.

* * *

A transit van pulled into the kerb. The words 'Blues Domination Society' were painted along the side. The Hawaiian shirt got out and took a couple of strides. His steps faltered, and he went back to check that the doors and windows were locked. You could never be too careful.

He popped into the pub.

Sammy was standing in a doorway across the road. He was trying to keep a low profile, but it was difficult. He had Malcolm's phone balanced on his shoulder, and he was having to shout into it.

'Mich?...Mich?...we're oan...action stations!...eh?...aye, ACTION ST...Mich?...ach, fuck it.'

Ten minutes later, Moose came marching down Victoria Street. He had his eyes trained on the van. There was no messing about, no furtive looks over the shoulder. Within seconds he had the door open and the engine started, then the van was gone.

Sammy was taken aback by the skill the boy had displayed – he was only, what, 14? Technically, he shouldn't have been driving. Then again, technically he shouldn't have been stealing the Blues Domination Society's van.

Sammy legged it back to the flat.

* * *

His purchase was folded up neatly and laid with a pat on the counter.

'So that's the wet suit,' said the assistant, and brushed her fringe out of her eyes. 'You're sure you don't want the flippers?'

He had been doing a bit of reading on the subject. It was called a wet suit because the material soaked up water when immersed, providing a layer of insulation. He concluded that it would also create an airtight seal.

'You're sure it's top quality?' he said.

'SBS surplus, sir. Nothing better. I should know, I do a bit of diving myself.'

'Really?' he said. 'Scuba or muff?'

'Eh...'

'Now what I really need in order to achieve Nirvana is a gas mask.'

The assistant, poor girl, pointed shyly to a battered arrangement hanging over the door. It looked like an elephant's head had been nailed there last century and left to shrivel.

'Oh, dear me, no,' he said. 'It's all dry and cracked. What about one of those with the plastic windows over the eyes?'

'Sold out, sir,' she said. 'Blame it on the Iranian Embassy, then there was that Lewis Collins film...'

This was a setback. He'd already tried the store in Nicolson Street. They were sold out, too. This was why he was all the way down here, almost in Leith.

'Do you have any idea where I might find one?' he said.

The girl phoned round.

'No dice.'

He would have to improvise. He looked at the thing hanging over the door.

'You wouldn't have any Vaseline, would you?' he said. 'To fill in the cracks, you understand.'

* * *

There was a bit of a commotion going on outside the pub. Sammy told Mich to pull over, and rolled the window down. The Hawaiian shirt was in heated conversation with a policeman, and he was getting things off his chest.

'But it's fu' ae oor stuff! Fuckin' drums an' amps an' guitars! We're talkin' aboot a fuckin' fortune!'

Now, now, thought Sammy. Don't exaggerate. Fast Chuck's gear wasn't worth tuppence.

He got out and told Mich to park down in the Grassmarket. The policeman looked like he was on a YTS, and it was obvious from the way he was scratching his ear that there was nothing he could do. Sammy bypassed them and went inside. Even though it was early, there were already a few Blues Domination Society fans in. He knew they were Blues Domination Society fans because it was written all over their T-shirts, the wankers.

He pulled up a stool at the bar.

'Cannae stay away fae the place?' smiled the barman. He already had a glass angled under the tap.

'Aye,' said Sammy. 'Looks like ah missed aw the action, though.'

The barman was trying not to laugh.

'Some cunt hijacked the band's motor,' he said. 'The singer's oot the front daein' ae's nut.'

'Aw, right,' said Sammy. 'So that's whit aw the noise wis aboot.'

He sipped his beer slowly, watching the barman washing glasses and serving the odd customer. The boy was taking his substitute manager status seriously – he had the key to the till on a chain round his neck. Mick Robertson had obviously left strict orders.

It was difficult to decide if a decent interval had passed.

'Here,' said Sammy, after he'd ordered another half. 'Whit yez goannae dae fur music the night?'

'Fucked if ah ken,' said the barman. 'Ah'm huvvin' enough bother makin' sure these cunts dinnae start pocklin'.'

There were two other boys on duty, both of them leaning on the other end of the counter, picking their noses.

Sammy sniffed.

'Ah'm in a band,' he said.

'So?' said the barman.

Sammy's heart was thudding through his jumper.

'We can play here the night if ye want,' he said. 'It'll no cost ye anythin'.'

The barman seemed to be thinking about it. The place was beginning to fill up.

'Whit kind ae music dae yez dae?' he said.

'Eh, blues,' said Sammy. 'Amongst other things.'

'Are yez any guid?'

We hud a five grand recordin' contract, ya fuckin' tube, thought Sammy. Of course we're fuckin' guid.

There was a ruckus at the door, and the Kaptain's Kabin regulars trooped in. Moose must have got back to Dalkeith. The word was out, and they'd piled onto the first available bus.

Sammy looked at the barman and smiled.

'Ask them how guid we are,' he said.

The barman was looking.

'Well, ah don't know...'

They were crowding round the bar, slapping Sammy on the back. Sammy leaned over the counter.

'This lot drink like fish,' he said.

'Well,' said the barman. 'Ah suppose so.'

Moose appeared at the edge of the crowd. Sammy tipped him the wink. They'd have the gear set up in no time.

* * *

'Very punctual,' said Plato.

'Good evening,' said Terry, and glanced at Morag, who was sitting in the corner.

He turned to Plato.

'You can't possibly be serious...'

Mr Kwak came crashing through the door.

'Ah, our Asian accomplice,' said Plato. 'Do come in.'

Mr Kwak parked himself against a bookcase. His head was lolling on his shoulders. He was having quite a night.

'So, everyone, meet Mr Kwak. He's the final member of our little outfit.'

'But he can't even speak English!' said Terry.

'What?' said Plato. 'You've met? Splendid. I find diagrams are good. You show him where to go, and he goes, usually with a wide smile of gratitude, which is rather encouraging. Being unable to articulate his misgivings, he doesn't. The archetypal soldier, in other words.'

Slight inflation of the truth never harmed anyone, Plato reminded himself. Mr Kwak could always be relied on to locate the late night shop in Lothian Road when the Left Bank's customers ran out of

Gauloises. Even when he was pissed. Perhaps he should have got Mr Kwak to do the pub. Oh, well. Too late now.

He noticed that Terry had turned his doubtful stare back to Morag.

'Don't be taken in by Morag's demure appearance, either,' he said. 'There's a tiger roaring away in your tank, isn't that right, Morag?'

She blushed, and began to squirm in her chair, her mouth working on silent vowels.

Plato sighed.

'It's not an essay question, Morag,' he said. God, but she was slow. He knew that if anyone was going to fuck up, it was her.

'How do we get in?' she suddenly asked.

Plato coughed. Time to get serious.

'Informed sources tell me,' he said, 'that the place is, appropriately, trussed up like a turkey.'

He pulled on a cord dangling from the shelf behind the desk. A map unfurled, with a path drawn in red felt tip.

Terry scoffed.

'Which Primary school did you nick that out of?' he said.

Plato ignored the comment. His intelligence work, he felt, was impeccable. He'd bumped into Rimmer at Cowdenbeath Raceway two nights before – it was a Monday meeting, and Robert Bruce had romped home, battered but victorious, in all his races. Quite a profitable evening, in fact, although Rimmer had yet again been in a depressed mood, chainsmoking like a condemned man. Plato had tried to glean details of that drunk acquaintance of his, the ex-SAS ambulance driver, but seemingly he was out of town working for a bus company. Fair enough, Plato had thought, it must be hard finding satisfying employment when you're a retired assassin, especially when your speciality is sliding down ropes into Belfast housing estates.

Perhaps it was all for the best. The objective was to give Terry what he wanted then disappear before the metaphorical smoke settled; Plato's sudden absence would be met with prepared sympathy at the University – he'd already started a whisper round the department concerning his mother's health.

'Let's get back to the plan,' he said, and drew their attention to the chess clock.

* * *

He was on a long weekend. Another one. He dropped off a load of Japs at Trafalgar Square then parked the coach round the back of the Strand. He hoofed it over to Soho. There was something he was dying to try out.

Rimmer had mentioned that, if he ever got the chance, he should visit the Isle de Feu in Dean Street. It might bring back fond memories of Paris.

It only took him five minutes to locate the bar. In fact, he spotted it from the other end of the street. The guy with the bullwhip was a dead giveaway.

'Do you do Coprophagy?' he asked the barman. You'd bloody better, he thought. It had cost him a fiver just to get in the door.

The barman put down the glass he was polishing and leaned across the beer taps.

'What was that, chief?' he whispered.

'Coprophagy,' said Vic. 'It's an acquired taste. Fucking ace, though.'

He was taken through the back yard to a basement establishment. There was a sign over the door. The Morris Dancer.

They did Coprophagy all right.

* * *

They played a stormer. Even the hard core fans with the T-shirts were nodding their approval. When Baz got his harmonica out and started Layla, they nearly creamed their pants.

They did Walking On The Moon. Baz had splashed out on an effects box from Jackie's, and it sounded like The Police had come to Edinburgh and got psychedelically stoned. Sammy clocked the Blues Domination Society sitting in the pulpit, listening to what was what and checking out the audience reaction. The drummer caught Sammy's eye, raised his glass and winked. The dickhead in the Hawaiian shirt was trying to do the same to Mich. Fast Chuck wasn't shy. He came over and stood at the side of the PA, paying close attention to the riffs. Amid the deafening applause and cheering at the end of the song, he beckoned Baz over and shook him warmly by the hand. Mr Invisible was just behind him, nodding.

Twenty years of hard work had finally paid off. Sammy's band were playing the biggest venue in Edinburgh, and they were bringing the house down.

They could do Wednesday nights no problem.

He filled his lungs and smiled the biggest smile in the world.

Then Mick Robertson kicked Bear off the stage.

* * *

Vic was led down, down, down into a dungeon that was lit by a green bulb in a wire case. He tried not to trip on the rubber sheeting that was stretched from wall to wall.

There was a kitchen sink in the corner, but the place smelled like a toilet. Maybe there was a problem with the plumbing; water was dripping somewhere.

'Where's the bar?' he asked the young man at his shoulder who, for some reason, was unbuckling his belt.

'Never mind a bar,' he said, as his jeans fell round his ankles. 'I'll 'ave a log as thick as your arm in a minute. Oi! Julie! Bring on the Fairy!'

'It was Coprophagy I wanted,' said Vic, sensing that there was a bit of a misunderstanding going on.

An emaciated girl, presumably Julie, appeared in the doorway.

'I'll do it if you want, Colin,' she said. 'I 'ad a bogging souvlaki last night at Yanni's.'

'Nah, you're all right, girl,' said Colin. 'Just get us the squeezy bottle.'

She raked around under the sink.

'Will Safeways own brand do?' she asked. 'We're out of Fairy.'

'Champion,' said Colin, and turned to Vic. 'Nice girl, eh? She's me sister. Yours for twenty nicker. Thirty if you want me to join in.'

Julie squeezed her bottle. It whistled and wheezed, and a caterpillar of green bubbles oozed from the nozzle.

Vic was still wondering where the beer taps were.

Colin threw his jeans into the corner and squatted on the floor. He wasn't wearing underpants.

'I think we should discuss prices before she squirts that up my arse,' he said.

Vic began to shake.

'It's twenty for the scat,' said Colin, 'and a tenner for a wrist job during the performance. A Rotherhithe Steamer will cost you fifty...'

The sound of an army of boots came thudding down the stairs.

'...but if you 'ang on a tick, the Chelsea Pancake Crew will do you for free.'

Shaven heads and leather vests came pouring through the door.

Colin looked apologetic.

'They don't like refusals,' he said.

Vic knew he was in deep shit.

He soon would be.

* * *

'What are those?' said Morag.

There was a bundle of clothes on Plato's chair. He'd get back to the chess clock in a moment.

'Ah,' he said. 'I'm glad you asked.'

Not surprisingly, he had found nothing suitable next door; the shop's niche was 'Old Men's Castoffs', not 'Urban Guerrilla'. Fortunately, however, one of his Honours students worked part-time in the Army and Navy in Nicolson Street, and had acquired three sets of SAS surplus combat fatigues.

He handed them round.

'I'm a size fourteen,' said Morag.

It might have been a problem, but they were going on a mission, not taking part in a fashion show. The overalls were huge, made for special forces soldiers, not Wee Morags.

'They'll be too long in the arms,' she said.

'You can roll the sleeves up,' said Plato.

'But they'll still be too long in the...'

'You can roll the legs up as well!'

'Iranian embassy, yes?' said Mr Kwak. He was looking good in his balaclava.

'Is this what I think it is?' said Terry, and patted the chess clock.

Morag shifted in her chair and began to wring the sleeves of her overalls.

233

'It's quite a subtle design,' said Plato, proudly. 'When you press the button, the clock begins to tick. So.'

He pressed the button.

'When the flag falls, the circuit is completed, and a series of sparks is relayed to the, er...I hesitate to use the word 'explosive'.'

A camping gas canister was taped to the side of the clock.

'It'll never work,' said Terry. 'Do you expect the sparks to ignite the gas through the metal?'

'It's how they do it in Athens!' Plato protested with what, he was sure, was a convincing level of indignation. If it worked, it worked. If it didn't, and it most certainly wouldn't, he would still have honoured his end of the bargain.

Mr Kwak was trying on his bullet proof vest.

'You need something more flammable,' said Morag.

'Like a rag soaked in petrol,' said Terry.

Plato shook his head.

'Too smelly,' he said. He'd thought about that.

'Just so long as it burns,' said Morag.

Plato and Terry stared at her.

'Whatever,' said Plato. 'You can set the timer to anything up to an hour. Give yourselves time to get away. The point is it would not be wise to be in the building when the straw...'

Morag gasped.

Plato coughed.

'Leave it to me,' said Terry. He made for the door, the chess clock under his arm.

Oh, dear, thought Plato.

'SAS, yes?' hissed Mr Kwak through his respirator.

'Yes,' said Plato. 'Very.'

* * *

'But ah wis tryin' tae help ye oot!' Sammy shouted.

'Don't you try an' bullshit me ya four-eyed wee cunt!' said Mick Robertson. 'Ye think ah'm fuckin' daft?'

It would have been the interval, but the gig was over. Bear had disappeared.

'How many times dae ah huv tae tell ye, Sammy? If ah want tae employ a midget, ah'll open a fuckin' zoo.'

Baz cleared his throat.

'Take it easy there, Mick,' he said. 'Show a bit ae respect, eh?'

'Wh...!!?'

The punters had been tuning in, but it was their Wednesday night, and they wanted to hear music, not an argument. They were crowding round the bar, getting their drinks in for the second half.

Mick Robertson had a look round the pub.

'Well,' he said.

The Hawaiian shirt was approaching.

If ae asks if they can yaze oor stuff, ae can go an fuck aesell, thought Sammy.

'Seein' as the freak's done a vanishin' trick...,' said Mick Robertson. '...ah hear ye can sing, Sammy.'

Sammy smiled. He was up for it. Too right he was.

He got back in behind his drums. He nodded to Moose, and got the microphone set up next to him. They'd start off with Sultans of Swing, then move onto...

Baz was winding his guitar lead round his arm.

'Baz!' Sammy shouted.

He came over.

'That's me, man,' he said. 'If you want tae stay here an' play fur this cunt, oan ye go. But that's me...ah'm no lettin' um talk aboot Bear like that...'

Sammy stared at him.

Mich unplugged her bass.

'Mich? Whit ye daein', doll?'

'Think, Sammy,' she said.

He tried to.

'But it's the Prezzie Hall!' he pleaded.

'Yeah,' she said. 'And Mick Robertson's a fucking bastard.'

CHAPTER 19

He lay in bed and stared at the ceiling. The sheet, stained with sweat and worse, was wrapped around him like a shroud.

There was no point getting up. Geeky was still out of town. He'd be back in a few days.

'That's yin thing aboot Lanzarotti,' he said. 'Plenty totty!'

Sure, thought Terry. Geeky looked like he'd been standing in front of an open fire for a week. He had the pulling power of a charred pepperoni stick.

'Anyway,' Geeky said. He looked furtively round his room. 'Here's that, eh, message ye asked me aboot.'

Terry prised off the lid. He lowered his head carefully into the tin.

'It smells like pl...,' he said.

'...aye,' said Geeky, and scratched his nose. 'Ah noticed that an' all. They pit that in tae fool the sniffer dogs.'

It was business as usual in the Left Bank. Almost the end of term, and everyone was downing alcohol by the gallon. He found a space at a corner table, and laid his satchel carefully between his feet. It was the Yah contingent, with those loud voices, as if the place had been taken over by donkeys. The men all looked like Terry, and the women were beautiful. In a parallel universe, he was sure, the one where he got no less than his due, he would be taking one of them home tonight.

Something soft brushed against his shoulder; a petite behind in a green mini skirt. Green tights.

He inhaled perfume.

A woman sat on his knee. Her face was vaguely familiar. She was well gone, sucking on a bottle of Pimms.

'I like my men wasted,' she slurred into his forehead.

Terry cupped her face in his hands, and his tongue dragged a groove from her chin to her cheekbone.

Her eyes floated around, trying to focus on him.

'I always had a thing about you,' she said.

'Really?' said Terry.

This was more like it. His hand explored the pert firmness of her left breast. What a change from the slack udders he had been kneading at the Kaptain's Kabin. Even Mich had been a disappointment.

He smiled, and his hand moved under her skirt. Her crotch singed his fingers. She closed her legs on him and stuck her tongue in his ear.

'Hey, steady on, there,' said some floppy-haired boy on the other side of the table.

Terry looked up.

'What was that?' he said.

The boy ignored him, and reached over the table.

'Come on, Pippa,' he said. 'I think you've had enough.'

Terry's knuckles cracked off the young man's nose.

They left, the whole Yah lot of them, dragging Pippa behind them.

He finished his drink on his own.

'It's the star of the show!' exclaimed Plato, with a little too much excitement. He looked flushed, twitchy, as if he were warming down from a particularly pleasurable bout of exertion, and couldn't wait for the next.

A Samsonite suitcase was sitting at the side of the desk.

This will be fun, thought Terry.

'Going on holiday?' he said.

'No,' said Plato, his mouth twitching into a grin. 'Whatever gives you that idea?'

'Yeah, right,' said Terry, and pulled a bottle of whisky out of his satchel. Plato's discomfort was a joy to behold. 'Drink?'

'No, thank you,' said Plato. 'I'm, er, driving.'

237

Aren't you just, thought Terry. He opened the bottle and helped himself to a generous mouthful.

'Mmm,' he said. 'One of our better single malts. Not very Rock 'n' Roll, but a versatile drink all the same. Wouldn't you agree?'

The only sound was the babble of conversation from the bar.

Plato dragged his suitcase round behind the desk.

'You must have a lot of dirty washing in there,' prodded Terry, gently. He knew that Plato was for the off – a week before the end of term indeed. Pressing family business at home? Probably not. Terry had taken a walk round a few city centre estate agents and had seen what was on offer. Gaffs like Plato's were quite rare, and the ones that were available were on sale for fifty to fifty five grand. He had obviously come to some sort of agreement with The Reverend – and for more than fifty five grand. Plato may have been a lot of things, but Terry didn't have him down as a masochist.

'How much?' asked Terry. 'Sixty, sixty five thousand?'

Plato flushed crimson.

'Don't worry,' Terry laughed. 'I'm not going to steal it.'

That seemed to relax him. Plato smiled like an idiot. It was unbelievable.

'Yes, indeed,' he said. 'Dennis brought it round this afternoon, as agreed. It turns out he's a gentleman – a rough diamond, as it were. Sid wasn't with him, I noticed.'

'No,' said Terry. 'He had a bit of an accident.'

'Oh, really?' said Plato. 'Not of the golfing kind, I trust?'

'No,' said Terry. 'Although we might blame it on a careless driver.'

Plato chuckled.

'A shame he didn't bring a lawyer with him,' he said. 'I signed my name 'Donald Duck'. Of course the ownership of the property still resides...'

Morag appeared at the door, dressed from top to toe in her combat gear. She looked like Minnie Mouse in mourning. Mr Kwak lurched through the space at her side. He was completely tooled up. He flicked open his holster, poked around inside, then pinned something on his chest. A little tin star. 'Sheriff', it said.

'Milky Bar Kid, yes?' he smiled.

Plato reclined in his chair and rested his feet on his case.

'I have a good feeling about tonight's soiree,' he said.

'Me, too,' said Terry.

Morag put her hand up.

Terry snorted.

'It's not a fucking tutorial,' he said. Christ, what a balloon.

'It's about the buses,' she said.

Silence. Even Mr Kwak seemed to be listening.

She rubbed her breasts in a completely asexual fashion.

'Well,' she said. 'I mean getting from here to the, eh...'

What? thought Terry. She wasn't expecting them to get the bus, was she?

Mr Kwak struck a pose in front of the window. He stared down his reflection.

'Yeah, you,' he said. 'You wanna piece me? You wanna some?'

Terry reached for the bottle.

Plato tut-tutted.

'Really, Terry,' he said. 'Do you think you should? Drinking while on active service?'

Terry didn't like the hint of sarcasm.

'Do you think it'll make any difference if we're pissed?' he said, and gestured at Mr Kwak. 'He's already out of it. As for you, Morag, I think a drink would do you the power of good.'

Someone rapped loudly on the door. Plato's leg jerked so violently that he almost kneed himself in the face. He moved the suitcase behind his chair.

'Enter!'

A man stood in the doorway. He was wearing a black beret, and his overcoat went down to his ankles.

'Ah, Daniel,' said Plato nervously. 'Yes.'

'Who the fuck is this?' said Terry.

'You're, er, rather early,' said Plato.

Daniel did not look comfortable.

'Just to say that we're still on for...' he said, and slipped a paperback book out of his pocket.

Plato made a strange sound somewhere in the back of his throat.

'Yes, lovely, lovely,' he said. 'I'll see you later. Morag, if you'll

239

take Daniel and Mr Kwak through to the bar? Terry and I have something we need to discuss.'

They had to drag Mr Kwak out.

Plato waited until the door clicked shut.

'If you'll just slide the bolt home, Terry. We don't want anyone else barging in uninvited, do we?'

'No,' said Terry. 'We certainly don't.'

Plato pulled a big white hanky out of his pocket and mopped his brow. Daniel had certainly had an effect on him. And everything was on for later? And the ownership of the bar still resided with Plato. What was it Rimmer had said? A greedy fucker. It was all Terry could do not to laugh.

'I see you've also got your luggage with you, Terry,' said Plato, wiping the back of his neck. 'Though not quite as chic as mine.'

Terry laid his satchel on the desk. He'd got a fright when the slapping had started through in the bar, but he'd had everything under control.

'Yes, indeed,' he said.

He produced his package, wrapped in a William Low's plastic bag.

'Late night shopping, Terry?' said Plato.

'Hardly,' said Terry. He pulled off the lid. 'I've been advised not to arse around with any of the wires,' he said.

Plato leaned in for a closer look.

'Ooh,' he said, 'that's a smell that takes me back a few years – pl…'

'Yes,' said Terry. 'It's not important.'

Although Terry had passed his IPM, he hadn't paid much attention during the practicals. It was all very technical. There was something that looked like a circuit tester connected up to one of those large 9 volt batteries they used to put in radios. A jumble of wires of different colours. Then something that looked like a blunt pencil stuck into a block of blue plasticine.

'I feel the Family Circuit biscuit tin lends a certain juxtaposed homeliness to the whole affair,' said Plato.

Terry slid the lid back into place.

'Ten out of ten for presentation, by the way,' Plato added.

'Yes,' said Terry. 'And so much more effective than your chess clock, I'll bet.'

Plato's head twitched in what looked like a gesture of agreement.

'I won't ask you where you got it,' he said.

Terry grinned.

'Look,' said Plato, and started with his hanky again. 'I, er...have you really thought this through, Terry? I was expecting you to come up with a variation on a Molotov cocktail, not something out of an IRA arms cache.'

He suddenly wheeled round in his chair.

'Christ!' he said. 'Are you sure you weren't followed here? Special Branch could very well be watching the building right...'

Terry laughed. He wrapped up the bomb and slipped it back into his satchel.

'That thing,' said Plato, his finger shaking. 'You could...'

'Kill someone?' said Terry. He put the bottle of whisky in his satchel, too. Better not forget that. 'Do you think so? That's refreshing.'

Plato's eyes darted round the room. His hand went behind his chair, and his knuckles rapped against his suitcase.

'No, Terry,' he said. 'No, no. I forbid it. I won't have you planting bombs...'

'What do you mean you forbid it?' Terry laughed. 'Do you think you can tell me what to do?'

'Well, if you do this, and I strongly advise you not to...'

Terry was still laughing.

'You haven't got a say in the matter!'

'I'll make sure you don't graduate!' said Plato. 'I'll...I'll...tell them you didn't write any of those essays, it was all Lloyd's work, and as for the fake exam marks...'

Terry pulled the satchel over his shoulder. A week before, he couldn't have cared less. But where he was going, with Plato's help, a degree was a very necessary piece of paper.

'Oh, no, Plato,' he said. 'That will all go very smoothly. You seem to forget that we have an agreement.'

'.....'

'Although I admit that what's his name, Daniel, is a late addition to the mix. There's going to be lots of pyrotechnics tonight, eh?'

241

'.....'

'And at the risk of labouring the point, remember that I also have friends who make bombs, and I've made sure they know your name, and where you're headed. Get me?'

'Where I'm headed?' said Plato, his voice suddenly falsetto. 'I don't know what you mean.'

Terry leaned on the desk.

'I don't know why you didn't just drive down to Hull and get on the ferry,' he said. Booking a ticket was a bit clumsy.'

'.....'

'The weasly guy in the travel agent's? Stinks of pepperoni? He's a valuable acquaintance.'

'.....'

'You should always cover your tracks,' said Terry, making for the door. 'You fucking amateur.'

Plato got unsteadily to his feet.

'Look, Terry, you're going to ruin everything. I...'

The suitcase.

'Perhaps if I offered you something...'

Terry slid back the bolt.

'Meet me at the east end of Great King Street at 2am,' he said. 'Believe me, you'd better be there.'

'But you can't...!'

'Be there,' said Terry, and pulled the door shut behind him.

They hiked the two miles to the Queen's Buildings. Terry made sure that Morag had the bomb securely fastened to her back. If they got stopped by the police, he would vanish.

Mr Kwak was behaving like an arse. He had his gas mask pulled down over his face, and was darting into the shadows between the lamp posts. When he started scrabbling over the rubbish skips in Mayfield Road, Terry got hold of him and told him to calm down.

The security inside the campus was conspicuously discreet. They would have to be careful, though. Mr Kwak stopped and took a leak against a tree. Morag stopped, too, and started crossing herself. Perhaps, thought Terry, I should take her along later – she'll clash nicely with The Reverend's Protestant intolerance.

'Catholic?' he whispered, having made sure there were no guards prowling.

'No,' she said. 'Itchy overalls.'

They moved further into the darkness, Mr Kwak really getting into it. He started hopping around between the buildings, pulling out his water pistol and challenging imaginary bad guys.

Terry gave him a slap.

They moved slowly along the back of the Institute. The side entrance to the Kinlochleven Suite was only a few yards in front.

Morag pulled back her cuff and pressed a button on her watch.

'It's half past twelve,' she whispered.

Terry removed the satchel from her back.

'Don't worry,' he said. 'It'll all be over soon.'

He looked at the lock on the door jamb.

Shit. He'd forgotten about that.

Then he remembered something.

'Morag,' he said. 'You haven't got your library ticket on you, have you?'

Of course she did. She'd probably been in the reading room till throwing out time, her frumpy commando look drawing stares from all the other spastics.

He slid the card into the metal slot.

There was no sound, no bleep, no ker-klunk of sliding bolts.

He tried again.

Still nothing.

The door was already ajar.

He located Mr Kwak's sleeve and pulled him close.

'Come with me,' he said. 'Morag, you stay here and keep your eyes peeled.'

He crawled into the building, making sure that Mr Kwak was well to the front. They negotiated a few corners, the place almost in total darkness. Mr Kwak suddenly stopped and turned. He lifted up the bottom edge of his gas mask.

'Student prank, yes?' he said. He sounded hopeful.

Terry said nothing. He was too busy straining his ears, trying to pick up any noises. He clicked on his torch, and told Mr Kwak to do the same.

All clear.

The new animal enclosure was a vast shell of a place, with exposed girders across the ceiling and metal bars sectioning off the pens. It was completely empty, apart from a mountain of hay bales stacked at the far end.

Terry stood up and moved across the floor. When he was half way to the other side, he saw himself step on his own shadow, which quickly grew larger and stretched all the way to the opposite wall.

Someone had opened a door behind him.

'I say,' echoed a posh voice. 'What the blistering hell do you think you're doing?'

A tall man was silhouetted in the doorway, the light from the room behind him flooding the enclosure. He took a step inside. He was dressed in a diver's wet suit, and had a coil of mountaineering rope round his shoulder.

Mr Kwak was hissing rapidly inside his mask.

'Ooh,' said Rimmer, and approached. 'You seem to have reached the point where I'd like to be. Mind if I borrow this?'

He yanked the mask off Mr Kwak's head. It must have been sore; Terry heard Mr Kwak's ears snapping back into place.

Rimmer turned the mask over in his hands.

'You wouldn't believe the trouble I've had trying to locate one of these things,' he said.

Mr Kwak whimpered, and looked at Terry.

'Sorry about the ears,' said Rimmer. 'But they tell me it really does add a certain *je ne sais quoi* to the *frisson*.'

Terry just stood there.

A scratching sound.

The three men looked down.

Morag came crawling through the door and looked up at Rimmer.

'Are you with us?' she whispered, her voice echoing round the enclosure like an extended sigh.

'What?' said Rimmer. He looked at Mr Kwak, then Morag, then Terry. 'Ah, yes, we could start a club, couldn't we? Terry could be President – he's certainly dressed for something more, how should I put it, office based.'

Terry was wearing his suit under his overcoat.

244

Rimmer flap-flapped bare-footed over to the wall, leaving a trail of wet footprints behind him. He unscrewed the filter on the gas mask and turned on a tap that was jutting from a metal support. The water spat out, then stopped, the tap sneezing spray. He screwed the filter shut tight.

'Is this an end of term prank, Terry?' he said.

Mr Kwak looked around, nodding furiously.

'Or perhaps something more sinister?' Rimmer added.

'You've got a cheek to ask,' said Terry. 'What the fuck are you doing here, as someone once said.'

'Touché, Terry. But let's remember, I'm only here because you suggested it.'

'What?'

'Anyway,' said Rimmer, and pulled the mask onto his forehead. 'I have something I really must be getting on with. If you need anything, please don't disturb me. I'll be taking a shower.'

He turned to leave.

'And another thing,' he said. 'Feel free to turn a light on. The security firm are on strike.'

He closed the door behind him.

'I heard voices!' said Morag, her face illuminated in the beam from Terry's torch. Mr Kwak ran for it. Terry let him go. The sooner they got this over with, the better.

They climbed over the bars into the pen at the far end. There was nothing to it. He laid the torch on one of the bales, took out his bottle and filled his mouth.

Then he started dousing the hay.

Something snorted.

'What was that?' said Morag, and farted.

Terry put the empty bottle back in his satchel. He reached into his pocket and pulled out a gleaming new Zippo.

Another snort. Louder.

General Charles de Gaul appeared round the side of the hay bales. From the size of the erection he was trailing beneath him, he had just been woken from a very pleasant dream. He took a heavy step towards Morag.

'Check out the size of that!' she said.

245

Yes, thought Terry. And by the look of things, it's all for you.

Morag farted again.

The General began to paw the ground, inching his bulk towards her.

'I think he likes it when you do that,' said Terry.

'I've just wet myself,' she whimpered.

'Don't move,' said Terry.

'.....'

He looked around, and flicked the lighter.

'I'm going to open that big door in the wall,' he said. 'When I say go, run like fuck. For the door.'

The General was moving from side to side, his penis swaying.

'Are you ready, Morag?'

'Hu-hurry...'

The huge door swung outwards.

'Now!' shouted Terry, and threw his lighter into the hay.

He sprinted all the way out onto West Mains Road. He didn't hang around to see what happened to Morag. In any case, there wasn't enough time.

He flagged down a taxi and waved a twenty pound note in the driver's face.

'The New Town,' he gasped, and slumped across the seat. 'I'm in a hurry.'

There were lights on in the church. His plan had been to leave his present at the door, but this was an opportunity too good to miss. The vestibule was empty, but he could hear something going on in the main hall. The balcony would give him a grandstand view.

Despite the main doors being open, this was obviously a private affair.

It looked as if a dust sheet had been draped over a bulky piece of furniture.

They must have been on a table – the altar, perhaps? The Reverend was on his knees, engaged in sexual intercourse of a doggy-style nature with Miss Chang, who appeared unemotional, if compliant. Only their heads were visible, their modesty spared by a vast swathe of multicoloured robes.

The Reverend pumped Miss Chang as Dennis pumped the organ.
'Ms Tonner!' shouted The Reverend.
She continued playing – something whimsical – Mozart?
'Ms TONNER!'
Dennis collapsed into a chair, and the music waned.
'Ms Tonner,' The Reverend complained. 'Can't you play something a little more *rhythmic*?'
Dennis waved a hand from between his knees.
'Come on, Eck, I've been at this for twenty...'
'Yes, Dennis, thank you for your input, but the point is that the job can only be done successfully if my wife and I orgasm simultaneously. I have explained this.'
Miss Chang groaned. It wasn't pleasure.
Dennis was still bent double.
'If you want her to start enjoying herself,' he said, 'give her a slap. That's what I did to mine, and she dropped four kids.'
He should have set the timer for five seconds and thrown the bomb over the balcony, but that would have been too indiscriminate. Added to that, he wanted his father to suffer, and killing him would defeat the purpose.
Clunk-clunk. Wheeze.
'Oh, that's more like it, Ms Tonner!' said The Reverend. '...and 2 and 3 and 4 and *On-ward Chri-stian So-ho-ho-ho-ldiers*...faster, Ms Tonner...oh, yes!...harder, Dennis!!...*a-With-The-Cross-Of-JEEEEE-SUS!!!...*'
Terry crept back out to the stairway. There was a door set into the wall. It must have been the bell tower. It was exactly what he was looking for.
It smelled musty; claustrophobic. Light from a streetlamp was filtering in through arrow slits in the masonry. Something fluttered round his head, but he did his best to ignore it. Geeky had assured him that things would go with an especially loud bang, probably leaving an extensive crater, depending on where the bomb was planted. Terry wasn't interested in craters, not any more. He set the timer and wedged the bomb into a crack in the stonework. Hopefully, the tower would collapse into the street. There might even be secondary damage, a fire, even. Whatever happened, the church would

no longer be giving him the finger from afar. Only the clenched fist would remain.

Shouting in the vestibule.

Scuffling sounds, then more shouting.

Dennis was at the bottom of the stairs, yelling into the phone. He wanted an ambulance. Heart attack. Before he'd hung up, the whole of the interior of the church was flashing blue from the lights out in the street.

Leather soles running up the main steps.

'Is The Reverend Kinlochleven here?' barked a voice.

'Fuck, that was quick, Sergeant,' said Dennis. 'But it was an ambulance I wanted.'

'What?'

'An ambulance. For E...The Reverend. He's having a heart attack.'

'What, did the fire brigade phone him here?'

'Eh?'

Terry looked over the banister. Ms Tonner was dragging his father out of the hall, pulling on the loose material from his robe.

'Could ye give me a wee hand here, Dennis?' she puffed. 'He's awfy heavy.'

'Is that The Reverend?' said the Sergeant.

'Dehehehehennnissss...'

'I'm here, Eck.'

The Reverend was struggling for breath.

Hang on, daddy, thought Terry. The night is young.

'Didchoo...didchoo...mmmbulance?'

'Aye, Eck, don't worry. It'll be here in a minute.'

The Sergeant leaned in, taking control.

'Sorry about the delay in getting here, Reverend,' he said. 'But we've been busy with an incident up Mayfield Road. A bull trying to copulate with a rubbish skip, would you believe.'

'.....'

The Sergeant coughed.

'Sorry to hear about your fire, sir,' he said.

The Reverend drew in a laboured breath – it sounded like it might be his last.

'Wh...?'

The Sergeant turned to Dennis.

'I thought you said he knew?'

'What fucking fire?' said Dennis.

'Up at the Queen's Buildings,' said the Sergeant. 'Someone started a fire in that new shed they've been building. The flames are fifty feet….' He looked at his watch. 'It'll be gutted by now, right enough.'

The Reverend groaned. Good, thought Terry. Hang on.

'Tehh...terr...'

'What's that, sir?'

'Tehh...terr...'

'Aye, sir, terrorists all right, those animal rights idiots, I'll bet. No respect for private property whatsoever.'

The screech of brakes outside.

The paramedic, a woman, wasted no time getting him trussed up.

'Tehh...terr...'

'Right here, dad,' said Terry, and elbowed Dennis out of the way. He knew he shouldn't be doing this, but he couldn't help himself.

He leaned over The Reverend's helpless form.

'Don't worry, Sergeant,' he said. 'I'm his son. Do you mind if I say a few last words?'

He whispered into The Reverend's ear.

'Tehh...terr...,' he mocked. 'Yes, you're fucking right it was me. And in about tehh...ten minutes, your church is going to blow sky high.'

He laughed softly, and stroked his father's brow.

'I'm insane,' he said. 'And guess what? You've got a bomb in your belfry.'

'Tehh...terr...'

'Have a nice life.'

'Tehh...'

'What's left of it.'

'T...'

'You fucking *nothing*!'

They pushed the stretcher into the back of the ambulance. Miss Chang, wearing a white nightshirt, climbed in, too.

Terry watched it roar off down the street.

'Can I offer you a lift to the hospital, sir?' said the Sergeant, and wiped tears from his eyes with a paper tissue.

'No, thank you,' said Terry. 'I'll make my own way there.'

The engine was running. Plato was shaking like a leaf.

'A lot of, er, emergency service activity tonight, Terry,' he said.

Terry glanced round the interior of the car. The suitcase was on the back seat, badly hidden under a tartan blanket.

He smiled.

'Plato,' he said. 'Shut up and *drive*!'

Radio 4 was as clear as a bell until Maastricht. Then it hissed for ten minutes and turned into something else. Brass bands with accordions.

'Do you speak German?' said Terry. He wanted to hear the news, although he knew that Scotland being featured was a bit of a long shot.

Plato moved around in his seat. His head twisted slightly on his neck.

Don't worry, thought Terry, your case is still there.

'How far do you intend going?' said Plato.

Terry didn't have to think about it.

'All the way,' he said.

Plato groaned.

They drove on in silence. Plato obviously knew the road – perhaps he'd made the journey before, but it wasn't long before his head began to nod over the steering wheel. Terry took over. He tried his best to keep going south east.

He pulled off the motorway near Frankfurt, and left Plato dozing in the back with his suitcase in his arms. He took the car keys with him. The service station was plush. He bought two sets of clothes and got changed in the toilet. He decided to hang on to his suit – he would be needing it.

There was still no news from Edinburgh. Then again, the papers were a day old.

He placed his plastic bags in the boot and closed it with a thump.

'Ah, Terry,' yawned Plato, lifting his head off the suitcase. 'Where are we?'

Terry was twisting the lid off a bottle of Pro Plus. He tossed a can of Coke over the back of the headrest.

'Still a way to go yet,' he said. 'Cheers.'

He drove for the rest of the day, his foot to the boards to keep up with the traffic. When they got to Munich he took a left turn – he doubted if Plato's car would be able to manage the Alps.

He got lost.

'Oh, for God's sake, Terry,' Plato protested for the hundredth time. He was back in the passenger seat. In fact, he'd been back in the passenger seat for the last twelve hours, and he'd been nipping Terry's head for most of them. 'Let me drive.'

'Take it easy,' said Terry. 'We'll get there.'

By the time they got to Venice, Plato was in a lather.

'That has got to be the biggest bloody detour in the history of motoring,' he said. 'I mean, *Graz*, for crying out loud!' He leaned over and tapped the dashboard. 'Pull over at the next petrol station. I'll let you pay again.'

'We could have gone through Yugoslavia,' Terry reminded him.

'Oh, Terry,' said Plato. 'Be serious.'

They parked in the floodlit forecourt of an Esso garage near the harbour. The cafeteria was almost empty. Plato got a plate of spaghetti off the hotplate and went to sit at a corner table, his suitcase trundling unsteadily behind him. It was a good job it had wheels – he was having trouble just tilting it a few inches off the floor. Terry plumped for something wrapped in plastic that claimed to be a potato baguette.

There was a rack of newspapers at the cash desk.

Edinburgh got a mention in the Times, Telegraph and Guardian. There was a Daily Record buried at the back. It was the same story, only this time it was all over the front page. He tugged the paper open and raced through the other pages. Bastard!

He threw the paper across the table.

'You've made the national press,' he said.

Plato pushed his plate slowly to the side. His eyes scanned the page; they stopped and lingered on one of the photographs. He stroked the caption with his fingertips, then burst into tears.

'Oh, God,' he moaned. 'What have I done?!'

Terry looked around. The other customers were just leaving.

'Well, if you're going to play with fire...,' he said. There had been nothing, absolutely nothing about the Kinlochleven Suite, nor about his father's church.

Plato raised his hands slowly and gripped the hair on the sides of his head; he began to tug rhythmically.

'I… told… him…'

He was gnawing the words through clenched teeth.

'… to… take… the… night… off… the… deaf… old… '

Terry squinted at the photographs. The first showed a scowling man – Daniel Miller, 35, according to the caption. The Firestarter, obviously. The second was one of those classic newspaper shots that accompany bad news – it was completely out of focus, as if it had been Xeroxed from a sodden bus pass.

It probably had.

'...ohhhhhhhhhh....,' went Plato.

'Who's the old man?' said Terry.

Plato inhaled, then let out a juddering sigh. He directed a shaking finger at the photo.

'It's…my…,' he groaned.

Archie Buchanan, 75.

'What?' said Terry. 'Do you...did you know him?'

Plato dragged his eyes from the picture.

'Know him?' he said. 'It's…my…*fath*….'

Ah.

'Sorry to...,' said Terry.

Plato pushed himself away from the table. He tried to lift his case.

'Come on,' he said.

Terry had just got his fingernail under the cellophane of his sandwich.

'Eh?'

'We'll need to go back,' said Plato.

Terry slid the wrapping down the sides of the bread.

'How do you work that one out?' he said.

'Give me the keys,' said Plato.

'I'm eating,' said Terry, and bit off a mouthful.

'Give me the keys!'

Terry manoeuvred the bolus of bread to the side of his mouth with his tongue.

'Sit down, Plato,' he said. 'Let's not be rash.'

Time to improvise.

There was a payphone at the other end of the cafe. Terry stabbed the numbers until he got a ringing tone then listened to a man shouting at him in incomprehensible Italian for two minutes. Even when the line went dead, he kept his ear to the phone. He nodded and mumbled rhubarb into the mouthpiece. Yes. Yes, I know. I could just walk out to the car and disappear into the night, but I'm not a total animal. Besides, I'm enjoying this.

He nodded a final time, delivered a warm thank you, and hung up.

Plato, crying quietly into his hanky, watched him approach.

'There's a flight to London leaving in half an hour,' said Terry. 'Come on, you can get a ticket at the check in desk.'

He had to support Plato all the way to the car. The man was devastated, as well he might be. Terry had a grip of the suitcase.

Fate seemed to be playing along; the airport was signposted. They skidded to a halt outside Departures. Plato slowly got out of the car, but reached back in to unlock the back door.

Terry grabbed his hand.

'Leave the case, Plato,' he said. He had to shout. The whine of jet engines was loud. 'You'll do yourself an injury.'

'I'll risk it,' said Plato, and pulled up the button on the window ledge.

'Look,' said Terry. 'It's heavy. You know that. If you try to lift it you'll give yourself a stroke.'

'I'll risk it,' said Plato.

'Oh no you fucking won't,' Terry murmured. He looked at his watch. 'Leave it where it is for now,' he said. 'I'll park the car. Go and get the tickets. You'd better hurry. I'll be along in a few minutes.'

Plato's hand was still on the lock.

'What?' he said. 'Are you flying back, too?'

Terry smiled at him gently.

'You're in no condition to travel all that way on your own,' he said. 'We can get the car later.'

Plato nodded, and withdrew his hand.

'You're a good man, Terry,' he said, and sobbed as he was engulfed by another wave of grief. 'I...I can trust you, Terry?'

Terry nodded.

'All the way,' he said.

The door clicked shut. Plato walked slowly to the entrance. He didn't turn back to wave.

All the way, Terry said to himself, and slipped the car into gear.

* * *

The fire destroyed the animal enclosure, and there was extensive smoke damage to one wing of laboratories. The electronic sprinkler system had come on, but there had been a problem with the plumbing. The damage wasn't irreparable. However, the Inauguration would have to be put back a few months.

It was a week later that a guard from the new security firm found a corpse hanging from a shower head in the boot room. Although they had assumed duties the day after the fire, it was obvious from the state of the areas of exposed skin around the neck and groin that the body had been there for some time. The rubber clothing had been keeping the smell in. So had the gas mask.

The constable who was called to the scene had bad acne; he must have been given special permission to go on his own.

This'll be fun, thought Vic.

He was back on the job, despite the pain in his liver. The doctors had told him that he needed complete bed rest, but he had checked himself out of the hospital and driven the bus – slowly – back up the motorway. London hospitals had a strange regimen for dealing with hepatitis. Vic knew that a big creamy pint of Edinburgh Guinness was what he was needing, not a bonemeal enema twice a day.

He was back on the sauce, too. With a vengeance.

They regarded the corpse as it swung gently on its rope. A window was open high on the wall, and there was a draught.

'It's usual in these cases to cut the victim down,' said Vic.

'Eh?' said the constable. He looked as if he was going to be ill; his plukes were a funny shade of green. 'Nobody said anything about that.'

Vic tut-tutted.

'They told me not to touch anything,' said the constable.

The body continued to gyrate slowly. The shoulders were hunched forwards, the right hand just touching the shining conglomeration of rainbow coloured flesh that was hanging from the gusset of the wetsuit.

'But he might not be dead yet,' said Vic.

The constable started fiddling with the noose, his eyes on the striplight in the ceiling. He tripped over something on the floor – a wee hoover.

'I'll have to remember that for later,' he said. 'The Sergeant'll be needing it for evidence.'

He stumbled against the body, setting it swinging. He caught it by an arm, but had to hug it to make it stop rotating. His nose was pressed against the raw patch on the neck where the rope had been rubbing.

'Chrissss....!' he exhaled, and reeled backward. He must have caught a noseful.

Vic handed him a Swiss Army Knife.

'Great things, these,' he said. 'A blade for every occasion.' He nudged his first aid kit and his ECG with his foot, although he knew he'd be needing neither. They'd only be required if the constable cut himself badly with the knife.

The corpse hit the floor with two damp thuds. The shower head spat once in protest, then hissed, then stopped.

Vic got down on one knee. When he'd stopped wobbling, he dragged the ECG over to the body. He didn't connect it up, but he switched it on.

'It works on radio waves,' he said, and stifled a laugh.

The machine was making a continuous whining sound. He gently touched the corpse's throat, next to the raw patch, and turned to the constable with a surprised expression.

255

'Jeepers,' he said, in an American TV accent. 'He's gahn.'

The constable sobbed, once.

Vic cut off the mask.

'Well,' he said. 'I think that's conclusive.'

The face was bloated purple, almost black, and the eyes were completely distended, lying on the cheeks like bloodshot golf balls.

The constable vomited over the wee hoover.

'I've heard about this from colleagues down sou...,' Vic began. That took the humour out of the situation right away. 'This is probably the first case north of the border. Take a good look. That's history, that.'

It was perverse, he thought, though not as perverse as what he'd been through in the Morris Dancer. Maybe he would pull a fast one on Rimmer the next time he saw him, and tell him that autoasphyxiation was a French beer. Maybe not, though. It didn't sound very French. Come to think of it, neither did Coprophagy. The old wanker. He'd get him back one day, that was for sure.

The constable wiped his chin on his sleeve and, after a few attempts, managed to flap open his notebook. His eyes darted to the page, then to the walls, then to the ceiling, and back to the page.

Fair enough, thought Vic. It wasn't a pretty sight.

A buzzing sound.

A bluebottle emerged dizzily from a welt in the turgid cock.

'Any idea of the......probable...?'

Poor wee bastard, thought Vic. For sure he hadn't joined the force for this.

'Aye,' said Vic, and zipped up his anorak. 'Wanking from a gibbet. Oh, don't write that down, for Christ's sake!'

The constable was swaying, his pencil tracing nothing on the page.

'Asphyxiation,' said Vic, before the boy fainted on him.

'How do you spell...?'

Vic sighed.

'A – S – P – H – ...'

CHAPTER 20

It was a scorcher. Dug's ears were peeling, even though he was in the cab. The laddies had been threatening revolt all afternoon, and Mac had made a point of staying with them, much to Dug's relief. It was obvious that he wasn't cut out for man-management, even if the men were only fifteen years old.

He was feeling pleased with himself, though. He'd been driving the tractor up and down the D-field since dinner time, and he hadn't run over anyone. At lousing time, Mac told him to take the tractor up the road. Dug, yet again, refused. Fair enough, he had his Provisional license, but there was no way he was going to drive on the main road without L-plates.

Mac cursed and told eveyone to get into the van. The laddies piled into the back. Dug and Judd, as the oldest, were allowed to sit up front.

Dug soon had his Scotsman spread wide.

'Get this,' he said with a chuckle. 'Some poor so and so copped his lot. He jumped out of an aeroplane and his parachute failed to open. What a way to go, eh?'

Mac cleared his throat.

'I saw that story in the Record,' he said. He changed up to third, and the gears crunched.

'Aye,' said Judd, stretching an arm so that the newspaper ended up crumpled in Dug's face. 'It's the bounce that kills ye.'

Dug thought about it for a second then burst out laughing. He didn't mind his Scotsman getting crushed, of course he didn't. You couldn't get annoyed with Judd. His one-liners were priceless. Dug had started writing them down in a wee notebook back at the farm.

Judd lit up.

'Dinnae smoke that doon tae the choaklit,' Dug smiled. 'Ye get cancer that way.'

It was a line he'd heard Judd using with the laddies, in the hope they would leave him part of their fag to suck on. But Judd was staring at him, his eyes moving slowly towards Mac.

Mac cleared his throat. He changed down to second. The gears crunched, louder this time.

'Cancer's no joke,' he said. 'The way it eats away at ye, like...'

'Sorry to interrupt,' said Dug, 'but you're wrong there, Mac. It's a mistake a lot of folk make. The cancer doesn't actually eat away at anything...'

Judd grabbed the newspaper and started rustling the pages.

'Shut it,' he said.

'...I wrote an essay on this in second year. Biology. Or was it Physiology? Anyway, the cancer cells multiply out of control, so they're not eating away at anything per se. If anything, it's quite the opposite...'

'Is that right, Professor Dug?' said Mac. 'Don't you sit there and try to tell me about cancer. I nursed my mother for three year, and had to hold a sanitary towel to the hole in her throat...'

'...aye, right, Mac, but you're talking about trachaeotomy incisions. I'm talking about...'

Judd kicked him.

The van jolted to a halt in the yard. The laddies immediately piled out and started slapping the sides. Judd would have got out, too, in fact he shoved Dug, but he was stuck in the middle of the front seat.

Mac leaned on the steering wheel. He was fuming.

'You shouldn't be here, Dug,' he said. 'Cutting cabbages with these laddies? You should be sitting in an office somewhere making a thousand pound a week.'

Dug couldn't have agreed more. But he was only filling in till he heard from the teacher training college. It was a cliché, of course. Those who can't do...

'Sorry to hear about your mum,' he said, but his words were silenced by the slam of the door.

Judd was trying to fold the newspaper back into shape. He gave up, and passed the mess back to Dug.

'He wis aw fur you, ye ken that?' he said.

Marie came round with the wage packets. She left Dug till last, as usual. He knew why. She didn't want the laddies seeing how much he was getting paid for the same work.

'What's been going on?' she said. It was safe to talk. The laddies had disappeared on their bikes. 'Mac's in quite a state.'

Dug counted his money. It gave him somewhere to put his eyes.

'Blame it on me and my big mouth,' he said.

They walked round to the house.

'Terry phoned,' she said.

'What?!'

It was three months since he'd disappeared.

'Where is he?!'

'He wouldn't say – just that he was far away, and not to worry. He seemed rather keen to know how his father was. And his church. I can't think why.'

Right, thought Dug. There was no love lost there, that was for sure.

'By the way,' she said. 'The results are out. I opened Terry's. He passed.'

Of course he did, thought Dug.

'I left your mail in your room.'

'Thanks, Marie.'

They were standing at the back door. She stopped, and turned to face him.

'There's something else, Dug,' she said.

'Oh?'

He felt himself blushing. It was always awkward being alone with her like this. She was a good looking woman – 'the epitome of beauty', he'd written in a poem. He was suddenly consumed by that feeling of excited dread: he didn't know if she was going to ask him to sleep with her or send him packing. As always, of course, it turned out to be neither.

'Yes,' she said. 'There's going to be a memorial service for Roger Rimmer. I'm sure there's something about it in the things they sent you from the University, although that's a mere formality. I'm organising it.'

'.....'

'Could you come with me, Dug?'

'Well, I...'

'We're having the service in the Kinlochleven Suite, before the Inauguration.'

'Well, I don't...'

'The thing is, Terry mentioned that you might want to say something. In fact, he almost insisted. Something about a conversation you had at the RAF, whatever that might mean. Maybe I didn't hear correctly – there was a terrible crackle on the line.'

He found what he was looking for exactly where he knew it would be, on the last page of the booklet.

BSc General Science

Crighton, Andrew McDonald
Grassom, Margaret Cecelia
Kinlochleven, Terence Alexander
Lloyd, Douglas in absentia

After the conferment of degrees, refreshments will be available for Graduands and guests in the Cheviot Carvery.

Douglas Lloyd, BSc. It sounded good, to the uninitiated. He knew it was nothing to shout about. It was no coincidence that the result was on the last page. He would be the last to receive his degree. The lowest of the low. That was why he'd told them he wouldn't be going.

He couldn't see Terry turning up, either.

Poor old Margaret Cecelia Grassom.

There was something else in the envelope.

Ward 13
Edinburgh Royal Infirmary.

Dear Dug,

Just a quick note about the reference you asked for. I have filled in the form, recommending you as a person who is hon-

est, candid, of good-will and as someone who values communication. I think you would make a good teacher. I gave you an A rating. (Not an A+, I'm afraid, but I'm sure it will do the trick.)

By the by, if Terry Kinlochleven gets in touch with you, you might like to ask him about a friend of mine, Mr Samsonite, who went missing.

Yours, philosophically, aye,
   Plato Buchanan

PS Congratulations on your degree.
PPS Morag sends her regards.

Good old Plato.

There was another letter. It was addressed to Dug, Songwriter, The Farm With The Castle, Loch Leven, Fife.

There was a card inside.

Sammy and Mich request the pleasure of your company at their WEDDING in Dalkeith Registry Office at 5pm on Friday, July 17th, 1987.

Live music, dancing, food and drink will follow at the Kaptain's Kabin, Dalkeith TILL LATE!!!

This was a surprise. He'd bumped into Sammy just before he left Edinburgh, and they'd ended up back in Marchmont. Sammy had told him about the old flat being burned down, then asked him if he'd seen Terry recently. Seemingly, things weren't going too well with the band, and they were looking for another singer. He had made them some tea, and then pulled out a big cardboard box from behind the couch. It was full of records. He'd passed one of them to Dug. ***Drive!*** It said. ***Bayonet Practice (Livingstone/Rimmer/Birkett/Lloyd.)*** Sammy had told him that the records were numbered. Dug's was number 7. Then he'd told him there were 193 left in the box, and burst into tears.

There was nothing about the memorial service. There was nothing about the Inauguration of the Kinlochleven Suite, either. Dug wasn't invited. He'd be there, though. Too right he would.

Luckily, the place was almost empty.

He laid his bag on the floor and ordered a double Isle of Jura.

He could feel the customers staring at him, sitting there in their three-piece suits, the money dripping off them. Even the barman was having a quiet titter. He wondered why Terry had ever bothered with the place.

Someone began whistling Scotland The Brave, which everyone found amusing.

He downed his drink in one and nearly choked.

'Fuck yez,' he rasped, and made for the door.

He had to come back for his bag.

They found that funny, too.

He told the taxi driver to let him off at the Institute of Animal Science, as close to the entrance as possible. He pushed his way through the wall of bodies gathered outside, but a space was quickly cleared so the Quinties could get a good deek at his legs.

'For fuck's sake, Lloyd, what are you *like*?!'

He tried to ignore it. Luckily, they soon had something else to gawk at. A Midnight Blue Audi Quattro growled to a halt in front of them. The windows were tinted black. Dug moved forward and escorted Marie to the area of grass that had been set aside for floral tributes. She laid a wreath next to the others and bowed her head in silent prayer for an old friend she hadn't seen in years, and would never see again.

Dug wiped a tear from his eye.

The comments were still audible.

'Dug,' Marie whispered. 'It's a memorial service. Do you really think Highland dress is appropriate?'

He knew he looked like a complete dork. Even the guy in the kilt shop had been pissing himself.

'I'm going to a wedding later,' he explained.

She smiled at him.

'Thanks for coming,' she said, and took his arm.

Silence reigned as he accompanied her back to the entrance, but not for long. People began to point over their heads, out towards West Mains Road. A helicopter came buzzing into view, and hovered a couple of hundred feet over the Institute. As it began its descent, the floral tributes began to dance around all over the car park.

So did Dug.

Marie didn't stay to watch.

. . .

The Reverend had his face pressed to the window. His fingers were in his ears; the hire company hadn't seen fit to provide headphones for the passengers, and the noise inside the cabin was an incessant, deafening drone. Dennis had located the sick bag in the back of the pilot's seat before they had taken off, and was enjoying the flight even less than Miss Chang, who was being leered at by the retardantly recuperating Sid.

Something was going on down at ground level.

An idiot in a kilt was chasing Rimmer's wreaths around the car park, the tartan billowing around his waist, his red underpants flashing like a danger sign in a lingerie shop.

The Reverend thumped Dennis on the elbow. He had to shout.

'Tell the pilot to get this damned contraption on the ground before I am completely upstaged!'

Dennis leaned over the back of the pilot's seat and yanked at his headphones. The helicopter lurched to the side and went into a spin. The emergency was only momentary; the pilot soon had things under control and he began a slow descent, but not before the back of his fist had hit Dennis in the eye.

The helicopter bounced once, and they were down. There was a slight delay while Dennis wiped the blood off his face with the side of the sick bag.

The Reverend stood in the doorway and surveyed the scene. He had decided to dress for the occasion. After much thought, he had plumped for his blackest of black robes, an InVestments-4-U Grief Chief, full length. It had been intended as a dignified nod to the deceased, but when he observed the state of the car park he realised he should have worn his suit. It was as if Rimmer had taken the chance to cock a final snook at his magnanimity. There were flowers scattered all over the place. It looked like the aftermath of a rampage through an open air market.

263

This was supposed to be Alexander Kinlochleven's day, not Roger Rimmer's. The planning for the Inauguration had been a drain on him, both mentally and physically. It hadn't been easy to organise something on such a grand scale while hooked up to an oxygen supply. His doctor had suggested that perhaps he should let Dennis take over the planning, and The Reverend had laughed so much that he thought he was having another heart attack. No, no, no. The Inauguration of the most expensive asset the University of Scotland had seen in years required The Reverend's personal attention. Then his damned ex-wife had got in touch, demanding that they should put on some kind of service for Rimmer. He had acquiesced; indeed he had turned that side of the affair over to her. He didn't have the strength to argue with the woman.

He would mumble something about the fruity old goat then get on with the real business.

He held out an arm, and Dennis helped him down the steps.

Sugden was waiting for him at the entrance, bent from the waist at a commendable ninety degree angle. On closer inspection, it was apparent that his head was gradually moving even lower.

Good God, thought The Reverend. The little freak is going to kiss my boots.

'Oh, get up, for goodness' sake,' he said. He hauled a sleeve over his forearm and proceeded into the foyer. He had hardly put his foot over the threshold when he realised that this was going to be a total balls-up.

The Agrics' Theatre was packed. There was standing room only. All the big wigs from the University were there, applauding like seals in the front two rows. With a flourish of his robes, The Reverend took his seat in their midst.

'Are you comfortable, Reverend?' said Sugden. 'There's certainly a bumper turnout...'

The Reverend cut him off.

'Forgive me for pointing this out,' he said. 'But this is the Inauguration of the Kinlochleven Suite today, is it not?'

Sugden was dry washing his hands.

'Yes, that's right, Reverend.'

'Ah, yes, I thought so. So why the blazes are we sitting in this dump of a canteen instead of over the road?'

'Well, yes,' said Sugden. 'Bit of a problem with the builders, Reverend. On strike, I'm afraid. Health and Safety won't let us put anything on until the scaffolding comes down...'

The Reverend shooed him away. He caught Dennis's eye. It wasn't difficult – it was looking decidedly puffed up.

'My wife?' he asked.

Dennis looked further along the row.

'Aye,' he said. 'Still looking good after all these years.'

'Dennis,' said The Reverend, with a huge, forced smile. 'When you've finished ogling my mistake of yesteryear, would you please fetch my wife?'

Miss Chang was standing nervously by the doors. Sid was behind her. He raised a crutch and poked her in the back.

There was a growl from the other side of the theatre. The Reverend looked over, and saw a line of shoulders rolling inside double-breasted suits.

Miss Chang was guided into the seat next to her husband, and Sid hobbled over to a space that opened up for him near the wall. Feet scuffled, and he disappeared like a ball being sucked into a rugby scrum.

The Reverend scanned the faces in the room, behind him and along the walls, but there was no one of note. He'd had a strange feeling that his errant son would put in an appearance, but that, it seemed, was not going to transpire. There were certainly a lot of ruffians in the place, especially that crowd Sid had gone to stand with. He hadn't been fooled by the shiny suits. He knew working class unemployed when he saw it. Friends of Rimmer's, no doubt. He always liked a bit of rough. It had been the man's undoing.

A guitar and microphone were set up on the stage. The Reverend's lip curled. His ex-wife had gone totally over the top. Two hunched figures climbed the steps. They went straight into a jangling ditty that soon had half the theatre sniffling into their cuffs. The dignitary to his right, presumably a Physics professor judging by the hair, leaned in and whispered 'Cat Stevens', whatever that was supposed to mean.

265

Having no option, he subjected himself to the rest of the performance.

His neighbour leaned in again.

'Father and son,' he whispered, his voice catching in his throat.

What was he talking about? There was no way this pair were father and son. Even for them to pass for brothers would have required a gargantuan dose of imagin...

Hang on...

There was something about the guitarist's eyes, and the other one, the Special Needs case...

Oh, what? he thought.

It was a good job their mother hadn't come along. The Reverend had invited her, but she had said she had put Roger Rimmer behind her years ago. And anyway, a young man was coming round at eleven to cauterise her bellows.

They finished the song. The last note from the guitar rang round the theatre and faded to nothing.

'That was for our dad,' said the singer.

There was a muffled sob, as if someone was in pain.

It was like something out of This Is Your Life, thought The Reverend. Totally crass. Perhaps Rimmer was going to come storming into the theatre with Eamon Andrews by his side carrying the big red book. We fooled you all! The boys trudged off the stage. Look at the state of them. Rimmer was better off dead. A couple of wasters, and no mistake, although it had to be admitted that the older brother had quite a voice.

There was another sob, and the suits shuffled audibly.

'Shut it,' someone said, and a foot stamped on the floor.

The stage was empty.

The Reverend strode to the microphone.

'If you'll all look out of the window,' he said.

They did.

'That's the new Kinlochleven Suite,' he said. 'Funded entirely by me. I now declare it open.'

He headed straight back to his chair.

Sugden stood up and looked around, nodding, smiling and applauding. He was the only one.

The Reverend's neighbour leaned in again.

'Reverend,' he began, 'I'd like to offer my hand. Donald Ilium, Dean of the Faculty of Science. Strange we haven't met until now, but there's…'

'And?' said The Reverend.

The Dean looked over his shoulder and winked at whoever was sitting behind him.

'We were expecting to hear a few words about Roger Rimmer,' he said. 'Rumour has it that the two of you had quite a history. I don't know much about the way things work in your church, I'm an atheist myself, but I must say that a few words from your esteemed self would, er, help to put the record straight.' He beckoned Sugden over and whispered something in his ear.

The little ferret mounted the stage and approached the microphone.

'Ah, yes, Reverend,' he said. 'Perhaps you would like to say something about the, er, dear departed. Not my idea, of course, but the powers that be...'

The Reverend yawned.

'I don't think so,' he said. He looked at Miss Chang. 'I think we're all done here.'

The singer was crying in the corner.

An emaciated boy in a kilt bounded up the steps and nudged Sugden out of the way. When the wolf-whistles had died down, he tried to begin.

'If I could have everyone's attention,' he said.

'Ye've already got it!' someone shouted. Laughter.

'Road map!'

'Yes, very good. Now, Reverend. My name is Dug Lloyd, and I'd like to say something about Roger Rimmer.'

The dignitaries shuffled in their seats. The Reverend could feel their eyes on the back of his neck. This was preposterous. After all the money he'd sunk into this place! He got up and headed for the door.

'Not so fast, Mr Kinlochleven,' said Dug.

The microphone was loud, but he kept walking. Miss Chang was still in her seat. She could catch up in her own time.

267

'Mac?' said Dug.

A large man blocked the doorway. The Reverend stared at him.

'Mac?' he said. 'It's been a while. Still cutting cabb...'

'Sit down, Eck,' he said. 'Ye owe Roger that much.'

It was hard for him to argue. There was a young man standing there, too. He looked like Popeye. He was brandishing a torque wrench. The Reverend suddenly felt very uncomfortable, as if he were back in Numpty, only this time there would be no way out. He returned to his seat. His chest was beginning to throb.

'Sitting uncomfortably?' said Dug. 'Then I'll begin.'

'It's Terry's old flatmate,' said Dennis, as he made for the exit. 'Back in a minute.'

. . .

Mich was staring at Jackie. He couldn't take his eyes off the Asian woman in the front row. His hands were down his trousers, and he was fumbling, his whole body contorting. Eventually, he extricated Alec Dick's new shillelagh from his trouser leg. Mich shook her head and checked her watch. She still hadn't been to the hairdresser's, and her dress was still being altered, but what could she do? She couldn't have let the boys down, not today. She'd heard, as had all the Kaptain's Kabin regulars that were leaning against the wall, what this man Kinlochleven had done to Baz and Bear. Not only that, most of them, even Sammy until recently, lived in Kinlochleven owned flats, and were sick of being hassled by Dennis. There was another sob, and more shuffling of bodies as they took turns stamping on Sid.

. . .

Dug was scrabbling about for something in his sporran. People began to giggle. He unfolded a piece of paper.

'Get on with it!' someone shouted.

'Firstly,' Dug said, 'that was a lovely musical tribute from Baz and Bear of Drive!. Please put your hands together...'

The applause stuttered into life, but soon grew into the real thing.

The Reverend looked slowly round the room.

'And, yes, a large Institute of Animal Science thank you to the Right Reverend Kinlochleven for his eloquent, if laconic, eulogy.'

That was enough. He didn't need this little oik taking the piss out of him. He looked over towards the exit. Mac shook his head.

The boy was getting away with the sarcasm. The crowd seemed to love him. If he'd asked them to jump up, clap their hands and dance a jig, they would have done it. It was the kind of rapt worship The Reverend was all too familiar with.

'We all agree that it was very fitting of His Graciousness The Eminence Kinlochleven to speak here today.'

The dignitaries nodded. The Dean patted The Reverend on the knee.

'After all,' Dug continued, 'he was responsible for Roger Rimmer topping himself.'

The Dean withdrew his hand at once, and wiped it on his jacket. Sugden was standing at the side of the stage making rapid cutting motions with his hand across his throat. He looked ridiculous. He strode to the middle of the stage and clumped his hand over the microphone. From the front row, however, his voice was audible.

'Eee, Dug,' he said. 'Why don't you fook off back to whatever hole you crawled out of this morning?'

Dug slapped his hand out of the way and pulled the microphone off the stand. He began to pace the floor. The boy, The Reverend noted with discomfort, had all the makings of an Evangelist.

'Ah, yes, Doctor Sugden. Today's grand prizewinner. Park your arse until I've finished.'

'Now joost you look 'ere!'

'Sit doon!'

It was the suits.

'Ya fuckin' English poof!'

'E's not even a true Scotsman!' Sugden shouted. 'We all saw his scarlet knickers in the car park!'

The Dean sighed.

'How undignified,' he said. 'It appears Doctor Sugden is still striving for equilibrium after his dip in the Channel.' He leaned in. 'Are you sure he's the man to head up the Suite?' he said, then rubbed his hand on his jacket again.

269

Sugden stormed off the side of the stage. He didn't get very far. The audience were in uproar at the sight of the curtains billowing as he tried to locate a door backstage. There was none. He decided to play dead. The toes of his shoes could clearly be seen sticking out at the bottom of the material.

'That's better,' said Dug, and waited for the laughter to die down. 'Now, to business. I was asked to come here today.'

The curtain moved.

'No you bloody weren't,' said a muffled voice.

'Oh, but I was,' said Dug. 'It was Terry Kinlochleven's idea…'

Oh, Christ, thought The Reverend. A twinge shot across his chest and a memory of that night flashed into his head; he'd been straining to make his mouth work while lying in the back of the ambulance, but whatever it was they had injected into his arm had made connected speech impossible, even though he'd been conscious throughout. He had spent a fitful twenty four hours in hospital waiting for word of his church, but there was nothing – perhaps they didn't want to break the bad news while he was in such a delicate condition. He'd eventually managed to get a message out to Dennis to go and check the belltower, and within the hour the clown had blagged his way into the intensive care unit with a large biscuit tin. He tried in vain to tell Dennis to be careful – they had just given him another injection – but before he could muster the strength to pull the blankets over his head, Dennis had ripped open the lid. A cloying aroma immediately filled the room. Even though there were tubes stuck up his nose, he recognised it from years back, and it was accompanied by a mental image of a small boy moulding little animals in his hands. One whiff was all he needed to realise that the whole affair was a hoax. He'd certainly fallen for it. Play-Doh doesn't make for the widespread devastation his shit of a son had alluded to while wishing him a pleasant death.

A pain shot down his left arm like a skewer.

'…we'll get back to Terry later,' said Dug. 'What about poor old Roger Rimmer?'

Where the hell was Dennis? The helicopter would be able to get him to the Infirmary in minutes...and this little bastard would be getting his legs broken later, that was for sure.

'First of all, there's been a lot of talk about the way Dr Rimmer died, and if it really was suicide. After all, he didn't leave a note.'

A feeling of being crushed, that unbearable heaviness on his chest. It was happening again. The Reverend twisted his lips into a plea for help, but all that came out was a hiss.

'Shh!' said the Dean, and rubbed both his hands on his trouser legs. 'I've got money on this.'

'But he didn't have to leave a note,' said Dug. 'He told me he was going to do it. He did it because of...'

The Reverend gasped, and slumped back in his chair. Dug was looking directly at him, his eyes bulging.

'...because of *you*, Reverend. How does that make you feel?'

The Dean slapped his hands together.

'I bloody knew it!' he laughed, and turned in his seat. 'A definite Durkheim scenario, you heard the boy. I'll see you all in The Confessional later – cash only, if you please, gentlemen.'

The Reverend keeled over, coughing through the pain. He felt someone tapping him reluctantly on the back.

'Best to get it all up,' said the Dean.

He managed to twist his head to the side. Dennis was at the door, with Mac's hand over his face. Popeye had the torque wrench pressed into Dennis's ear.

'First of all,' said Dug, 'you cheated Dr Rimmer out of his share of the Numpty gold mine. Isn't that right?'

No, no, no! Christ it was sore. It was a business transaction. Rimmer should have been more careful.

'Then you stole his wife and children.'

No! Mary Tonner had thrown herself at him. She'd been a cracker in those days, a real goer. It hadn't been his idea for her to bring her kids with her. That's why he'd had them packed off to a home.

One of them was a dwarf, for Christ's sake.

'Which brings us back to Terry. You tried to destroy his life, and you made a pretty good job of it. No one, not even his mother, has any idea where he is.'

The Reverend tried to fill his lungs. It was like inhaling scalding lumps of coal.

'He had it coming to him!' he gasped.

'What?' said Dug. 'Because he poked...'

He tried to get to his feet. He grabbed hold of Miss Chang's wrist and stumbled forwards, hauling her out of her chair.

'And you're a slumlord!' Dug shouted. 'Ask them!'

The suits were advancing in a line. What was Sid doing curled up...?

It felt like his heart was trying to burst out of his neck.

'De-he-he-nissss....'

He stumbled again, pulling Miss Chang across the floor.

The suits descended on him.

'De-he-he-nissss!'

'Don't worry, Eck! I'll save you!'

There was a moment of silence. Then Dennis addressed the suits.

'What have you done to my laddie?' he demanded. 'Eh? Where is he?'

The Reverend tried to take a breath.

'On...th...floor...!' he gasped.

'Sid?' said Dennis. 'Sid! Get up ya useless...'

A thump. Dennis didn't get to finish the sentence. Someone was pulling at Miss Chang. It was Marie, leading her out of the melee, and out of the building.

The Reverend turned back to Dennis, but all he saw was a large fist growing larger and larger, the letters L – O – V – E tattooed across the knuckles.

* * *

The reception at the Kaptain's Kabin was wild, which was what everyone had been expecting. Drive! were doing the music. By half past two, it was only the hard core that were left. Jackie was sitting in on drums. Sammy was lying slumped in front of the stage, blotto, muttering to himself.

'...no a fuckin' weddin' band,' he slurred. 'We're no...'

Mich had just finished mopping up a pool of vomit near his hand. She put her arms round him.

'Come on, you,' she said, and pulled him to his feet. 'They're going to play our song.'

·272

She had given her bass to Dug. He had been as high as a kite since his speech that afternoon, and was ready for anything.

'Take Me Home,' she said, trying to keep Sammy vertical.

Dug looked puzzled.

'Don't worry,' she said. 'It's Phil Collins.'

That didn't help very much. Dug rubbed the fretboard.

'Just play the same note all the time,' she explained.

She guided Sammy onto the dancefloor, but decided it would be a good idea to stay close to the edge in case he needed to sit down. Dug was managing to keep up with Baz, although it was a pity about Jackie on the drums.

''Scuse me,' said Malcolm, cutting in. 'But is this a gentlemen's excuse me?'

She lowered Sammy into a chair.

Malcolm soon had a grip of her.

'Ah've been waitin' fur a slow yin,' he informed her breasts. He leaned in. 'Ah saw ye wi' yer squeegee there,' he said.

Mich drew back so she could see him.

'Ah want tae pit ye oan ma books,' he said.

She drew back even further. God, his breath was foul.

'What?' she said. 'But the contract with the band was cancelled...'

'Naw, hen,' he said, and gave her a nip.

Someone was shouting. Even over the racket Jackie was making, it was audible.

'Fuckin' liberty! Ma fuckin' weddin', tae...that's...ma fuckin'...'

Over Malcolm's shoulder, Sammy was swaying towards them.

Baz launched into Joy Division.

Dug stopped playing.

'Just do a Phil Collins!' shouted Mich. She could feel Malcolm's fingers roaming the back of her dress. She tried to push him away... something was pressing into her shyuck.

Bear went straight into the chorus.

Sammy fell over.

'Naw, hen,' Malcolm growled. 'Ma other books...'

CHAPTER 21

The village was called Panorama, which was appropriate, given the view.

He leaned on the telescope and trained it down the side of the hill. The city was a shimmering haze in the distance, the buildings barely discernible under a forest of TV aerials. He panned round, following the main road, and spotted a Coast Guard motor launch bouncing across the bay. He had to smile. Cops and Robbers.

Chase me.

Catch me.

See what I do.

Crack-crack-crack!

It was a sound he was slowly getting used to. The trigger happy guards at the radar station further up the mountain liked to let off a few rounds in the midday sun. Another burst, and he looked up behind the villa.

The dome, as was its wont, protruded from the summit like a huge nipple.

All that surveillance equipment, he smiled, and no one knew where he was.

No one could find him.

Jasper was down in the yard, polishing the car. He whistled while he worked, a man happy with his lot, taking a pride in the day's chores.

The past year was a blur, a temporary setback; an aberration of the real man. He was finished with Scotland, of that he was more than sure. From now on, there would be no restraints. The sky was the limit. Here, he could be someone.

Here, he could be anyone.

And this heat!

He stepped into the lounge and slid shut the balcony door. A wave of air-conditioned coolness lapped over him, making him shiver. His heels clicked rhythmically across the marble and he sat down at the piano. He sorted through the piles of paper and found the list of names.

He had fooled them all.

He wasn't who they thought he was.

He wasn't a singer, for a start.

He certainly wasn't a pianist, although he was working on it.

He was beginning to suspect what he really was. In fact, it was more than a suspicion.

His mother had been a mine of information. His father, it seemed, wasn't dead yet. There had been no news about his church, either, but then that had come as no surprise. He had scanned the English newspapers for a month after he left Edinburgh, and there had been nothing about an explosion in the New Town. It couldn't have been that the Bomb Squad had got there – that would have been news. No. Geeky had sold him a dud. Maybe one fine day Geeky would be over here on business with Travel Ecosse, in which case Terry would introduce him to Jasper, then politely ask for an explanation.

Perhaps not. After all, things had turned out rather well. He was sitting at a Steinway grand piano, for Christ's sake.

And what about Rimmer killing himself? The man had always been an accident waiting to happen, although Terry fancied that he was the only one who knew it was an accident. He'd been trying to christen the Kinlochleven Suite, that was all, and something had gone wrong. Maybe he had slipped. Rimmer and his artificial vagina. He was better off dead.

He wondered if Dug would go to the memorial service. Probably. Dug was an aspiring poet of the romantic sort, who actually believed that friendship existed. One word from Terry, especially if passed on by his fragrant mother, and the boy would be running, all too willing to make a fool of himself. Who ever heard of it – doing someone else's University assignments for them! Talk about arrested development. And he had received absolutely nothing in return. Perhaps that was what friendship was – giving without taking. But that sounded uncomfortably Christian for Terry's liking. And anyway, who was Terry to philosophise on the nature of friends? He didn't have any.

His plan – plan D, wasn't it? – had been to get a job in one of the thousands of English schools in the city, and he'd heard that a degree, any degree, was essential. In reality, however, the bosses weren't fussy. They would employ anyone. Even Jasper had been offered a job, and one look at Jasper would have sent the kids screaming for their mothers.

As it turned out, of course, Terry didn't need to find a job.

He'd paid up the lease for the next twelve months, and there was plenty left over. His bank manager, a moustachioed chump in a linen suit, loved him. His eyes had lit up at the sight of Terry pushing wad after wad of twenty pound notes across his desk. His confidentiality had been secured with a not insubstantial gift in a brown envelope. Plato wouldn't miss his cash. He would have his hands on all that lovely insurance money by now. Terry wondered if the old fool would be able to keep hold of it – and keep away from Dennis.

Terry wasn't a thief. The way he looked at it, he was keeping the money in the family.

He fashioned a G minor chord on the piano. He'd started lessons, although he knew he wasn't practising as much as he should. He'd been listening to a lot of Poulenc recently, and had told Jasper to make a tape of the organ concerto for the car. Music was becoming ever more important to him, although he would never again be taking an actively public role. He had come through that stage.

Poor old Sammy, the disaster headed nowhere fast. The forty-year-old still living in the teenage dream. And just like every teenager's dream, it would never come true. Sammy would never play the Prezzie Hall. Everyone knew that Sammy had shot his bolt. It was a shame he refused to accept it.

There was one name left on the slip of paper.

Terence Kinlochleven.

He drew a line through it.

It was as easy as that.

He laid the list in the ashtray and sparked a match. The paper curled at the edges, flared for a moment, and was gone.

Terence Kinlochleven is dead.

Long live...

He had adopted the accent of an English lord. It hadn't been difficult. His private school education had given him a head start. He would listen to the BBC World Service and hone his vowels to perfection. It was all acting, and he, as everyone knew, was one hell of an actor.

International Playboy or Enigma?

He laughed out loud.

Time for a song!

Twenty one today, twenty one today...

No. Not that. Too difficult. What was that annoying tune everyone played? Chopsticks? How did it...

Ah, yes. Miss Chang.

Who cared? She was a victim. A classic doormat.

He slammed the lid shut.

Doormats get stepped on.

They rolled to a stop in a clearing. The dust settled, and the sky burned white over the pine trees. Through the heat, insects crackled like gunfire.

He watched from the car while business was taken care of.

An old man was standing at the side of an ancient motorcycle. The rust had been painted over with turquoise emulsion, to little effect. He handed something to Jasper then opened his arms wide, his palms empty.

A tap on the window.

'He's having trouble keeping up,' said Jasper.

Oh, Lord, he thought. Not again.

'Tell him it's quite all right, Jasper,' he said, and adjusted his sunglasses with his middle finger. 'I'm a reasonable man. I'm sure we can work something out.'

The old man was almost crying. He touched Jasper on the arm; perhaps it was a gesture of thanks. Then he looked over at the car, and raised a hand in greeting.

277

Jasper dead-legged him.

He went straight down.

Through the heat, the insects continued their song.

The car moved off.

'Jasper?' he said. 'Let's take a drive around town. I really think I should get out more.'

'You got it, chief.'

'Lovely,' he said.

The tyres churned the shingle. He looked out of the back window, but all he could see was dust. The opening bar of Poulenc's masterpiece suddenly filled the interior of the car, and in the few beats of that defeaning minor chord, he was sure – no, he *knew* – that he was destined for greatness.

You're a good man, he said out loud, but his words were drowned in the music.

The irony wasn't lost on him. Perhaps we all turn into our fathers, sooner or later. Maybe that's what they want. He nodded to himself. It was as good a starting point as any.

They drove down the winding road to the city, the detached villas slowly merging into the ghetto.

So many strangers, he thought.

It would be easy to get lost here.